Five Years and 2,000 Miles

Ivy Duncan

First paperback edition January 2024

Cover Illustration by Athena Dela Victoria
Edited by Amy Snyder

ISBN 979-8-9899850-0-5

To those who have been encouraging me to write for years.

CHAPTER ONE

LEO

Senior year, according to others, went too fast. Leo didn't agree.

He'd asked his friend Colin about it over lunch on the first day of school, wondering why everyone seemed down. Usually, Leo was the quietest at their table, so he'd felt uneasy when his small group of friends had sat silently as they processed what it meant to be high school seniors.

"It's the last time for everything," Colin had answered. *"Aren't you a little sad?"*

No, Leo wasn't. Leaving high school was part of the natural progression from child to adult and being sad about it wouldn't make a difference.

Thankfully, the dim mood had faded. Now, mid-way through December with semester exams fast approaching, his friends were back to their normal, lively discussion.

Instead of discussing the end of their time at Edgewood High School, they spoke about what came next: college. Three in their group of five had made their decisions already, deposits sent to reserve a spot at their chosen universities. The remaining two were unsure of where they'd spend the next four years. Leo was in this second group.

That lunch period, his friend Benjamin—the other indecisive one—was being cajoled into explaining how far along he was in the decision-making process.

Leo ignored the chatter as he mulled over a text from his French teacher, Michael Bradford. They often messaged each other, so getting a text from him wasn't concerning. What gave him pause were the three simple words of this text.

Michael: Coffee after school?

Michael reached out to him with the offer of *coffee* only when there was something specific to tell him. He contacted Leo to do other things frequently. *Dinner* wasn't alarming; that message came at least once a month and often resulted in Leo venturing to the apartment Michael shared with his husband, Ian. Even *Come to my classroom after school* didn't make him think twice.

But *coffee* . . . To Leo, coffee seemed like what you would drink when you wanted to talk about something serious. He imagined his parents had discussed their separation over lattes.

The first time Michael invited Leo to a café was to share that he'd asked Ian to marry him. Back then, this information warranted *coffee* because of the slightly embarrassing history between Leo and his teacher.

For Leo's entire life, the Bradford house was a few blocks down the street from his own. Every Saturday, Michael Bradford came by to teach French to Leo and his younger sister, Elizabeth. Michael was eight years older and attractive. It didn't take Leo—young, *gay* Leo—long to figure out he felt something toward him. He wasn't sure what anymore. In his freshman year, Leo began to realize that he had been calling his attraction to Michael *feelings* to avoid addressing actual emotions.

The revelation hadn't come until later in Leo's freshman year—not until after he'd learned of Michael's plan to marry—so their afternoon of getting coffee to discuss the news ended with Leo awkwardly sitting in the passenger seat of Michael's car, refusing to talk as he was driven home.

This *coffee*—whatever it was Michael wanted to talk to him about— couldn't result in a situation as uncomfortable as that, Leo was sure. Still, he didn't want to wait the rest of the day to find out, so he finally texted back:

Leo: Sure, but wouldn't it be easier to come to your classroom right now?

An answer in the form of small lettering below his message stated that the text had been read. No actual reply came.

"Who're you texting?" Colin asked. "New boyfriend you've neglected to tell us about?"

The suggestion made Leo frown. Throughout his high school career, he had managed two relationships—both with boys, and both failures. At the end of the first relationship, Leo did the dumping, and in the second, he was the one getting dumped. He felt indifferent about the endings, no matter who brought them on.

His friends called him cold for this. Leo didn't agree. He'd dated both boys because he was unsure of how to reject them, and when he conducted a breakup, he was quite gentle with it. As far as he was concerned, whether he had romantic feelings was out of his control, and not wanting to date someone he had little interest in didn't make him *cold*.

"I'm texting Michael," Leo told Colin. He continued to eat the salad he'd started on before the concerning text arrived. "Why would I want a new boyfriend now? In eight months, I'll be starting college."

"Like any of your relationships have lasted that long," his friend Elijah said. Leo dismissed the statement, not seeing why it mattered.

When he said he would be starting college, he didn't mean he wanted to avoid being in a relationship when he left. Leo had five months left for him to secure his place as third in their graduating class, and he couldn't afford to let his grades slip, costing him the hefty scholarship that Edgewood offered its top three graduating students. In addition to that, he would be moving out of his mother's house. They had agreed it would be best for him to live on campus, given he sometimes indulged in antisocial tendencies. He didn't want to waste any of the time he could spend with his family on a relationship guaranteed to fail.

"Mr. Bradford?" asked Colin, as he always did when Leo referred to their teacher by his first name. "I always forget you're friends. You go weeks without mentioning him outside of class, and then you call him *Michael* and it throws me off."

When discussing French class, Leo was careful to refer to Michael as Mr. Bradford. It was more professional and the girls in his class wouldn't glare at him for being informal.

"I don't know if *friends* is the right word," Leo said. All three boys at the table—had his friend Jackson been at school that day, he certainly would have done the same—fixed him with the same *teenage-boy-head-in-gutter* expression. He gave them a disappointed look. "He's like an older brother."

"Who you find attractive," Colin added.

His friends didn't know about his past crush on Michael, but Leo supposed it wouldn't be difficult to presume that he was attracted to their teacher. That man attracted everyone interested in men. It wasn't only Michael, either. All the Bradford sons were enthralling.

Growing up, Leo had been jealous of the Bradfords. Leo had black hair and brown eyes, and he didn't think it was fair that he was stuck with that underwhelming combination while there were seven boys down the street with dark hair and golden or periwinkle eyes. Over time, Leo realized that not having an eye-catching appearance was far from the worst thing. Actually, he learned to appreciate and prefer it.

"I said brother for lack of a better term," Leo defended.

Colin grabbed Leo's water bottle to pull at the label. "Anyway, have you thought more about where you'll go next year?"

Leo had, and he didn't mind discussing it if it meant they dropped the topic of Michael. "I've narrowed it down to four," he admitted, holding his hand out for his drink.

Colin laughed. "I started with four schools."

"Well, he applied to the most schools out of all of us," said Benjamin. "You had a lot of options. How did you get down to those four?"

Leo was unsure what he was searching for in a university other than an astrophysics program. Luckily, Edgewood provided each student with money to apply to their top five schools, so maximizing his options wasn't nearly as expensive as it could have been.

"We only toured six schools, and of the six, those were the ones I liked the most," Leo answered unenthusiastically. They were all great schools but something seemed to be missing. He couldn't put his finger on what. "I don't know how I'm going to choose."

"I feel the same," Benjamin said, followed by, "Dude, stop. You're making a mess." This was directed at Colin, who had taken to shredding the detached water bottle label, creating a little mountain of paper scraps. Leo let his gaze linger on the destruction before eating a cucumber out of his salad.

He tuned out the bickering that began. It wasn't of interest to him, and there were so many other things to think about.

The end of high school, which he was apparently supposed to be upset about. Maintaining his rank in his class. Which school he would go to. What he was even looking for in a school...

Coffee.

"You haven't come over for dinner in a few weeks," Michael said as he raised his mug to his lips. "What's up with that?"

Leo leaned back in his chair. This clearly wasn't what Michael had brought him there to discuss, and he wondered how long he should allow him to avoid the conversation.

"I've been studying a lot lately," Leo said, deciding it wouldn't hurt to play along for a little while. "And I guess Lizzy and her new boyfriend aren't as insufferable as she and her other boyfriends have been." In the past when he'd dropped by Michael and Ian's apartment, it was often to get away from whatever relationship his sister was currently in.

Lizzy had started high school this year—not at Edgewood, because she'd failed the entrance exam, to their mother's disappointment. And although Leo didn't like to admit it, his sister was quite beautiful and had her fair share of suitors because of it.

She had terrible taste in boys, always bringing home the most obnoxious guy who expressed interest in her. This time it was a kid a year younger than Leo who was absolutely terrified of him. Because of this, Lizzy and her boyfriend spent most of their time in her room.

"Does that mean you approve of this one?" asked Michael.

"No."

Chuckling, Michael looked out the window they had sat beside. "And what about college? You still struggling to pick a school?"

"I've narrowed it down to four."

"Which ones?"

Leo listed off their names.

"All in Illinois, huh? How'd you decide on those?"

Leo took a sip of coffee and burned his lips. "I don't really know why I narrowed it down to those. I like the campuses, but that isn't a concern of mine. I don't know what I'm looking for in a school so it's making it hard to choose one."

"I'm glad you're not taking the decision lightly." Michael sounded distant.

Leo didn't respond. He felt as if they'd made enough small talk. It was time for Michael to tell him why he was there.

Michael met his gaze evenly. "We're moving, Leo."

"Oh." Leo could handle that. If they were leaving Illinois for somewhere else in the Midwest, Leo was certain he would still make the time to visit them, and if they went even farther than that—say, either coast—he'd be able to take a summer road trip. It would be fine. "How far?"

"We're leaving the country." It was quiet then, the sound of a coffee grinder filling in the space. "Ian got a job at a restaurant in France."

Leo didn't know what to say. He felt his lips moving, searching for a shape that seemed right. He came up empty.

Michael smiled sadly. "I know this must seem a little unexpected, but I assure you, it wasn't a hasty decision. It's been a dream of his ever since he finished culinary school, and we've been talking about it for a while."

"When is this happening?"

"After the school year ends."

There were many more questions Leo wanted to ask, but the next thing he said wasn't any of them. "I don't have a passport. How am I supposed to visit you without a passport?"

Michael looked surprised, then amused. "We thought about that, actually. The paperwork is at our apartment, so you have to come by for dinner soon. We thought it would be a good eighteenth birthday present. You know, since I'm not going to date you."

"Ugh, shut up," Leo groaned. He managed a smile. "You're really moving to Europe?"

"We are."

"Wow," he said. "How are you not absolutely terrified? I mean, your entire life is here. What are you even going to do? You're a French teacher."

"I'm going to teach English," Michael said. "It'll be an adjustment, but I'm willing to make it." He smiled down at his coffee. "I don't want to gross you out with old married couple sap, but my entire life is here until Ian is somewhere other than here, and then my entire life moves to wherever he is. Of course I'm scared. We both are, but we're also really excited. It'll be uncomfortable for a while, because there's no way monumental change won't be uncomfortable, but that doesn't mean it's bad. It'll be good for us to start over somewhere new."

Leo pondered these words. *That's it.*

When Leo got home, he went straight to his bedroom, ignoring his sister calling after him from the living room. He took a seat at his desk. It was organized neatly, all his books stacked against the wall and his pencils and pens in their holder. The only things out of place were the four acceptance letters on the desktop.

In that moment, he ignored them, pulling open his desk drawers one at a time until he found where he'd discarded the letters from the schools he had ruled out. For the first time since they made their way into the drawer, he removed them.

He was searching for the first letter he'd gotten back, the one he'd barely read before dismissing. The only reason he'd even applied to the school was because of his mother's insistence.

Am I really doing this? he wondered, finding the crinkled paper and stopping to study it. He remembered looking it over the day it came in the mail. This time felt different.

His fingers curled, further wrinkling the paper. Michael and Ian were moving to Europe. He could manage this.

He found his mother sitting at the dining room table, a novel open in front of her.

"Hey," she greeted when she caught sight of him. "You didn't come home right after school. Were you with Colin?"

"Michael and I got coffee," he answered, putting the letter down and sliding it over to her. "This is where I want to go."

Surprise showed on her face as she read the school's name at the top of the paper. "Are you sure?"

Nodding, Leo pulled out the chair across from her. As he sat, he kept his eyes on her face, observing her reaction. He knew this decision was unexpected, and the last thing he wanted to do was upset his mother. While she had been the one to recommend the school to him, he was positive she wouldn't be excited about the distance. "I think I need to do this. I'm sorry it took me so long to decide."

There was a minute of tension in which neither of them spoke. Then she folded her book shut. "I guess I'll call your father."

CHAPTER TWO

LEO

Eight Months Later

"Why don't you rest here for a bit," Leo's father suggested, hovering awkwardly in the doorway of the room that had been designated as *Leo's*. It was strange to have a room that was *his* at his father's house. His stepmother even painted it for him; a mint green she thought he would love, which was ironic since he was colorblind.

He was only staying with them for about a week before moving to campus, but he could appreciate the gesture and enjoyed having a place to hide when he got overwhelmed.

His father and stepmother, Meredith, were both nice people, and after years of trying to get Leo to visit their home, they were so incredibly pleased to have him there that sometimes they couldn't stop themselves from hovering. He endured it as much as he could, and then a little longer because he felt guilty about his unexplained and abrupt departure five years ago when he'd last visited, but he needed a break sometimes.

"It's been a long morning," his father said, knocking his fist against the doorjamb before finally leaving him on his own.

It *had* been a long morning, the longest since he arrived in California three days before. They'd spent the past few hours shopping for Leo's dorm room. He had most things already, but he'd put off purchasing the bigger items in Illinois. Everything left on his list had now thankfully been found, leaving him, and his bank account, thoroughly exhausted.

Leo went to the bed and lay on his back above the covers. It was cold in the house, though in contrast to the heat outside, he quite enjoyed the cool air blowing from the vent by his bed. He would appreciate it while he could. In five days, he would move into a small room that lacked air-conditioning.

A room that was only half his.

So far, he communicated with his roommate—*Justin Morris*—through messages. They discussed only two topics: who was bringing what for their dorm, and the times they began class in the mornings.

Leo ended up using the school's random roommate selection. It was fine. Who he shared a room with didn't matter. At least Justin seemed like an okay person. They probably wouldn't have any problems.

Leo rolled onto his side to stare out the bedroom window. All he could see was the roof of the house across the street and a blue sky.

Morgan should be going to college, too. I wonder where he's going.

Since arriving, Leo caught himself thinking about the other boy often. It was hard not to when most of the memories they shared took place right outside his window.

Days ago, when he was first shown to this room, his father left him alone to unwind from the trip and emotional exhaustion of saying goodbye to his mother and sister. Leo had stood in front of his window, staring at the gray house down the street. Seeing it again confirmed the accuracy of his memories. The only thing missing was the boy jumping down the porch steps on his way over. *Morgan.*

What does he look like now? It's been five years. Would I recognize him? Would he recognize me?

Leo spent a lot of the time in his room standing in front of the window asking himself these questions. It was happening almost subconsciously, his feet taking him there before he even considered looking outside. Sometimes he'd stare at the house and watch—*hope* might have been a better word—for Morgan to come out (he hadn't yet), and other times, Leo would look up and down the street and reminisce on the events from years ago.

He could view many memories from his spot in front of the window, and when they came to him, he thought about them thoroughly, as if confronting them now could resolve the guilt he felt for his behavior at the end of those two weeks.

Still, Leo was happy he wasn't able to see the small house built into the tree in Morgan's back yard. He wasn't quite ready for that memory yet.

"Hey, Dad?" Leo began, twirling his fork around in the spaghetti his father prepared for lunch. His dad was a good cook, but Leo missed his mother's food terribly and had to resist the urge to make a face with each bite. "Do you remember that kid I was friends with when I visited?"

They didn't talk about his visit often, and both his father and stepmother paused, sharing a quick look. "Yeah. Morgan Sloan. What about him?"

"I was wondering if you knew where he was going to school," Leo admitted, taking another bite of pasta. He felt their gazes linger on him.

"I haven't heard anything," his father eventually said. "The Sloans haven't lived on this street for years. They moved a few neighborhoods away into a smaller home once both of Morgan's sisters moved out."

Disappointed, Leo mumbled, "Oh."

I've been watching that house for no reason.

"I'm honestly surprised the two of you didn't keep in touch. You seemed really close," his father said.

Meredith smiled warmly. "He was very fond of you."

I know, Leo thought. He nodded and turned back to his food, hoping the heat he felt in his face wasn't visible to them. *That's why I left.*

It was awkward then. Leo knew it was his fault for acting strange, but he didn't know how to fix it. He simply curled his fingers tighter around his fork until his knuckles cramped and waited.

His father broke the silence. "Do you have all your textbooks already?"

Leo quickly swallowed his most recent bite. "Yeah."

"If you'd like, in the future you can ship your books here and we'll hold them for you. It'll free up some space in your suitcase."

Leo's situation still didn't feel real to him, so the idea that he'd be returning later sounded strange. "Oh. Thank you. I'll remember that when I'm ordering books for next semester."

Across the table, Meredith smiled. "I don't think we've discussed the courses you're signed up for, have we? You're majoring in astrophysics with a minor in . . ." Her eyes flicked over to her husband.

"Astronomy and mathematics," Leo's father filled in, grinning as if this made him proud. Maybe it did.

"That's wonderful," Meredith claimed, grabbing another piece of garlic bread from the basket on the table. "Tell us about your schedule."

He didn't want to talk, but it was probably good practice for him. In less than a week, he would live in a place where he knew absolutely no one, and talking about himself would be necessary to make friends.

"I'm signed up for physics and astronomy, and I'm taking political science and psychology to cover some of my core credits," Leo said. "Three classes on Monday, Wednesday, Friday and one on Tuesday and Thursday, with my physics lab Tuesday nights."

"That's a pretty tough schedule. I'm sure you'll be able to handle it. Your father mentioned that your high school had you taking all honors and college courses by your junior year and you still finished third in your class. That's impressive," Meredith praised.

Horrible at taking compliments, Leo ducked his head and mumbled a weak "Thanks."

"Your sister is starting there this year, isn't she?" asked Meredith.

"Yes," he confirmed, though he was sure she already knew this. Lizzy was close with their father and Meredith. At least once a week she took it upon herself to reach out to them, so they were pretty up-to-date on her life.

When Lizzy didn't pass Edgewood's entrance exam the year before, their mother was understandably upset. His sister hadn't failed because the test was too hard; she failed because she would rather spend time with her now ex-boyfriend than study. As punishment, their mom labeled the boy a major distraction and forbade him from coming to their home. The relationship ended only a few short weeks after this rule was put in place, and it appeared Lizzy was unwilling to risk such a thing with her current boyfriend, because she threw herself into studying for the test and scored even higher on it than Leo had.

"She doesn't want to go, because her boyfriend won't be there," Leo said.

His father shook his head. "Well, that's always been your sister."

Meredith launched into a story about choosing the wrong college because of her high school sweetheart, leading to her transferring a semester in. Leo half listened as he finished his food, nodding when she told him it would be nice to go into Freshman year single.

"It'll be like a fresh start," she said, smiling warmly at him. All of her smiles were warm. He didn't remember that from when he was a kid, but he was positive she'd been kind to him back then as well.

"Yeah," Leo acknowledged, not because he particularly cared whether he was single as he began his undergrad but because a fresh start was the whole point.

Chapter Three

Sloan

"Are you sure this is a good idea, Morgan?" his mother asked, turning in the passenger seat to look back at him.

The use of his first name peeved him—he'd been going by Sloan since his freshman year of high school and he would prefer it if his parents called him that—but he knew it was useless to correct her.

His mother continued. "This seems too soon, doesn't it? I mean, you've only been dating for a year. Maybe you should try this next year." The way her sentence ended indicated there was more she wanted to say, and he would bet his life it was going to be something like, *when your relationship is more of a sure thing.*

While he understood her concern—a year wasn't long to be dating someone before moving in together, especially at eighteen—it was unnecessary. Everything was going to be *fine.*

How could it not? It's Drew, he thought fondly.

"Mom," Sloan began, smiling widely at her so she knew he wasn't sharing the same doubts. "I'm positive, so don't worry about me."

"I—"

He cut her off with a chuckle, turning to peer out the window at the apartment building as his father pulled into the parking lot.

"I know, Mom." Curling his hands into fists out of both

nervousness and excitement, Sloan studied his new home. He'd turned eighteen over a month ago, but it was only at this point that he felt like he was becoming an adult. "You can't help worrying about me because I'm your son. This isn't something you need to be concerned about, though. Worry about me adjusting academically, not my living situation."

Academics was what he spent the last month brooding over, the fear triggered when he opened a package addressed to him only to reveal his extremely heavy biology textbook. *"How am I supposed to learn all this in a semester?"* he'd stressed to his parents over supper many nights, the book open on the table beside his plate.

"It looks scary now because it hasn't been taught to you yet," his mother would say some nights, and on others, *"Please stop bringing that book to dinner."*

Most people probably could have consoled themselves, or at least accepted their fate, in the time he had been angsting, but classes started in five days and he still felt a concerning amount of discomfort whenever he looked at that damn textbook. God, he hated biology, and absolutely resented that it was a necessary part of what he wanted to do with his life.

"You're going to be fine, Morgan," his father assured. "You've always been a good student, and you're willing to work hard. Just don't let living with your boyfriend distract you from your studies." At this, Sloan wrinkled his nose and opted not to respond. He still didn't feel any better about his crisis, but he was going to take things one step at a time.

The first step was moving in, and he texted Drew to notify him of their arrival.

"Is Andrew going to come help us with your stuff?" his mom asked. "If not, we might have to make two trips."

His father pulled the car to a stop by the front entrance.

"He's coming. I texted him so he should be down in a second." Sloan tucked his phone into the pocket of his shorts and craned his neck to see into the back seat.

Unlike most first-year students, Sloan wasn't bringing much with him to college. Drew had been living in the apartment for the past two years, and there was no need for additional furniture. When Sloan suggested they get a new couch because he didn't like the orange color of the one in the apartment, Drew got weird about it, so he'd dropped the topic.

Sloan had packed only clothes, necessities, and a few succulents he didn't feel comfortable parting with.

It was only a minute before Drew came to open the door. The sight of his boyfriend made Sloan grin and he exited the car to greet his new roommate.

They hadn't seen each other in a few weeks. Summer had been difficult with Sloan working full time to convince his parents he was mature enough to make his own decisions and move in with his boyfriend.

Drew didn't get it. *"You're going to be eighteen when you move in. Why does it matter what your parents think?"* he always asked when Sloan explained why he couldn't come visit, too busy with work. Sloan doubted that his words got through to Drew at all. By that point, Drew had been a proper adult for three years, so of course he didn't understand Sloan's desire to still have his parents' approval for big decisions.

"I'll get used to it," Sloan assured when his boyfriend expressed concern. *"I'm gonna need a little time to adjust to them not being in charge. I want to know that they're okay with this."*

Then, every time, because he didn't think the joke ever got old, Drew would say, *"Whatever. As long as you don't feel the need to call them whenever we have sex to ask for permission."* Sloan would chuckle along—not because he thought it was funny, he was just expected to—and then thank his boyfriend for being so amazing and understanding, promising to take off work soon and come visit.

This wasn't something he'd have to worry about anymore. Long gone were his days of visiting. Drew's home was becoming *their* home, and if things went well—which he was expecting them to—Sloan would stay for summers as well. He wouldn't need to take time off to visit Drew. His boyfriend would be there when he came home.

"Hey babe," Drew welcomed, grinning when Sloan didn't even bother to shut the car door before throwing his arms around him. With a soft sound that told Sloan his boyfriend was pleased, Drew gripped his hips and pressed his lips against his temple.

Yeah, Sloan thought, pulling away from the hug, reluctantly since it had been so long since he'd last felt those arms around him. *This is a great idea. There's no reason to worry.*

"Hello, Andrew," Sloan's mother greeted, joining them outside the car. She pushed shut the door her son had neglected to close with a warm smile on her face. It was hard to imagine that a minute ago she had been expressing her concerns with Sloan's choice of living arrangement.

Sloan stepped out of the way so his mother could hug Drew.

"How have you been?" she asked. "I don't think we got to see you the entire summer. Every time you two got together, Morgan wanted you all to himself."

This wasn't actually true. Every time they got together, Drew insisted Sloan come to him for purposes of *privacy.* "*I want him all to myself. You know we don't get to see each other often*" was easier to explain to his parents.

"Oh, I've been fantastic," Drew answered, winking in Sloan's direction when their gazes locked. "Even better now that you've delivered my new roommate."

His mother's expression shifted to something a little warier as Drew reached out to brush his knuckles against Sloan's forearm. The touch made him shiver, his breath hitching.

"I'm expecting you to take good care of him," she managed.

It wasn't that his parents didn't like Drew; it was just that there were some things about him they weren't sure of yet. This was understandable. Sloan and Drew had only started dating about thirteen months ago, and

Sloan's parents had had very few chances to get to know him. Sloan was sure they would come around eventually. Already they'd made improvements, having given their blessing for Sloan to move in with Drew—something they most definitely wouldn't have done if they'd still felt the way they had about him in the beginning.

His parents' previous blatant dislike for Drew could be traced back to the day they all met.

During Sloan's junior year of high school, when he was still trying to decide what college to attend, his parents took him on plenty of school tours. It was on a tour that he first encountered Drew, who was working as a guide at the university over the summer. Sloan was sure he would never forget the way the older boy paused in his introduction of himself upon laying eyes on him.

During the tour, Drew had been completely professional, the perfect gentleman Sloan came to know and love. When they hung back at the end of the tour as Sloan's parents used the bathroom, Drew stared him straight in the eye and asked, *"So how much do I need to beg before you give me your phone number?"*

The answer? Not at all, though Sloan teased him for a minute before giving in and passing his digits off to the college sophomore.

It only took about two weeks for his mother to discover that the reason her son was spending so much time on his phone was their tour guide, and she'd been less than pleased. *"How do you know he doesn't give all the kids he shows around his number, Morgan? He's a college boy. They do stuff like that because they're only thinking with their—"*

"He's different," Sloan always promised when the topic came up. *"Drew's not like that."*

Drew not being like that was something his parents were still coming around to on their own. Seeing that Drew was serious enough about their relationship to want to share an apartment with him seemed to help the cause.

Sloan could hardly wait for the day his parents finally saw in his boyfriend what he did, because Drew actually *was* different. There were so many things about him that made him special, and Sloan knew how incredibly lucky he was to have him in his life. Of *course,* Drew could take care of him, and his boyfriend told Sloan's mother as much with a gentle "I will. He's in good hands." As he spoke, Sloan's father finally got out of the vehicle. Drew's green eyes raised to regard him. "Hello, sir. How was the ride up?"

"Smooth," his father answered. Sloan was fully prepared for the man to launch into a soliloquy about how wonderful his SUV was. Instead, he asked, "Are you ready for your final year?"

"As ready as I'll ever be," Drew responded, smiling politely. "It's not really my final year, though. I'll still have two more after I complete my undergrad working on my masters." The prospect of continuing school after college made Sloan want to cringe, and he reminded himself this was something he too would need to get through in order to become a doctor. His mood worsening at this, he let out a sigh only his mother was attentive enough to catch.

The noise must have been mistaken as discomfort from the heat, because she suggested, "Shall we grab boxes?" with a gesture toward the back of the car. "It would be nice to get into the air-conditioning."

"That's a great idea," Drew agreed, following Sloan's father when he rounded the car to the trunk.

His dad opened the door, revealing Sloan's three large bins and five plants.

"Wow, you brought a lot," Drew said. "I thought we talked about how I already had all the stuff we need."

"Ah, yeah, sorry," Sloan apologized, smiling sheepishly. "I have a lot of clothes, and the plants go where I go so my mom doesn't kill them." His mother rolled her eyes.

It was funny, since she always hated when he rolled his eyes. It had to look incredibly similar on his face as it did on hers. Most things about them were the same: dark blond hair, gray eyes, the shape of their mouths. She was just mirroring the expression she disliked so much on her own face.

A laugh left Drew. He slipped his arm around Sloan's waist, pulling him close to his side. Warm lips pressed a kiss to his cheek. "It's okay. I'm not at all surprised. I'm sure we'll be able to make it work."

Sloan's father distributed his things among them and they all followed Drew to the front door. Sloan went in first, then hesitated, glancing at the keypad on the wall. "What are you waiting for?" Drew asked. "They emailed you the code, didn't they?"

Even though Sloan had been visiting Drew at the apartment building for over a year, his boyfriend had never shared the code to get inside. It wasn't because Drew didn't trust him, Sloan was sure. Drew just didn't like to break rules, even for the sake of convenience. Now that Sloan filled out all necessary paperwork and made his first rent payment as an official resident, he finally received the code in an email from their landlord.

"They did," Sloan confirmed, setting his bin down and pressing in the five-digit code. "It just feels strange actually putting it in for the first time after all my visits." The lock clicked. Sloan held the door open for the three of them to enter before him.

As Drew passed by, he took a second to press a kiss to Sloan's temple. "Welcome home."

The four of them got dinner, and afterward, Sloan's parents drove them back to the apartment building. Drew bid them goodbye before leaning over to quietly ask Sloan not to take too long. As he went up to their apartment alone, Sloan and his parents climbed out of the car to exchange hugs.

He embraced his mother last, knowing she would want to hold on to him a little longer. When he pulled away from her, she still didn't let go. Her hands remained on his arms. She seemed conflicted, her eyes glassy with tears. "You're happy, right?"

"Yes, I'm happy," he answered. His insistence didn't seem to convince her because her worried expression didn't change. "Mom . . . is this about Margo?"

Immediately, she turned her face away, answering without words.

Margo was his beloved cat, a gift from his parents for his thirteenth birthday, and until two months ago, the plan had been to bring her to school with him. Originally, he was planning to live in the dorms and worried the cat wouldn't be able to adjust to the smaller space, but when Drew said, *"Why don't you just move in with me?"* Sloan thought this solved the problem.

But then there was a bigger problem. Drew didn't like cats, and he didn't want one in his apartment. For about a week they discussed it, and decided that Margo would remain at Sloan's parents' house for the first year and then they would discuss the topic again over the next summer. Maybe then Drew would feel comfortable referring to it as *their* apartment, not just *his*.

"Mom, it's fine. I mean, it's not like I'll never see her again."

"You cried when we left this morning because of that damn cat."

He laughed, then pulled his mother back in for another hug. "You're going to take good care of her for me, so it's fine."

This time, when he pulled away, she let him go. "Call us," she demanded.

Nodding, he forced a smile. "I will."

She reached out to touch his arm again and said, "Okay, love. Be safe."

His heart hurt as he watched them climb back into the car, but he didn't let the sadness show until they had driven far enough away they could no longer see.

***

When Sloan got up to the apartment, he went to the bedroom to unpack. As he passed the bathroom, he could hear the hiss of the shower on the other side of the door.

He sorted through the first bin of clothes, putting things away in the closet and dresser and making sure everything was incredibly neat so his boyfriend didn't realize he was on the messier side just yet.

It was seeming like he may actually finish unpacking before bed, already halfway through the second bin, when he uncovered something unpleasant. With a heavy sigh, he freed the sizable biology textbook from the bin. He brought it over to the bed and took a seat on the edge of the mattress. In a sort of dread-induced trance, he stared blankly at the book.

When Drew walked into the bedroom a few minutes later with wet hair and only a towel around his waist, Sloan was still seated there. At the sound of his boyfriend, he raised his head and smiled so Drew didn't pick up on his discouragement.

"What are you doing?" Drew asked. He came to stand in front of him, eyes on the book. "Are you excited?"

Sloan didn't respond right away, afraid that if he was honest, it would disappoint Drew. Still, he decided he didn't want to start off being an actual adult by lying to his partner. "I'm kind of worried, actually." He brushed his thumb over the top left corner of the book's cover, where it was scuffed from the previous owner. He bought all used books for the semester, finding the price to be far more reasonable that way. "I don't know. Sometimes I feel like a bio major doesn't suit me."

"Nonsense," was Drew's curt response. He took the textbook from him and dropped it in the bin. "You'll be fine if you apply yourself. Are these the hangers you brought?"

Caught off guard with the sudden subject change, Sloan frowned. "What?" With one hand on the towel to keep it around his waist, Drew bent down and pulled a blue hanger from the bin. "Oh, yeah. Those are my hangers. Why?"

"They don't match mine."

Sloan glanced toward the closet, where he could see all of Drew's clothes on white hangers. "Oh, no, they don't. They're hangers. Are they supposed to match?"

It didn't seem like it would matter, though Drew was looking at him as if it did. "Well, I'd prefer if they did," he claimed. Something about his voice told Sloan he should care as well.

Still, he didn't, but it wasn't a big deal, so he gave a shrug of his shoulders. "Oh. Okay. We can stop somewhere tomorrow and get more."

"Alright," Drew agreed, dropping the hanger and coming to sit on the bed beside him. "We might be able to find a place where you can walk in and get your hair cut, too."

"My hair?" He'd been putting off getting a haircut for a while, liking it a little wilder. He thought it fit him better.

Reaching out to pinch a blond strand between his fingers, Drew said, "It's getting long. Your bangs must hang in your eyes when it's wet. There's no reason for you not to cut it."

Sloan shrugged, because it did hang in his eyes when it was wet. "Yeah, sure."

Smiling, Drew leaned in to connect their mouths for the first time in nearly a month.

And *god*, it felt good. With a soft sound of pure content, Sloan melted into his boyfriend. His fingers reached up to rest on Drew's bare chest as his lips were pressed apart. This surprised him. Drew wasn't a huge fan of open mouth kissing—*"It feels too wet,"* he'd said the last time Sloan asked about it. Sloan found this disappointing, so he eagerly kissed back while he could.

After a few brief moments, Drew pulled away. "Let's have sex."

Startled by the forwardness, Sloan's eyebrows shot up. He turned to look at all he had left to unpack. "I don't know . . ." he trailed off. "It's just . . . it's been a long day and I should probably unpack tonight so these bins aren't in the way."

Not listening, Drew stayed close, the hand on his leg moving to touch more intimate places. "Come on," he urged, thumbing the button of Sloan's shorts. "Relax."

I can take care of it later, Sloan told himself, turning his face toward the persistent man and allowing himself to be pushed back against the mattress. This was what adults in a relationship did.

Chapter Four

Leo

Even though he was trying to think about anything else, Leo was having a hard time ignoring it.

The *heat*.

It was sweltering, causing his hair to cling to his temples and his clothes to stick uncomfortably to his body. When he moved, the fabric would temporarily pull from his skin, only to be glued to another part of him with sweat. Every shift made him painfully aware of how damp the sheets below him had become. He'd only moved in that morning and he would already need to wash his bedding. When he managed to find the washing machine, that is. That'd have to be done later. It was far too hot to explore the building yet.

Moving in turned out to be a non-event. He and his father only needed about twenty minutes to unload the car. By the time they had finished, Meredith had already assembled the futon and put the sheets on his bed.

His father and Meredith left shortly after, wanting to be out of the way before Leo's roommate made an appearance. They both pulled him into hugs on their way out, even though they were all gross from the heat and humidity trapped in the small room. To his surprise, he actually felt sad watching them go. Overall, he enjoyed the week he'd spent with them.

Once they were gone, Leo started to hang his shirts in the wardrobe sandwiched between the end of his loft and the wall. Only about half of them found their place before he decided it was simply too hot to function and climbed into bed.

Thankfully, the heat was the only thing about the room he couldn't handle.

The space was small and he cringed at the idea of sharing it with another person, but it was clearly divided with the lofted beds on opposite walls and the desks underneath them. The wardrobes were awkwardly at the end of the beds, unable to fit anywhere else because the futon took up so much space along the back wall. Beside the futon on Justin's side of the room, there was enough space for a mini fridge. The dorm was *cute*, to use a word of Meredith's. Another had been *cozy*.

Cozy but *hot*. Groaning, Leo sat up and pushed a hand through his hair, trying not to think about how sticky it felt. Would he be able to stand it for three and a half months? His father insisted it would cool down in a few weeks when the temperature outside grew milder, but he was having a hard time foreseeing that, too busy focusing on how to not die in the present.

Usually, Leo spent most his summer in the AC since he naturally ran warm. Winter was his season. It always had been. *So why am I going to school somewhere it doesn't snow?*

He took out his cell phone and texted his sister this question. Then, because he hadn't spoken to Colin in a few days, he sent his friend a message asking how move in went.

Colin moved into his dorm the day before. While Leo wanted to text him right away to see how he was faring, he knew Colin was probably busy making new friends already.

The thought made Leo's eyes shift over to the door. His father and Meredith left it open upon leaving, at his request. It was apparently what everyone did for the first few days after moving in, welcoming people into the room so meeting neighbors was easier.

Leo was playing along because he thought that more air circulation might make the temperature in the room drop.

His phone buzzed in the palm of his hand, and he raised it to look at the screen.

Colin: Went well. Call tonight?

Leo: Yeah. I'll call you, though. Have a freshmen group meeting tonight with my floor and I have no idea when it's gonna be done.

There were still no messages from his sister. This was unsurprising. He talked to his mother that morning, and she mentioned Lizzy's boyfriend would be over.

Sadly, he was out of distractions, so he went back to agonizing over the heat and considering how expensive it would be to buy a window air conditioner.

He didn't know how long he'd been there melting when a boy with dark brown hair walked into the room. He was carrying a large plastic bin, much like those Leo had used to move in.

Pulled from his daze and slightly alarmed, Leo sat up. At the sound of the creaking loft, the kid's eyes found him. They were blue. "Hi," the brunet greeted, studying him with mild interest.

Wrong room? Leo wondered. *Looking to make friends? Justin?*

"Hey," he offered.

"The door was open."

"It's hot."

The other boy chuckled and set the bin on the floor. "It is," he agreed, scanning the room. "I noticed. Hot air rises, though, so why are you lying in your loft?"

Not wanting to admit it was because he was afraid of leaving sweat marks on the light gray futon, Leo answered, "I figured since it's the third floor, it wouldn't make much of a difference."

"That's probably true," said the boy, not yet confirmed to be Justin, as he crossed the small room to look out the window. "You didn't bring a fan, did you?"

"No," Leo admitted somewhat miserably.

The boy smiled. "Yeah. Me neither." He turned toward Leo's loft and outstretched a hand. "I'm Justin."

An older man walked into the room with a bin identical to the one Justin had been carrying. Leo spared him a glance, assuming he was a member of Justin's family, given his roommate's lack of alarm. He shook Justin's hand.

"Leo," he offered back.

The man he presumed to be Justin's father lowered the bin he was carrying and then looked to Leo. "Hello. Are you Justin's roommate?"

"No, he's a random kid hanging out in my roommate's bed. *Yes,* he's my roommate, Dad," Justin answered for him. Uncomfortable in the way he often was around new people, Leo shifted awkwardly on his mattress.

"I suppose that was obvious, huh?" Justin's dad said.

Not wanting to lie there lazily while they brought everything in, Leo offered, "Do you need any help?" It came out weak. He felt far too tired to be helpful.

This must have easily been detected, because Justin chuckled and shook his head. "Nah, man. You're all good. You should probably find a building with air-conditioning and hang out there for a while. You look like you're gonna have heat stroke."

As Justin and his father left the room, Leo wondered why he hadn't thought of that already.

Leo figured it was a good time to find all his lecture halls. The buildings were likely air conditioned, so he could cool down as he searched.

He was trying to locate his schedule on his phone when it rang. *Lizzy* appeared at the top of the screen.

"Hey," he greeted after answering, hesitating on the path through campus where it diverged to the right toward a large building. The name

Marvin Science Center was displayed in silver letters above the entrance. "Oh."

"Oh?" Lizzy echoed. "What's that mean? What are you doing?"

He started toward the building. "I'm looking for my classrooms. The science center is close to my dorm."

"That's nice. How is your dorm? Dad and Meredith called, and Mer said it was cute. She's more optimistic than you, though, so I wanted to know what you thought."

All the doors to the science building were locked when Leo tried them. An examination of his surroundings revealed a small device for him to swipe his ID card.

"It's fine," he answered, running his card through the scanner. There was a moment in which he thought it hadn't worked, then all the doors clicked.

"*Fine*," Lizzy repeated, exasperated.

"It's nice."

She sighed. He was only vaguely aware of her annoyance with him, too focused on the cold air washing over him.

"I don't know what you want me to say to you. It's small. My roommate is moving into it right now. I'll send pictures once everything is set up," Leo promised.

"Ohhh." There was a brief silence, and Leo used it as an opportunity to find the room numbers on his phone. When she spoke again, her voice sounded distant. "Is your roommate hot?"

Without having gotten the needed information, he returned his phone to his ear. "Lizzy, *no*," he scolded. "You can't date my roommate. Off limits."

"I wasn't asking for *me*," she insisted, sounding amused as she always did when Leo added a new person to his list of people she wasn't allowed to date. Really, it was a list of people who weren't good enough to date her. He was going to keep that to himself. "Besides, I already have a boyfriend."

"Lizzy," he groaned, not considering her suggestion. "Shut up. Don't say stupid stuff like that. Now be quiet for a second. I need to check my phone for room numbers" She groaned, though didn't speak until he finished and said, "Hey, I'm back."

"Why is me suggesting you get a boyfriend a stupid idea?" she demanded, prepared to fight with him if he'd allow her to.

He ignored the question as he started down the hall.

"*Leo.*"

"I'm not looking for a boyfriend, Lizzy," he insisted, his voice lowering as he passed a girl sitting on a bench outside of a classroom. "That's not why I'm here. I'm here to get my degree and to—"

She interrupted, finishing the sentence for him. "Be *boring.* Yes, I know." That wasn't what he was going to say, and he rolled his eyes. "Leo, this is it."

Confused, his eyebrows drew together. "Huh?"

His sister's voice took on an excited tone. "This is the *year!*"

"The year of *what?*"

"You getting your cherry popped!" she exclaimed before making a popping noise.

"Oh, for crying out loud—" Her laughter interrupted him. Flustered, he nearly missed the door to his physics classroom. "Lizzy, stop."

"You can't waste college, Leo," she lectured, as if she had some higher knowledge about how he should live his life. "I know what you're thinking right now, but all jokes aside, you need to try and make friends. You can't be lonely all four years. New start means new friends."

The worry in her voice made him feel uneasy. "I know," he grumbled, continuing on to find his astronomy classroom. "I'm going to try. You know I'm not great at that stuff."

He really wasn't. The only reason he had his friends in high school was because Colin found him endearing and didn't leave him alone.

"Leo, everyone is in the same boat as you. They're all looking to make friends." Lizzy's voice was suddenly soft. He felt embarrassment settle in the pit of his stomach at his transparency. Luckily, she knew him well enough to know that was about as much of the topic as he could handle and easily changed the subject. "So, how was it staying with Dad?"

"Oh." He stepped into the stairwell and startled at the sound of the door shutting heavily behind him, echoing throughout the well. "It was nice, actually. Weird, since it seemed like both of them really wanted to bond with me, but I get why. I feel more comfortable around them now than I did a week ago."

"That's good," Lizzy assured, and he could hear the smile in her voice.

His sister was one of the only people who knew about what happened that summer he was supposed to spend in California. She never pushed Leo to share the story with their father, but she made it known that she wanted Leo and him to mend their distant relationship.

"Meredith is nice, huh?" she prompted.

Leo hummed thoughtfully in agreement, thinking of the hug he'd received from the woman earlier that day. "Yeah. She's great. Very welcoming."

He reached the top of the stairs.

The first room he came across was the one he was looking for, and he made note of the location. The obvious next step in his quest was to leave the building in search of Winston Hall, where his other two classes would be held. Instead, Leo wandered, not willing to part with a temperature he felt comfortable in just yet.

When he didn't say something else right away, Lizzy ran out of patience. "Hey, what are you doing?"

"Finding my classes," he answered. "I told you that." He slowed to a stop. At the end of the hall was a small study space with a window overlooking campus. There was a couch that appeared long enough to fit him, and the space was empty. "Maybe I'll take a nap."

"You're going back to your room?"

"No." Leo continued down the hall. "There's a couch here."

"So, you're going to sleep on it? Leo, what if somebody kills you?"

He couldn't help chuckling at this. "No one's going to kill me. There's no one even here." At the end of the hall, he looked over his shoulder to make sure that was true and then approached the couch. "I don't think you understand how hot my room is." He lay down on his back, head propped against the armrest with his eyes closed.

She snorted. "Okay, dork. Send me pictures of your room when you get back to it, okay?"

"Yeah, sure. You're going?"

"Well, I'm not going to waste my time talking to you if you're going to fall asleep on me," she said. "Besides, Dennis is over and he's hanging out in the living room with Mom, so I should probably make sure he's okay." She paused, then, "Love you, idiot."

"Yeah, love you too," he replied. "I'll send you pictures later tonight."

"You better." She hung up without a goodbye. She'd never been good at those.

He dropped his phone on his chest and crossed his arms over his stomach. It was nice talking to her, even though their conversations were never long. He always felt better after they spoke.

Leo wasn't comfortable enough to fall asleep. The way he was lying made his neck hurt, and when he slid down the couch so his head was flat, he found it wasn't any better because his feet hung off the end. Still, it was preferable to his dorm room, so he stayed and looked out the window with half-lidded eyes at the campus he would come to know over the next four years. Being there almost didn't feel real. He'd spent so long preparing for this chapter of his life, but he still didn't know how to feel about arriving at it.

Excited, probably, though that wasn't the word he would use to sum up his feelings. What he felt was anticipation.

Sighing, he directed his gaze upward. His whole body tensed at the sight of a pretty blonde girl peering down at him with curious brown eyes. "What are you doing?" she whispered. He sat up quickly.

To hide his flushed cheeks from her, he faced the window. "I'm sorry."

"No worries!" she assured, seeing him making room on the couch as an invitation to round it and sit beside him. "I was surprised to see you here, is all. I moved in yesterday and this is where I've been taking all of my naps." As she spoke, Leo studied her. Two things surprised him.

The first was how open she was being, giving her words to him like they cost her nothing, like she wasn't afraid to say something stupid or embarrassing that would make him judge her. *That's how most people are,* Leo reminded himself. It always struck him as strange.

The second thing was how pretty she was. Her blonde hair was clipped out of her face with hairpins and her eyes were wide and warm. It wasn't often that Leo was caught off guard by a girl's appearance like this. His sister was beautiful, so he was used to seeing a pretty girl, and he was gay, so girls rarely piqued his interest long enough to give them more than a glance.

"So, are you a freshman this year?" she asked.

It seemed they were going to make small talk. He didn't like small talk much, but it had to happen before they progressed to an interesting conversation. "Yes."

"Cool! Me too." She pulled her legs up onto the couch, folding them on the cushion in front of her. "I moved in yesterday because I'm in the honors program. Our freshman experience began last night. Yours starts tonight, right? Or are you in the honors program, too?"

He wasn't, mostly because he waited too long to apply and missed the deadline. "I'm not. I start tonight."

"That'll be fun. It kinda sucks at first since everyone is overwhelmed by living in a new place and stuff, but the people I've met from our class are nice so far," she told him. "I'm just excited to start classes."

Her words died then and she looked at him expectantly, probably waiting for him to ask the question that clearly came next. "What's your major?"

Her face lit up. "Biology! I'm pre-med, actually. What about you?"

"Astrophysics," he shared.

Despite the lack of information, she seemed intrigued. "Graduate school?"

"Probably," he answered. "It's hard to tell at this point."

"That's super cool!" she insisted. "Oh, I don't know your name. I'm Colette." She held out a hand. He shook it.

"Leo," he responded, pulling his hand back.

"So, are you in here to get away from the heat?"

"I am," he admitted, staring forward blankly. *More words,* he reminded himself. "I was shocked by how hot my room was." A laugh left her, the sound pretty.

"Yeah, my room is really awful as well. Where are you living?"

He had to think about it, not yet familiar with the names of the buildings. "Warner."

Her nose wrinkled. "All boys, huh?"

"Yeah. I didn't know that until I moved in."

"Didn't they talk about it during your school tour?"

"I didn't get the chance to tour," Leo admitted. "I actually ruled this school out at first and made a split-second decision to go here." Even if he hadn't, he was pretty sure he wouldn't have gotten to tour. Plane tickets were expensive, after all.

Her eyebrows raised. "Oh? Why'd you rule it out? It's a great school."

"It was my farthest option from home," Leo answered vaguely. "I was reluctant to be so far from my family."

"That's understandable." She seemed thoughtful.

Leo was surprised that their conversation was carrying on for so long. He'd been expecting to sit there in silence uncomfortably after exchanging names.

Colette continued. "I only grew up about twenty miles away, but I didn't stay for my family. I've been in this area my whole life and I love it. I couldn't imagine being anywhere else."

Suddenly, Leo missed home.

"Oh, hey!" she said eagerly, distracting him from the pang in his chest. "Is this your phone?" She leaned down—which was impressive given how she was sitting—and picked his phone up off of the floor, where it must have fallen in his haste to sit up.

"Oh. Yeah." He accepted it and noticed the time. It was only four thirty, and his meeting with his freshman experience group wasn't until six, but he still wanted to eat and shower before then. "I should probably go."

"Oh, really?" she asked, sounding disappointed, though not managing to look anything other than content as she stretched out across the couch as soon as he rose from it. "Well, I guess I'll see you around, Leo. It was nice talking to you."

"Yeah," he agreed, watching enviously as she easily curled up on the couch. "I'll see you." He actually kind of hoped he would.

He thought about their conversation the entire way back to his dorm room, wondering if he said the right things at the right times and hadn't completely put her off to the idea of socializing with him again. Lizzy would be proud.

Maybe I'll like the people here, he thought hopefully.

A minute later, when he unlocked the door to his room, he was greeted by the unmistakable scent of marijuana. His roommate was sitting on the futon, clearly stoned.

Or maybe not.

CHAPTER FIVE

SLOAN

Sloan was ready for his first day of classes. His hair was cut to Drew's liking, he had the dreaded biology book in his backpack, and he woke up with his first alarm, which didn't always happen. To his horror, his chemistry class was scheduled for the earliest possible time block, so at eight a.m. he pulled himself out of his and Drew's bed and filled an incredibly large travel mug with freshly brewed coffee.

Initially, he was planning to drink it throughout all three of his morning classes, but by the time he made his transition from chemistry to biology, it was almost gone.

A girl named Colette—a blonde with a zest for the morning he found off-putting—was in both science classes with him. He walked with her to biology, listening as she explained her whole planned-out future. It sounded strikingly similar to his own—bio, pre-med, medical school, internship, residency . . . so many years of so many things—and listening to her talk about it made him feel even worse.

"Are you okay?" she asked him suddenly, cutting off from her speech about which hospital she would prefer to work at. "You look like you're gonna pass out."

Groaning, he raised a hand and rubbed his tired eyes. "I'm not, sorry. I'm really not a morning person and I hate biology with a passion."

"Didn't you just tell me you're a bio major?" She reached out and took his travel mug from the side pocket of his backpack. "Oh, my god! Was this full? You drank this much coffee already? Don't you need to pee or something? Coffee is really acidic. I think you're gonna get sick."

He chuckled and took the mug back from her. "I don't, and I'm not."

"You know we have lab tomorrow at eight, right?" she reminded.

"Yeah, I know." Thankfully, both of his labs took place on Tuesday, and all of his classes were Monday, Wednesday, and Friday, so he could sleep all day Thursday if he pleased. "I'll try to go to sleep early tonight."

They reached their classroom and Sloan opened the door for her.

She continued on with their previous topic. "Okay, so what's your issue with biology, then? Should you really be majoring in it if you hate it that much?"

"I don't actually hate it," Sloan grumbled, following her into the classroom.

There was only one other person in the room so far, a boy wearing a red baseball cap pushed down enough to shadow his eyes. He looked somewhat familiar. Sloan was pretty sure he had been in their previous class as well.

As he trailed Colette, assuming they'd sit together to continue their conversation, they passed by their classmate's table. Sloan noticed that the boy appeared to be sleeping.

He and Colette found seats on the left side of the lecture hall. Immediately, Colette turned in her chair to look back at the sleeping boy. "God, I can't stand people who don't take things seriously."

"If I'm being honest with you, I wish I were him right now," Sloan said, completely serious. Still, Colette laughed as if he were making a joke and went to pull the much-hated biology textbook out of her bag. The sight of it reminded him of her previous question. "Oh, it's not like I have a genuine issue with bio. I'm just not good at it, so it's hard to stay motivated."

"Then why did you choose biology as your major? You said you were pre-med, right? There are other things you can major in to prepare for medical school. What about chemistry or psychology?" She arranged a bunch of colored pens in rainbow order on the tabletop.

"I would if I thought they'd be any better. I'm not good at science stuff in general," he admitted. Her hand paused, hovering over a purple pen. He raised his eyes to look at her face, and she was staring at him like he was crazy. "Look, I know that sounds stupid, but I'm gonna work really hard. I may not be excited for this class, but I'll get through it." He was repeating Drew's words to her, words that were said to give him confidence, though they sounded pathetic coming from his own lips. "I just want to be a doctor."

"I'm sure you'll be able to do it." Her voice was softer then. It was clear she was trying to be supportive. "Bio has always been my favorite subject, so if you ever need help, let me know, okay? Here, give me your phone. I'll put in my number. It would be nice to have someone to study with."

He unlocked his phone and handed it to her with a smile on his face, happy he already met someone to struggle through his least favorite class with. "That would be great."

More students entered the room, talking far too loudly for how early it was. He was absently watching them come through the door when Colette's voice reached him again. "So, is that your boyfriend?" She placed his phone on the table between them. It was still lit up, displaying his lock screen photo of him and Drew.

They were standing outside the apartment building, and Drew's arm was thrown around Sloan's neck, pulling him close so he could kiss his cheek while Sloan grinned at the camera. He loved that picture.

"Ah, yeah. It is," he confirmed nervously, reaching out to grab his phone and returning it to his pocket. Usually, he didn't reveal his sexuality so quickly, but he wouldn't lie. He knew Drew would be upset if he learned Sloan denied their being together.

"Aww," Colette offered, leaning on the table with her elbow. "That's cute. You two look happy together."

Relieved, Sloan smiled. "We are. I actually moved in with him last week."

"Oh?" Colette's eyebrows raised. "Wow. That's kind of serious, isn't it? How's that going?"

"It's good." Living with Drew was fun. They ate together, slept together, went on walks together, showered together—not all the time, just when they were in the mood to—and Sloan loved every second. "Great, actually. We get to spend all of our free time together. For the entirety of our relationship, we had to do long distance. It's nice having access to him whenever I want."

She looked intrigued, and Sloan was more than happy to keep talking.

"Drew—my boyfriend—goes to school here as well. He has an apartment right off campus that he's lived in ever since we met. I'm from about an hour south of here. Close enough I could come and visit some weekends, but I definitely wanted to see him more than that."

"That must have sucked," she sympathized.

He bobbed his head in agreement. It *had* sucked. That didn't matter anymore. They were together now, and would continue to be.

"You said he goes to school here? What year?"

"It's his last," Sloan explained. "He's planning on going to grad school in the area next year, so it shouldn't affect our relationship too much, other than him being busy."

Glancing forward as their professor approached the podium at the front of the lecture hall, Colette quietly asked, "Did you come here because of him?"

"Not really."

The woman up front began to speak. They both fell silent to listen.

As Professor Larson went over their syllabus, Sloan thought more about Colette's question. It wasn't exactly true that he hadn't come to their school because of Drew, but he didn't want her to think he was another kid basing life-changing decisions off of a boyfriend. She had to know as well as he did they were at one of the best schools in the area for a bachelor of science degree. If it hadn't been, he wouldn't be going there, even if Drew was—though that was the precise reason his boyfriend went there as well. To Sloan, it was okay that he considered Drew heavily in his decision, because it was the best school he'd gotten into.

Biology class went quickly. For a minute after they were dismissed, Sloan stared at the few notes he'd written in horror. He was blowing it out of proportion—they'd only covered vocabulary—but he spent so long dreading the class that he couldn't help it.

I don't know if I'm going to be able to do this, he thought.

Beside him, Colette was packing her backpack. "Do you have a class after this, or would you like to get coffee or something? I can explain what she went over." He didn't know if he should be concerned that she knew he was an idiot or thankful she saw he was struggling and offered to help.

"Thanks, but I actually have political science right after this," he answered, finally folding his notebook closed and pushing it into his backpack. "Could I text you later, though?"

"Yeah, for sure. I have Ancient Civilizations at one thirty, then I'm done for the day." She didn't rise from her seat even though her things were packed up. "It's kind of rough you have three classes in a row right in the morning. Is polisci your last class of the day?"

"I have a four-hour break and then Basic Statistics at three thirty."

As he zipped his backpack, she sympathetically patted his shoulder.

He checked his watch. "I should go. I have to get to Winston Hall for my next class." As he rose, he pulled one strap of his backpack over his shoulder. "I'll talk to you later, Colette."

"Bye, Sloan," she replied, smiling and raising her hand to wave. Feeling content, he returned the gesture.

As he left the classroom, almost giddy, he wondered whether it was normal to be so excited about making your first friend at college.

He found his political science room less than a minute before class was supposed to begin. The small lecture hall was almost full. Not wanting his classmates to notice his near tardiness, he took the seat closest to the door.

This professor, a man who seemed to be in his late fifties and was *exactly* what Sloan had been expecting, began the class by taking roll call. While this was incredibly boring to sit through, Sloan didn't mind having a few moments to decompress after biology.

He was simply relaxing with his eyes closed when the professor called a familiar name. "Leo Meyer."

Wait, what?

"Here," came the response, sounding just as bored as Sloan felt. Curious, he sat straighter in his seat, suddenly alert. His gaze moved throughout the room.

There was no way that Leo was there. It must be someone with the same name, because the Leo Meyer he knew was from the Midwest and there was *no way* he was in California studying at the same school as him.

But he *was*. He was sitting a few rows from him in the room's center aisle. Sloan could perfectly see the side of his face, a face that was unmistakable to him even after so many years. *He's here*, Sloan thought, staring at the boy from his past in wonder. *He's actually here.*

Absently, when he heard his name called out, he responded, "Here," watching Leo carefully to see if he showed any sign of recognition. He didn't seem to be paying attention. He stared forward, his expression blank, as if he too wasn't excited to be there.

Probably not a political science major, Sloan noted, amused.

The professor finished his list of names and put a slideshow on the front screen. Sloan was aware of everyone around him beginning to write, but he found he could not join them, unwilling to look away from the boy he never thought he would see again. An intense feeling of relief washed over him, as if all this time he'd been waiting for Leo to come back into his life. There were so many things left unsaid between them. Sloan owed him an apology.

He stared openly and for a long time, fascinated by the things in Leo that had changed—no, *matured.* He looked so much older, *handsome* rather than cute. *Has it really been five years?* It felt wrong that so much time had passed since their last encounter. Even though they only knew each other for a short time, Sloan could remember wanting to be with Leo forever. They had talked about staying in contact way back then, before he went and ruined everything.

This is my chance to make it better, he told himself. *This is my chance to be his friend again.*

From the corner of his eye, he saw the professor change the slide without him having written any of it down. He forced himself to look at the front of the classroom, comforted by the fact that Leo would not disappear again.

Does he even remember me? he wondered. *He must.*

I was his first kiss, after all.

Sloan thought about it throughout class. About how he wouldn't move when the professor dismissed them. He'd wait for Leo to leave and when he was close enough, Sloan would reach out and gently touch his arm to get his attention.

It didn't happen like that.

All through class, he kept thinking of the look on Leo's face after he kissed him, clearly concealed panic. He made the mistake of pretending not to notice, simply telling himself it was first kiss jitters and Leo would get over it.

The memory drove him from his seat as soon as they were

dismissed. Sloan left the classroom first.

Not yet, he thought. *I'm not ready to know if he hates me.*

Chapter Six

Sloan

Five years ago

Toward the end of Morgan's seventh grade year, two new kids came to his neighborhood.

The girl looked to be a little younger than him, and often played with the elementary aged children on the block. The boy kept to himself. Whenever Morgan saw him, he was sitting on the steps of a porch down the street reading. He was Morgan's age, his mother had told him. The son of one of their neighbors visiting for the summer.

There was nothing particularly interesting about the boy. He had black hair and pale skin and clearly enjoyed reading more than anything else. Morgan would have liked a friend in the neighborhood since all his school friends lived too far away to hang out on weekdays, but he doubted this boy would be interested in anything he wanted to do. For the first few days after noticing him, Morgan hardly thought of him.

That all changed the Sunday before his second-to-last week of school. Morgan had been taking a walk around the block with his mother when he noticed that the boy had moved from his spot on the porch to kneel in the grass along the Meyers' front walkway.

As they got closer, Morgan could see that he was drawing on the sidewalk with chalk. Curious, he looked to see what the boy was making as they passed the house and noticed that he was writing something.

Morgan's feet stopped. His mother came to a stop as well, a few paces ahead of him. "Morgan?" she asked.

"I'll come home in a little while," he told her, already cutting across the Meyers' lawn.

The boy didn't look up, not even when Morgan took the final steps toward him. He was either too distracted by the task before him or simply did not find Morgan's presence interesting enough to acknowledge.

Morgan stopped off to the side so he wouldn't be in the kid's way. He directed his attention to the ground to see what had been written. He frowned upon realizing he wasn't able to read any of the words. The letters seemed to be all out of order. "What is that supposed to say?"

The kid ceased writing and looked up at him, revealing his face. From afar, Morgan had thought he was plain. Up close . . .

Pretty, he thought, his throat closing and his heart pounding. The reaction confused him. He wondered what it meant.

Mr. Meyer's son squinted at him for a moment before dropping his gaze and continuing the movement of his hand.

Morgan feared he wouldn't receive a response. Then, the boy claimed, "It says, *I hate it here,* in French."

Eyebrows furrowing, Morgan turned his head to better look at the letters. "You know French?" That seemed weird for someone their age. The boy didn't answer. "You know, it doesn't really rain here often. That's going to be there for a while."

"Good."

Morgan had been expecting a longer answer. "What's your name?"

A beat of silence. Then, "Leo."

"Do you go to school, Leo?"

"Yes. I'm missing the last weeks of the year for vacation."

Lucky, Morgan thought.

"Why do you always sit out here by yourself?"

"Why does it matter?" Leo shot back. After an uncomfortable pause, Morgan took a seat on the pavement across from him and grabbed a pink piece of chalk from the beat-up box. He drew a sun. When he raised his head, Leo was looking at him, dark eyebrows pulled together. "Why'd you sit down?"

"Because I'm always by myself, too," Morgan answered.

"So?" Leo didn't seem to care.

Morgan wondered if he should give up and leave Leo alone, but the boy was already far more interesting than he'd been expecting. He wanted to know more about him.

"So," Morgan continued, tossing the piece of chalk into the grass so it didn't break before wiping his hands on his shorts. "Let's do something together."

CHAPTER SEVEN

LEO

It probably shouldn't have surprised him as much as it did, but after a week of classes, Leo could determine that college was absolutely draining.

For most students, it was probably the workload and time management that depleted their energy, but these were things Leo was already used to from high school. They were not his problem.

His problem was that desperately, Leo missed being alone.

Everywhere he went, there were people. When he was in class, there were his classmates; when he was in the cafeteria eating, there were the students talking around him; and when he was in his room, there was Justin.

He didn't mind Justin, really. They talked little, which was actually preferable, and when they did talk, it was never about anything that made him uncomfortable. Justin smoked a lot, sure, but he always did it by the window, so he wasn't hotboxing Leo in their room. On top of that, he bought air fresheners—as well as a fan, though this was probably more because of the heat than the smoke—so the room didn't smell.

Still, they weren't at the point where Leo could consider Justin a friend, which was where the other half of his problem came into play.

While Leo missed being alone, he was absolutely fed up with being lonely.

He needed to make friends and didn't know how to. It seemed to be too late. All the people around him had already established their little groups and were no longer looking for anyone else to be a part of them. Sometimes he even spotted Justin around campus with two other boys, the three of them always laughing about something. The word *jealous* was not one Leo used to describe himself often, though he felt something akin to it every time he went to eat lunch by himself after seeing Justin with his friends.

It was his own fault, really. Leo had the opportunity to try to make a friend. Multiple times he'd seen the blonde from his first day on campus, and each time she met his eyes, she would wave. He always returned the gesture and considered going up to her, but he didn't know what he would say, or if she even wanted to talk to him. Maybe she was being polite by waving and would find him approaching her to be bothersome. Even though he wanted to talk to her, it was a risk he never took, afraid to make her uncomfortable.

It was because of his lack of friends and inability to put himself out there that when he returned to his dorm on Friday, it was with the mindset that he would have nothing to do that weekend except homework.

"Hey, man," Justin greeted when Leo pushed open the door. He was seated at his desk, hunched over an open textbook. Not for the first time, this surprised Leo. Although he appeared uncaring and laid-back, Justin was clearly devoted to his education and spent much of his time between getting high—and while high, Leo noticed a few times—completing class work.

"Hi," Leo responded, aware of how miserable he sounded. After toeing off his shoes, he went to drop his backpack by his desk and clambered up into bed. It was hot as always, so he lay above his covers on his stomach.

"Long day?" asked Justin. Leo wondered if he was imagining the concern in Justin's voice. He hoped so. He already felt like a child with his mother constantly checking in on him. His roommate worrying about him as well was not a comfort.

After a pause, Leo answered. "It's been a long week."

Justin chuckled as if he too was having the same issues. "Well, we have fourteen more of those to go," he reminded.

The idea of fourteen more weeks of this was terrifying. Not for the first time, he wondered if he should have gone to school with Colin or chosen to study online. These thoughts weren't exactly welcome. They often led to him being angry with himself for wishing to take the easy way out, but sometimes he couldn't help thinking them.

"Are you gonna go out tonight?" Justin asked.

Astounded, Leo pushed himself up on his elbows to look down at Justin, who had turned so his back was to him. The question was so ridiculous he thought Justin must have been joking, but it was impossible to tell without seeing his face.

He asked as much.

"Uh, no?" Justin said, and Leo could see his pen pause. "Why would I joke about that? I'm genuinely curious."

Leo's surprise shifted to perplexity. "Why would I be going out?"

"There's lots of reasons," Justin claimed, dropping his pen. He leaned back in his desk chair enough that the front legs lifted from the ground. "It's the first Friday of the semester. Lots of people will go out. There's gonna be parties all over the place."

There are? Leo wanted to ask. He stopped himself, aware that he would be admitting he hadn't been invited to any. In all honesty, he didn't want to go, but he felt it would be embarrassing to say he didn't even have the option of going because no one reached out to him about it.

"If you've had a long week, it might be a good way for you to blow off some steam," Justin suggested, finally turning to look at him. Their eyes met, and it occurred to Leo that this was his invitation. "Come on. It'll be fun. You haven't gotten out much, so it'll probably be good for you."

So, he noticed, Leo thought, keeping his face completely neutral as he stared back at his roommate. Shame rose within him. How could Justin not have noticed? Leo didn't leave their room for anything other than food or class, and Justin had to have seen him alone around campus just as Leo saw him *not* alone.

He knew Justin wasn't trying to make him feel bad with his words. Still, he kind of *did*, exposing to Leo that he wasn't the only one aware of how lonely he was becoming and would continue to become without some kind of interaction. Justin was only trying to be nice. While that was mortifying, it was nearly impossible to say no to.

"Fine," Leo agreed, looking away. It felt like he was giving something up by agreeing, like he was admitting to his weakness. "I'll go . . . where exactly is this happening?"

"One of the campus houses. You can walk there with me. Do you need alcohol? You have to bring your own."

"No, I don't need alcohol," he answered, dropping back down on the mattress.

Leo had a certain philosophy that he should try things at least once to better understand them. There were exceptions to this, of course. He would not attempt hard-core drugs or have sex with a woman . . . not that he'd ever slept with a man, either. Alcohol was already crossed off his list, and he had no interest in trying it again anytime soon. After tonight, he guessed he could eliminate parties as well.

The conversation was over then. Justin went back to focusing solely on his homework, and Leo typed a message to his sister. The party wasn't exciting to him, but he knew Lizzy would want to know about it.

Leo: Guess what I'm doing tonight?

Lizzy: What???

Lizzy: Stop using formal punctuation at the end of your texts, you seem passive aggressive

Leo: I'm going to a party.

Lizzy: OH MY GOD ARE YOU SERIOUS!!!!

The walk over was filled with Justin speaking and Leo making the occasional noise to let him know he was listening.

After five minutes of this, Justin asked, "You really don't enjoy talking about yourself, huh?"

Leo sighed and shook his head. "There's not all that much to say," he admitted, which was his first full sentence since they left their dorm building. "Will I get kicked out if Campus Safety comes and catches us?"

"Kicked out of the party?" Justin asked. "If Campus Safety comes, the party is over—oh! You mean kicked out of school, don't you?!"

Leo wasn't able to dignify this with a response before Justin laughed, throwing his head back in his amusement. Startled by the sound and the fact that he had been the one to cause it, Leo blankly looked at the boy beside him.

When Justin laughed he was attractive, Leo realized, or he would have been if he wasn't wearing a jacket—it was almost eighty degrees outside even with the sun having set, so he looked ridiculous—with its pockets stuffed full of beer cans. "No, you won't get kicked out of school," Justin answered finally. "Oh, my god, Leo. They'll give you a warning at first. Besides, if Campus Safety comes, just run. You don't get in trouble if they don't catch you, and you should have a better chance of getting away since you're gonna be one of the few sober people there."

This was news to him. Maybe he should have assumed as much with common sense. "I will?"

Justin smiled and shook his head. Leo was pretty sure it was at his naiveté and not in answer to his question.

He was beginning to regret coming along. It didn't sound like it would be fun to spend the evening with a bunch of drunk people. "Oh."

"You might actually find it easier to talk to people if you know they're drunk," Justin said. "A lot of people won't even remember what you say to them."

It occurred to Leo that maybe this would not be the best place to meet people. If they weren't even going to remember him in the morning, what was the point? He didn't share this thought out loud, assuming Justin would laugh at him again. Instead, he said, "I'm not worried about talking about myself."

"No? I thought you were. I mean, I know absolutely nothing about you, and we've been living together for a week." They were nearing the end of the campus houses, so Leo suspected they were getting close. It seemed strange that he couldn't hear any music yet.

"I didn't realize you wanted to know things about me," Leo said. Justin gave him a dry look. "What? I didn't."

In a way that implied it was obvious, Justin said, "Of *course* I want to know things about you." Leo's eyebrows raised. "Don't you want to know things about me?"

If he was being honest, he hadn't really thought about it. "Well . . ."

"Leo, we live together. We're supposed to accumulate information about each other so we're not strangers the entire time. So we're comfortable living together," Justin explained. Leo must have made a concerned face, because he immediately added, "I'm not saying I find it uncomfortable to live with you, I'm just saying it's kind of weird that we have to live in the same space for the next few months and I don't even know where you're from or what you're studying."

"Oh." He considered this. "I don't mind—"

"We can talk about this later," Justin cut in. He reached out to grip Leo's arm, forcing him to a stop. "We're here."

Leo examined the house with a frown. "We are?" Faintly, he could pick up on the sound of a beat. It wasn't nearly what he had been expecting. "I don't hear much."

"You're not supposed to," said Justin, nudging him up the driveway rather than the walkway to the front door. "I've been told that the few houses with basements on campus are where most of the parties are so it doesn't get too loud. That's how you keep Campus Safety from coming. We have to go in the back door. It's suspicious if a bunch of students are coming in and out of the front."

"How do you know all of this?" Leo asked, following him to the back of the house where a group of seven or so were standing by the door. They all had beer. Other than that, they didn't seem suspicious, their voices clear but quiet, obviously at ease with their breach of campus policy.

"I grew up in a college town," Justin answered without explaining what that meant. Before Leo could ask, his roommate's name was being spoken by someone in the group. Justin grinned in that direction with a little "Hey, man."

A boy split from the huddle to meet the two of them halfway. Nervously, Leo glanced at the back door, wondering whether Justin was expecting him to go inside alone.

"Why are you standing outside?" Justin asked the person who'd approached. It was dark out, so Leo couldn't tell the exact color of the boy's hair or eyes, but he knew the stranger was looking back at him curiously.

"Too hot in there," Justin's friend answered. Leo cringed, sick of the heat. "Who's this?"

"Ah, my roommate." Justin turned to Leo and held out his hand. "Give me your phone."

"Why?" Leo questioned, though he did as asked without hesitation.

"Don't you need to unlock it?" Justin asked.

Leo shook his head. "No. I don't have a passcode."

There was a pause in which Justin deadpanned. He repeated what Leo said as a question. "You don't have a passcode?"

Positive he had spoken clearly the first time, Leo made a face at him. "No. Why would I?"

Both of the boys laughed. Justin's friend asked, "Don't you have things on your phone you don't want anyone else to see?"

"No?" Leo replied, unsure. He watched Justin create a new contact. "Why? Do you have things on your phone like that?"

"Oh, shit yeah," the boy claimed, grinning at Leo in a way that made him nervous on top of curious. "I have a lot of—"

"Stop that sentence," Justin interrupted. Leo looked at Justin's friend just long enough to catch his mischievous smile before his roommate was thrusting his phone back at him. "Okay. You have my cell number, so if anyone tries to abduct you or like . . . threaten your innocence or whatever, just send me a message and I'll find you." While Leo had known that he and Justin wouldn't be together at the party, he'd been hoping Justin would take him inside and show him where to go.

"Ah, the basement door is on the other side of the kitchen," Justin's friend chimed in. "Can't miss it."

"Thanks," Leo offered sincerely, sliding his phone into his back pocket. He left the two of them, trying to appear confident as he walked away.

When he pulled open the door, a wave of sound finally hit him and he stepped inside despite his unease.

Even though Leo hadn't known what to expect, he hadn't thought he'd be stuck watching over a drunk girl only twenty minutes after arriving, covered in the beer she'd spilled all over him.

Her name was Kenni, and she appeared to alone. It would have been easy enough to leave her to fend for herself—desperately, Leo wanted to return to his dorm—but he thought about what he'd want someone to do if they found Lizzy in a similar situation and knew he had to stay.

He had given her a cup of water and helped her to a seat at the table in the dining room. Thankfully, the room was empty except for them, so he didn't have to worry about other people as he watched her and thought about how to resolve the current situation.

"Drink," he told Kenni when he realized she hadn't yet, crouching in front of her so he was looking up at her face. She stared back at him with large eyes as he took the cup from her, holding it to her lips. "Come on. You'll feel better in the morning if you do."

"What will you give me in return?" she flirted. He didn't answer, only pressed the cup against her mouth until she took it from him and finally began to drink. This was a relief. Getting hit on was something he wasn't used to, and he didn't know how to respond.

"Hey, do you have any friends you could call?" Leo asked. He stood and crossed his arms over his chest, hating the wetness of his shirt on his skin.

Kenni blinked up at him. "Hmm, I don't want my friends," she protested after a moment of thought. "I want to spend time with you."

"I don't think that's a good idea," Leo responded, bringing his hand to his forehead to push his hair back. It felt damp, reminding him that the house was horribly hot. "Shouldn't we at least reach out to your friends and let them know where you are?"

This time she didn't even consider his words, merely shook her head and raised the cup to drink again.

He didn't know what to do. He was unwilling to just leave her behind, aware of what could happen to her, but he also knew how bad it would look if he attempted to help her to her dorm and was caught by Campus Safety smelling like beer and escorting an intoxicated girl home. For the sake of the college's female population, he hoped the officers would intercede, though at the same time he didn't want to get written up for underage drinking while he was completely sober and had good intentions.

"And what do we have here?" an unfamiliar voice asked. Justin's friend from earlier was standing across the table from them, watching with a grin. "You don't seem like the type of guy to pick up girls"—*What did that mean?*—"but good going, man."

"I didn't pick her up," Leo said, looking back at Kenni. She had ceased drinking and turned in her chair to gaze at the boy addressing them. "She's too drunk to get picked up. She needs to go home."

Justin's friend moved around the table to stand beside him. "Huh," he voiced, eyeing Kenni up and down. "Well you're very pretty." She broke into a smile at the compliment. "Why'd you drink so much?"

"Because my parents won't yell at me back in my dorm room," she answered.

Justin's friend chuckled and held his fist out toward her.

"I feel that." She bumped her knuckles against his. Leo watched them with a frown. "So," the boy began, now addressing him, "why didn't you take her home, Justin's roommate?"

"Leo," he corrected. "And I don't know her, that's why. I just met her tonight."

"I see." Leo lifted his head to meet the boy's eyes. They were an interesting shade of brown. "I'm Max." A hand was outstretched, and Leo shook it hesitantly. Something about his expression seemed to amuse Max, because he chuckled. "No need to look so wary. I saw you seemed overwhelmed, so I thought I'd come over to help."

This warranted no reaction from Leo.

Surely Max was expecting some gratitude, but he didn't seem upset to have received none. Instead, he cracked a smile. "I'm happy I found you."

Unsure of what that was supposed to mean, Leo's eyebrows furrowed. His gaze dropped when Kenni grabbed the front of his shirt. "That makes it sound like you were searching for me," Leo pointed out, though he suspected this was exactly why Max had chosen those words.

This theory seemed more plausible after the cryptic response he received. "It does, doesn't it?" From the corner of his eye, Leo shot the boy a glance, only to find him looking back down at Kenni again. "And what is your name, beautiful?"

"Kenni," she told him happily. "Can I go home with you?"

Leo's mouth opened to protest this—he didn't know how being

friends with Justin spoke of Max's character, and he wasn't about to take any risks—but Max beat him to it. "Not tonight. Maybe some other time when you're in the right mindset. Alright?"

"Okay!"

Max's eyebrows shot up at the enthusiasm, and he withdrew his phone from his pocket, typing in the passcode before creating a new contact. "Hey, put your number in here," he instructed. She took the device from him, fingers slipping from their hold on Leo's shirt.

Leo thought of pointing out that she was possibly too drunk to do this successfully. Instead, he inquired, "Did you come over to hit on her?"

"Not at all," Max said. "I actually didn't even see her at first. Like I said, I noticed you looking concerned. I came over to see if you were alright, and then I noticed you were in the company of a pretty girl and I seized the opportunity." Max smiled as Kenni gave him his phone back. "Thank you. Now why don't you drink some more water?" For some reason, she listened to him right away. Honey brown eyes focused back onto Leo. "So, you're Justin's roommate. I've been wondering what you were like. I didn't expect this."

This made Leo feel self-conscious and he averted his gaze. "I—"

"It's not a bad thing," Max assured. "You're interesting." There was no obvious response to this, so Leo remained silent. It did not deter Max. "What's it like living with Justin, then?"

Leo shrugged. "It's fine. He's quiet and he studies a lot. We go to bed at pretty much the same time."

"And the weed smoking doesn't bother you?"

"Not really," he admitted. "As long as I can breathe, I don't care." In front of them, Kenni hummed a cheery tune. "What do you think I should do about this?"

"I don't know," Max said.

"I thought you were coming over to be helpful," Leo reminded under his breath.

Max laughed. Maybe he really did find Leo interesting. "You can wait until someone she knows comes to get her, or until you find someone you trust to leave her with." The idea of waiting wasn't one Leo liked—he was tired and hot and just wanted to get out of there—and Max must have been able to tell. "You want to head out already? You haven't been here all that long."

"I don't like parties," Leo said. "I'd like to go back to—"

Kenni dropped her water and it splashed all over the front of her shirt.

"Aww," she whined. Leo sighed and lifted the empty cup from where it had fallen on her lap. "Now I'm wet too."

Max's eyebrows shot up, but he didn't make the joke Leo suspected he wanted to, probably for his sake. "Here, give me the cup. I'll go fill it," he offered, holding his hand out. Leo handed it over with a thank you.

When Leo turned back to Kenni, he noticed she appeared to be completely unconcerned with the fabric sticking to her obscenely. Pulling at the front of his own shirt so it wasn't plastered to his stomach, Leo thought that maybe there were some advantages to getting drunk after all.

He opened his mouth to ask how she was feeling, but before he could, a hand came to rest on the crook of his elbow. Startled by the sudden touch, he turned quickly and came face-to-face with Colette. She smiled at him. "Hey, Leo, how's it going?"

Thank god.

"Hey, do you think you could do me a favor?" he asked her desperately, aware that he was possibly being rude and ruining his only chance of a friendship on campus. He was far past the point of caring.

Coming there had been a mistake.

"I need to get out of here. She's very drunk, and I don't want to leave her by herself. Would you be able to stay with her?" He wasn't exactly sure why he trusted Colette to watch over Kenni—he knew her about as well as he knew Max—but he did.

Please say yes.

"Oh!" Colette looked at the girl, eyebrows drawn together in confusion. "Um . . .sure? I just came over here to tell you that a friend of mine wants to talk to you."

"Oh?" Leo couldn't imagine who her friend would be.

"Yeah. He's right over—" Colette turned and pointed into the next room. Leo's eyes followed the direction of her finger. From where they were standing, the only thing that could be seen was an old couch, and it was completely empty. "What the hell? He was right there!"

"That's okay," Leo assured. "Next time, I guess. I'm gonna go. Thanks a lot." He glanced toward the kitchen, where he could see Max by the sink, cup in hand as he talked to a girl with short hair. Leo doubted the boy would mind if he left without saying goodbye. "Bye, Kenni. Thank you, Colette."

Kenni snapped to attention. "You're leaving?"

Leo didn't answer her. He left without another word to either of them. He knew he should take the back door as Justin told him to, but he slipped out the front, anyway. The party suddenly felt unbearable and he desperately needed to get away. It felt like he was suffocating.

As he walked home, covered in beer and upset for a reason he didn't fully understand, the pathetic-ness of the entire night hit him. His fingers pressed on the outline of his cellphone in his pocket, wondering who he could call.

Lizzy might tease him, not because she was mean but because she really wouldn't understand that he was actually distressed, and his mother would be too sympathetic, which would only make him feel worse. Michael and Ian were probably still asleep, and Colin would be out at a party he actually enjoyed, surrounded by new friends.

Leo called no one.

There was no one to call.

Chapter Eight

Sloan

On the first Friday of the semester, Sloan found himself at a party.

He hadn't been particularly interested in attending, but Colette was, and she begged him to join her. It wouldn't be her scene, he could guarantee it, but he agreed to go anyway.

They stood in the basement for thirty minutes hollering to be heard over the music before Colette suggested they retreat upstairs to where it was quieter.

"Why don't we go somewhere else?" Sloan practically pleaded as they made their way to the first floor.

Colette looked back at him. "Do you not like parties? If you don't like parties, you could have said so."

"I don't *dislike* parties," he answered. It was the truth, even though it sounded a bit like a lie. Most of the time, he didn't mind parties. Sometimes he even enjoyed them. It was just that this was his first college party and Drew seemed put out about it even though he refused to admit that was the case. All night, Sloan's phone had been riddled with text message after text message, and his boyfriend expected him to respond to each of them immediately. "I don't mind staying longer if you want to. It just might be hard to find a place to talk."

It wasn't. She led him into the nearly empty living room and pulled him over to the couch.

He was happy he met Colette. They were fast friends, spending Monday evening going over biology and then talking in the library until the surrounding people got annoyed by their laughter. Ever since that night, he and Colette spent much of their free time together.

"Of *course* he's here," she said, sounding bothered. Sloan raised his gaze from his phone to look past the dining room into the kitchen, where he could see the tired boy from chemistry and biology arrive through the back door.

"Maybe you should go talk to him," Sloan suggested. He finished typing his message. "Develop a truce or something." During the past week, the boy caught on to Colette's distaste of him and began to playfully taunt her. Like now, when he caught them watching and one of his eyelids dropped in a wink. Colette huffed while Sloan let out a laugh.

When he looked back down, he saw he'd received another message from Drew.

Colette noticed as well. "You know, you're not going to have any fun if you spend the entire night with your eyes on your phone."

"Aww, am I not giving you enough attention?" he teased, only to receive a soft elbow into his side and a pointed look when he raised his head. "I know. He worries sometimes, and I can't control that."

"Worries about what?" Colette asked. "You are in *very* capable hands, he must know. Or he *would* know if you'd let me meet him."

This was something she had been asking him persistently since Monday night, and he was still holding off on agreeing. "*Drew is really busy,*" he always told her, which was true, but that was only half of it. Drew was busy a lot, and Sloan wanted him to himself when he wasn't.

"You'll get to meet him," he promised her. "If you ever come over to the apartment he could be there, depending on the time. On weekends, chances are he'll be home unless he has a golf thing."

"I'll come over tomorrow!" she said, taking it as an invitation.

Sloan shook his head. "Not tomorrow. I'll let you know when it's a good time."

"Tomorrow isn't?"

The past week he'd barely seen his boyfriend between golf, class, and Drew hanging out with his friends. Saturday was going to be his day with him. "No, not really." Sloan looked up from his phone again. That's when he saw him.

Leo was there. At the same party as them. *At a party.* This surprised Sloan, though he supposed that maybe over the past five years Leo had become a vastly different person, one who didn't shy away from social situations. It seemed unlikely from what he'd seen in class so far—Leo appeared to be as antisocial as ever—but it was a possibility.

One that should be considered, because there he was, standing in a house full of people, his expression troubled as he gazed down at a girl sitting in a chair before him. *He's still so pretty,* Sloan thought wistfully, resisting the urge to sigh.

In his hand, his phone buzzed with another text. He didn't read it right away, eyes glued to Leo. The shock of seeing him in California had yet to wear off. He felt it never would.

Sloan wondered if Leo knew the girl he was with, watching as he crouched in front of her to hold a cup against her lips. Maybe they were friends, or maybe Leo was just looking out for her because he was that kind of person.

"You know," Colette began, bumping into him again with her elbow. "For someone with a *mysterious* boyfriend who probably doesn't even exist—"

"You and I have known each other for five days, and he is very busy—"

"*You* are sure staring at Leo quite intently."

Sloan turned to her, his eyebrows raised. "You know his name?" he asked. It was quite obvious she did. What he should have asked was *how.*

"Yeah. I met him on freshman move-in day," she answered. "Why? Are you interested? He seems really sweet. I can introduce the two of you."

"I don't need you to introduce me," Sloan said. He looked back to the dining room. A boy had joined Leo, and he watched them talk with interest. "We already know each other. When we were kids, he came to California to visit his father who lived down the street from me."

"Came *to* California? Where is he originally from?"

Absently, he replied. "Illinois."

Her eyes got wide. "What's he doing here?"

"I don't know. I noticed he's in my political science class on Monday. I haven't spoken to him yet," Sloan admitted. "Did you learn anything when you two talked?"

"Not a lot. He didn't seem like the type to talk about himself," Colette said. "He lives in Warner Hall, he's an astrophysics major, Um . . .he wasn't going to come here since it was his farthest option from home, which I suppose makes sense now."

"Yeah," Sloan agreed breathlessly. Leo being there felt like a dream. For nearly two years after Leo left, Sloan fantasized about them meeting in the future. It'd been so long now that he'd given up hoping.

"So why haven't you gone to talk to him yet?" asked Colette.

Sloan wondered if he should tell the truth, and then determined there was no reason not to. "Because five years ago I kissed him, and he freaked out and left California the next day. I haven't seen him since. I'm worried he wouldn't want to talk to me after that."

Colette seemed intrigued. "You kissed him? On the mouth?"

"Yeah. It's not that big of a deal. We were thirteen and it happened once. It's not like he's my ex-boyfriend or anything." He watched as Leo addressed the boy standing beside him. Sloan wanted to know how well they knew each other. He could have been mistaken, but it seemed the unknown boy was fond of Leo, his eyes lingering when Leo's attention moved elsewhere. "Besides, he's interesting to watch from afar, you know. He's . . ." Trailing off, he glanced at Colette from the corner of his eye. She grinned at him in a knowing way, and he huffed. "Calm down.

I love my boyfriend very much. I'd just like to be Leo's friend again and apologize for taking his first kiss."

"You should try to talk to him, then! You won't know if he doesn't want to talk to you until you try, and if he seems bothered, you can leave him alone."

"I don't know."

"Oh! That kid left." Standing from the couch, Colette announced, "I'm gonna go get him." She left before Sloan could fully process her words and protest. The warmth rising in his chest told him he wouldn't have, even if he had the chance to.

The feeling grew as he watched Colette get closer to Leo, reaching out her hand to touch his elbow. *This is it,* Sloan thought, biting his lip. *I'm going to get to talk to him again. I'm gonna learn if he still hates me after all these years—*

The phone in his hand buzzed, and this time it didn't stop right away. A call. Sloan hoped it was his mother. If it was his mother, he could ignore it and call her back tomorrow.

The name on his screen said *Drew.* Of course it did. Why would his mother be calling him so late at night, when she was usually asleep? For a second, he considered ignoring it and waiting for Colette to bring Leo over to him, but he could imagine how Drew would react if he didn't answer. Sighing in disappointment, he shot one last look at the pair in the dining room before answering the call and rising from the couch. "Hey, Drew. What's up?" he greeted, trying not to sound put out as he pulled open the front door and stepped out onto the porch, away from the sounds of the party.

"I'm just checking in. Am I not allowed to check in? I want to make sure you're safe," Drew defended in his ear. Sloan squeezed his eyes shut. The disappointment of not getting to talk to Leo slipped away, replaced with guilt. *I can just talk to him when I get back inside.*

"Thank you. Of course you're able to check in. I want to talk to you." Sloan tried to peer through a window into the house. The blinds were drawn.

"Good. How's the party?"

This question annoyed him—they'd been texting about it all night, so Drew must already know—but he didn't let it show. "It's good. Loud. Colette and I moved to the living room so we could hear each other talk."

Drew responded, but Sloan wasn't listening. The door to his right opened, and Leo walked past without looking in his direction. He was leaving, Sloan realized, and he opened his mouth to call after him.

He stopped when Drew said, "Babe? Are you alright?"

"Yes," Sloan breathed. It felt like a lie. He watched Leo walk down the street, getting farther and farther away from him. "Sorry. Something just distracted me for a second."

"Oh? What was it?"

"It was nothing," Sloan insisted. "I saw someone I knew leaving and I was gonna say goodbye, but they're gone already."

"Oh, I'm sorry, babe. Go hang out with your friends. Just keep in touch, alright?" Sloan hummed in agreement, no longer eager to return inside. "Come home soon, please. Don't forget we still have plans tonight . . . and I miss you."

"I know. I miss you too." He lost Leo in the darkness down the street. "I don't think we'll be staying much longer." *Suddenly, I don't feel like there's a reason to.*

When he went inside, it didn't take him long to find Colette. She was standing exactly where Leo had been with the mysterious brunet boy beside her. The girl Leo had been watching was still in the chair, her eyes on Colette, who was saying something to her. When Sloan joined them, Colette fell silent and swung a fist to punch him in the arm. "What the hell, dude! You *ran* away!"

"Drew called me, so I stepped outside," he admitted, smiling at the pretty woman in the chair. "Who's this?"

"Her name is Kennedy. She's super drunk," Colette said. "Leo was watching her—"

"Where'd he go?" the drunk girl whined. "He was so cute and tall. I even offered to go home with him and he left me here." Kennedy looked like she was going to cry.

"Hey, it's okay!" Colette said cheerfully. "We'll take you home." Sloan raised his gaze to regard the boy standing with them and was surprised to find him already staring back. They held eye contact for a moment before the brunet sighed and looked at the cup he was holding.

"I wasn't gone for that long," he said. "Do you think he left because of me?" He directed the question at Colette, who made a face that perfectly expressed her confusion as she turned to him.

"I don't know. He seemed kind of overwhelmed. Were you the one to overwhelm him?"

"I don't think so," was the response, spoken with little confidence. "I came over to help because he already looked overwhelmed. Maybe he's just not good with drunk people." The boy looked at Kennedy—who seemed to have recovered from her sadness—and then blinked as if he suddenly remembered something. "Oh." He offered the cup to her. Before she could take it, Colette intercepted it. "Woah, calm down. It's just water."

With an expression that showed doubt, Colette studied the cup suspiciously. "*Just* water?" she asked. "Are you friends with Leo?"

The brunet made a face that suggested he hadn't been expecting to be asked such a thing. "Why? What's that have to do with anything?"

"I might trust you if you're friends with Leo."

He appeared to be contemplating. "Hmmm, no. I'm not friends with Leo, though it would be easy enough for me to lie, so that wasn't a great question to judge my character. I didn't drug the water or anything, if that's what you're thinking. It's not hard for me to pick someone up with this face." He grinned, as if showing his potential. Admittedly, he was attractive, and Sloan observed this for a second before looking to see Colette's reaction. She was staring at the kid as if he were crazy.

Chuckling, the boy raised both of his hands. "Okay, well, on that note I'm gonna go find the people I came here to spend time with. Have a nice night." His brown eyes shifted to Kennedy, who Sloan would bet money wasn't even listening to him. "Kenni, I'll call you." With that, he left.

Huffing in exasperation, Colette set the cup of water on the table, apparently still not trusting the contents. "I wonder if he was trying to pick Leo up."

"Oh," Sloan voiced, eyebrows drawing together. "But he told Kennedy he would call her . . ." Even as he made his point, he was thinking of the way the boy had looked at Leo earlier.

"He left because I'm not pretty," Kennedy suddenly declared, not specifying which man she was referring to. Sloan felt fingers tug at his, and he glanced down to see that Kennedy had taken his hand. "Is that why he left? Is it because I spilt my beer on him? I said I was sorry and hugged him."

"Kennedy," Colette began, only to be spoken over.

"Do *you* think I'm pretty?" Kennedy asked Sloan.

"You're very pretty," he admitted. Kennedy squeezed his hand tighter. "I'm also gay, though."

Kennedy sighed and released her grip.

"We should get her home," Colette said, reaching out for Kennedy's hand and trying to pull her to her feet. Kennedy refused. "Come on. We'll walk you back to your dorm to make sure you get there safely."

"No," Kennedy protested, shaking her head. "I came here to find someone to sleep with." The bluntness of this made Sloan's eyebrows raise and Colette look slightly horrified. "I can't leave without—"

"Yes you can!" Colette declared, crouching so she was directly in front of Kennedy's face. "You are a strong, independent, beautiful woman and you don't need a man to make you feel validated."

"Wow, Colette," Sloan managed, while the drunk girl simply accepted this with a nod.

"Okay. You guys can take me home." Kennedy stood, and Colette grinned at Sloan, proud of herself. She reached out and grabbed Kennedy's arm.

"Where do you live?" Colette asked, leading her toward the back door.

Sloan trailed them, not at all minding that they were leaving. Drew would be in a good mood for the rest of the night if he returned so soon after their call.

After Kennedy mumbled a response to the question, Colette turned to him. "Are you okay with this? If you want to come back, we can. Or I can take her by myself, but I'm a girl and it's dark outside, so I don't like that option."

"You're not going by yourself," Sloan dismissed. "I honestly don't mind cutting the night a little short. I feel slightly bad that Drew is sitting home alone, especially since he was so understanding when I asked him if I could come." Colette didn't respond and he wished he could see her face as she walked ahead of him. "Colette?"

"Oh. Sorry, I was thinking."

Sloan adjusted his pace so he was walking beside her. Kennedy was on her other side. Either out of kindness or worry that Campus Safety would come and stop them—probably both—Colette linked her arm with Kennedy's, supporting more of her weight as they continued toward campus. "I understand. You miss your boyfriend. I'm happy you could come with me, though."

"Me too." He smiled and bumped his shoulder into hers. He was glad Drew gave him the okay to go along.

They walked in silence for a minute, just listening to Kennedy hum an upbeat song. It was comfortable. A light breeze had picked up, making the walk back not nearly as warm as the walk there. "Hey, I'm sorry I couldn't get Leo to stay." Colette sounded regretful.

"Oh. You don't need to be sorry about that. It's not like you told him to leave."

"No, I know. I am still sorry," she said, reaching out when Kennedy nearly fell off the sidewalk to steady her. "Your expression when you saw him . . . I don't know. I haven't seen many people look at someone like that."

Shocked by this observation, Sloan needed a moment to respond. "We're just friends, Colette." After the words were spoken, he realized they weren't right. They *weren't* friends. Right then, they were nothing, and it was killing him.

"I know," she insisted, turning to smile at him. "I didn't mean it romantically. I know you have Drew. It just looked like you wanted to be near him. Like you couldn't stand the fact that he was so close and not with you. I really think you should talk to him, Sloan. Be his friend."

"I—" *want to so bad,* he was about to say, but a voice calling out interrupted them.

"Kennedy?! Is that you?" It came from a boy who was walking down the sidewalk toward them. "Where the hell have you been? I've been looking all over for you." He stopped a few feet away, gaze moving between Colette and Sloan. "Who are you guys?"

"We found her at the party," Colette answered cautiously. Sloan studied the tension on her face, eyebrows raising at her tone. "She's really drunk so we're walking her home."

"Oh, thanks. I know how difficult she can be when she's trashed. I can take her off your hands," the boy offered, taking a step toward Kennedy, who pulled away from Colette. Instead of going to him, she crouched to look at a bug on the sidewalk in awe. "Oh, my god, Ken. How much have you had to drink?"

"Um, I don't know if I feel comfortable letting her go with you," Colette interrupted, moving to protect Kennedy with her body. "We're almost to the dorms already so we can get her there safely."

The boy had been moving down to collect Kennedy, and now look alarmed that his path had been blocked. He narrowed his eyes at Colette before breaking into a smile.

"Thank you for being concerned, but you really don't need to be.

She's my best friend. Kenni, tell them," the boy instructed. Kennedy looked up from the sidewalk and grinned, her eyes barely open.

"That's Oli," she said happily, reaching around Colette to hold her hand out. Oli stepped into the grass to take it, then helped her to her feet. "You found me!"

"It's Oliver, actually," he told Sloan and Colette, his gaze on his friend as she bent over to brush dirt off her skinny jeans. Sloan wasn't concerned about Oliver having lied to them. His worry for the girl could be seen easily in his expression. "Thanks for looking after her. We were at a party down the street, and when she gets really drunk she runs, and I went to the bathroom for like a *second*—"

"I got lost," Kennedy interrupted, and Oliver sighed, shaking his head. "But look! I made us new best friends!"

"Oh, really?" Oliver asked, smiling at her as she wrapped her arms around his neck. "Tell me either of their names." As he said this, he scooped Kennedy off her feet, picking her up as one would a sleeping toddler, an arm behind her back and the other at the fold in her knees.

"Their names are . . . hmmm. . . Ryan and Kelly."

"Those aren't your names, are they?" Oliver inquired, amusement clear in his voice. Sloan shook his head as Colette let out a breathless laugh.

"He's Sloan, and I'm Colette."

Oliver smiled pleasantly again. "Well, Sloan and Colette, thank you for keeping an eye on her. I can't believe I misplaced her already and its only week one. Come on, Kenni. Let's get you to bed." He went in the direction he had come from, toward the dorms. Over his shoulder, Kennedy waved goodbye.

Colette let out a sigh. "Drunk people are exhausting." She reached down to take Sloan's hand, urging him to walk once more. "Are you okay walking me the rest of the way?"

"Yeah," he said. "Of course."

It was a short walk, and before long they slowed to a stop in front of a dorm building. Colette turned to him, their clasped hands hanging between them. "Thanks for inviting me," Sloan said.

"Yeah." She paused, turning her face to look at the building. "No chance that I can convince you to take me to your apartment right now to meet Drew?"

That was probably a bad idea. Drew mentioned earlier that he wanted to have sex when he got back. If Sloan delayed it by bringing Colette with him, his boyfriend would probably be peeved. "You'll get to meet him, I promise," he assured, chuckling when she let out a groan at his roundabout way of rejecting her.

"*Fine.*" It was good-natured, though, because she laughed and dropped his hand to hug him. Sloan gladly returned the gesture. "You should talk to Leo," she said into his shoulder. "I don't think he has many friends here. You should reach out to him."

"I will," he agreed, stepping out of the hug and grinning at her. "I'll figure it out."

"Soon?" she asked hopefully, and he nodded. It would have to be soon for his own sake. "Good."

He waited for her to get inside before turning around to cut back across campus.

Soon.

Chapter Nine

Sloan

"So!" Colette began, flopping into the seat beside him, her expression expectant. "How'd it go?"

Of course, Sloan knew what she was talking about—she'd asked him the same question every day since the party last Friday, and that was now a week ago—but it didn't feel like part of the game if he didn't respond with, "*How'd what go?*" as he had every other time she'd asked.

Immediately, she deadpanned. He gave her a grin as he brought his coffee to his lips.

"So, you *still* haven't talked to him?"

"You know I haven't. The only chance I have to talk to him is in political science, so I haven't had an opportunity since we discussed this yesterday."

"Sloannn," she groaned, punching his arm lightly a few times as he ignored her and searched through his notebook for the next clean page. "It's been a week, and you said soon! Do you even know what that word means? Come on. You should reach out to him today. It's a Friday, so if you don't talk to him, he's going to spend another weekend all alone. We're going to watch movies with Kennedy and Oliver tonight, remember?"

On Tuesday after lab, Colette apparently had run into Oliver and

Kennedy at the campus coffee shop and they exchanged phone numbers. On Wednesday, Sloan had lunch with the three of them, and they'd made the plans for a movie night. He'd been looking forward to it.

"You should invite Leo to join us!" Colette continued. "It'd be fun. He already kind of knows Kenni."

Shit, Sloan thought, grimacing as he turned back to her. "I forgot to tell you I can't go anymore."

"Oh?" Colette's lips pulled into a frown. "You asked Drew and he said *no?*" Something about her voice worried him, and he quickly corrected the miscommunication.

"When I asked him, he told me he had actually been planning a date for the two of us tonight. While I like you guys, I love my boyfriend and we haven't gone on an actual date since I moved in."

Sloan waited anxiously for her to respond, hoping it was a good-enough excuse to back out of the plans with their new friends.

"That's okay," Colette said eventually. "I understand. That's a good reason to blow us off."

Before he could thank her, their chem professor began to speak about the assigned homework. While Colette struggled with being quiet most of the time, she didn't have this problem during class. For the time being, their conversation was over.

Class was uneventful as usual. The only time it got remotely interesting was when their professor asked a question and Colette, confident as always, had thrown her hand in the air with an answer on her tongue, only to be wrong. This encouraged the boy who deeply irked Colette to raise his hand and state the correct answer. With a little huff, Colette turned to look back at him, as did Sloan, curious to see what the boy's response to her fierce glare would be. He winked, just as he had at the party a week before, and Colette turned away, cheeks pink with rage.

"What exactly is your problem with him?" Sloan asked her after class as they walked to the bio room, multiple paces behind the boy in question so he couldn't possibly hear them.

"He takes no notes," she complained. "He just sits there with his notebook out and listens. His eyes aren't even open half of the time! I think he's asleep!"

And how does this affect you? Sloan wanted to ask, but he knew he shouldn't. Colette, while very nice and understanding, had a certain way of doing things, and she seemed to think everyone else's way was inferior.

"Well, he's clearly studying. I don't think he answered a single question wrong yet."

She clicked her tongue dismissively, the look of annoyance still on her face. "Okay, so about Leo," she began, easily moving on.

Sloan sighed. It wasn't that he didn't want to talk to Leo, but he'd agonized over how to go about it so much in the past week that the idea now exhausted him. "No, don't make that sound. You still never confirmed if you would talk to him today."

"That's because I don't know," Sloan answered, slowing when they reached their classroom. "It's not as easy as you make it sound."

"I thought you decided you weren't going to worry about him not wanting to talk to you."

"It's not that," he dismissed. They moved toward their seats at the far end of the room, walking in front of the irritating—in Colette's opinion, not his own—boy's table. Not for the first time, Sloan noticed the boy's gaze lingering on Colette as she passed. "Well, it's not completely that. I'm still concerned he's going to want nothing to do with me, but I understand I won't know until I talk to him. I'm just not sure how to approach him."

Colette took her seat first and turned to look up at him. "Just go up to him."

With a frustrated huff, Sloan sat beside her. "I can't do that in the middle of class. I need a reason to. And I can't catch him before class because I don't have time, and I feel awkward waiting for him in the hall afterward. I sit by the door, so I guess I could catch him on the way out, but it would be weird to stop him in front of the door, because then he'll be in people's way. I don't know the right way to go about it, I guess. I know it sounds stupid."

"Oh." She frowned, still probably not understanding his dilemma. "When I met him, he was trying to take a nap on a couch upstairs. Maybe you should try to look for him up there."

"Of course you interrupted his nap," Sloan responded, not without fondness. "I'm not going to wander around upstairs waiting for him to come sleep. He probably hasn't tried that again since you ruined it for him. I will talk to him today, though. Okay? I'll wait for him in the hall after class or something."

"I think that's a good choice," she said. "I'm expecting him to hang out with us soon. What kind of movies does he like? I'm planning on making movie watching a common thing."

As Sloan removed his biology notebook from his backpack, he asked, "How do you know he's going to want to spend time with us? Maybe he won't want to be friends."

"But we're cool!" Colette protested. "I think we'll all be great friends!"

Sloan wished he could be as optimistic as she was, but he wasn't so sure. His past actions toward Leo could have been enough to make Leo steer clear of him, even after all these years.

This is it. This is my chance.

Halfway through political science, the professor described a partner project. The words "You'll be able to choose your own partners when I'm done explaining the project" had Sloan's eyes focusing on the black-haired boy sitting a few rows away from him.

He was nervous, though more than that, excited. *I'm finally going to talk to him again.*

The girl beside Leo turned her face toward him, probably considering him as a partner. With a small huff, Sloan zipped his backpack and pulled it over his shoulder. He was going to ask Leo to be his partner before she built up her nerve. There was no time to be nervous.

For the next five minutes, their professor explained the project to the class. Sloan barely listened, his body positioned on the edge of his seat.

I have to get there before she asks him. If I know Leo, he'll say yes to whoever asks him first, and it needs to be me.

He considered that maybe he didn't know Leo. Maybe he *would* say no, though Sloan told himself it was okay if he did. It would confirm to him whether his presence was wanted. This almost seemed easier than simply talking to Leo and trying to sense how he felt. When they were kids, Sloan often had trouble reading him. This would be a way to give Leo an easy out.

"I'll pass out papers once you're situated. I don't mind you moving seats to sit with your partners," Professor Smets finished, gesturing a hand to indicate they were free to carry this out.

Without hesitation, Sloan launched himself from his seat and finally closed the distance between him and the boy he'd never been able to forget.

Chapter Ten

Leo

Leo hated partner projects in general, but he feared this one would be especially difficult, given he didn't know anyone in his political science class. It seemed like it would be easiest to ask the person beside him to be his partner, and he turned to greet his neighbor for the first time when the sound of someone dropping a textbook on his table startled him into looking upward.

The first thing he noticed was gray eyes. Then, the warm smile, as well as the fact that the face before him was familiar. *Oh.*

Leo felt his eyes get wide. "Morgan?" he asked, aware of the disbelief in his voice.

It wasn't an actual question. Of course it was Morgan.

"Wanna be partners?" Morgan asked, his voice deeper than it had been the last time Leo had heard it. Overwhelmed and unsure of what to say, Leo glanced off to the side. His seat neighbor—a girl, he noticed now—was sliding from her chair, leaving it open.

"I guess," Leo responded, looking back at Morgan. Him being there didn't feel real, as if Leo was having another dream in which they were reunited. He felt he would wake up soon and Morgan would be gone.

Morgan smiled as if relieved, and it was then that Leo noticed he'd been nervous about asking.

Why? Leo wondered as Morgan rounded the table to take the seat beside him. *Did he think I would say no to him? Doesn't he remember I could never say no?* "Uh," Leo voiced, struggling to think of what to say. He looked at his old friend, only to have his mind go blank when he caught Morgan already staring back.

They held eye contact for long enough that if it had been anyone else, Leo would have been uncomfortable. But it *wasn't* anyone else. It was Morgan.

Morgan, who went out of his way five years ago to befriend him after noticing him alone all the time.

Morgan, who pulled Leo along with him everywhere during their short friendship, treating him as a necessity to his adventures.

Morgan, who'd curled up next to him the night they slept in his tree house and asked Leo if they could be friends forever.

Morgan, who once kissed him with a tenderness Leo didn't realize a twelve-year-old boy was capable of.

Morgan, Morgan, Morgan.

The man before him differed from the Morgan in his memories. His blond hair was a tint darker and cut shorter. His face wasn't as round, baby fat long gone. The gray eyes were still the same, the almost-blue color unchanged, but something about them seemed older. They gave away less than they used to. Before, Leo had been able to read Morgan so easily, even on the day they'd met. Now, he couldn't tell what Morgan was thinking as he stared back. This Morgan and his Morgan didn't seem like the same person.

Swallowing heavily, Leo forced his eyes away. "You go to school here?"

"Nah," Morgan answered, sounding on the verge of laughter. If he did laugh, Leo wanted to witness it, so he glanced back at him. "I'm just visiting."

"What?"

Morgan laughed. "Sorry. I was teasing. I go to school here."

Starting at the front of the room, their professor began to hand each pair an instruction sheet for the project.

"It's okay," Leo said.

"Me going to school here is okay?"

"No. I mean, *it is*. That's not what I was talking about. I don't mind the teasing. I'm just not used to it." *Anymore,* he tacked on in his head.

Will I get used to it? Is he going to stay around long enough for me to? That wasn't fair. Morgan hadn't been the one to run away in the past, so Leo had no right to expect that of him now.

"I'm surprised to see you," Leo offered.

"You haven't noticed me around campus?"

"No. But if I'm being perfectly honest, I wasn't ever paying much attention. You knew I was in this class though, right? Why didn't you say anything sooner?" Leo asked.

This time, when their eyes met, it was only for a moment. Morgan was the one to look away. "Oh, well. I wasn't sure you would want me to."

Why wouldn't I want you to? Leo was going to ask. Before he could, their professor interrupted, placing a worksheet on the table. It was probably a good thing he hadn't asked. It wasn't clear yet if Morgan was comfortable discussing what had happened between them. Leo hoped he would be. He wanted to apologize for his behavior at some point, now that he had the chance.

"Well, you're not the only one surprised. Actually, between the two of us, I figure I should be more shocked. You're a long way from home," Morgan pointed out. "How'd you end up here?"

At first, the answer he thought of was *to meet you again*. He managed—thankfully—to keep it to himself. It wasn't the truth, not really, but now that Morgan was right there in front of him, it kind of felt like it was. He'd been looking for something, and now, with Morgan's sudden reappearance, he considered the possibility it had been him. "Um, I wanted a fresh start," he managed. "This seemed like a good place for that. It's far away from home, but my dad's close in case I need anything, so my mom was okay with it."

There was a pause in which Morgan examined the direction sheet. Then he asked, "Is everything alright?"

"Why wouldn't it be?"

Morgan's eyes raised from the paper. "Well, I didn't know what kind of fresh start you were hoping for. I thought maybe something happened."

"Oh. No. Nothing happened. I felt like something was missing. I needed something to change and I couldn't decide what, so I changed everything."

Morgan smiled again. "How's that going?"

"It's—" Only negative words came to mind. The idea of sharing them embarrassed him. "*Different*," he settled on. "It's taking me some time to adjust. I like the location despite the heat, and my classes are enjoyable." Morgan's eyebrows raised. The expression on his face was nearly transparent then, save for the faint blush across his cheeks, as if he was feverish or overwhelmed. Leo could relate to the second thing, his heart pounding in his chest. "Not this class."

Yet another smile opened Morgan's lips to display his white teeth. Before Leo could appreciate it, Morgan's face turned away to look at the instructions again. It was taking him a long time to read them, but Leo was happy he wasn't the one attempting to. He doubted his ability to focus right then.

"Well, at least this project doesn't seem too bad," Morgan claimed, glancing at the face of a smartwatch on his left wrist. "Class is almost over, though and we haven't really discussed it yet. Are you free after this? Do you want to go to the library and work out a plan?"

Leo wasn't exactly sure what expression came over his face at the suggestion. The blond must have interpreted it as wary because he was quick to add, "Don't look so unsure, Leo. I'm not going to try to kiss you."

The words didn't process right away, Leo too focused on the sound of his name leaving Morgan's lips. When he finally considered the rest of the sentence, he let out a sigh.

The mention of what occurred between them years ago was a comfort. It was nice to know that they would not pretend it had never happened. "I'm not unsure," he said. "I was just thinking that I haven't been to the library yet since I don't know where it is."

The end of his sentence was cut off by their professor dismissing them. Leo packed his books into his backpack. "We can do that, though. You'll just have to lead the way."

Mild surprise crossed Morgan's face. "Oh. I can do that. You haven't explored campus at all?"

"I only found the places I needed to be," Leo admitted.

Morgan chuckled. Leo thought he looked happy.

They left the room together, and then Morgan led him to the right.

"Where do you go between your classes?" asked Morgan.

"My dorm."

"You must spend a lot of time with your roommate, then. How is he?"

Leo shrugged, thinking of Justin. "He's nice enough. Smokes a lot of weed."

This was apparently funny, because Morgan laughed.

The sound stirred something within him, and it took Leo a moment to place the feeling. Just like Morgan, he was happy.

Leo chewed his lip to refrain from smiling. *Happy.*

For the first time since school began, he didn't feel lonely.

The library, Morgan explained, was four floors. When he asked Leo which floor he would prefer, Leo answered confidently, *"The one with the least amount of people."* He got a pleased smile in return.

They sat at a table near the library's large front windows.

Morgan removed the project handout from his backpack and slid it across the table to Leo. "I've been hogging this," he said. "Do you know what we're supposed to be working on?"

"Kind of," Leo answered. "I listened to about half of what Professor Smets said before I got bored and stopped." He lifted the paper to look it over.

"We only need to talk about how we want to present the information," Morgan explained. Immediately, Leo's eyes dropped to the bottom of the paper to see if it said anywhere that they would need to present in front of the class.

Thankfully, he saw no such instruction. After reading the details, it occurred to him that maybe he and Morgan had little to discuss, and going to the library to prepare may have been unnecessary. "Um, should we do a slideshow?"

"Sure!" Morgan agreed, and Leo lowered the paper enough to look at him over it. Morgan leaned against the table, his elbow propped up so he could rest his chin against his fist. "Now that that's covered, tell me how you ended up an astrophysics major."

Certain he had not mentioned his major, Leo frowned. "How do you know that?"

"Ahh, well, you see," Morgan began, eyes shifting away as if he feared he'd made a mistake. "You know Colette, right? We're friends and she mentioned it."

Leo wasn't sure what he found more unexpected: that Morgan and Colette were friends or that they had been talking about him. "Oh," he offered. "How did that come up, exactly?"

"We saw you at the party last Friday and we briefly discussed how we both knew you. She ended up telling me your major," Morgan explained.

The answer made sense. It also made Leo regret leaving early Friday night. Instead of admitting this, he moved on to the original question. "I'm in astrophysics because I like physics and astronomy. That's probably the most boring answer possible, but it's the truth."

Morgan made a thoughtful noise, seeming satisfied.

"And what are you majoring in?" Leo asked.

When they were kids, Morgan wanted to be an actor, so Leo was completely unprepared to hear the words, "Biology. Pre-med. Chemistry minor." Another thing Leo recalled from their short friendship was that Morgan was enthusiastic about most things. This did not seem to be one of them. Perhaps the slight personality shift that came with aging accounted for this, but Leo doubted it. Morgan looked a little crestfallen compared with the minute before.

Leo looked back at the paper in his hands, using it as an excuse to break eye contact. "I was never good at biology."

"Me neither," Morgan responded miserably. "Colette is practically dragging me through that class, and it's only the second week. I'm getting a little nervous . . . *more* nervous, I guess, since I never felt *good* about it."

"Do you like it?" Leo questioned, interested in the answer. Never before had he liked a subject he wasn't good at and couldn't imagine majoring in one. But, he supposed, as long as you enjoyed it and didn't mind putting in the extra work . . .

"Not really," Morgan admitted, rendering him speechless. There didn't seem to be anything he could say in response besides *Then why are you majoring in it,* but he thought it might be rude.

Before it could get awkward or Leo's hesitance could be noted, Morgan's attention was drawn away from him when a semi-attractive boy came up and placed his hands on the blond's shoulders. At first Morgan startled, his eyes widening, but then he tilted his head back to see who it was and relaxed. With some discomfort, Leo noted the unknown man was staring pointedly at him, eyebrows furrowed to form an expression of displeasure. "Oh, you scared me," Morgan greeted, lips curling.

This statement went unacknowledged. "Who's this?" the angry-looking interruption inquired, brows pulling together even more when Leo stared back with a blank expression. He didn't know how to react to someone who clearly disliked him despite not even knowing him.

"Leo," Morgan answered, head still tilted back. Leo eyed the way the standing man slid a hand to the side of Morgan's neck, the touch tender. "He's in my political science class and we're partners on a project. We actually know one another a bit from when we were kids, though." Morgan lowered his head to meet Leo's eyes. "Uh, Leo, this is my boyfriend, Andrew."

This shouldn't have been a shock, considering how they were touching each other. Still, the information surprised Leo. His eyebrows shot up for a second before he made his face neutral again. It seemed he'd been unable to do this quickly enough because the man behind Morgan tensed.

Morgan chewed his lower lip.

A hand stretched out across the table toward Leo, the same hand that had just been pressed to Morgan's jaw. "I go by Drew," the boyfriend said. Leo shook his hand.

"It's nice to meet you," he offered, not because it actually was—the man had spent the entire time glaring at him—but because it was clearly the appropriate thing to say.

With a nod, Drew's hands returned to Morgan's skin and his eyes dropped to regard his boyfriend. "Sloan, will you be ready for our date by the time I get home later?"

Sloan? Leo thought, watching the couple with interest until Morgan's hand came to rest atop Drew's. The gesture was too personal for Leo to feel comfortable observing.

"Of course. I haven't forgotten," Morgan answered.

"Perfect." There was a sigh, and when Leo glanced up again, he saw Drew's hands slip from Morgan's shoulders. "Okay, well, I'm meeting Simon for lunch before class, so I should go. I'll see you tonight."

"Yeah," Morgan agreed with a smile. Leo was only aware he was staring again when Drew's eyes met his. Typically, he leaned more to the passive side, especially around new people. Right then, though, Leo felt like looking away would mean losing, so he held Drew's gaze.

Something sparked in Drew's dark eyes, and he ducked down and kiss Morgan full on the mouth. This seemed to startle Morgan, because his eyes grew incredibly wide.

A feeling stirred within Leo, but it wasn't what he thought it would be. His expectation had been to feel jealous or bitter. That wasn't it. All he felt was a second-hand embarrassment that made him shift uncomfortably in his seat.

The couple parted, and Drew said his last goodbye before leaving the table. Morgan watched him go with worry clear on his face.

Why do you look so concerned right now? Leo wanted to ask. He thought the answer might be *Because my boyfriend hates you,* so instead he asked, "Why does he call you by your last name?"

Gray eyes flicked back to him, tense expression melting away. "Sloan? Everyone calls me that now. That's what I go by."

"Oh," Leo voiced, wondering how many times he'd called him by his first name so far. "I'm sorry. I didn't know." Morgan—*Sloan,* he supposed—looked at him curiously, his wide eyes and downturned lips making him look innocent in a way he never had when he was younger.

"I don't mind," he assured. "Call me whatever you want." Like with Drew, Leo found himself unable to look away, though it was completely different. This time, he didn't feel like he would lose if he averted his eyes. He just sensed he would regret it.

"I see . . ." Leo trailed off, pressing his lips together. "Well, he seems nice. Good for you, I guess?"

Sloan chuckled. "Thanks. What about you and the guy you liked? Did you two ever work things out?"

"We didn't. He's actually married now and lives in France."

"Aww, that's a shame. I was rooting for ya." This was doubtful. If Sloan had been hoping for Leo to have a relationship with someone else, he probably never would have kissed him. Disbelief must have shown on his face, because Sloan laughed.

That sound made Leo think of summer days long ago.

CHAPTER ELEVEN

SLOAN

"Welcome home!" Sloan greeted when Drew came through the front door with his golf clubs. Usually, he left them in his locker in the sports center. Their presence told Sloan his boyfriend came straight home from practice at the course. "How was practice?"

"It was alright," Drew answered, not looking at him. He leaned his clubs on the wall by the door and toed off his shoes. "What have you been doing?"

Sloan looked at the biology textbook in his lap. "Studying for the last twenty minutes. Before that I was on the phone with Nicole, but she had to go to some study group thing." Nicole was his best friend from back home. She'd started college that week and had called to complain about her new roommate.

When Drew didn't respond, Sloan turned to find his boyfriend's eyes narrowed. "What is it?"

"That shirt. I'm not a huge fan of that color on you. It makes you look pale," Drew claimed. Concerned, Sloan dropped his chin to look at himself.

He was wearing a light-green button down his mother had gifted him for his birthday. It was his favorite color, and he liked how the shirt looked on him, so he tried not to appear too hurt by Drew's opinion of it. "Oh . . . Alright. I'll go change quick and then we can—"

"Actually, I'm going to take a shower first," Drew interrupted, walking toward the bedroom.

"We have a reservation, right? At the library you made it sound like I had to be ready when you got home. Do we have time?" Sloan looked over the back of the couch to watch Drew go through the open door of their room.

There was a pause, and then Drew agreed quietly, "I did say that." Sloan had a suspicion that Drew said it only to bring up their date in front of Leo. He was jealous. "We still have a bit of time, so I'm going to shower since I didn't at the gym. I'll be quick. Change your shirt?"

"Sure thing," Sloan confirmed, smiling at Drew when he emerged from the bedroom in hopes it would reassure him. Drew's expression didn't change.

With a soft click, the bathroom door closed between them. Sloan squeezed his eyes shut, a quiet swear leaving his lips. It was never good when Drew got in these moods.

Not wanting to forget and peeve his boyfriend further, he went into their bedroom and changed out of his button-down. As he pulled on a maroon shirt he knew Drew liked, he wondered why he hadn't considered it earlier. If he had, Drew might have been a little happier.

Drew didn't speak again until they were in the car on their way to the restaurant. "So . . . where are we going?" Sloan asked, hoping to break his silence.

"You'll see when we get there," Drew replied. "It's not too far. Only ten minutes or so. You'll like it. Don't worry."

"I'm not worried about not liking it," Sloan assured. He pulled his lower lip between his teeth. He didn't want to say the wrong thing and worsen Drew's mood. "I was just curious. Um . . .how was your day today? You said practice went alright. What about the rest of it?"

"Fine."

Sloan frowned. "Huh?"

"I said it was fine," Drew repeated without enthusiasm.

Apparently, he wasn't about to cooperate. "That's all you're going to give me to work with?" Sloan questioned softly after a moment of silence.

"What do you mean?" As he spoke, Drew kept his eyes fixed on the road even though they were stopped at a red light. "I didn't know you needed stuff to *work* with. We're in a relationship. Do you not know me well enough to keep a conversation going?"

He isn't being fair. "Are you going to be like this all night?"

"Be like what?"

"Are you going to keep ignoring me?"

"I'm not ignoring you," Drew grumbled.

Sloan felt his patience wearing thin. "Well, you're not really talking to me, either."

Drew looked out his window, hiding his expression. Nothing was said. The light turned green.

They'd just made it through the intersection when Sloan snapped. "This is because of Leo, isn't it?"

Immediately, Drew gave up on pretending not to be mad. "Why didn't you tell me you were with another guy? You didn't come back to the apartment, and you didn't text me—"

"We were in the library doing schoolwork," he defended patiently, not wanting to give in to his own frustration. "You don't get upset if I don't tell you when I'm doing homework with Colette."

"Colette is different."

"Because she's a girl?" Sloan asked, already knowing that was the reason. "You really don't trust me enough to not be worried when I do homework with another guy? I love *you*, Drew."

"It would have been nice if you mentioned it," Drew shot back.

Taking a deep breath, Sloan refrained from responding. Sometimes, just having discussed the problem without even resolving it would make Drew relax for the rest of the night. He hoped this would be the case.

Sadly, Drew didn't seem to want to let it go. "And how come you didn't mention you had a boyfriend? Seems like a kind of important thing to forget."

"I didn't forget about you. It hadn't come up in conversation, and it's not like he was hitting on me. It would have sounded like I was bragging if I suddenly started talking about my boyfriend out of nowhere. I didn't want to make him uncomfortable—"

"Why?" Drew inquired. "Why does that matter?"

Exasperated, Sloan answered, "Because he's a person, and I don't go around trying to make other people uncomfortable. He's shy and wouldn't know how to react."

"Well, that's not really your type, is it?" Drew responded unkindly.

Sloan's jaw dropped in surprise before he clenched it tightly and faced the other direction. They didn't speak for the rest of the ride.

Their silence continued throughout their meal and the drive home. By the time they got back to the apartment, Sloan was exhausted from the tension. He watched as Drew kicked off his shoes and took a seat on the couch. When his hand reached out for the television remote, Sloan realized he had to say something or they wouldn't speak for the remainder of the night.

"Can we please not do this anymore?"

Drew shook his head. "I don't know what to say to you when you don't even recognize what you did was wrong." He finally met Sloan's eyes. It was obvious what he was expecting to hear.

"I'm sorry, okay? Next time he and I work together, I'll text you and let you know. And I should have told him about you right away. I was too focused on our project." There was a pause in which Sloan waited anxiously for his boyfriend's response, and then Drew nodded once. Sighing, Sloan went over to join him on the couch, leaning into Drew's side. He felt guilty. He knew Drew had been looking forward to their going out, and he had prevented them from having a good time. "I'm sorry I ruined date night."

For a long moment, silence stretched out between them. Then Sloan felt Drew's hot breath on his neck. "Make it up to me?" he suggested softly.

It wasn't hard to read between the lines.

With a nod, he slipped off the couch onto his knees, moving to kneel between Drew's legs, which parted for him without instruction. They had done this enough times that it was well practiced.

Even though Sloan didn't want to, he wasn't about to deny him. If it meant they weren't fighting, he'd do anything.

Chapter Twelve

Leo

"Hey," Justin said to get his attention, raising his chin to look at him in his loft. "You wanna come out tonight? I know you said yesterday you weren't feeling it, but it's a whole new day."

"What?" Leo pushed himself up onto his elbows. "You're going to another party?" It was Saturday, and Leo understood Saturday was a typical party day. Still, Justin had gone out the night before, and two parties in one weekend sounded like hell. Leo was still worn out from the previous Friday.

"Yeah," Justin confirmed, not sounding enthusiastic. "I am. I have nothing better to do. Want to come along?"

Lowering himself back onto his stomach, Leo said, "Not really."

Justin smiled. "That's alright. I figured that would be your answer. I wasn't sure if I should even ask you at first. Max kept telling me to check with you, and I thought it was worth a shot." At the mention of Justin's friend, he shot his roommate a confused look. "Yeah, I was surprised too. Are you two friends or something?"

"Uh, no?" Leo denied. "I mean, we talked at the party last Friday, and now he waves to me if he sees me around campus, but I don't think I'd call him my *friend*."

"Strange." Justin took out his phone and sat on the futon. "Hey, what's your fact for the day?"

Ever since Justin pointed out that they knew nothing about each other, they had been sharing a fact about themselves every day. "I'm not good at coming up with them. You go first and I'll think about it."

"Okay . . ." Justin trailed off, considering.

Every day during this conversation, Leo wondered if he should tell Justin that he was gay. He was worried about how Justin would take it. Not that he thought it would disgust him or that he would act cruel afterward; he just wasn't positive Justin would be comfortable living with him.

"Well," Justin began. "My favorite food is lasagna, but only when my dad makes it."

"Didn't you say that one earlier in the week?" Leo asked, sure he'd shared with Justin his love for mac 'n' cheese, and he usually based his facts off of his roommate's.

"Ah, no. Earlier in the week I told you my favorite dessert, and you told me your favorite food because you said you didn't have a favorite dessert. Clearly you haven't been paying attention."

"I can take notes if it's that important to you, but it would be weird to have a paper with a bunch of facts about you on it," Leo said, making Justin laugh. "I don't retain information about people unless I think it's important." *Depending on the person,* he considered adding. He didn't, afraid it might come off as saying that Justin wasn't important enough for him to remember the little things.

There were only a few people over the years who got that treatment: Michael, Ian, Colin . . . *Morgan.*

Justin's fact didn't give him any insight for what his own should be, so Leo hesitated. "I'm not good at talking about myself—"

"Leo."

"I can speak French?" he offered after a pause.

"Really? Like you can actually speak and understand it? Or do you mean you took French through high school, because in that case, I can speak Spanish."

Leo shook his head. "My French isn't perfect, but I had someone teaching my sister and me from a young age and could probably be considered fluent? I don't speak it a lot. No reason to around here. I mostly just watch movies in French and read books."

Justin appeared to be intrigued. "You have a sister?"

"Yeah."

"Older or younger?"

"Younger," Leo explained. "She's fifteen."

"What's she like?"

For a minute, Leo thought of how to answer. "She can be a little wild."

"Oh? How so?"

Leo groaned. "She makes poor decisions. She always has some annoying boyfriend and goes to parties a lot. Just last week, my mom caught her smoking a cigarette, and they got into a big fight." Most of his text messages from his sister lately were about this issue, so it made sense it was the first example that came to mind. With Lizzy, there were many others.

"She's that different from you, huh? You'd think she'd be similar because she was raised by the same people."

"Maybe. She was too young when our parents split to remember what it was like. I tried to be a good kid for my mom after that, not wanting to give her anything else to worry about, but Lizzy ended up being double the work anyway."

Justin shifted on the futon. "Um, your parents are separated?"

"Divorced." It wasn't a big deal anymore. No longer did the idea of discussing it make him upset. "I was a kid when they split. My dad and stepmom live here, and my sister and I live with our mom in Illinois."

"*That's* where you're from?" Justin asked loudly. Curious, Leo lifted his head to look at him, eyebrows raised. "Sorry. That volume was unnecessary. I'm surprised, is all. That's farther than I was expecting.

How'd you decide to come here? I can't imagine being so far from my family."

"Well, like I said, my dad is here, and I felt like I needed a change. A friend of mine was uprooting his life and moving to Europe, and when we talked about it, he was so optimistic, even though he was scared. I thought, if he was doing that, I could move to California and start over too. I miss my mom and sister, though, and I'm not all that close with my father."

This time, the silence between them stretched out even longer, long enough that Leo figured Justin wasn't even going to respond. By the time his roommate's voice reached him, he was reflecting on his words, wondering what required that much contemplation. "Well, if I can do anything to make your fresh start better, let me know."

Leo didn't know what Justin could do besides take him to more parties, so he said, "Yeah. Thanks."

Justin chuckled. "Sometimes you're so easy to read."

After Justin left, Leo thought about Sloan again.

Seeing him had been a shock, and he still couldn't believe that they ended up at the same school. He was glad, though. It had been nice to do something away from his room with a friend for a change.

Friend. He considered the word. *Is that what we are? Friends.*

They'd been on that path when they started working on the project, but Leo wasn't sure if they still were. He kept remembering the way Sloan's boyfriend looked at him—with utter disdain—as well as Sloan's response to that look.

After all this time, it would be nice to be friends with Sloan again, but Leo didn't want to cause any problems. Hopefully, if their friendship was going to be an issue, Sloan wouldn't approach him again. It wasn't like they exchanged numbers, anyway. Silently parting ways once more would be easy enough.

Tangled somewhere in his sheets, Leo's phone rang. He felt around for it, happy to be distracted. Thinking about Sloan's expression when Drew walked away made him feel uneasy.

When he answered the video call, Michael Bradford's handsome face was framed on his screen. "Hello," Michael greeted with a grin. "You look well. We haven't talked in a while, so I thought I would check in." This was true. It had been over two weeks since they'd spoken, the last call coming in while he was still at his dad's house.

"You guys have been busy," Leo said, sitting up so he didn't strain his neck.

"*We've* been busy? *You've* been busy, college kid."

Leo shrugged, wondering whether he should admit to Michael just how much free time he actually had.

"Well, how are you? How has school been?" asked Michael.

"Good," Leo said. "My classes are good. It's been rough socially, I guess. Not that anyone's mean or anything, I just don't know anyone." Sloan came to mind then. "Well, almost no one."

Michael's eyebrows drew together. "What's that mean? You made friends?"

"Uh, not really . . ." Leo shifted his gaze away. If he was going to talk to anyone about this, it would be Michael. "Do you remember when I went to visit my dad the summer after seventh grade and I made that friend?"

"Oh, the kid you had a crush on." Michael sounded quite happy to make the accusation.

Glaring at the screen, Leo denied it. "I did not."

The response was immediate, possibly because Michael was expecting Leo's rejection. "You did too."

Leo shook his head. "It doesn't even matter. Anyway, he goes to school here and we're working on a project together for class." That reminded him. He was planning on finishing it during the weekend so he didn't have to worry later. Maybe that's what he'd spend his night doing.

Michael suddenly seemed excited. "Oh? That's great! Are you two gonna go on a date?"

Leo's eyes grew wide at the misunderstanding.

"Leo's going on a date?!" a voice yelled from somewhere off Michael's screen. Michael smiled at who Leo assumed was his husband. This was confirmed a moment later when Ian's face popped into view. "You have a date? Is he cute?"

"No," Leo denied before realizing he didn't specify which question he was answering. "I mean . . ." Whether or not he found Sloan cute didn't matter right then. "It's not like that. He has a boyfriend who I'm pretty sure doesn't like me."

"He has a boyfriend?" asked Michael.

At the same time Ian said, "He doesn't *like* you?" The couple shared a glance. "How could he not like you? Even I like you, and the first time we met you were completely disagreeable."

"I don't think he liked that I was with his boyfriend," Leo explained. "We were doing homework and catching up in the library, and his boyfriend showed up and seemed displeased by my presence." Leo thought of Drew's hands on Sloan and Sloan's shocked expression when he was kissed. "He kept touching him and kissed him in front of me, and it was uncomfortable. Morgan seemed startled, so I'm guessing he was just doing it because I was there."

"Ah, well, that's awkward," Michael agreed. "At least you have a friend, though." Leo didn't respond. "What? You guys aren't going to be friends?"

"I don't know. If his boyfriend doesn't like me, why would he reach out to me again? He probably only approached me in the first place because he feels bad for kissing me, but that's not a big deal. I don't understand why he would continue to talk to me if it's going to make things more difficult for him. What if his boyfriend gives him shit for it?"

It was Ian who responded, sounding concerned. "Then he's not a good boyfriend."

Leo shook his head. "That's none of my business."

"Don't you care about him?" Michael asked. With a heavy exhale, Leo squeezed his eyes shut. It wasn't that simple.

He cared about Sloan, though he still didn't feel it was his place to make judgments about Sloan's taste in men.

"He's important to me because of the time we spent together as kids, but I don't know him now, and I can't start acting like I know what's best for him," Leo said. "It's not like I have feelings for him and I'm jealous because he's dating someone else. I just don't want to cause any trouble, so I think it's best if I stay out of it."

"Leo . . ." Ian trailed off. They were worried about him making friends, he knew. Ian's expression was troubled.

Michael looked more annoyed than anything. "How's that fair to him?"

"What do you mean? Fair to Morgan?" It felt better to say Morgan than Sloan. He supposed it wouldn't matter soon if his prediction was right. Then he'd have no reason to use either.

"Yes, to Morgan," Michael confirmed. "So, he doesn't get to be friends with you because you're deciding what's best for him without even talking to him first?"

Leo glanced away and grumbled, "How do you expect me to talk about it? I'm guessing he doesn't even want to be friends with me. We're just partners on this project."

"Okay, well, say he wants to be your friend," Michael suggested. "What are you going to do then?"

"I don't know." Now both men on the screen looked annoyed. "Are you suggesting that I be friends with him even if I know it'll cause issues for him? Doesn't that make me a bad friend? I'm trying to do what's best for him."

"Why do you immediately assume that's not you?" Ian asked, the question mumbled. Leo's eyes widened at the implication.

"It's not your choice to make. He's the one who gets to decide if it's worth it," Michael added.

Leo considered this. "I don't want him to think being friends with me was a mistake." If Sloan decided to reconnect with him and had problems with his boyfriend because of it, wouldn't he eventually regret befriending Leo again?

"You have to make your own decisions, Leo," Michael said. "I just hope you have enough common sense to get all the information before you condemn relationships that haven't even begun."

"Consider it, okay?" Ian suggested, smiling at the camera. "You're too young to have regrets."

"I already have regrets involving Morgan," Leo reminded.

"That's right." Michael was speaking so quietly it was almost hard to hear him. "You were the one who ran away, Leo, not the other way around. Learn from your mistakes. Don't repeat them."

Chapter Thirteen

Sloan

"You're acting all excited," Colette accused, looking at him instead of the worksheet they were supposed to be completing. "You're all twitchy. Did you have too much coffee this morning?"

"What?" Sloan stopped tapping his leg beneath the table and checked the watch on the back of his wrist. "Oh. I didn't get up in time to make coffee this morning. I'm looking forward to next hour, is all."

Her expression was knowing. "Ah, Leo?" Sloan studied her out of the corner of his eye cautiously, not liking the way she said Leo's name in a teasing sort of way. "What? I think it's nice you're excited to see him."

"He's just a friend," Sloan was quick to remind, the sentence coming out easily as he'd said it multiple times to his boyfriend that weekend.

Colette's eyebrows shot up. "I know. You've said that and I believe you. It's okay to be excited to see a friend, too. I'm excited to see you before we have this class."

"Oh." He glanced at the worksheet. It was supposed to be finished before the end of class, but Colette didn't seem too concerned about it. "Sorry. When Leo and I were at the library doing our work, Drew saw us and we kinda got in an argument over it. It's fine now, but if he heard someone imply that I might have feelings for Leo, or that Leo might have feelings for me, he'd probably get angry."

"You guys got in a fight over *Leo*?" Colette sounded as if she couldn't believe Leo was the kind of guy to be fought over. "It's not even like the two of you are close friends. Why was he bothered?"

Sloan let out a sigh. The jealous side of his boyfriend wasn't something he enjoyed discussing, and he didn't want Colette to judge Drew because of it. "Drew can be possessive when it comes to certain people. I don't really know what triggers it. In high school, he got weird about a couple of guys I worked with. It can be troublesome." Sloan checked his watch again. *Five minutes.*

"So," Colette began after a minute of work. "What'd you do all weekend then? I know you went on your date Friday night. What about Saturday? Why couldn't you come with Kenni and me to that party?"

Distracted by a question on the worksheet, he didn't look up while he replied. "Ah, well, I kind of ruined our date Friday night, so we ended up having a weekend date."

"A weekend date?" she echoed, sliding the paper away from him to erase what he'd just written and correct it. "What does that entail?"

"Sex and food," he admitted with a shrug, frowning at the new answer on the paper. He shifted his gaze to the front of the classroom, where their professor was collecting worksheets.

A surprised laugh left Colette. "I'm still waiting to meet Drew, you know."

Sloan rolled his eyes. "Oh, my god, you'll meet him, okay? I promise. He wants to meet you, too. His schedule is just really awkward." This wasn't exactly a lie. Drew *had* expressed interest in meeting Colette, though only after Sloan suggested it multiple times and got annoyed with his boyfriend's lack of response.

"Huh," was all Colette said, writing the last answer on the page in time for their professor to come by and collect it, dismissing them for the day. "Well, enjoy your time with Leo. Wanna get lunch when you're done with class?"

"Sure," he agreed, pushing his pencil case into his backpack. "Can I see if he'd like to come as well?"

"Of course. I'll be in the hall after class waiting for you."

"Great." They walked out of the room together and parted ways in the hall.

Sloan got to class a full three minutes earlier than usual. Leo was there already, his head pillowed on his folded arms. The chair beside him was empty. Without a second thought, Sloan approached.

When he dropped into the seat to Leo's right, Leo's eyes cracked open, looking directly at him. As if surprised by his presence, Leo sat up straight. "Morning," Sloan offered pleasantly.

"Hi," Leo said with a soft voice. It soothed the few nerves that accompanied Sloan's excitement.

"How are you?"

"I'm—" Leo cut off, his eyebrows drawing together as if he'd spoken before actually evaluating how he was and needed a moment to think about it. "I'm alright. What about you?"

"I'm good." Sloan shifted in the chair to find the most comfortable position with his lower back ache. "Tired, but I'm always tired at this time. Not exactly a morning person, you know?"

Expression thoughtful, Leo admitted, "I remember that about you."

Sloan bit his lip to hide a smile. "So," he began, and Leo's eyes snapped up to meet his. "When are we gonna work on our project? I know the rest of the work can be done separately, but it might be smart to do it together so we can make sure we're consistent with format and font and stuff."

"Oh. I already finished my half," Leo claimed, suddenly studying the table with great interest. Sloan raised his eyebrows. While the project was simple, it was tedious. It would take some time to complete, and he wondered why Leo rushed when they had the next couple of weeks to get it done. "I shared the slideshow with you so you can look over what I did. I don't care if you want to change anything. I'm not good at design."

"I'll take a look at it," Sloan offered. "When'd you get it done?"

"Saturday night," Leo answered, watching him from the corner of his eye. He seemed more skittish than on Friday. Sloan hoped it wasn't because he was making him uncomfortable.

"Oh . . . so you didn't go out on Saturday, then? What about Friday night?"

Leo made a face. "I didn't go out at all this weekend. It's not really my scene."

Sloan thought of Leo at the party the previous Friday. "Yeah, when I saw you last weekend, I thought you seemed a little out of place."

Leo's eyebrows pulled together. "I've been thinking about that," he admitted, watching the front of the room as their professor wrote on the board. "That party. If you saw me, why didn't you come and say something? Why did Colette come to talk to me? I would have stayed if it were you."

"Oh." *I thought you wouldn't want me to*, he was going to say before recalling Leo's confusion when he suggested something similar last Friday. "I got a phone call and stepped outside, so Colette went up to you instead." These events were out of order, but Leo didn't need to know that.

Sloan saw an opportunity. "Speaking of phones, may I acquire your cell phone number?"

"What? Why?" Leo sounded defensive.

Slightly discouraged, Sloan dropped his gaze. "To work on the project."

"I finished my part of the project," Leo reminded. He was still a weird mix of perceptive and clueless, easily reading Sloan's discomfort while not understanding the cause.

"Right. Well, then I'd like your phone number so we can do something together as friends sometime."

Immediately, Leo shifted in his seat. "Oh."

"Is that okay?" Sloan asked. "I mean, we don't have to if you don't want to. I understand if you want nothing to do with me, but I promise you, I'm in a healthy relationship, so I'm not going to do anything to you … not that I would if I wasn't in a relationship."

"I'm not worried about that," Leo mumbled. "I'm surprised, is all. We know nothing about each other anymore. Things have changed."

"Well, that's why I'm suggesting you give me your phone number, so I have a way to contact you. Then, we can arrange a time to get together and talk about everything that's changed," Sloan suggested. "Look, Leo, I'm not going to force you to give me your number. Can I ask why you're hesitant to, though? Do you think us being friends again would really be that bad?"

"I don't think it would be bad at all," Leo said, reaching down between them where his backpack was and pulling out a notebook. "That's not the issue." Sloan watched him flip to a blank page and write ten numbers in neat handwriting.

"What's the issue then?" he asked, smiling at the paper. After five years, Sloan finally had a way to contact him.

Leo tore the paper from his notebook and gave it to him. As Sloan was folding it to fit safely in his pocket, Leo caught him off guard by saying, "Your boyfriend didn't seem too happy to see you with me. I don't want to cause any trouble."

"Drew?" he asked, voice hoarse. *So he'd noticed, then.* Of course he had; Drew wasn't exactly subtle. Sloan cleared his throat. "Don't worry about him. Sometimes he gets weird about stuff. He's totally harmless. Us being friends won't cause him any trouble—"

"No," Leo interrupted. "I'm not talking about causing *him* trouble."

It took Sloan a moment to understand what Leo was implying. "Oh … well, it won't cause me any trouble, either."

Sloan was surprised Leo worried about him. It was sweet, though misplaced.

At the front of the room, their professor began to speak. Gently,

Sloan nudged Leo with his elbow. "Is it okay if I text you?"

Leo's lips curled up slightly. Sloan wanted to stare. He looked pretty when he smiled. It was a shame he didn't do it more often. "I wouldn't have given you my number if it wasn't okay," said Leo. His brown eyes shifted back to their professor then, but Sloan didn't have it in him to pay attention.

He was far too happy to get distracted by a boring class.

Sloan was only reminded of lunch when he passed Colette in the hall as she rushed toward the classroom he'd just left. "Sorry I'm late," she said. It was quickly followed by "Where's Leo?"

Sloan grimaced. "I forgot to ask him."

She lightly punched his arm. "Are you serious? How could you forget?"

"I was so happy he gave me his number that I wasn't thinking about lunch."

She sighed and grabbed his arm to pull him toward the closest exit. "Give me his number."

"What? Why would I do that?"

"Um, because you don't have a monopoly on him?" Colette said, sticking her tongue out when he frowned. "Just give it to me. I'll text him right now and see if he wants to meet us."

"Oh. I can do that," Sloan offered, though when he removed the paper from his pocket, she was quick to snatch it from him.

He made no move to take it back. "Don't harass him too much, okay?"

She snickered, eyes down on her phone as they walked. "What kind of person do you think I am?"

She handed him the paper back, a smile on her lips. He took a moment to study the number. *Leo's number.* When they were kids, Sloan asked Leo if they would stay in contact when Leo returned home. That was before summer even really began, and he wrongly assumed he would have more time to get Leo's contact information.

Content, he carefully tucked the paper back in his pocket.

CHAPTER FOURTEEN

LEO

On Wednesday, Sloan once again claimed the chair beside him in political science class.

"Is this your seat from now on?" Leo asked, trying not to sound hopeful.

"Yeah," Sloan confirmed, turning away to rifle through his backpack. "Is that okay with you?" He must have assumed it was, because he continued to unpack.

"You can sit there," Leo granted. "I was hoping you would."

Sloan's smile made Leo wonder if all the other smiles Sloan had given him counted. They barely compared to the expression presented before him right then. In that moment, Leo somehow achieved making Sloan so happy that he absolutely beamed. If Leo had still been debating whether to keep his distance, he was sure this display would have completely swayed him. Seeing Sloan look that overwhelmingly delighted filled him with a feeling so pleasant, he was instantly addicted. The second the smile slipped in order for Sloan to speak, Leo craved to see it again.

"I'm glad," Sloan said, voice cheerful, completely unaware of Leo internally struggling beside him because *what the fuck was that?* "The next time Colette and I get lunch, you should come with us. She was bummed when you couldn't join us on Monday."

Leo already knew this, since Colette had told him as much over text. "Sorry about that," he offered. "By the time I saw her message, I had already heated up leftovers in my dorm."

"Don't apologize. It's my fault. I was supposed to invite you during class, but it slipped my mind." Sloan seemed genuinely upset with himself. "Oh. I hope it's okay that I gave Colette your number."

Leo shook his head. "I don't mind. She's already texted me quite a bit."

"I can tell her to stop."

"No," Leo said quickly. "Don't. It's really fine."

Leo actually enjoyed Colette's messages. At first, they hadn't been about anything important, just small talk, but their topic has somehow shifted to Drew, and Leo had admitted his concerns about causing problems in Sloan's relationship to her. It felt good to talk about it with someone who knew the full situation, and she'd made him feel better by claiming Drew probably didn't like her either, given how frequently he texted Sloan when they were together. She wasn't going to let it bother her, and she advised him to do the same.

At the front of the classroom, their professor began to speak.

After a minute, Sloan nudged Leo with his elbow and addressed him at a whisper. "Wanna get together to do something soon?"

Leo's gaze slipped over to him. "What would you want to do?"

Sloan shrugged. "We could do anything. Watch a movie? Eat something? Work on homework? I don't know. What'd you do with your friends from high school when you got together?"

Leo glanced to their professor, still not listening to anything the man was saying.

"I didn't really do anything with my friends outside of school besides homework," he admitted, thinking of Colin. In the back of his mind, Leo made a note to text him soon and ask how he was doing.

Sloan was quiet for so long that Leo peeked curiously at him, only to find Sloan looking back with a quizzical expression. "I like movies," Leo told him.

Sloan's lips curled into a smile. "Great. We'll watch a movie then. Does tomorrow evening work for you? I'll have to talk to Drew first to make sure he has nothing planned, but I don't think he does."

"Tomorrow works fine."

"Cool. I'll text you later to confirm."

"Sure." From the corner of his eye, Leo watched as Sloan finally let himself get absorbed in the lecture. He didn't join him, instead staring forward blankly as he thought about their plans.

Would they go to his and Justin's room to watch this promised movie, or would Sloan invite him to his place? Would food be involved, or should Leo eat beforehand?

Usually in these kinds of up-in-the-air situations, Leo would become unsure and regret agreeing to go, but right then, all he felt was excitement.

Because finally after five years he was getting another chance.

They were going to walk together until they went separate ways, though it became apparent about halfway to the cafeteria that they were going to the same place.

"Who are you meeting?" Sloan asked. "I'm going with Drew. He starts class next hour, so we overlap on lunch time. Usually I make him lunch, but I looked online at the menu for today and they have some of his favorites, so he said he'd meet me."

Suddenly nervous he was going to be in the same place as Sloan's boyfriend again, Leo voiced, "Oh," unenthusiastically. It had the potential to be a good thing. Maybe Drew would be different this time around and not look so angry. Leo doubted it. Still, it was reassuring that Sloan didn't seem concerned. "I'm actually eating by myself. I have my first physics exam coming up, so I was going to study while I ate."

"Oh! You sure? You can sit with us if you'd like."

"That's alright," Leo was quick to assure. "I still get weird around new people, so it'll be easier for me to eat by myself."

"How do you expect to get used to new people, then?" Sloan asked. While it would have been a valid argument if he'd been presenting it as such, he phrased it like an innocent question.

"I guess I don't," Leo admitted. Sloan said nothing about this, but he did smile.

When they arrived at their destination, Drew wasn't there yet. Sloan followed Leo to a table with the promise to leave as soon as his boyfriend arrived.

Leo didn't say it out loud, but he didn't mind the company, and when he returned from getting a plate of food, he was pleased to see Sloan still seated where he'd left him.

It was only when he was putting his plate down that Sloan looked up from his phone and noticed his return. "Thanks for letting me sit by you. For some reason, sitting alone in public places like this makes me self-conscious."

Leo removed his notebook from his backpack. "I could see that."

"You feel that way too?"

"Not really. I don't have the kind of face that distracts people."

Sloan's lips curled up. "You think I do?"

"I think you always have."

It only occurred to Leo that this might have been a stupid thing to say when Sloan flushed. Feeling his face warm as well, Leo quickly dropped his gaze.

There was a minute of silence in which Leo found the page of his notebook he needed to study the most.

Sloan cleared his throat. "Astrophysics, huh? Do you like it?"

"Of course I like it. That's why I'm studying it. Why?"

The look on Sloan's face changed to something insecure. Leo thought of their conversation in the library and Sloan's admittance that he didn't actually enjoy biology even though it's his major.

"Hey . . ." He considered that he maybe shouldn't ask, but Sloan was now looking at him expectantly. "Why are you majoring in bio?"

Sloan shrugged and turned to look at the people filtering into the cafeteria. "I don't know. I mean, being a doctor would be cool, right? I'm just not very good at biology and it's hard to enjoy sometimes." Sloan cut off, his gaze dropping, eyes unfocused. "Drew says I'm probably not applying myself as much as I should, and I guess that's maybe true. It's just hard to fully apply yourself to something you're not even interested in."

It was strange to see Sloan express a concern with such a distant look on his face. Given his personality and behavior, it was so easy to believe he had no problems. That having an easy life made him able to smile like that. Seeing him struggle made him more impressive and confusing.

"Morgan, I—"

"Oh!" Sloan cut in. It occurred to Leo that he accidentally referred to him by his first name. Before he could apologize, Sloan was explaining his surprise. "There's Drew."

Leo only needed to search for a moment before he spotted the brunet approaching, his expression tense at the sight of them together. Concerned, Leo glanced at Sloan, who'd raised a hand to wave.

"I'll talk you later, okay?" Sloan spoke without looking at him. "I'll text you about our plans for tomorrow." With that, he rose from his seat and pulled his backpack up onto his shoulder. He went to greet his boyfriend with a large smile on his face.

Drew wasn't looking at Sloan. Instead, he was staring past him at Leo. Their eyes met. Leo looked down at his notebook.

They must have gone off to sit somewhere together. Leo didn't bother to see where, worried he would catch that unfriendly gaze again.

He was distracting himself from any unpleasant thoughts about Drew with his notes when the chair across from him abruptly pulled out. Startled, he looked up and met Justin's eyes.

"Uh," Leo began, only to be cut off as Max took the seat beside him.

"Hey, Leo, right? Remember me? We met at that party," Max said, grinning. His teeth were very white.

"I remember." Leo looked to his roommate. "What are you doing?"

"Are we not allowed to sit here?" Justin asked, pulling apart a breadstick and eating it in pieces.

"You can sit where you want," Leo said after a pause, dropping his eyes to his own plate of untouched food. It was probably cold. He didn't mind; he wasn't hungry anymore.

Leo pulled his physics notebook a little closer to himself.

"I saw you and thought I'd ask what your fun fact for the day is," Justin said.

Without raising his head, Leo asked "We're doing this now?"

"What are you guys talking about?" Max questioned, leaning just enough to the side that his elbow was pressing into Leo's arm. Confused by the proximity, Leo looked down at where their skin touched. He didn't put any distance between them, not wanting Max to think he was uncomfortable when he wasn't.

"Leo and I are trying to get to know each other better so we share one thing about ourselves a day," Justin explained. "And why shouldn't we do it now?"

"I don't want to bore your friend with unimportant facts about myself."

"Oh, I am definitely interested," claimed Max. His knee bumped against Leo's beneath the table

Frowning in his direction, Leo said, "Justin, you go first."

His roommate sighed, but must have been expecting as much, because he confessed, "I'm weirdly proud of my hair," without pause.

Leo's eyebrows raised, but he didn't have anything to say about this.

"Your turn," Justin urged.

Leo considered his own appearance, hoping to use Justin's fact as guidance as usual. His appearance never bothered him all that much—

he was tall enough, just over six feet, and he didn't mind his dark hair or dark eyes—but it also wasn't something he took pride in. When he said as much, Justin grinned.

"I guess you just have to come up with something else then."

He thought for a minute, and then Max asked, "Instead of you coming up with something, could I ask you a question?"

"Dude, this has nothing to do with you," Justin protested.

Ignoring his roommate, Leo nodded. "That's probably easier for me." Max appeared to be pleased while Justin rolled his eyes.

"Well then, what's your major?"

It was an easy question, and Leo couldn't keep his content out of his voice when he answered, "Astrophysics."

"I already knew that," Justin grumbled.

"How does one get interested in that?" asked Max.

Leo hadn't been expecting follow-up questions, but he didn't mind the conversation. "I got interested in astronomy when I was younger, and I wanted to do something related to it."

"What's your star sign?"

"That's astrology, and I'm a Sagittarius."

Max propped his elbow on the table and leaned heavily against it, his body turned toward him. "Wow. That's not what I thought you'd be. I'm an Aries, and a computer science major, in case you were wondering."

Leo hadn't been, but now that he knew Max was a STEM major, he found himself asking, "And what's your minor?"

Justin seemed surprised by Leo's interest. Max smiled.

"Math minor."

Nodding, Leo told him, "I'm a math minor as well. What class are you in?"

"Calc two." Max sounded less than pleased. "It kills. What course are you in?"

"I'm not taking a math course right now."

"How'd you swing that?" Max inquired. Again, his leg knocked against Leo's. "I thought you had to take a class for your minor?"

This was supposed to be the case, so Leo made a noise of agreement before explaining his situation. "I'm ahead because of my high school courses. I've already taken Calc two, so if you have questions, let me know. It's been a while, but I still should be able to do it."

"Ah." Max finally looked away from him, taking interest in his food for the first time since sitting. "I'll probably take you up on the offer of help, actually. You should give me your phone number."

"Can't you get it from Justin when you need it? If I give it to you now and you don't end up having a need for it, then you'll have my number for no reason."

Max made a face. "Is that a bad thing?"

"I don't even think I have your number," Justin chimed in, eyes moving between the two of them. "I gave you mine the night of the party, but you never used it so I don't have yours."

"Oh." After a moment of consideration, Leo removed his phone from his pocket to text Justin. "What if you get locked out?"

"Awww, it's almost like you care about me!" Justin teased, earning a deadpan look that he laughed at. With a quick head shake, Leo brought his focus to his phone to complete his text.

He didn't mind Justin and Max sitting with him, even though he wasn't getting his work done. It was nice to not be lonely.

"Oh, hey, Max," Justin began as Leo returned his phone to his pocket. "Isn't that the girl you hooked up with this weekend?"

This didn't concern or remotely interest Leo, so he looked at his physics notes again. He only made it through a few lines when the sound of his name pulled his attention to the conversation. "What?"

"Ah, I was telling Justin about how I met her when you two were together," Max said.

"Met who?"

"The girl he slept with," Justin explained, talking around a mouthful of food.

"Kenni," Max continued. "She was the girl you were with—"

Leo didn't need to hear more to know who he meant. "I remember. We weren't actually together. She spilled her drink on me, so I got her water." It didn't shock him that Max ended up seeing her again. They'd exchanged numbers after all. "Glad it worked out for you."

Max and Justin both made equally annoying snorting sounds. "Leo, it's not like they're dating or anything. They only had sex."

"Ah." Leo began to ignore them again. It wasn't any of his business, but he didn't understand why anyone would want to have sex with someone they weren't in a relationship with. To him, that seemed like far too personal of a thing to share with just anyone.

He got through a few more pages of notes before he realized Justin and Max had fallen silent. Curious, he raised his head and noticed both of them looking past him to the end of the table.

When he turned, he was greeted with the unwelcome sight of Drew. "Oh," Leo managed, already having a bad feeling about the upcoming interaction. "Hi."

"Leo, right?" Drew asked, intense gaze unwavering. Like when they first met, Leo was filled with the sense that breaking eye contact would mean losing, so he stared back as he nodded in confirmation. Drew smiled. It wasn't the pleasant, sincere expression Leo was used to seeing on Sloan's face. "Do you have a moment to talk? I was wondering if we could discuss your intentions with my boyfriend."

Shock rendered him speechless. Somehow, he kept his expression blank, giving Drew nothing to take satisfaction in.

"Ah, so you're not going to reply? That's fine. I only need you to listen," Drew claimed, his cheerful voice contradicting the hard look in his eyes. "You don't need to tell me your intentions, because they seem quite obvious to me by now. I would just like to clarify that he's dating me, and has been for quite some time now, so I suggest you back off. He's not interested in you, so don't waste your time. Alright?"

While Leo was aware he was supposed to respond, he remained silent. He wondered if Sloan was watching this interaction occur. It didn't seem like the kind of thing he would let happen without saying anything, though Leo didn't know if Sloan was afraid to stand up to Drew.

The silence stretched on. Still, Drew didn't leave, watching him expectantly, waiting for a response. It felt like another contest, but if losing meant Drew would go away, it was probably worth it.

Before he could decide, Justin cut in. "You've said what you needed to say, right? So fuck off, man." Drew looked away first, his composure fracturing for a second as he stared down Leo's roommate. It was tense enough that Leo feared the two of them might fight or something, but then Drew huffed, shaking his head as he backed away from the table.

No one spoke until he was out of hearing distance. Leo dropped his head into his hands to breathe out a soft swear.

"Dude," Max said, elbowing him. "That man is going to punch you in the face at some point. I can feel it."

"That's probably true," Leo mumbled, lifting his head and watching Drew's retreating form. "How bad does that hurt? I've never been punched in the face before."

The answer didn't come right away, Max probably debating whether he should tell him the truth or not. "Well . . . it doesn't feel good," he admitted finally. Leo sighed. "You hit on his boyfriend?"

"No," Leo denied. "I did nothing. We just know each other from when we were kids."

"Did anything happen back then?" asked Max.

"I mean ..." Leo glanced at his roommate. "We kissed once, but I don't know if his boyfriend knows. We were thirteen, so it barely counts."

Justin wasn't paying attention to him, still watching Drew leave.

"Justin." Leo hated it had to be brought up this way. "That's okay, right?"

His roommate sounded confused. "What's okay?"

Max, who seemed to perfectly understand what Leo was saying, let out a snicker. "He's asking if it's okay that he likes boys, Justin."

Leo breathed out a sigh of relief that he wouldn't need to say it himself.

"You like boys?"

"I just told you I kissed one," Leo said.

"Yes, but you didn't say you liked it."

Leo didn't respond.

"Oh. Well, that's fine. Why wouldn't it be fine?" Justin asked. "Have people not been fine before?"

"Probably," Leo admitted. "I don't know. I never cared about what anyone thought besides my family and friends, and they were all fine with it. It's important this time around though, because we live together, and I don't want to make you uncomfortable."

Humming, Justin twirled his fork in the spaghetti on his plate. "Well, ignoring that you obviously excluded me from the category of *friends*, it's really okay. I'm not at all uncomfortable. The rules for the room gotta stay the same though: no having sex when I'm in there."

"That is a great rule!" Max declared. "My roommate literally does not give a shit if I'm there or not. When the bottom bunk moves, so does the top."

This seemed like a lot to unpack, so Leo ignored it. "That's not going to be an issue," he promised Justin. For the first eighteen years of his life he had gone without sex, so he figured he'd be able to refrain when Justin was around . . . if he ever got someone to do it with, that was. He wasn't optimistic.

"I do have a request," Justin suddenly added, looking very serious. "Leo, that asshole does not deserve a boyfriend. Do not back down because of him, alright?"

Sloan: Tomorrow night works for me! Still good for you?

Leo: Rain check? My roommate asked me to help him with something.

"Leo," Justin groaned, right in his ear, startling him into sitting up. Justin was in his desk chair facing him, right behind where Leo's head had been resting on the futon a second before. "That's him, right? I don't approve of you using me in a lie to get out of something I completely support!"

"So, you read my texts now?" Leo grumbled.

"Leo."

"I know, alright!" he snapped, lying down on his side and pulling his legs to his chest. "I'm not going to stay away from him completely, and I'm not afraid of Drew. I just think, for Sloan's sake, it would be better if I avoided doing things with him one on one. Then at least Drew won't be able to say anything to him about it. He'll only be angry at me."

A groan came from Justin. Leo didn't bother to look at him. "That's not going to last long, you know. Eventually you're going to get close enough that you avoiding being alone with him will be obvious. You'll need to tell him why."

He was probably right, but Leo wouldn't think about that yet. "I'll address that when I get to it," he mumbled. "I'll figure it out along the way."

Chapter Fifteen

Sloan

After his morning classes on Friday, Sloan stopped by the campus convenience store to buy something for lunch before making his way back to his apartment. During political science, he asked Leo if he wanted to get lunch, but he had stared at Sloan with wide eyes for a moment before giving an excuse. *"I'm tired, so I was planning on going back to my room to take a nap."*

The night before, while Drew was at practice and Sloan was lounging on the couch, he wished Leo hadn't needed to cancel their movie night. It seemed kind of strange, Leo making plans with his roommate when he said the time worked for him, but Sloan was happy to hear he did things with other people. Still, he wanted to be with Leo too, so he decided he'd ask him in class about maybe rescheduling for the weekend.

It hadn't gone according to plan. When Sloan suggested they get together sometime over the next couple of days, Leo had asked in a small voice, *"Just the two of us?"*

It had taken Sloan a minute to respond, wondering why Leo said it like it was a bad thing. They were friends, and wasn't it normal for friends to do things together without others? Eventually, after determining that Leo must have taken something the wrong way, Sloan had clarified, *"You know I'm not hitting on you, right?"*

It was awkward after that. Leo shook his head, mumbling about how he understood that before cryptically claiming, *"I'm not sure if it's the best idea."* They hadn't spoken for the remainder of class, and at the end, when Sloan bid him goodbye, Leo appeared inexplicably upset.

Huffing in irritation at the recent memory, Sloan unwrapped his sandwich, hoping he didn't run into Drew on the short walk to their apartment. His boyfriend would probably scold him for eating while walking, claiming it unsanitary or dangerous in some way. Sloan's impatience when it came to food often bothered him.

As he bundled up the plastic wrap, he thought about what possibly could have gone wrong with Leo. Whatever it was, it was probably the reason Leo canceled on him Wednesday night. What could have happened between the time they parted in the cafeteria and the time Leo texted?

Taking the first bite of his sandwich, Sloan thought about talking to Leo on Wednesday and how easy it felt to fall into conversation with him. They had been perfectly fine then and hadn't spoken at all in between. It didn't make any sense.

Unless . . . Leo's concern was still about Drew. Could he be worried about Drew having seen them sitting together in the cafeteria? It wasn't a big deal that time around, because Sloan had been sure to text his boyfriend that the two of them were together. If that was the problem, Leo was overreacting. Sloan was willing to update Drew on his whereabouts, so he had nothing to be angry about. Maybe he should let Leo know . . . but if he was wrong and it was something else bothering him, it would be a little awkward to have brought it up.

Frustrated, Sloan chewed so hard his jaw ached. There was no reason for them not to be friends—no good one at least—so why was Leo acting strange?

For the past five years, Sloan had been waiting for Leo. He refused to make the same mistakes he had as a kid. He wouldn't fuck things up again, and he wouldn't let Leo run away without having a conversation with him first.

By the time Sloan got to his building, he'd finished his sandwich and was instead occupying his hand with his cell phone.

There was a message from Drew, claiming he had already left to go study in the library before class, one from Colette asking him how political science went and if he and Leo had any weekend plans, and multiple messages from Nicole begging him to call soon.

Because his boyfriend was the one most anticipating a response, he sent him a message first, letting him know he was back at the apartment. Then, because she would give him insight on the Leo situation, he called Colette.

It rang for about a minute. By the time she answered, the elevator had dropped him off on his floor. "So, I'm guessing Leo couldn't get lunch if you're calling me, huh?"

"Good guess," Sloan answered, holding the phone to his ear with his shoulder as he fumbled with his keys. "I'm almost at my apartment now. I think I'm going to lie on my couch and contemplate what the hell went wrong."

"What do you mean? Wasn't he just busy this afternoon?"

"He said it wasn't the best idea for us to hang out," Sloan explained, unlocking the front door. Once he was inside, he kicked it shut more aggressively than Drew would have appreciated.

"Are you okay?"

"Yeah, sorry." He toed off his shoes, throwing his backpack onto the floor at the end of the couch before collapsing across it on his stomach. "I don't know how to approach this."

"Don't give up!" Colette insisted. "When he and I text, I can tell he wants to be friends with you—"

"I know he does."

"What happened, though?"

As he lifted his head to adjust the couch pillow, Sloan grumbled, "I don't know. I'm assuming it wasn't a sudden change of heart and that something actually happened, because Leo wouldn't do something without a reason, you know?"

Colette hummed out her agreement.

Sloan continued. "He seemed fine when we were talking. I told him more about my struggles with my major but didn't get to hear his response. Maybe he thinks I'm pathetic."

"Stop," Colette snapped. "That's not the reason. What's something else that could have happened?"

"The only other thing I can think of is that when I went to join Drew, Leo might have thought Drew was angry or something," Sloan explained. "He didn't look all that happy, but I wouldn't say that he looked *angry*. He had no right to be angry. I told him beforehand that I was sitting with Leo. Besides, if he's upset, he usually has no issue mentioning it to me. I told Leo it wouldn't be a problem. It's just frustrating."

"That's understandable," she sympathized. "You want me to come over?"

"You're not busy?"

"Nah," she denied. "My afternoon class was canceled because my professor is sick. I'm free for the rest of the day. I'll come over—" The end of her word cut off suddenly. "Um, is Drew there?"

Earlier in the week, Colette came over to study and finally got to meet Drew. It had been awkward and probably not what Colette was expecting because she became quieter in conversations about his boyfriend and asked far fewer questions.

"He's not," Sloan admitted. "Why do I get the impression that if he was, you wouldn't be coming?"

To his surprise, Colette chuckled. "Ah, well, he seems kind of territorial. Besides, I don't want to take up any of the time the two of you get together. College is busy, and I can't imagine how difficult it is to find time for each other." Not believing the second half of this to be sincere—he was pretty sure she was just saying it so it didn't seem like she disliked Drew—Sloan hummed. "I'll head over now. Are you hungry? I haven't eaten yet so I'm gonna stop at the store on the way over. Want me to get a pizza to share?"

"Colette," Sloan groaned. His stomach still felt empty despite having just eaten. "Have I mentioned how much I love you yet? No hetero."

This warranted a full-out laugh, and Sloan smiled along. "I love you, too. I'll text you when you need to come open the door."

Drew smelled a bit like alcohol when he came home. Sloan didn't mention it. When Drew was tipsy, he forgot about his distaste for cuddling and let Sloan curl up against him on the couch as they watched television. They didn't talk, but that was fine. Sloan was content to close his eyes and breathe, taking in the scent of Drew's cologne with each steady inhale.

The only problem was that Sloan couldn't stop thinking about Leo. He and Colette had talked about Leo that afternoon, though they hadn't come up with a solution beyond not giving up. *"If you keep asking him to do stuff, he's bound to agree eventually,"* was what she had suggested. Sloan wasn't so sure about this. Even so, he was going to keep inviting Leo to hang out, regardless of the previous answer. It was important for Leo to know that Sloan didn't have the same concerns.

Sighing, Sloan leaned heavily into Drew's side to free his phone from his back pocket. Drew groaned at the added weight but didn't protest.

"What are you doing?" Drew asked, dropping his head on the top of Sloan's. It seemed like a sweet gesture to get closer to him, and Sloan thought that it was somewhat, but he also knew it was easier for Drew to see the screen of his phone that way. "Who are you texting?" His breath smelled like the cocktail he had drank earlier, and Sloan wished he was smelling his boyfriend's cologne instead of the bittersweet scent of a mixed vodka drink.

"Leo," Sloan admitted, though he had the messages between them open and Drew could clearly see this for himself. It didn't bother him that Drew was reading his messages. He never said anything he would need to hide from him, anyway.

"Why are you texting him?" asked Drew, now nuzzling the top of his head.

"I wanna see if he can do something this weekend," Sloan admitted, thumbs moving over the keyboard. He typed out a quick message—a simple, *Come on, are you free tomorrow?*

"You know, I thought we could have a nice weekend in, just the two of us," Drew claimed.

"We can," Sloan agreed. "But you have practice this weekend, and I get lonely here by myself." Drew made a soft noise Sloan recognized as indifferent. "It doesn't matter, anyway. He's going to say no." As he was saying this, his phone buzzed with the awaited message.

Leo: Sorry, can't.

Sloan was pretty sure the word Leo really wanted to use was *shouldn't*. Frustrated, he went to respond—*plead*—for Leo to reconsider. Drew closed his hand over the top of his phone, pulling it from him. He tossed it to the end of the couch where Sloan couldn't reach it.

"Stop," his boyfriend grumbled, leaning back against the cushions and patting Sloan's shoulder comfortingly. "You know I don't like it if you're on that thing when we're together."

Because he was annoyed, Sloan wanted to argue and tell Drew he didn't see the problem because it wasn't like they were really doing anything—if his phone was going to distract him, it'd be from the television, not Drew—but he bit his tongue, knowing this would only result in them fighting. "Sorry," he offered eventually. "I wanted to check with him again to see if he changed his mind."

"Again?" Drew echoed. "You already asked him?"

"Yeah. In class today."

"And what'd he say?"

"That he didn't want to," Sloan admitted sadly. "I don't believe him."

There was a moment in which the only sound in the room was the TV. Drew sighed. "Why are you trying so hard with that kid?" he asked, squeezing the arm around Sloan's shoulder a little tighter so they fit together snugly.

"I don't think he has many friends here, and I don't want him to be sitting in his dorm by himself all the time."

"And how is that your problem?" Drew inquired. Holding back a noise of annoyance, Sloan squeezed his eyes shut. He loved his boyfriend, but sometimes Drew failed to be understanding when it came to things not directly related to him.

When he replied, he had to try to avoid sounding peeved. "Because I care about him, Drew," Sloan stressed. Immediately, his boyfriend tensed. "I don't mean it like that, and you know it." To be reassuring, Sloan patted Drew's leg. "You know I meant as a friend. When I was a kid, all of my friends lived far away so I was lonely. One summer, Leo came to visit his dad, who lived on my street, and I wasn't lonely anymore. If he's feeling that way now, I want to be the one who makes him feel less lonely. I owe it to him."

Once again, there was a pause. "Well," Drew began. "You can't push it, okay? If he keeps saying no, I think you should leave him alone. The last thing you want to do is make him uncomfortable, right?" He pushed Sloan's hair off his forehead, making room for warm lips to press there for half a second.

Sloan closed his eyes. Drew was right in that Sloan didn't want to make Leo uncomfortable, but his boyfriend didn't fully understand. Sloan was confident Leo wasn't avoiding him because of discomfort. He'd figure out why, no matter how long it took, and then he would do his best to fix it.

Chapter Sixteen

Leo

On Saturday, Leo brought his laptop to the lounge in his dorm to do homework. He told Justin he needed a change of scenery, but in reality he just wanted to go somewhere he wouldn't notice his roommate—albeit subtly—pitying him for his lack of plans.

He was a few hours into a research paper when he received a text from Colette asking him to meet her in the science center. There was no reason not to accept her invitation, so he sent back a conformation text and packed up his things.

When he returned to his dorm room, Max, Justin, and a black boy Leo recognized but didn't know by name were squished together on the futon. Startled, they looked up when he entered, all appearing guilty. Doing something suspicious, he supposed, though he didn't care enough to ask.

"Ah, hey," Justin greeted. "Finish your paper?"

"No." Leo dropped his backpack by his desk. He had the intention to leave right away, but when he turned, he caught Max's eyes and paused.

"You staying? We can make room," Max offered. It sounded ridiculous coming from the boy sandwiched between two others on the futon, clearly uncomfortable. "I'd even let you sit on—"

"Stop it," Justin cut in. "I'm not gonna let you come to our room anymore if you make my roommate uncomfortable."

Max didn't seem at all concerned, throwing his head back to laugh. "Aw, he's not uncomfortable. Right, Leo?"

"I'm not," Leo said.

"You *want* him to hit on you?" asked Justin.

Leo shook his head. "I didn't say that, either. I'm not staying, though."

Justin's eyebrows raised. "Where are you off to?"

"A friend asked me to meet them."

"Is it the boy whose boyfriend is a total prick?" Max asked.

"It is not," Leo answered, thinking about Sloan. He felt guilty for lying to him the day before, especially when he wasn't sure he was doing the right thing. He would ask Colette her thoughts on the matter.

"Are you still serious about staying away from him?" Justin sounded exasperated. "You're letting him win, Leo."

"It's not a competition," Leo protested, and Justin made a face that showed he disagreed. "I don't mind losing once in a while anyway, and it's not like I'm giving up completely. I'm just going to avoid spending time with him alone so his boyfriend isn't so mad."

Justin shook his head. "So, you're appeasing him, then? By acting this way, you're making it seem like his boyfriend has a right to get angry when the two of you are alone together, which he doesn't because you're not doing anything wrong."

"I'm still trying to figure everything out," Leo defended without passion. "The reason I'm leaving is to go talk about it. I'd like to avoid getting beat up if at all possible."

"Ah, I highly doubt that dude is gonna beat you up," Max said.

"No?" Leo glanced toward the door. He didn't want to leave Colette waiting too long. "Didn't you say he would punch me in the face?"

"Yeah, but that was before I realized where I knew him from. He looked kind of familiar to me. I didn't figure it out until I went to class yesterday and saw him in the math building. He's one of those super annoying engineering majors who talks about it loudly a *lot*. Computer science is in the same building, so I actually see him quite a bit. I'm guessing that grad school is in his future plans, and he's not gonna jeopardize that with an assault charge. He's all bark and no bite," Max explained.

It was a relief, though at the same time, Leo felt bothered. He hadn't wanted to admit it to himself before, but he had been hoping Sloan's boyfriend wasn't smart. He had wanted to be superior to that asshole in some way.

Leo's lips pulled into a frown. "Oh, I guess that's good."

"Why don't you look happier?" Justin asked. It was a fair question.

He didn't acknowledge it. "I'm going to be late," was all he said before grabbing his keys and slipping out the door.

When he got to the couch on the second floor of the science center, Colette was already there. He hoped she hadn't been waiting long.

He said as much when he took the seat beside her. She looked up from her phone to smile at him. "No worries. I've actually been here for a couple of hours. I was studying and fell asleep for a while."

"Do you sleep in public places often?"

"No. Only when my roommate has someone in the room and I'm tired," she answered. "I sleep only here, though. Few people come this far down the hall, so it's often empty."

Leo nodded in understanding. It seemed like a good place in the conversation for the small talk to end, but he was unsure how to continue when he didn't know the reason she asked him there. "Uh . . ."

"You're wondering why I reached out to you, right?" He nodded. "I guess I wanted to see whether it was really just Sloan."

Confused, Leo's eyebrows pulled together. "What?"

"Well, you're not doing things with Sloan. He and I talked, and he said you were avoiding him. I wanted to see what was going on and if you're okay. Did something happen?"

He wanted to tell, but he worried what Drew said to him would get back to Sloan. At the moment, it wasn't Sloan's problem to deal with, and Leo wanted to keep it that way.

His unease must have shown on his face, because she added, "You can talk to me about it, you know. I won't tell Sloan if you don't want me to. I know you don't want to cause him any trouble, and neither do I."

He believed her, and he was happy he did, because he really wanted to talk to someone besides Justin about what had happened. "Drew approached me during lunch on Wednesday to tell me to back off."

Colette's brown eyes got huge. "He fucking did *not!*" she exclaimed, making him wince at the volume. "Oh." Her hand flew up to cover her mouth. "Sorry. I was surprised."

"Yeah," Leo agreed. "Me too. I don't know what to do about it, but I'm not completely avoiding Sloan. I thought it would probably be best for us not to do things alone together. That way Drew can't hold anything about our relationship over him."

"This is all ridiculous," Colette accused, and he winced again, believing he was about to be lectured. "Oh, sorry. I don't mean you. I know you're doing your best. I'm talking about Drew. I can't believe him! Being friends with you would make Sloan happy, and you're stepping back because you want what's best for him, while the asshole he's dating is taking advantage of you being a good person to keep Sloan out of a relationship that would be good for him." They were both quiet for about a minute, and then she sighed heavily. "I promise I won't say anything, but are you sure you don't want him to know?"

Leo was sure. "It'll only result in a fight, and I don't want to cause any trouble."

"Okay," she agreed softly. "I think you should rethink not doing things with Sloan one on one. He's an adult, and he can handle his adult relationship on his own. You don't need to protect him from something he's chosen for himself."

"Yeah," he mumbled. "It's not my place, is it?" He might have been mistaken, but Colette looked sympathetic right then. "That's fine. That's how it's supposed to be." She hummed in response, as if she didn't quite believe him.

Leo remembered something else he wanted to discuss. "Hey, you're a bio major with Sloan, right?"

"Yeah. Why?"

"Well, I was wondering if you were able to figure out why he's majoring in it. We talked about it for a bit, and he didn't seem at all enthusiastic."

"Ah." The concerned expression on her face told him she had noticed this as well. "I didn't understand it at first either, because he clearly doesn't enjoy it, but I think I kind of get it now. Earlier this week, I ended up going over to their apartment—"

"Sorry, whose apartment?" he cut in.

"Oh. Sloan and Drew's. They live together in a place off campus. You didn't know?"

"No." He decided not to think much of it.

"Oh, well, yeah, they live together. Anyway, while I was over there, we were doing homework and he made a comment about disliking bio and doubting his ability to do well, and Drew launched into this whole lecture about how society needs doctors and people who will work hard to become them." She looked flustered. "It would be one thing if Sloan was miserable, but he's *not*. He's actually happy there, even though Drew is constantly correcting him on everything."

She paused to take a deep breath. "And seriously, it's *everything*. Sit up straighter. Don't check your phone when you're studying. Maybe you should use a green highlighter instead of the blue one because blue looks bad. And Sloan just *agrees* with a smile on his face like he doesn't even realize. I even gave him a pencil with sharks on it, and Drew told him he shouldn't use it because it's *childish*. Sloan told me not to mind him on that one and said some shit like *Sometimes he forgets that we're not even real adults* and then he didn't use the pencil!"

Colette had mentioned lots of details that Leo thought to focus on, but he found himself asking, "A pencil with sharks on it?"

She rolled her eyes. "If you come watch movies with us sometime, you'll understand. It's infuriating." A long sigh left her. "It has to bother him, doesn't it? Being treated like that? Like he isn't good enough and needs to make corrections?"

"I don't know. I'd think it would bother him, but maybe he's used to it. Maybe he doesn't even notice it anymore." Leo thought of Sloan and couldn't even imagine what Drew thought needed to be changed. "I don't know, Colette."

Her eyes met his. "At some point he's going to realize it isn't healthy and he could be happier with someone else. He's got to. And we have to be there for him when it happens. Alright?"

"Alright," he agreed.

She smiled, but Leo wouldn't describe the expression as happy. "Thanks," she said. "I think he really needs us, Leo."

He liked the idea of being needed by Sloan. He just wished the situation was different.

Leo was lying in his bed, staring blankly at the ceiling as he thought about what the atmosphere of Sloan and Drew's shared apartment must be like, while the boys sitting on the futon discussed whether they should get high. The answer to that question would be *yes*, Leo was pretty sure, but he didn't mind their conversation as background noise. It gave him something to focus in on when he got irritated by his own thoughts.

This happened about every five minutes or so, and he felt the emotion beginning to tighten his chest when Justin asked, "Hey, Leo, do you care if we smoke in here?"

"No," he answered, turning to look down at them. Only Max met his eyes. "Doesn't really bother me." Nodding, Justin got up from his seat and went over to his desk. He pulled open the middle drawer and rummaged through it.

"Thanks, man," he said, and Leo nodded, gaze moving back to the ceiling.

Did they share a bed? Did they have sex? Leo wondered. *Probably.*

"Wanna join us?" Max questioned. It took Leo a couple of seconds to realize he was asking him, and he sat up to stare at the two boys on the futon. They were looking back at him. Max was smiling widely, and Justin's other friend, who Leo overheard being referred to as Jared, seemed curious.

"Dude," Justin said, returning to the futon and pulling the ottoman—Justin had bought it last week to stash alcohol in—toward him. He had a little tin container, and he opened it carefully. "He's not gonna want to get high with us."

"Why not?" Max asked. "Have you ever tried it before, Leo?"

"No," he admitted. "I haven't."

Justin joined the other boys in looking up at him. "Are you actually interested?"

"I don't know," Leo answered unconvincingly. All three of them chuckled. "It's not that I want to. I'm curious, and I like to try everything at least once." *And,* he added, just for himself, *maybe it'll get me to stop thinking about Sloan being in a relationship with an asshole.*

A teasing smile slid onto Max's face. "If you tell me the things you haven't done before, I'm pretty sure I could help you out," he offered. Justin drove an elbow into his side. "God, I'm joking! Leo, you in or not?"

"Yes," he responded without really thinking. Justin's eyebrows shot up. Max made a whooping noise. "Is that okay?"

"Yeah, man," Justin said, groaning when Max pushed on his arm. "Hey, I'm trying to roll this."

"Do it at your desk," Max demanded. "Let Leo sit there."

About to protest, because this seemed unnecessary, Leo opened his mouth. Justin spoke first. "Ugh, fine. Leo, get down here."

As he climbed down the end of his loft, Leo wondered if this experience was something he should share with Lizzy, or if it would only encourage her.

He sat on the futon beside Max and pressed his sweaty palms against his jeans. He felt incredibly nervous.

This must have been obvious, because Max reached out and laid a hand on his forearm. "Hey, don't worry about it. You ever smoked a cigarette or vape before?"

"No," Leo answered, sounding as anxious as he felt. "Why? Should I have?"

Max shrugged carelessly, the exact opposite of Leo. "No, it'd probably be easier for you not to cough if you had, but you'll be fine. You get used to it pretty fast."

Curious, Leo watched what Justin was doing. His fingers were rolling the material into a thin tube with care and experience. When he was about to reach the end of the paper, he lifted it to his mouth and pressed it to his tongue. "That helps it stick," Max explained.

Nodding, Leo inhaled and wrinkled his nose. He was used to the smell already from living with Justin, but he felt more aware of it now that he would be joining them.

"Okay," Justin said, holding the joint in one hand and fumbling around for his lighter on his desk with the other. "So, when you inhale, you kinda want to hold it for as long as you can before exhaling. That'll help you get high." Locating his lighter, he left his desk to sit on the ottoman directly in front of Leo, holding the joint out to him. "Take it."

"I'm going first?" Leo asked, accepting it and holding it between his thumb and forefinger. "I've never done this before. Why do I have to go first?" His eyes flicked over all of them. "You all staring at me like that doesn't make me feel any better about this." Only Jared, looked away.

"Want me to go first?" Max offered. Leo turned to nod at him, only to find honey brown eyes focused on the flame of Justin's lighter as he lit the end of the joint still pinched between Leo's fingers.

"Um," Leo voiced, unsure. Before he could put his hesitance into a sentence, Max was reaching out and grabbing his wrist, pulling his hand close to his face. Surprised, Leo watched as Max leaned toward his hand and closed his lips over the end of the joint, eyes becoming half lidded as he inhaled. In that moment, Leo found himself shockingly attracted to the other boy, and he continued to observe him after Max had pulled back to release a long breath of smoke, seeming incredibly content. When he finished, his eyelids lifted again, gaze fixed on Leo.

"Did that help?" he asked, and Leo looked at the hand still around his wrist.

"Not really," he answered. "But I'll try it." The fingers slipped away, and he raised the burning joint to his own lips. Looking at Max made him feel nervous—he wasn't used to people who were so open about their interest in him—so he focused on Justin as he finally took his first inhale.

Immediately, the smoke shocked his lungs, and he coughed it out. "Ah, fuck." Jared and Max both laughed, Max's hand coming to pat his back. Justin smiled at him and took the joint, taking a quick hit before passing it off to Jared. It all seemed kind of unsanitary.

"Deep breaths. You'll be fine," Justin told him. "The second time will be better because you know what to expect."

"Here," Max said, taking the joint from Jared and handing it back to Leo right away. "Breathe in slowly. Don't force yourself to hold it in too long if you can't."

"I'm regretting this already," Leo grumbled. Still, he did as instructed and managed with only a few small coughs on his exhale.

"Yeah," Justin said, looking oddly proud. "Just like that."

They continued on like that, passing it between them until Max burned his fingers and swore. They took a break as Justin prepared another. At that point, Leo didn't feel great, but as he had the first—and only—time he got drunk, he didn't want to be the one to bow out first. Every time Max asked if he wanted more and pressed something against his lips, he nodded and inhaled until his state became apparent.

"Uh, are you okay?" Max asked. Leo didn't bother to open his eyes at the question. "Hey, Leo, look at me."

"How much did he smoke?" Leo heard Jared ask. A second later he felt hands on his face, lifting his head.

"Leo, open your eyes," Justin instructed, and he somehow managed, blinking at his roommate. "How do you feel?"

He thought about it, closing his eyes again. "Awful."

"He is so fucking high, man," Jared summarized, and Justin sighed heavily enough that Leo felt the breath on his face.

"*Max*," Justin groaned. "You were supposed to be watching him."

An answer came from his direct left. "Shit, man, I'm sorry. I'm stoned. I wasn't paying super close attention. When I asked him if he wanted more, he said yeah."

"Am I going to die?" Leo cut in to ask, his throat scratchy and dry.

"You won't die from getting too high," Justin promised. "It fucking sucks, but you won't die." Humming in acknowledgment because the idea of speaking made him feel dizzy, Leo let his head fall back again.

The level of sound in the room decreased then as the three boys, who apparently weren't at all afraid of dying, spoke in whispers. He didn't know how long he'd been in that state when Max lightly pressed his shoulder. Startled, Leo jerked.

"Woah, sorry. I just wanted to let you know your phone buzzed in your pocket. You didn't feel it?"

He hadn't, but that wasn't surprising. Leo's whole body felt like it was vibrating. "Hmm, could you check it for me?"

"Fuck, he's so baked," Justin groaned.

"You sure the message isn't gonna be something you don't want me to read?" Max teased. Leo managed a grunting noise in response.

"Alright, alright, one second." Patiently, Leo waited for Max to speak, barely feeling him carefully removing Leo's phone from his pocket. "It's from someone named Sloan. They want to know if you really can't hang out tonight. What do you want me to say? That you're busy?"

"No," Leo protested. He didn't want that. Right then, he wanted to see Sloan. He wanted it more than he felt he'd ever wanted anything before. "No, I want you to tell him to come over."

There wasn't a response for a moment—Leo assumed Max was typing—and then Justin said, "Leo, that might not be the best idea. It's better to not be in a room full of other people when you're like this, and our dorm isn't that big."

Too focused on moving his tongue around, trying—and failing—to wet his incredibly dry mouth, Leo didn't reply right away. When he finally did, he said something that was honest in a way he typically avoided. "I don't care. I want him."

CHAPTER SEVENTEEN

SLOAN

Despite what Drew said the day before about them spending the weekend together, he texted Sloan halfway through golf practice to let him know he'd be getting dinner and going to the bars with some of his friends. This was fine, but it meant Sloan would be spending his night alone, so he responded to Drew saying he would probably do things with his friends as well.

He messaged Leo first, asking if he'd changed his mind about hanging out. Not expecting the answer to be yes, he was going to send Colette a text as well, but he received Leo's response before he could. Less than fifteen minutes later, he was knocking on the door to the dorm room that Leo had told him to come to.

It sounded like Leo had other people in the room, and he wondered if he was about to meet Leo's roommate.

The thought made Sloan consider his own roommate. *Drew's not going to be happy I came out like this.* Before leaving, Sloan hadn't bothered to put in contacts, and, according to Drew, Sloan's glasses should be worn only in the apartment. There wasn't anything that could be done about it right then, so he dismissed the thought before it could cause him anxiety.

The person who answered the door wasn't Leo, but he was someone

Sloan was familiar with. The brunet boy from chemistry and bio—the one Colette was often frustrated with—stood before him, seeming equally confused by his presence. They looked at each other for what felt like a long time, and then understanding shone on the guy's face. "Ahh, you're here for Leo? I'm his roommate."

"Oh," Sloan voiced, wrinkling his nose at the smell of marijuana coming from inside the room. He remember Leo saying his roommate smoked a lot of weed. "Um, I don't actually know your name."

"Oh! I'm Justin." He pushed the door open farther and gestured for Sloan to come inside. "And you're Sloan, right? That's what Leo called you."

"Yeah . . ." Sloan trailed off as his eyes landed on Leo. He was sitting on the futon, appearing completely out of it. Beside him sat a boy with light brown hair who Sloan immediately recognized from the party the first weekend of school. He was turned toward Leo, one hand stretched out as if he meant to touch his forehead. He froze when he spotted Sloan watching, fingers not quite making contact.

"I'm really sorry about this," Justin said, closing the door. "Apparently Leo's never gotten high before and he ended up smoking too much so he's fucking tanked. I wasn't sure if you coming over was the best idea, but he wanted you to."

Should have known something was up if he agreed to hang out with me.

Still, he didn't feel at all bitter about it. Honestly, at the moment, he was quite content knowing that Leo wanted him there in any state of mind.

"I think Max, Jared, and I are gonna step out and go get food or something. It'll be easier for him if there's less people here," Justin explained. "Are you okay to look after him? It'll probably be super uneventful."

"Yeah, that's fine," Sloan answered, toeing off his shoes.

"I still don't think we should leave," the boy on the couch beside Leo said. "This is my fault. I should be responsible for him."

"Responsible for *him*?" Justin echoed under his breath, just loud enough for Sloan to pick up. Curious, he glanced between Leo and Justin's friend, who was clearly interested in him. He'd have to tease Leo about that some other time. "Max, come on. Let's go. Leo's fine. Right, Leo?"

Without opening his eyes or changing his expression, Leo's hand lifted to give them a thumbs-up. Amused, Sloan smiled. He couldn't help thinking about the few times he'd gotten high in high school. It wasn't something he wanted to relive, especially since he had a terrible reaction the third and final time. Just looking at Leo told him it would be some time before he tried something like this again.

"Fine," Max said.

As Justin and his friends fumbled about by the door, Sloan took the seat beside Leo. "Hey," he greeted. Leo lifted his head, eyes cracking open to meet his. They were red. "How are you feeling?"

Leo reached out and pressed his palm against Sloan's forearm. It startled Sloan—not the touch, but the heat coming from it. "I'm freaking out," Leo whispered, staring forward to where Justin was trying to find his keys. "How do they do this all the time? I feel like . . ." He trailed off, his eyes sliding shut.

"We're gonna head out now," Justin announced. "Um, if you need anything, Leo has my number, and his phone doesn't have a passcode. Leo, want us to bring you back something to eat?"

Beside him, Leo's breathing picked up slightly. "I think he's good," Sloan answered for him, moving off the futon to pull open the mini fridge. As he grabbed a bottle of water, he heard them leaving the room. "Hey, do you want water?"

"Morgan, I might be dying."

"You're not dying," Sloan assured, smiling at the use of his first name. "Here." He sat beside Leo again. "Drink." He helped Leo wrap his hand around the bottle and pushed the dark hair off his warm forehead. "You're going to feel better in the morning. You just smoked too much pot."

"How do I make it stop?" Leo asked miserably. "I don't want to be like this anymore."

"You have to ride it out." A horrified noise left Leo, and he shook his head as if he were rejecting this. "Do you want to lie in bed?"

"I don't know." Leo took a drink of water, his hands shaking.

"When I first came in the room, I thought you were already sleeping."

"No," Leo denied. "I was trying to relax so the anxiety didn't get so out of control in front of them." As he said this, Leo's spilled water onto his lap. "Oh. I'm sorry."

"Well, you didn't spill on me." Sloan took the bottle from him to avoid further accidents and placed it on the floor.

"That's not what I meant. I know this probably wasn't what you had in mind." Leo took a deep, shaky breath. "They asked me if I wanted to join them and I've never smoked before, and they enjoy it so I thought maybe it would be fun but I . . . I can't calm down." His voice verged on panicked.

Sloan thought back to the final time he had gotten high, when he felt incredibly anxious and needed to relax. He had been with Nicole, and he recalled her giving him something to focus on to help him forget the paranoia.

"Hey, does being close to me make you uncomfortable?" He hoped the answer to the question was no.

Leo shook his head. "Of course not."

"Okay." Pressing back against the futon, Sloan removed his phone from his pocket and gestured to Leo. "Lean on me so you can see my screen." He searched for what he thought were calming videos online. It only took him about a minute to find a channel filled with videos about how random objects were made. Hoping it would be helpful to watch something that required little energy to focus on, he played the first one.

Leaning into his side, Leo questioned, "How is this supposed to help me?"

"Just try to watch it and don't think about anything else, okay?"

With a sigh, Leo's head dropped onto his shoulder. Sloan tensed for a second before relaxing. It was fine. He didn't mind Leo using him as a pillow. It actually gave him hope things would be normal from then on out. This seemed like good friend-level support.

They fell silent, listening to the soothing sound of the woman's voice coming from his phone. Over time, Leo's breathing steadied, the subtle trembling of his fingers on his own leg ceasing. These signs of improvement kept Sloan from answering all the messages from Drew coming in on his phone, worried that in the time he'd have to take to respond, Leo would return to his state of panic.

Sloan had texted Drew before leaving the apartment to let him know where he would be, so at least his boyfriend wouldn't be worried about him. He'd undoubtedly be peeved with Sloan not answering, but he'd text him back when he could and clear everything up.

After some time—the length of eighteen of those videos—Justin and Max returned. Their other friend wasn't with them.

For a few seconds after they entered, they studied the sight of them on the futon while Sloan stared back. Justin smiled as he shut the door. Max didn't exactly look pleased to see Leo perfectly content with his head on Sloan's shoulder. Sloan was more amused than concerned about it, since he knew Max was getting the wrong idea.

"Thanks, man," Justin offered, not bothering to take off his shoes as he moved farther into the room. "Do you want me to take over? I understand if this isn't how you want to spend your Saturday evening."

"Nah, I'm alright," he assured. "I don't know if you've heard about it, but he's been avoiding me lately, so I'm planning on holding this over his head." A huff left Leo at that, and Sloan grinned. "Besides, I'm kinda worried he might freak out again if I move."

Justin's eyebrows raised. "He freaked out?"

"Ah, just a bit," Sloan answered. Justin's gaze lingered on them before flicking over to his friend.

"Well, alright then. Max and I can hang out in his dorm. It'll probably be easier if it's quiet in here."

With a nod of agreement, Sloan dropped his eyes to his phone as another message from Drew came through. From the corner of his eye, he glanced at Leo. He wondered if he'd noticed the incoming notifications, but doubted it when he saw Leo's glazed-over look as he watched the video. A narrator was explaining how springs were made, and the sight of the machine coiling the metal was hypnotizing.

"Max? Let's go," Justin said, reaching out to grab his friend's sleeve. Curious, Sloan looked between the two of them, noticing the way Max stared back at him. "Max? What are you—"

"Can I ask you a question?" Max said to Sloan.

Smiling a bit, Sloan said, "You can ask, but I'm pretty sure I know what you're going to say. It's about our relationship, right?" he asked, and Max's eyes averted. Even though he seemed embarrassed, he didn't deny it. "We're friends. I have a boyfriend, and I'm pretty sure Leo's available." Leo had no reaction to this, which meant either it was true, or he wasn't paying attention.

"Max—" Justin began, only to be cut off again.

"Okay, thanks," Max offered, nodding in Sloan's direction. For some reason, he didn't look like he felt any better about the situation. "Justin, let's go. You can stay in my room tonight."

"Max—" Sloan didn't get to hear the rest of his sentence as Max pulled Justin from the room, closing the door behind them.

This was all very interesting to Sloan. First, Justin, the boy who drove Colette near insane, was Leo's roommate. Then, one of his close friends was interested enough in Leo to get jealous over Sloan's proximity to him. Max didn't seem like a bad guy. Maybe Sloan could convince Leo to give it a try. It would probably be good for him.

For another hour they sat like that, Sloan's phone automatically cycling from one video to another. Every once in a while, they got a repeat. Leo didn't seem to notice.

It was when Sloan noticed how long Leo's breaths had become that he spoke again. "Hey, do you want to get into bed?"

It took Leo a moment to respond, and when he did, he sounded perfectly relaxed. "I don't know." He spoke at a whisper. "I feel better but I'm afraid to move. My body feels tired."

Sloan thought for a minute. "Here. Hold my phone."

With a noise of agreement, Leo took the device and lifted his head from Sloan's shoulder. Rising from the futon made Sloan groan, his limbs protesting after not moving for so long.

"What are you doing?" Leo asked.

"Getting you a pillow and blanket," he answered, reaching up to the loft on the left. "This is your bed, right? I was guessing this was your side because the desk is so clean." Leo made a little grunt in agreement.

Sloan pulled down the necessary bedding and laid it on the futon beside Leo. "Sleep there tonight. That way, if you get sick you don't need to worry about getting out of bed."

"Get sick?" Leo sounded worried.

"Yeah. When I got too high, I ended up throwing up. You seem to have passed that stage, so I wouldn't worry too much about it." Leo regarded him in a way that made Sloan feel like all his feelings and thoughts were out in the open. Instinctively, his body tensed.

"Alright," Leo agreed, eyes flitting away. They were open a little wider than they had been earlier, but he still looked stoned out of his mind.

Fingers wrapped tightly around Sloan's phone, Leo lay down onto his side with care. When his head met the pillow, he extended his hand with the phone in Sloan's direction. "You can take it back. Thank you."

Sloan returned from having turned off the light to accept the device. "You're okay now?" he asked, itching to check his messages from Drew.

"I feel really paranoid, and I don't think watching a video on how to make bubble gum is gonna change that," Leo said.

Sloan made no move to check his messages.

"You've been high before?" asked Leo.

Sloan took a seat on the floor, the futon against his back as support. "Yeah. In high school. I didn't do it often, but my best friend was always curious about stuff and didn't want to do things alone."

"High school," Leo said, sounding wistful. "It feels weird to think about high school now, doesn't it?"

Sloan smiled. "What were you like in high school? I've thought about it, over the years."

"You thought about me?" Leo sounded surprised.

"Yeah," Sloan confirmed. "Of course. Did you not think of me?" He hoped Leo had. That would mean their friendship as kids had meant something to him as well.

"I tried not to. Thinking about you made me feel guilty," Leo admitted, his voice sad.

That wasn't what Sloan wanted. "What were you like in high school?" he prompted again. "What'd you do with your free time?"

"Homework," Leo answered, voice coming out slow. "I was pretty boring. My focus in life back then was my grades and securing a good scholarship for college. My school was really competitive, so that was my friends' focus as well. We didn't do much outside of school."

Sloan turned his head to look at Leo and caught him looking back. Leo's eyes slipped closed after a moment. Sloan continued to stare. He'd spent so long thinking of Leo as a child that seeing him older was fascinating.

"That's no fun."

"It was fine," Leo mumbled. "I got to spend a lot of time with my mom and sister."

"How's your mom doing with you so far away?" Sloan asked.

Leo's lips curled into a smile. "She misses me, but I think she's happy at the same time. She thought I would be the kind of person to stay in the same place my entire life."

"Is that bad?"

"Not for people who are able to be happy where they're from."

"You weren't happy?"

"I was indifferent, and I didn't want to live my life like that," Leo admitted. "Getting away was good for me. You can't expect things to change if you do nothing to make them change."

"Yeah." Sloan thought about this. "I suppose you're right."

He wondered what he wanted to change in his life. Everything seemed to be going fine at the moment, especially since he was almost positive this would be the turning point in his and Leo's relationship. Maybe he'd like it if his mother stopped babying him, but he felt like he addressed that by moving in with Drew.

Oh shit, he thought, fumbling with his phone again. *Drew.*

He'd been planning on texting him while talking to Leo before getting distracted by the conversation. "Hey, is it okay with you if I call . . ." He trailed off, eyes falling on Leo's relaxed face. He was asleep.

It was a good thing—he had been worried Leo wouldn't be able to sleep—but he didn't have time to be relieved. He quickly dialed Drew's number. Immediately, the call was picked up. "Where the hell are you?"

Sloan cringed at how pissed his boyfriend sounded. "I am so sorry. I'm still at Leo's." This was probably already known to Drew. He had the location of Sloan's phone and wasn't afraid to check it. "Leo smoked too much and wasn't feeling well, so we were watching videos on my phone until he calmed down." Sloan kept his voice quiet, and he threw a quick glance at Leo to make sure he was undisturbed. It would be easy enough to slip out of the room and go home. That would mean leaving Leo alone though, and he didn't want to do that. "I'm sorry, Drew. I don't think I'm going to be home tonight."

"Are you kidding me? Can't someone else take care of it? How is it fair to make you stay?"

"No one is *making* me. I don't mind being here with him, and I'd be worried if I left him."

"What do you mean, you *don't mind*? You'd rather be there with him than home with me?" Drew snapped.

Sloan squeezed his eyes shut. "Please don't start this right now."

There was a scoff in return. "It's a legitimate concern!"

"It's not," Sloan protested. "He's my friend and he's stoned. I'm not just going to leave him. That doesn't mean I wouldn't rather be with you."

"Then come *home*."

If there's one thing I want to change, it's the fact that my boyfriend doesn't seem to hear me.

"Are you even listening to me?" Sloan asked, not bothering to hide the frustration in his voice. "I *can't* leave him like this. What if he gets sick and chokes? What if he panics again?"

"And how is that your problem?" Of course Drew didn't get it.

Sloan couldn't think of a response that wouldn't further aggravate his boyfriend, so he spit out a rushed good night and hung up. For good measure, he turned his phone off, preventing him from seeing any more of Drew's messages.

He understood maybe it was shitty of him to have neglected Drew's wishes to have him home early and fail to text him about it, but Sloan couldn't believe Drew expected him to leave Leo in this state so he could go home, and they could, what? Sleep in the same bed? Have sex? They did that all the time. Leo wasn't like this all the time. Sloan should have been able to miss one night for the sake of his friend.

When he went home in the morning, he and Drew were going to fight.

Sloan really hated fighting.

The next morning, Sloan and Leo got breakfast at a restaurant off campus. They sat in a booth by the window and he put his phone face down on the table. It was still off, but he was sure it was filled with texts from Drew.

I'm being a bad boyfriend, he thought. A glance at Leo reminded him of how long he'd been waiting for this moment. Sloan shook his head, focusing on his menu. *I'm allowed to have breakfast with a friend without Drew making me feel bad about it.*

"Have you always worn glasses?" asked Leo, distracting him from his thoughts.

"No." Sloan turned his face away self-consciously. "I got them in high school. Most people don't know because I wear my contacts pretty much all the time. Glasses don't suit me, I think." Sloan wasn't actually the one who thought this. He had worn his glasses more than his contacts for the first year he had them, but when he met Drew, Drew made it known that he preferred the way Sloan looked in contacts.

Leo frowned. "I think they look nice."

"Thanks," Sloan mumbled. His face felt hot, and he wondered whether he was blushing.

"Hey." Sloan glanced up, but Leo was looking out the window as he spoke. "Thank you for last night. Really."

"Of course. Have I earned your forgiveness by now?"

Leo seemed surprised. "Forgiveness? For what happened when we were kids?" Sloan nodded. "There's nothing to forgive, Morgan. Is that why you thought I was avoiding you?"

"So, you admit that's what you were doing?"

Leo's eyes dropped to the table. "I didn't understand you or why you wanted to be friends with me when it seemed it could cause you problems. . . I still don't get that part, actually, but recently I wasn't trying to avoid you. I just thought it might be easier if we didn't do things together one on one. That's all you ever asked me to do, so I kept saying no."

"And I'm assuming by *cause me problems* you're referring to my possessive boyfriend?" Sloan asked. "I know how Drew seems. He's really not someone you need to worry about, though. Even if he doesn't like the idea of us being friends now, he'll get used to it. He'll have to. He and I . . . we're still pretty early in our relationship if you think about it, and he's going to have to learn to trust me and my feelings for him at some point. Our relationship won't be sustainable if he gets upset every time I make a new friend who is a boy." When he noticed Leo still looked nervous, he sighed. "It's not something for you to worry about, okay?"

"I know," Leo said. "I'm sorry."

"It's okay," Sloan assured. "Thanks for caring."

Finally, Leo looked at him through his dark eyelashes.

"*And,*" Sloan continued, "I know you said there's nothing to forgive, but I've been wanting to apologize to you for about five years now, so I'm going to—"

"Morgan—"

"Are you boys ready to order?" their waitress interrupted.

They took turns telling her what they wanted as she filled their coffee cups. When they were finished, she went on her way.

The second she was out of hearing distance, Leo told him, "You don't have to apologize for kissing me. I don't know if you recall, but you asked beforehand and I said it was alright. I've been meaning to say sorry for running away afterward when I panicked."

"It's okay." Sloan curled his hands around his coffee mug. "You know, I went over to your dad's house the next day to get you. You hadn't come outside yet, and I was concerned. Your sister answered the door and told me you left." The memory made Sloan smile sadly. He was pretty sure that was the first and only time he'd felt heart broken. "I'd pushed you too far. I knew you found it difficult to say no to me, which seems to be a thing of the past, might I point out. I shouldn't have asked if I could kiss you because I was doubting my sexuality."

Leo poured a creamer into his coffee and watched the liquids swirl together. "It's not a thing of the past. It's still difficult for me to say no to you. That's why I only did it over text. When you asked me to hang out in person, I didn't say no. I said it wasn't a good idea. If you had pressed it, I probably would have given in.”

"Huh. I'll keep that in mind," Sloan joked, laughing when Leo made a face. "Is it fair of me to ask you a yes or no question, then?"

"Probably not."

"Well, I'm going to anyway," Sloan said. Leo raised his gaze to look at him. Even after Leo admitted that rejecting Sloan was difficult for him, he still feared the answer he'd receive would be no. "We're friends now, right? Friends who'll do stuff together?"

Thankfully, Leo let out a chuckle. "Yeah," he agreed. "We're friends."

CHAPTER EIGHTEEN

LEO

Five years ago

"Leo. . . Leo. . . hey! Leo!" Morgan yelled, waving his hand in front of Leo's face to get his attention. They were lying in the grass in Morgan's backyard, staring up at the sky, and Leo found it easy to get lost in the clouds. "Are you okay? You seem like you're in a bad mood. Aren't you excited it's the weekend?"

"Every day is like the weekend for me. I have nothing to do," Leo reminded, sounding dry even though he actually was very much anticipating the next few days.

"I can't believe your parents were okay with you missing the last two weeks of school to come here," Morgan voiced, not for the first time. "I wish I didn't have to go to school. Then it'd be like summer already and we could do whatever we wanted."

While this did sound pretty nice, Leo only mumbled, "I still had to complete all my classwork," in response. Morgan made a face, probably because of Leo's attitude. "Sorry. My mom yelled at me this afternoon."

He's gotten in an argument with Lizzy, which ended with her calling their mother to tell on him and him getting scolded.

Morgan rolled onto his side to face Leo. "I thought you said you were her favorite."

"I am. She still scolds me sometimes," Leo said. "Don't your parents scold you?"

"Nah." Morgan shrugged the shoulder that wasn't pressed into the grass. "My dad isn't really one to scold, and if my mom is gonna fight with anyone, Nancy makes sure it's her."

Leo turned his face back up toward the sky.

"Well, anyway," Morgan continued, "I was saying that the stars are supposed to be super bright tonight."

"Okay? So what?"

"*Leooo*," Morgan whined, reaching out to tug on his sleeve. "Why don't you care about these things? Let's do something fun!"

"What do you mean?" Leo asked, enjoying the feeling of Morgan's hand, which had stopped pulling his shirt and instead rested against his arm.

The look on Morgan's face was the one he wore when he was going to suggest something out of Leo's comfort zone. "Let's sneak out tonight and go to the tree house!"

"To watch the stars?" Leo made a face that Morgan chuckled at.

"Yeah! Come on. It'll be cool. It's our first Friday night as friends, so we have to do something," Morgan insisted. There were so many reasons for him to say no. He didn't care about stars, and if they got caught, they'd be in trouble. He found himself mumbling *okay* regardless. That's what he always said. How could he not when Morgan looked so happy every time he did?

Late that night, Leo snuck out of the house. That was the simple part. The hard part was scaling the fence to Morgan's backyard.

At the top of the fence, he spotted Morgan on the other side, arms filled with blankets and a fluffy white pillow as he smiled up at him. "Are you just going to stand there?" Leo whispered, swinging one leg over the fence and then the other.

"How do you think I should help you?" Morgan asked, stepping back a few feet. "You have to jump."

Mumbling under his breath about how he was regretting this, Leo pushed himself off the top and landed on his feet before tipping forward and catching himself with his hands in the grass. "Morgan, this is a bad idea."

"Well, you're already over here. If you're about to back out, you're gonna need to climb back over the fence." He began to walk through his backyard. With a sigh, Leo followed. "Are your hands okay?"

"Yeah," Leo answered. "A little dirty but it's fine."

"Okay."

Leo didn't even need to see Morgan's face to know he was smiling.

"I checked the weather and it's not going to rain tonight. I thought we could lie on the deck." Morgan paused at the base of the tree and tilted his head to peer up at the tree house. They'd spent a couple of their afternoons up there already, and Leo was more than happy to stay out on the deck portion of the structure. The inside was quite stuffy.

"Yeah," he answered, raising a hand to stifle a yawn. He wasn't used to being awake this late. "Sounds good."

"Here." Morgan turned and pressed the pillow into his arms. "You can go first."

Leo did, struggling to keep the pillow stuck beneath his arm as he climbed the ladder. Morgan followed him.

There were a couple of minutes of arranging, laying down the pillow and blankets to make a somewhat comfortable bed, before they lie down side by side. Since there was only one pillow, they pressed together, shoulder to shoulder. It was nice.

"I was thinking of making popcorn," Morgan whispered. "But I think the popper would have woken my parents, and then everything would have been ruined."

"That's okay," Leo told him. "I don't need popcorn . . . this is actually kind of nice."

Humming, Morgan shifted under the blanket, his arm pressing harder against Leo's.

"Hey, Leo?"

"Yeah."

"Will we still be friends when you go back to Illinois?"

The question surprised him. Leo pulled his eyes away from the bright stars to watch the boy next to him. Even though it was dark, he could see Morgan perfectly. "I don't know," Leo admitted. Morgan didn't respond. "Do you want to be?"

"I still want to talk to you and stuff," Morgan insisted, also turning his face toward him. They were close enough that their noses were almost touching. "Don't you want to talk to me?"

"Yeah," Leo answered breathlessly, and Morgan's lips curled into a pretty smile. "I mean, I guess it would be kind of nice."

Morgan turned his face back to the sky. This slightly disappointed Leo—he really liked it when Morgan was looking at him—but a moment later he felt warm fingers slip between his own beneath the blanket. Face feeling hot, Leo looked upward. When the hand holding his squeezed, he squeezed right back.

That was the night he began to love the stars.

Saturday morning, the voice of Morgan's mother woke Leo. "I found them," she was saying to someone. "Why don't you give Mr. Meyer a call?"

Groaning softly, Leo turned away from the noise, pressing his face into something soft. Startled by the feeling, he cracked open his eyes. All he saw was blond hair. The night before came back to him. He turned his head again, blinking his eyes at the morning light as he came to his senses. Morgan's face was pressed against his shoulder, and from the sound of his breathing, he was still asleep.

"Leo?" Mrs. Sloan whispered. Leo looked toward her. Morgan's mother was peeking up at them, just far enough up the ladder that she could peer onto the deck. "Good morning."

"I'm sorry," Leo said immediately, trying to sit and failing with Morgan pinning him down. "Morgan, *hey*. Your mom is here."

"Good for my mom," Morgan grumbled against Leo's shoulder, his knees pulling up beneath the blanket.

"*Morgan*," Mrs. Sloan said, something about her voice sending chills down Leo's spine.

Her son must have heard it as well, because he shot up into a seated position, gray eyes wide. "I'm up!" he exclaimed, and Leo thought of the day before when Morgan said he didn't get scolded.

Sighing, Mrs. Sloan climbed the rest of the way up the ladder and took a seat on the deck. "You boys really scared us, you know that? Leo, your father has been looking for you all morning. If you guys wanted to have a sleepover, you could have just asked. You certainly didn't have to sneak out of your rooms and make everyone worry."

Ashamed, they both mumbled that they were sorry. Silence stretched between them.

Morgan's mother sighed and shook her head. "Did you guys have a good time?"

"Yeah!" Morgan answered with a grin. Apparently, he was no longer worried about his mother's anger. "The best."

"Yeah," Leo agreed softly, thinking of Morgan's hand holding his for most of the night. "It was fun."

Chapter Nineteen

Sloan

When Sloan returned home, Drew was sitting on the couch waiting for him. He was expecting a lecture the second he arrived, but to his surprise, the apartment remained completely silent as he shut the door and kicked off his shoes.

Unsure of what to do, Sloan paused at the end of the couch. Nothing happened. "Drew." Still nothing. "*Drew.*" Frustrated, Sloan took a seat. "Look, I'm sorry I haven't been answering your calls and messages since last night, but you have to admit what you were asking of me was unreasonable. I mean, he was miserable, and you expected me to leave him."

"You're *my* boyfriend, Sloan!" Drew yelled, loud enough that the neighbors probably heard. "How is it unreasonable that I want you here with me?!" Besides wincing at the volume, Sloan showed no reaction to being yelled at. Usually, he would shrink back or become submissive; this time, though, he would not let Drew get away with it. As he said to Leo, this was something he needed to confront if their relationship was to withstand time.

"You wanted me to leave him there by himself after I said I'd look after him."

"Why does he even matter?" Drew demanded, green eyes burning with frustration.

With a deep breath, Sloan forced himself to calm down. "He's my friend."

"Is he *just* a friend?" Drew shot back, turning his face away to scowl at the television.

"What exactly are you implying?"

"It's just that you seem awfully concerned for a friend," Drew accused.

"Because I stayed with him to make sure he was okay?" Sloan asked. There were three occasions that came to mind of Drew doing something similar for his male friends. Sloan had never felt upset or threatened by this because he trusted his boyfriend. He didn't understand why Drew didn't trust him as well.

"Drew, I'm not the kind of person who can leave someone behind and *hope* it all turns out okay. You know this about me! You said that's why I would make a good doctor, remember? Please don't turn this into something it's not," Sloan begged. Desperate, he hoped that would be the end of it.

The way Drew continued to clench his jaw told him it was just the beginning. "You've been interested in him this whole time. How can I trust you? First you didn't tell me that the two of you were hanging out in the library, then you're texting him when we're together and trying to get him to spend all this time with you, and then you choose him over me and spend the night with him! How do I know nothing happened? Was he really not feeling well, or did you just say that? How can I tell you're being honest with me?"

Flabbergasted, Sloan stared at his boyfriend, mouth agape. They already addressed them hanging out—which wasn't actually them hanging out—and Drew hadn't even seemed upset by his messaging Leo. Drew using these things as reasons not to trust him was so ridiculous it seemed unbelievable. "Don't you trust me at all?" Sloan asked. "We've been dating for a year, Drew. Do you really think that little of me?"

This clearly did not appeal to the part of Drew he was hoping it would, because his boyfriend huffed and shook his head. "You should have left him by himself."

"No," Sloan disagreed. To his satisfaction, his voice came out strong even though he felt like falling apart.

What does this mean for our relationship? he wondered, not feeling optimistic about the answer.

"No, I shouldn't have left him. I did the right thing, and you will not make me feel guilty about that. If I had to do it over, I'd do *everything* the same way."

Drew looked surprised. It didn't take long for his expression to morph into something of distaste. Neither of them spoke until the tension became unbearable.

Sloan sighed. "Drew—"

"I have nothing to say to you," Drew interrupted. "If you don't even understand what you did wrong, I don't know what to tell you."

Unwilling to sit there silently stewing in awkward, angry tension, Sloan rose from the couch and left the room. He went to take a painfully hot shower, as if the heat would melt away his problems.

When the tingling from where the water met his skin got too bad to ignore, he turned down the temperature. His problems were still unresolved.

That morning felt far away. It seemed impossible to feel this miserable after having such a great time with Leo. If he could go back thirty minutes, to when Leo asked if he wanted to hang out longer, Sloan would say *yes* instead of, *"I should probably get back to my boyfriend."*

That would only make things worse with Drew, Sloan thought. *It would only end up hurting more when I got back.* For some reason, it didn't convince him he had made the correct choice. He was happy in Leo's company, happy enough it almost seemed worth it to have Drew treat him like this. Maybe when he finished showering, he would send Leo a message and see—

I shouldn't think these things. That would make Drew more mad, and even if spending time with Leo would make me happy right now, I have to make some sacrifices for the sake of my relationship.

Lifting his head, Sloan let the water splash over his face. *"How can I trust you?"* Drew asked him. "How could you not?" Sloan wondered out loud. He raised a hand to push his hair off his forehead.

The bathroom door clicked. "Sloan, didn't I tell you to stop taking these showers? They can't be good for you," Drew pestered from the other side of the shower curtain. The urge to huff was barely resisted, but his eyes still rolled at the scolding.

"It relaxes me. You know that."

Drew didn't respond. Sloan could hear his boyfriend removing his clothes to join him. "Drew . . ."

"What?" Drew asked, and a second later the curtain yanked open. "Is the water still hot as hell, or can I get in without feeling intense pain?"

"I turned it down," Sloan admitted, moving forward so Drew had enough room to join him. He was still angry, but refusing Drew entry right then would be ridiculous, seeing as he already removed all of his clothing.

Drew stepped into the tub behind him and pulled the curtain shut. Paying him no mind, Sloan grabbed the body wash from the hanging shower caddy and shook it so it would come out more easily.

As he did this, Drew pressed himself against his back, his hands coming to hug Sloan around his waist. "Hey," he said into Sloan's neck, lightly kissing the skin there. "I don't like fighting with you."

"I don't like it either," Sloan agreed, popping open the body wash cap and spilling some onto his hand.

"Then let's make up," Drew suggested.

Sloan lathered his arms with the soap. He knew Drew was saying this not because he changed his view on the matter, but because he couldn't stand Sloan being angry at him.

"It's not that easy, Drew," he reminded.

"Sure it is." Drew grabbed the body wash from the caddy and put some on his own hand. He pressed his palm into Sloan's stomach before dragging it down at a teasing pace.

Oh.

"Drew—"

"Hmmm? You don't want me to?" Drew sounded as if he was holding in a laugh.

With a groan, Sloan squeezed his eyes shut and let his head fall back on Drew's shoulder. Chuckling, his boyfriend continued his ministrations.

"I love you so much it drives me crazy," Drew whispered in his ear, fingers stroking him how he liked.

"I love you too," Sloan managed. That was only a part of what he was thinking.

I love you too, but I don't know if this is the kind of love I want.

Apparently, Drew thought sex fixed everything, because when they got out of the shower, he went straight to bed and held his arms out. Instead of joining him, Sloan hovered in the doorway with his phone, texting Colette. "Come lay with me," Drew instructed, raising his head from the pillow to look at him. "Hey, who are you texting?"

"Colette," Sloan answered. "I'm gonna go study with her in the library."

As if startled by this, Drew sat up. Sloan was already moving back into the living room to grab his backpack and put on his shoes. "What? You weren't home all night! I missed you."

"I'm still annoyed with you," he called back, listening to the sound of Drew getting out of bed as he looked through his backpack to make sure he had the books he needed to study.

"You're serious?" Drew asked. "Sloan, I thought . . ."

The sound of his boyfriend trailing off made Sloan pause and lift his head. "You thought what? That if you could get me to put out, I'd suddenly no longer be upset that you have no trust in me and accused me of cheating on you?"

"I didn't do that."

Scoffing, Sloan turned back to his backpack and zipped it angrily. "Oh right. You didn't directly say it, it just was implied." He was slow in pulling the straps of his backpack over his shoulders, slow in slipping on his shoes, and slow in finding his keys, giving Drew an opportunity to say what he wanted him to say.

That he was sorry. Drew was *never* sorry about anything, and Sloan didn't think he should have to ask for an apology. It didn't seem like too much to ask that his twenty-one-year-old boyfriend could identify when he did or said something wrong and apologize for it.

Or maybe it *was* too much to ask, because Drew remained silent.

"I'll see you later," Sloan told him, feeling the urge to cry and refusing to let himself.

"You're wearing your glasses," was all Drew said in response, as if this could embarrass Sloan enough that he would end up staying.

It didn't. Instead, as he pulled open the door, Sloan recalled Leo telling him they looked nice.

Chapter Twenty

Leo

Leo did not know what to expect when Morgan invited him to an unfamiliar dorm room on Tuesday, but the door being answered by the brunette he'd watched over at his first campus party wasn't it. She looked really different, wearing a pair of black sweatpants and a large T-shirt, though she had a face he wouldn't have just forgotten.

She obviously didn't have the same recollection, because she looked him up and down with a sly smile before asking, "And who are *you?*"

Instinctively, he took a step back. Before he could even think of what to say, the door was pulled open wider and Morgan came into view.

"Leo!" he greeted with a grin.

"This is Leo?" asked the brown-haired girl, whose name he was having trouble remembering.

Morgan frowned at her. "You've met him before. At the first party of the year. The one we met at. He's the one who got Colette to take care of you."

"Well, why didn't you take care of me?" she asked. "We could have had fun." He recalled her saying similar things at the party. He also remembered, as an afterthought, that she and Max ended up sleeping together.

Interesting, Leo thought, eyeing her curiously.

"Kenni, leave him alone," a voice called from inside the room. *Kenni,* Leo thought, the name falling into place.

"Come on," Morgan said, reaching forward to grab ahold of his arm. As he pulled him forward, Kenni stepped out of the way with her hands held up, as if this was her physical representation of *leaving him alone.* Leo found himself in another overly hot dorm room.

It was cute, about the size of his and Justin's room. There were bunk beds and a small futon, where Colette was sitting. A black-haired boy sat on the bottom bed, and he raised a hand to give Leo a wave that somehow made him feel awkward.

"That's Oliver. He's Kenni's best friend," Morgan explained, hand sliding to wrap around Leo's wrist. "Come on. You can sit by Colette and me."

"Hey Leo," Colette greeted, patting the spot next to her.

"And you remember Kennedy, right?" Morgan asked, taking a seat and pulling Leo down beside him. "Even if she doesn't remember you." Morgan's hand slipped away from Leo's wrist, and he immediately brushed his own fingers there, wondering why his skin felt so hot.

"Yeah," Leo mumbled, watching as Kennedy joined Oliver on the bed. He felt uncomfortable as he always did around new people. Morgan gave him a reassuring smile before leaning forward to look around him at Colette.

"What are we watching? It's your turn to choose," he said.

Colette waved a remote around. Leo assumed it controlled the small television sitting on the desk directly across from them. That, as well as a small black box that appeared to be plugged into the television, were the only things on the desktop. Leo wondered where she—either Kennedy, or Kennedy's roommate—did homework.

"Be prepared for some quality television, you guys. Nothing like the shit you've made me watch so far," Colette said, sounding so sure of herself that Leo's eyebrows raised. It made him wonder what the others chose to watch.

As if able to read his mind, Morgan leaned over to explain. "Kenni chose a movie with no plot and a lot of eye candy, while Oliver chose an action movie that was kind of graphic. Colette enjoyed neither."

"Have you chosen yet?" Leo asked. The only answer he received was a grin.

"What are you gonna pick, Letti?" Kennedy prompted, leaning forward on the bed to better see the television screen as Colette searched through the streaming app.

"Something cute," Colette answered. "A nice rom-com to teach you how boys *should* treat you." At this, Oliver snickered and Kennedy stuck her tongue out.

"I should have known you'd choose a rom-com," Morgan teased.

She snorted. "Don't you go acting like you don't climb in my bed every Wednesday night to watch reality dating shows with me." To Leo's right, Morgan sighed heavily and dropped his head back against the futon. On the bed, both Kennedy and Oliver were laughing.

The group of four already seemed so comfortable with one another, so complete without Leo's presence. He didn't know how he was supposed to act so they would want him to come again. Nervously, he chewed his lip.

Colette chose some movie about a woman and her nerdy but hot best friend who she was to inevitably fall in love with. As she described earlier, it was *cute,* though not much of an attention grabber. Leo found himself disinterested within the first ten minutes, having already predicted the ending. Thankfully, the group didn't seem to follow the *no-talking-during-movies* rule, because there was a constant stream of chatter among them.

Leo didn't join in until Morgan nudged him with his elbow and said, "Hey. You should tell Colette who your roommate is."

He frowned and was about to ask why, but Colette was already asking, "Who's your roommate?"

"Justin Morris."

Colette looked at Sloan with raised eyebrows. "Am I supposed to know who that is?"

"He's that kid from chem and bio who bothers you so much," said Morgan.

This intrigued Leo enough that he completely abandoned the television screen to look at Colette. She seemed half shocked and half embarrassed by this information. "He bothers you?" Leo asked.

With a noise of distaste, Colette turned back to the TV. "He's just frustrating," she claimed. "It doesn't seem like he applies himself, and he doesn't even pay attention in class, but he's so good at everything. I don't like people like that, especially since I try so hard."

Leo thought about all the time Justin spent sitting at his desk in their room. "It might seem like he doesn't apply himself, but he actually studies all the time."

Colette was quiet for a minute. Then, she exhaled heavily and shook her head. "God," she muttered. "Why does that make me even more angry?" Morgan laughed. "Leo, hit him."

"I'm a pacifist," Leo explained, making no move to follow her command. Morgan looked incredibly pleased.

"Of course you are," Colette said, reaching over to poke a finger into his cheek. "I can't imagine you hurting anyone. Or anyone hurting you, for that matter."

Briefly, Leo recalled Max telling him Drew would punch him in the face, though that had been revoked on Saturday night.

"Oh, hey!" Colette continued. Her hand dropped. "I almost forgot. Yesterday I stopped by the teaching assistants' room, and Eric said there's gonna be another party this Friday at his place. We should all go."

"I'm in," Kennedy agreed immediately, not even taking time to think about it first.

Beside her, Oliver let out a groan. "I guess I'm going too then." He sounded less than thrilled.

"You don't need to babysit me," Kenni protested. On either side of

Leo, Colette and Morgan both made soft scoffing noises.

"Yes, I do," Oliver retorted. She appeared to be annoyed by this, even though everyone in the room—even Leo—agreed with Oliver. Before she could say anything about it, Oliver was addressing him and Sloan. "Well, Colette's clearly planning on going. What about you two? Are you in?"

Once again surprised he was being included, Leo didn't respond right away.

"Well, Drew's going to be gone Friday into Saturday this weekend, so I'll be able to go," Morgan answered.

"Why couldn't you go if Drew was still here?" Colette asked, sounding displeased.

Having no reaction to the distaste, Morgan shrugged. "Well, I'd have to talk to him first if he was home, is all. He'd be fine with it if he had nothing planned." Leo got the impression that Drew was a topic Morgan would prefer to steer clear of. Leo looked to the one person likely to know about it. Colette met his eyes before rolling her own.

"What about you, Leo? Are you gonna come along?" she asked, lightly bumping her elbow into his arm. "I think you should."

He thought about the last party he went to and how desperate he felt to get out of there after only a short time.

"I'm not sure".

"You should totally come!" Kennedy exclaimed. "It'll be fun! I'll dance with you the whole night. I promise." One of her eyelids dropped in a wink.

Without even looking at her, Morgan informed, "Kenni, he's *gay*." Kennedy didn't seem surprised, giving a shrug in response. "Leo, why wouldn't you come? Do you have other plans?"

"I don't," he admitted. "The last party I went to wasn't fun, though."

"But this time you'll be with *us*," Colette said, smiling in a way that made him feel warm. He glanced back and forth between her and Morgan, taking in their hopeful expressions.

"I'll think about it." Both of them grinned as if he had said yes, clearly confident in their ability to convince him within the next few days.

A part of Leo hoped they would.

Leo still had two hours before he needed to be at lab, so he and Morgan went to get an early dinner in the cafeteria.

"So," Leo began once they had sat down, "where's Drew going to be this weekend?"

"Ah, Drew?" Morgan said, almost immediately making Leo regret asking. "I don't know. Somewhere for golf, apparently. I don't always listen to him when he talks about it. I honestly don't find it at all interesting." After taking a quick sip of soda—probably to make the subject change less obvious—Morgan said, "You should come to the party on Friday. I think it'll be fun. I'd really like it if you came."

His mouth working faster than his brain, Leo questioned "Why?"

"I don't know. I just want to spend more time with you," Morgan admitted, somehow managing to not look even the tiniest bit bashful. It amazed Leo. He could never say something like that with such confidence.

"Oh . . . well . . ." He looked past Morgan and trailed off as he made eye contact with someone sitting a few tables away. It was Max, eating with a group of people Leo didn't recognize. The brunet smiled and waved.

Feeling awkward, Leo also raised his hand. He noticed Morgan's curious gaze then and lowered it quickly. "Sorry."

Morgan shook his head at the apology. "Who is it?"

"Justin's friend Max."

"He was there when you got high?"

Nodding, Leo fought the urge to cringe at the memory.

Morgan smiled. "He seemed like a nice guy."

"Yeah, I guess he is," Leo said. "I'm pretty sure he's having sex with

Kennedy."

"Oh." Morgan seemed concerned. "Does that bother you?"

Leo frowned. "No. Why would it?"

Gray eyes averted. "No reason."

They were quiet for a minute as they ate.

Morgan broke the silence. "Hey, could I ask you something I've been curious about?"

Leo shrugged. "Why couldn't you?"

"I was just wondering what ended up happening with you and that guy you liked when we were kids."

This wasn't what Leo had been expecting, so he took a moment to think of a response.

Morgan interpreted his silence as discomfort. "You don't have to answer."

"I don't mind answering, I'm just wondering if there's a way to tell you what happened without sounding pathetic." Morgan raised his eyebrows.

"Nothing happened. When I returned from California, I confessed my feelings to him, and he didn't return them, obviously, because he was an adult and I was a child. He kept tutoring me and was eventually my high school teacher, and I came to understand that what I felt for him was childish infatuation and not genuine feelings. Now I see him as an older brother."

Morgan's gaze lowered. "Huh" was all he said in response.

Leo was thankful that Morgan wasn't paying close attention to him. It meant he wouldn't be caught staring as he thought about his conversation with Michael the day Leo realized feelings weren't what he thought.

"*I know,*" Michael had said. "*I knew as soon as I heard you talking about that boy from California. At first, you were young and confused, and you mistook looking up to me as liking me, but once you returned from California, you were just using me as an excuse to avoid what you felt for him.*"

At the time, Leo said this was stupid. It hadn't been something complex like that, he'd simply mistaken his feelings as something more, he was sure. Now though, with Morgan sitting across from him again, he couldn't help but come to terms with the fact that Michael had been right.

CHAPTER TWENTY-ONE

LEO

Leo arrived to the party late that Friday.

He hadn't planned on going, despite assuring Morgan and Colette earlier that day that he would *probably* attend. It was Ian who talked him into it. Michael's husband had called to chat, and they discussed Leo's reasons for not wanting to go.

The first reason was that there would be people Leo didn't know, and the second was that there would be alcohol. Leo had gotten drunk once before in high school with his friends. It had ended quite terribly. He had no desire to repeat the experience.

Ian was very persuasive, and he told Leo he would only have to talk to his friends and that he could bring a water bottle and tell people there was alcohol in it so no one pressured him to drink.

And so, twenty minutes after ending the call, he was sending Morgan a message that he had arrived. He walked up the driveway of the house, a bottle of Dasani water in hand. It was unopened, and he wasn't exactly sure how he was supposed to convince people it was full of alcohol when it clearly was not, but he brought it anyway since Ian clearly knew more about these things.

There was no one outside like the first party he went to, and he relaxed, less worried about the gathering being broken up and getting in trouble. He grew even more comfortable when he stepped into the back hall and could hear only the faint sound of music from the floor below.

He was shutting the back door behind himself when his phone buzzed. The message was from Morgan.

Morgan: In the basement. Come down

He returned his phone to his pocket as he stepped out of the back hall into the kitchen.

He and Max spotted each other in the same moment. Max's lips curled into a grin.

He was alone in the room, leaning against the counter with a plastic cup in his hand. "I didn't know you'd be here tonight. Justin said you stayed in the dorm."

"Yeah," Leo confirmed, stopping in the middle of the kitchen. His eyes found the door he suspected went to the basement. Even so, Leo didn't move. "What are you doing up here by yourself?"

"I wanted water," Max answered, raising his free hand to wave Leo closer.

Leo hesitated, thinking that maybe closing the distance between the two of them wasn't a good idea. But he trusted Max, so he went to stand beside him.

"You came because of him, right?" asked Max.

Leo knew who he was referring to, but still asked, "Who?"

The smile Max gave him was sad. "Is it hard liking someone who likes someone else?"

Leo once again glanced at the door to the basement, this time with a different type of longing.

Max let out a sigh. "Hey, you want something to drink?"

"Oh." Leo clutched the bottle of water in his hand tighter, raising it for Max to see. "I have something."

Max stared at the bottle. "That's water."

They looked at each other. Leo kept his face blank although he was internally panicking while preparing himself for peer pressure.

It's fine. I'll just drink what he gives me and that'll be it—

"You don't want to drink?" Max asked.

"Uh . . . I'd prefer not to."

"That's cool," Max said, turning toward the cupboards. "If you don't want people to bother you about it, you should have a water bottle or something."

I thought I did, Leo almost said. After searching for a minute, Max pulled a reusable blue water bottle out of a cupboard and handed it to him. "Here. Put your water in there and no one will bother you. That's what most underagers drink out of if they bring their own alcohol, because no one can see what's inside."

"Thank you," Leo breathed, accepting the hard-plastic bottle and screwing off the top.

I am such an idiot.

Leo thought this for two reasons: First Ian obviously meant a reusable bottle and not branded bottled water. Second, Leo completely underestimated Max and assumed he would pressure him to do something he didn't want to.

Once he had poured his water into the bottle and twisted the top on, Leo noticed that Max was silently observing him. "What?" he asked self-consciously, raising his hand to rub at his forehead. "Do I have—"

"No," Max interrupted. "You don't. You look good. I'm glad you're here."

"Oh," Leo managed, confused. It seemed like Max was fond of him, though he knew Max was in some kind of relationship with Kennedy. Leo wondered if it would be okay to ask about her. Before he could decide, the door to the basement was thrown open, revealing a disheveled blond.

Everything stopped for a moment. Max and Leo both turned toward Morgan as Morgan looked back at them. He looked drunk, his cheeks flushed and eyes glassy.

Leo didn't realize how close he had been standing to Max until the boy beside him shifted away, raising a hand to rub at the back of his neck. "Ah, hey," Max greeted.

"Hi," Morgan responded, still looking back and forth between the two of them. His eyes eventually locked onto Leo's and he beamed. "I was trying to find you. Worried you got lost."

While still feeling quite dumb, Leo held up the blue water bottle and explained, "Just getting something to drink."

Moving farther into the room, Morgan raised eyebrows. "You're gonna drink?"

"It's water."

"Ahh." Morgan stopped in front of him. "Let me know if you decide you want something stronger." As if to show what he meant by *stronger*, he lifted his cup and shook it carelessly, sloshing dark liquid onto the floor. He didn't seem to notice. "They have wop downstairs."

"I don't know what that means," Leo confessed. Max and Morgan both chuckled.

"It's a bunch of alcohol and juice mixed together," Max told him. "It's in a bin downstairs."

"Is that sanitary?" Leo asked. Neither boy seemed concerned with this.

"There's so much vodka in there, it kills everything," Max claimed. "Except for like . . . drugs."

This didn't make Leo feel any better. Most negative thoughts left his head when Morgan reached out and grabbed his wrist. "Don't worry about it," he insisted. "A guy I know is making sure no one puts anything in it." Warily, Leo dropped his gaze to Morgan's cup. He said nothing else about the matter. "Come on. Let's go downstairs."

He let Morgan pull him away, looking over his shoulder as they went. Max seemed amused by this. "I'm fine," he assured, raising his hand in a wave. "I'll be down soon."

In the basement, Morgan led Leo toward a futon against the back wall, where Colette was sitting. She was alone but didn't appear to mind, a smile on her face as she watched Kennedy and Oliver dance.

When he and Morgan were close enough, Colette's attention shifted to them instead. "Leo, you came!" she exclaimed, speaking loudly to be heard over the music. Morgan, having spotted his two dancing friends, released Leo to join them. Leo took the seat beside Colette. "You almost didn't come, right?"

"Maybe," he admitted, eyebrows raising as she leaned into his side. She smelled like the alcoholic beverage Morgan had spilled on the floor upstairs. Thankfully, she didn't seem as far out of it as him.

"I'm glad you decided to, anyway. Sloan kept talking about how we were going to need to go to your room and get you if you didn't show up by eleven."

"Wow," Leo voiced. "You guys would go that far to get me to come?"

"Of course." Colette's smile was warm. "Hey." She tapped the top of his water bottle. "What're you drinking?"

"Water. Want some?"

"Oh, yes, please. I only had one cup of that stuff and it was much stronger than I was expecting."

He handed her the bottle and nodded toward Morgan. "How many cups has he had?"

"Too many. He's had a rough week," she explained vaguely before drinking from the bottle. Concerned, Leo watched Morgan for about a minute before gray eyes flicked back to him.

Embarrassed by being caught watching, Leo glanced away, giving his attention instead to his phone to text Ian.

Leo: I brought a water bottle.

Ian: Good!

Leo: No. Like, bottled water. I didn't understand.

The response didn't come right away, so Leo asked Colette about class. She was just getting into complaining about a failed chemistry experiment when Leo's phone lit up on his leg.

Subtly, so it didn't seem like he wasn't listening to her, he glanced at the screen to read the message.

Ian: Leo, I love you so much.

"Colette, do you want more to drink?"

The voice startled Leo. He glanced up to watch Morgan shake his now empty cup at them. Behind him, Oliver and Kennedy were waiting. The girl waved enthusiastically at Leo when their eyes met. Oliver just smiled.

"Oh. No, not really, but I'll come with you guys," Colette answered, handing Leo his water bottle and standing up. "Leo, you coming?"

Looking around at the crowded basement, Leo said, "I'll wait for you guys here." This didn't seem to be the answer Morgan wanted to hear, because he frowned. Still, nothing was said about it, and the four of them left him for the guy serving alcohol.

Leo was expecting to have at least a couple of minutes to himself, though after a matter of seconds, Justin was sinking down onto the futon beside him. During the week, Justin always looked tired, but on Fridays and Saturdays he seemed more alive. Right then, even though it was ten thirty, he looked more awake than Leo had seen in days.

"I'm surprised to see you here, but not surprised to see you sitting by yourself," Justin said. "You know Max would be by your side for the entire night if you asked him to."

"Yeah, what's with that?" Leo asked.

Justin sighed. "I don't know. Him and I haven't really talked about it."

Leo glanced toward the stairs and wondered if Max had come down yet. "Well, I'm not here alone. Sloan and them went to get more to drink." Justin gestured to the water bottle Leo was holding, as if to say *Not you too?* "This is water."

"Ah. Have you ever been drunk before?"

"Yes," Leo confessed. "It ended with me throwing up for hours and almost being taken to the hospital to get an IV."

"Damn." Justin sounded kind of proud. "Shit hits you different, huh?"

"Maybe," Leo acknowledged. "I get embarrassed when I look like I don't know what I'm doing, so I copy the actions of the people around me, and the people around me are idiots who are more experienced than me."

It took Justin a moment to process this, and then he broke out into a smile. "Did you just call me an idiot?"

"Probably." Leo couldn't help smiling as well. "Unintentionally, though."

"And yet you're not taking it back," Justin pointed out, not sounding at all offended.

Colette and Morgan returned then, Colette holding Morgan's arm in what looked like a friendly gesture, though Leo figured it was actually to steady him. "What are you doing here?" Colette asked Justin, eyes narrowed in a glare.

"Just visiting my roommate," Justin explained, not at all fazed by her cold behavior. "Is that alright with you?"

"Ack. How did someone like Leo get stuck with you for a roommate?"

"Oh my gosh, Colette," Morgan chimed in. "No fighting. We're gonna have a good night, remember?" Somehow, he sounded a lot drunker than he had five minutes ago.

"Yeah, yeah. We're having a good night," she assured, patting Morgan's shoulder and shooting Leo a look he assumed had to do with how drunk the boy was. "I'm gonna go dance with Kennedy and Oliver, alright? That way I won't feel the need to fight, because Justin will be far away from me." Justin let out an amused sounding huff.

Colette's hand slid from Morgan's arm as she moved toward the gathering of people by the speakers. Morgan hardly seemed to notice. He stepped so close to Leo that their knees pressed together. Saying nothing, Morgan extended his free hand toward him.

"Um . . ." Leo voiced, confused. Hesitant and hyperaware of Justin's eyes on them, he reached out to grab Morgan's hand. This seemed to be the correct response, because Morgan wrapped his fingers around Leo's and tugged a little. "What?"

"Come dance with me!"

Mildly horrified by the idea, Leo managed, "Huh?" Justin snorted.

"Dance," Morgan repeated, pulling a little more at his hand. Leo squeezed the fingers but didn't rise from the couch. Desperately he wished he was the kind of person who could dance and not worry about how he looked to others.

That just wasn't him.

"I'm not a dancer," Leo said, causing Morgan to pout. "I'm sorry."

"That's not something to be sorry for, I just want to do something with you," Morgan said. "What do you want to do?"

"I don't know." Leo lowered his gaze to their clasped hands. "I didn't come here because I wanted to go to a party and do the things people do at parties."

"Why'd you come?"

Leo thought it was obvious, especially to Morgan. "Because of you."

Grinning, Morgan released his hand and dropped into the seat beside him. On Leo's other side, Justin leaned into him and said in a low voice, only meant for him, "That was *so* gay."

"What?" Leo nervously glanced at Morgan out of the corner of his eye.

"I didn't know the two of you were together, man. Good for you," Justin continued. "Did this happen last Saturday?"

"What?" he repeated. This time Justin regarded him blankly. "We're not together. You've met his boyfriend."

At the mention of Drew, Justin's expression changed to one of distaste. They only met each other for about two minutes, though it had apparently been enough to make Justin hate him. "That's *still* his boyfriend?"

"Yeah," Leo confirmed, turning to look at Morgan. Gray eyes met his, and he wondered whether the drunk boy had heard any of their conversation. If he had, he didn't seem upset by it. "How are you feeling?"

"I'm great," Morgan insisted, making an *okay* hand sign while squinting his left eye. The expression indicated the opposite of the words, and Leo's eyebrows pulled together in concern. From over his shoulder came a laugh, and then Justin stood from the futon.

"I'm gonna leave you two be. I should go find Max, anyway."

"He was upstairs," Leo offered. Morgan enthusiastically said goodbye. After a quick thank you, Justin made his way toward the stairs.

Leo gave his full attention to the boy beside him. "Morgan, you don't have to sit here with me if you don't want to. I'm not exactly the most fun person to be around in these types of situations."

Morgan looked upset. "Hey, don't say that about yourself. What are you even talking about? I'm having a great time!"

"You're drunk," Leo accused lightly.

"Maybe, but I feel good," Morgan countered, smiling and leaning into Leo's side. "You know, I didn't think you were going to come."

"I know. Colette said you wanted to come get me."

"I did." He admitted it without shame. "I really wanted you to come, and you got my hopes up when you said you probably would . . . things are more fun for me with you around. Is that selfish of me? I didn't only want you here so it would be more fun for me. I want you to have fun, too."

"Oh . . . I think I'm having fun." The second the words were out of his mouth, Leo realized they were true. He *was* having fun. Even though he felt completely out of place, he was enjoying himself because Morgan was there with him. "It's fun. I'm having fun."

Alcohol apparently made Morgan feel happy, because he couldn't stop smiling. "Good. I'm having fun too."

***

Throughout the night, Morgan went through many stages of drunk, and Leo was beside him to watch them all.

There was the smiley drunk he had been as they talked on the futon, and then the barely-able-to-walk drunk as Leo practically carried him upstairs to get water. After that came sluggish drunk as they sat in the empty dining room together. It was at that stage when Leo told Morgan about his water bottle misunderstanding, and Morgan, unable to lift his head from the table, chuckled and mumbled, "Oh my lord, Leo, that's so damn cute," in a voice Leo could barely understand but was happy he could.

From then on out, it was a little more concerning. Morgan transitioned into dazed drunk, where he stopped listening and stared ahead blankly. Thankfully, Oliver came upstairs in search of them shortly after.

"Hey, you guys disappeared," he said. "Colette was worried—woah." He spotted Morgan and looked back at Leo, alarmed. "Is he alright?"

"I don't know," Leo admitted nervously, reaching across the table to press his hand against Morgan's cheek. "Sloan . . . hey, Sloan? Can you talk to me?" The response he received was mumbled and impossible to decipher. Sighing, Leo turned back to Oliver. "That's all he'll give me."

"Ahh . . . do you want help getting him home? I was going to head out since Kenni left a bit ago with some guy," Oliver explained.

Leo considered asking if it was Max. He didn't.

"Um, yeah, that'd be great," Leo accepted. "I was thinking of carrying him on my back, but I don't think I'm strong enough to make it the entire way."

Oliver nodded. "Well, I don't mind helping. Are you guys ready to go, or do you want to hang out longer?"

Leo was ready to leave, but he asked Morgan first before answering.

Morgan mumbled a single word, which made him easier to understand. "*Go.*"

"We're ready. What about Colette? We can walk her home on the way."

"I'll go get her," Oliver offered. "Even if she doesn't want to leave yet, I'm pretty sure she'll want to see you guys before you go."

"Alright, thanks."

Oliver left, and Leo began typing a text asking Justin if Morgan could crash on their futon. Before he could even finish the text, Morgan softly mumbled, "*Leo.*" Startled, Leo looked across the table at him. Morgan raised his head just enough to stare back.

Without sending the message, Leo returned his phone to his pocket and moved to the seat beside Morgan. "Yeah?" he asked, and Morgan sighed, resting his head back down, face turned toward Leo.

"I wanted to get drunk to feel better. It didn't fix anything. When I wake up tomorrow, things still aren't going to be okay," Morgan whispered, closing his eyes.

There was clearly something going on with him and Drew. Every time his boyfriend came up in conversation for the entire week, he'd been weird about it.

Leo didn't ask, worried Morgan would get upset in his current state. Instead, he raised his hand and pressed it against Morgan's cheek in a silent gesture of comfort. Light eyelashes fluttered at the touch, and Morgan raised his hand to rest it atop of Leo's, holding him there.

Oliver returned, Colette and—surprisingly—Justin following him. Justin halted in the doorway while Colette and Oliver came to the table. Colette laid a gentle hand against Morgan's back. "Are you alright?" she asked him. Apparently back to not talking, Morgan made a small groaning noise, fingers curling to grip Leo's hand.

"He's hammered, but he'll be alright. He's not unresponsive right now, I just don't think he wants to talk," Leo told Colette.

Morgan exhaled heavily. "I'm alright," he said, lifting his head and letting Leo's hand fall away. "I want to go. I don't feel good." His words were slurred but clear.

Colette addressed Leo. "Drew's gone tonight. Could he sleep at your place so you can keep an eye on him?"

"That was kind of the plan . . ." Leo trailed off, eyes finding Justin in the doorway. "Is that okay?"

"I don't mind," Justin assured. "I came up here to tell you that."

"Thanks. Colette? Are you coming with us or staying? We can walk you back to your room," Leo offered.

"Oh." Colette looked at the floor. "Um, I don't want to go yet… but I guess it would make sense for me to go with you guys—"

"I can make sure she gets home," Justin chimed in. After he said the words, he seemed as surprised as the rest of them. His gaze lowered. "If she wants to stay, I mean."

"I do," Colette confirmed, staring at the boy in the doorway. "Thank you." If it had been anyone else offering to get her home safely, Leo would have thought about it a little longer before agreeing. It was Justin though, and he trusted him, so he nodded in agreement before standing from his chair.

"Alright, Sloan. Let's go."

CHAPTER TWENTY-TWO

LEO

Everything was fine until they got outside of Warner. They had just reached the dorm when Morgan groaned, "I'm gonna be sick," and threw up on Leo's shoes.

There was a moment of silence in which they all stared at Leo's feet, and then Oliver breathed out, "Oh god, that's *so* gross."

This was an accurate statement, but Leo wasn't upset. He was just thankful Morgan hadn't thrown up right when they got inside. Also, it was a plus that he had missed Leo's socks, so the solution was simple.

"I am *so* sorry," Morgan gasped, sounding completely sober. Having no reaction, Leo stepped into the grass alongside the walkway to kick his shoes off. After grabbing them by the heel, he carried them to the garbage bin. "Leo . . ." Morgan trailed off as Leo came back to him and used the bottom of his own shirt to wipe off the drunk boy's mouth. "I am the worst friend ever."

"You're fine," Leo assured, shifting his eyes to Oliver. "Thanks for walking us back. I got it from here."

He carried Morgan up the three flights of stairs on his back, trying not to feel too offended when the drunk boy kept mumbling about how Leo was so much stronger than he looked.

The bathroom was thankfully empty, so there was no one to watch as Morgan stumbled his way into a stall and dropped to his knees, retching.

Leo dismissed himself and hurried to his room. He changed into a clean shirt, grabbed a bottle of water, and after a moment of contemplation, gathered the necessary items for Morgan to take a shower.

When he returned to the bathroom, Morgan was where he'd left him. He was sitting with his back against the side of the ugly beige stall, his head tilted back.

"Did you get it all out?" Leo asked. Gray eyes cracked open to look at him.

"I think so." Morgan's voice sounded better already, less affected by alcohol. Leo handed him the bottle of cold water.

"Oh. Thank you." He swished water around in his mouth before spitting into the toilet. "Do you hate me now?"

The question caught Leo off guard, but it didn't affect his answer. "No. Of course not."

Nodding, Morgan looked at the things Leo had in his arms. His eyebrows raised in question.

"I was wondering if maybe you wanted to take a quick shower," Leo suggested, feeling awkward to admit he had thought about Morgan showering, even though it hadn't been in a weird way.

"That's probably a good idea," Morgan agreed, getting to his feet with a groan. "I feel gross." He wobbled once he was standing, and Leo was quick to grab his arm. Morgan gave him a small smile and patted the hand that reached to help him. "I'm alright. I feel a lot steadier than before."

Nodding, Leo went to a shower and pulled the curtain back. It opened into a small stall for changing, with the actual shower curtained off. He set the pile of clean clothes on the bench there and stepped back, giving Morgan room to move past him after kicking off his shoes.

To his surprise, Morgan didn't pull the curtain shut between them.

Nervously, Leo shot a look at the door to the bathroom before turning to watch the drunk boy struggle to remove his shirt. This went on for far longer than it should have before Leo stepped back into the changing room and pulled the curtain shut behind him. "Come on, stop," Leo told him, reaching out to help Morgan free his arm from where it was stuck in his sleeve. "Raise your arms." He obeyed, and Leo easily pulled his shirt over his head.

Morgan's hair stuck up everywhere, and he pouted. "You're a mess," Leo told him fondly. Nodding as if he accepted this fate, Morgan let his arms fall to his sides. Without thinking too much about it, Leo carefully undid Morgan's jeans. "You're keeping your boxers on."

"That's fine," Morgan agreed, placing a hand on Leo's shoulder to steady himself as he stepped out of his pants. Once the jeans were free of his ankles, Morgan pulled open the shower curtain.

Leo stared at Morgan's back. He had a dark tattoo on his left shoulder. Leo recognized the pattern immediately. It was the constellation for Cancer, which Leo recalled was Morgan's astrological sign. He made a mental note to ask about it later, once Morgan was in a better mood and more open for conversation.

Morgan stepped into the shower, still wearing his socks and underwear, and leaned back against the wall opposite the faucet. When he made no move to turn on the water, Leo did it for him.

At the initial cold, Morgan hissed through his teeth, but he gradually relaxed against the wall again. Leo watched him, unable to ignore the way Morgan's boxers clung to his thighs, or the gentle jut of his hipbones. There were many lines and curves he'd never had the opportunity to see before. Leo wanted to stare.

But Morgan wasn't his to look at, so he forced his gaze away and cleared his throat. Grabbing the body wash, he held it out, waiting until he felt Morgan take it to withdraw his hand.

They stayed like that for several minutes, silently sharing the same space. Just as Leo began to wonder how long this would continue,

Morgan slid down the wall, closer to sleep than consciousness. Leo was quick to catch him, his entire top half in line of the shower's stream. Morgan's eyes blinked up at him, almost in a confused way. Leo shut the water off.

"Come on," he urged, grabbing the towel off the bench. He held it out toward Morgan. "You get dressed, okay? I'll be waiting on the other side of the curtain." Nodding, Morgan accepted the towel and wrapped it around himself.

Leo stepped out of the changing room and pulled the curtain shut between them. As he waited, he listened to the quiet sounds of Morgan dressing. After a minute, they were accompanied by a sincere "Thank you."

The voice echoed in the room. Leo dropped his eyes to look at his socked feet, thinking of his shoes in the garbage can outside. "It's no big deal."

"You literally carried me here, didn't freak out when I puked on you, and helped me shower."

"I didn't really help you shower," Leo protested. "Don't tell people that."

This made Morgan laugh. The sound relaxed Leo some. "Well, you at least made sure I didn't kill myself by knocking my head against the wall. I appreciate that."

"That's what friends do, right?" Leo didn't even need to ask if Morgan would have done the same for him; he already knew he would.

"I don't know. I've never been in this situation before," Morgan confessed. "I've never gotten drunk enough to throw up."

"Is everything alright?" Leo asked, wishing Morgan would confide in him.

Either Morgan was ignoring the question or pondering it, because he didn't answer.

The phone in Leo's front pocket—Morgan's phone, which had been handed over to him earlier after being dropped one too many times—

vibrated. He drew it out slowly, already knowing the name he'd see on the screen. "Drew's calling you."

"Don't answer."

Leo held the phone out in front of himself until the call went to voicemail. "Hey, Morgan?" he asked. "You don't have to say anything if you don't want to, but why don't you want to answer?"

"Because I don't want to talk to him," Morgan grumbled, clearly upset. "He's going to lecture me about being irresponsible for drinking, and I don't need that right now."

That was all Leo expected to get out of him, and he was about to tell Morgan he understood, but the sound of a shaky breath on the other side of the curtain froze the words in his throat.

"I'm not good enough, Leo."

"You are," Leo said without pause.

"No, I'm not. I never do anything right." The sounds of Morgan dressing ceased, and Leo wondered if it was because he was finished or because he stopped to talk. "I do *everything* he wants me to. I cook when he wants, I clean when he wants, I put out when he wants, even when *I* don't want to, and there's *always* something wrong with how I do things. Sometimes he doesn't even tell me what. He just looks at me with this expression and I *know* he's displeased." Morgan cut off. There was a little sniffle. He sounded even more sober than he had ten minutes ago. Leo couldn't find it in himself to feel happy about it, his mood dampened by the words.

"Why can't I ever do things right? And why is it that everything I want to do is *immature?* Why can't I watch the silly movies I want to watch? Why can't I read the books I want to read? Why can't I wear light green? What's wrong with light green? It's my favorite color. And why doesn't he ever say sorry when he's the one to do something wrong? Why am I the only one apologizing? I'm just so *tired*, Leo."

For a minute, Leo stood there with his eyes closed. *I wouldn't treat him like that.*

"You're good enough, Morgan," Leo assured, distressed by his own feelings. "He's the one who's not." The curtain pulled open, revealing Morgan standing there wearing only pajama bottoms. His eyes were swollen as he looked at Leo, but he didn't seem upset with him. "Are you alright?"

"I couldn't get the shirt on," Morgan admitted. "I'm still kinda drunk. I should probably throw up more."

"Okay." Leo leaned into the stall to grab the shirt. "Arms up."

Seeming displeased, Morgan raised his arms. Leo was quick to pull the shirt on over him, trying not to chuckle when the collar got stuck on Morgan's head and he had to be freed. "I feel like a child," Morgan grumbled, grabbing the towel and throwing it over his shoulders. He took a seat on the bench, peeling off his wet socks and putting his bare feet in his shoes when Leo handed them to him. When he finished, he relaxed against the wall. "This is embarrassing."

"It's okay," Leo assured. "I see this as us becoming even. You took care of me last weekend, so I'll take care of you this weekend."

Morgan looked at him with a serious expression. "Really, though. Thank you." He stood. His face was pale. "I'm really going to throw up, though, and that's embarrassing, so would you leave?"

"Uh, sure?" A frown pulled at Leo's lips.

"What?"

"I mean, you already threw up *on* me, so I don't get how throwing up near me is embarrassing, but okay."

"*Leo*," he whined, pushing him toward the door.

"Okay, okay. I'll go back to my room, alright? Come when you're finished." Leo left Morgan in the bathroom.

In the hallway, standing at the top of the stairs, was Justin.

They studied each other for a moment. Justin asked, "Why are you all wet?"

"Shower got me."

This seemed to confuse his roommate. The look only became more prominent when his eyes dropped to focus on Leo's feet. "Where the hell are your shoes?"

"They're in the garbage can outside. He couldn't wait."

Confusion shifted to disgust. "Ack, gross. Is he in the bathroom right now?"

"Yeah," Leo answered. "He wants privacy." They both hesitated for a second longer before starting toward their room together. "Did Colette get home okay?"

"Yeah ... I walked her back about ten minutes ago."

"Why'd it take you that long to get back here?"

"I ordered us pizza," was Justin's response, which didn't answer the question all that well, but Leo was still pleased. "I thought it would be good for Sloan to get something in his stomach if he can keep it down. It should be here soon. How long has he been throwing up?"

At their door, Justin took his key out. Before he could even try to unlock it, Leo reached out and opened it. "I stopped in here to get Sloan clothes for after he showered and left it unlocked."

"Ahh ... and you showered with him?" Justin asked, shooting a look at Leo's shirt before moving into their room.

"No. I reached into the shower to catch him when he almost fell," he explained. "And he hasn't been throwing up the entire time, if that's what you're thinking. He did when we got back, and he is now. He sounds much better than he did earlier."

Leo left the door cracked and went to collapse on the futon. The room was silent. At his dresser, Justin pulled off his shirt.

It was nearly impossible not to consider everything Morgan said about Drew. When he managed, for brief moments, to think about something else, it was the way Morgan told him he was cute at the party, or the way Morgan looked while standing in the shower with his eyes closed, or how much his heart squeezed when Morgan told him he was a good friend, because he wanted to be *more* than a good friend. He wanted to be a good *boyfriend,* and then he was back to thinking about

Drew again.

Leo wanted Morgan to be happy, and this whole time Morgan seemed perfectly content with Drew, but hearing him vent about all those things made Leo wonder whether it was possible to be happy in a relationship that made you feel useless.

"Fuck," Leo said without thinking. "What am I going to do?"

"Um . . .maybe change your shirt? You're getting the futon wet."

Leo hadn't even realized, and if he was being perfectly honest, he didn't care. "Not about my clothes, about Sloan."

"Ah," Justin voiced. "You have feelings for him."

"Justin, what do I do?" Leo asked, his voice quiet, not bothering to deny the accusation.

"I don't know," Justin answered, staring absently across the room. "I'm not very good at these things, either."

"Good at what things?" The question came as Morgan pushed open the door with his shoulder, his arms filled with the clothes he'd taken off to shower and a half-empty water bottle. He looked from Justin to Leo and then back again when neither of them answered. "Guys?"

"Justin ordered pizza," Leo spat out. "It'll help with your hangover if you're able to eat something."

"Oh! Thanks. I'm starving." Morgan moved into the room and turned to shut the door. Behind his back, Leo and Justin shared a look.

Fuck.

Chapter Twenty-Three

Sloan

Sloan's Saturday began with sunlight in his face and a splitting headache.

He let out a groan and pulled his blanket over his face to hide from the light, hoping to get a little more sleep. If he hadn't inhaled deeply right then, breathing in the scent of Leo from the blanket, he probably would have managed.

He did breathe though, and the memories from the night before had him jerking into a seated position to look around. Sure enough, he was on Leo and Justin's futon, both of them asleep in their lofts above him.

Beside him on the ottoman was a small bottle of pain killers. Thankful, Sloan took two before lying back down.

Now that he was sober, he could think about his most recent fight with Drew more rationally. It had been about something stupid, but he'd been so frustrated from the tension between the two of them the entire past week that he blew the whole thing out of proportion and ended up drinking too much because of it.

It would have been bad enough if it was only that, but then he had ignored Drew's calls the entire night. He should have answered, even if it resulted in him being scolded. Drew was probably just worried about him.

Guilt settled in his gut, the unpleasant feeling growing when he remembered the words he shared with Leo. He shouldn't have complained about Drew, no matter how frustrated he had been.

Sloan rolled onto his stomach and stretched to reach his phone on the corner of Leo's desk. A quick glance at the screen showed nearly twenty missed calls and even more text messages. "Fuck," he whispered, rolling off the futon and quietly crossing the room to the door. He slipped into the dimly lit hall and dialed Drew's number.

His boyfriend picked up within seconds, and Sloan cringed at his immediate question, "Are you okay?"

He was worried, Sloan thought. *I'm the worst boyfriend ever.*

"Yeah," he answered softly. "I'm alright."

"Why the fuck weren't you picking up? Do you have any idea how worried I was? I was debating driving back and missing my practice tournament to make sure that you were okay. You can't just do that, Sloan. It's fine if you want to go out with your friends, but you can't completely shut me out for the entire night. What if something bad happened? What if someone had taken advantage of you, or hurt you? What would you do then?"

Drew was probably trying to invoke fear, but Sloan felt nothing of the sort. There had been nothing to be afraid of the night before. He wanted to tell Drew this, tell him he'd been with Leo the whole time and was sure he wouldn't have let anything happen. He understood Drew's concerns—and knew that telling his boyfriend how much he trusted Leo probably wasn't a good idea—so instead he said, "I know. I'm sorry. I was upset, and I wasn't thinking straight."

"No, you weren't," Drew snapped, making him wince. "I understand that things have been difficult between us lately, but I need you to stop running away every time we disagree on something."

Sloan wanted to say that he didn't run away because they disagreed but because sometimes he didn't think he was wrong and didn't want to listen to Drew pester him until he apologized. Again, this wasn't the right thing to say. "Okay."

After a moment of silence, Drew let out a heavy sigh. "Well, I'm glad you're okay. I was worried about you. I barely slept."

"I'm sorry," Sloan apologized sincerely. "I love you."

"I love you, too." There was a brief pause. "Where are you right now?"

"I'm at Leo's," he admitted, glancing at the door. The room beyond still sounded quiet. "Last night I got sick, and my friends knew you were out of town for the night. They didn't want to leave me alone, so Leo took me back to his dorm."

"Of course he did," Drew grumbled, clearly less than pleased. The way he said it made it sound like he believed Leo had an ulterior motive, and Sloan bit his lip nervously, hoping his boyfriend wouldn't take a theory for fact. "How much did you have to drink? Do you remember the entire night?"

Sloan was quick to assure, "I didn't black out. I drank a lot, though. Too much."

"Without me there to make sure you were okay?" It was rhetorical, so Sloan remained silent. "That was irresponsible of you. You're lucky your friends were willing to look out for you. They don't care about you the way I do. You know that, right?"

"I know," Sloan agreed, hating the way the words pulled him down farther into his guilt. "They don't love me like you do." At this, Drew hummed in agreement. "I'm really sorry."

"For?" his boyfriend prompted. Sloan was familiar with this game. They often played it when Drew was frustrated with him and wanted to see if he could identify what he had done wrong.

Luckily, he knew exactly what his boyfriend needed to hear. "For not picking up your calls and drinking too much," he answered, his voice strong so Drew knew he was serious and not just saying it to appease him.

"*And?*" Drew added.

It took Sloan a moment to find an answer. "And for staying at Leo's without consulting you first."

"That's right," Drew praised. Still, he didn't sound pleased.

Sloan was sick of them fighting. Last week had been filled with minor arguments, all fueled by their unresolved dispute from the previous Sunday. He just wanted them to go back to normal. "Drew, how can I make it up to you?"

This must have shocked his boyfriend, because there was a full minute of silence before Drew said, "Oh," and then another minute of him thinking. "I'd like you to go to the apartment and wait for me to get back. We can talk then. Can you do that for me?"

Nodding even though his boyfriend couldn't see him, Sloan agreed, "Yeah. I'll leave right now."

"Thanks, babe." Drew sounded content. "Text me when you get home, okay?"

"Alright. What time will you be back?"

"Around noon," Drew answered. "I have to go. It's almost my turn. I'll see you soon. Love you."

"Yeah." Sloan wondered if he would ever tire of hearing those words. "I love you too."

Drew ended the call. Sloan gripped his phone tightly. His chest felt tighter than he thought it should after being presented with an opportunity to make up with his boyfriend. He dismissed the feeling, telling himself this was how it should be.

With that in mind, he went back into the dorm room to get dressed. If he didn't text Drew that he was back in their apartment in at least fifteen minutes, he would probably get another call.

His clothes from the night before were folded in a neat pile on Leo's desk, and he freed his jeans from the bottom of the stack. He was careful not to bump his head on the loft above him, less for the sake of his own head and more because he didn't want to wake Leo. They hadn't gone to sleep until well past one that morning, and he knew from Justin's teasing that Leo usually fell asleep around ten. It hadn't been his intention to keep him up so late, and at the very least he could avoid waking him.

He was buttoning up when he heard sheets shifting. Swearing to himself, he backed out from under Leo's bed and peered up at his friend. Leo's eyes were still closed, his face a mask of perfect sleep. He looked nice like that, a little more like he had when he was a kid, Sloan thought. If he was being honest, Leo looked nice most of the time.

"You're leaving?" a voice asked from behind him, startling him to the point of actually jumping.

"Ahh," Sloan mumbled, turning around. Justin was sitting up in bed, rubbing his eyes. "I woke you, then. I thought it was Leo who had moved."

"You didn't wake me," Justin corrected. "We forgot to shut the blinds last night. The sun woke me."

Sloan turned to the window but looked away when the brightness reminded him of his headache.

"So?" Justin asked him. "You heading out?"

"Ah, yeah. I keep thinking about my bed in my apartment and I can't resist."

"Is the futon uncomfortable?"

"No. It's not bad. It's just not my bed, you know?" He turned back to Leo's loft to grab his clothes and paused at the sight of the sleeping boy, dark lashes casting light shadows on pale cheeks in the morning sunlight.

"Are you going to wake him and say goodbye?" asked Justin.

"No . . ." Sloan trailed off, dropping his gaze from Leo's face. It felt wrong to look. "The reason he's so tired is because of me. I'll text him later to thank him again. When he wakes up, would you mention it for me?"

"Sure," Justin answered. "I'll let him know. You should still text him."

"I will." Bending, Sloan retrieved the borrowed pajama pants he'd kicked off and threw them over the back of Leo's desk chair. "Thanks, Justin."

"For what?" he asked, flopping down on his mattress.

"For letting me crash on the futon."

"No problem," Justin mumbled. Right after the words were out, his breathing grew long and steady.

Quietly, Sloan left the dorm room.

As he walked back to his apartment, he kept thinking of Leo the night before, standing on the other side of the curtain in the bathroom, telling him, *"You're good enough, Morgan."* It was sweet of him to say, and it had been enough to get Sloan to pull himself together in that moment, but Leo wasn't who he needed to hear it from.

When he woke for the second time that day, hours must have passed, because he could hear Drew in the living room. He pushed himself up, prepared to go greet his boyfriend. Before he could even get out of bed, Drew came to stand in the doorway. "Oh," he said at the sight of Sloan in bed. "Were you sleeping? I must have woken you with the front door."

"That's okay," Sloan told him, smiling. "How was the trip?"

"It was alright," Drew answered, taking a seat on the bed beside him. He seemed hesitant, regarding Sloan in a way that suggested he wanted to do something but was afraid he'd be rejected. "Sloan . . ." With a sigh, Drew leaned over to tuck his face into Sloan's neck. "I'm really glad you're home."

"I'm pretty sure that's my line," Sloan mumbled, sliding his arms around Drew's shoulders. Humming thoughtfully, Drew lifted his head and connected their mouths. He was expecting a quick kiss—most of their kisses were quick—so it surprised him when Drew's thumb came up to press into the corner of his mouth, guiding it open to slip his tongue past his lips.

The gesture made Sloan feel better. Drew kissing him with tongue was almost like an apology. Perhaps he felt bad about their argument the day before.

They carried on like that for a minute, pressed as close together as they could be. It was Drew who pulled away first, panting as he rested his forehead against Sloan's. Laughing softly, Sloan said, "That's how you should say hello to me every time you come home."

Drew chucked and leaned back, pushing the hair off Sloan's forehead with a gentle touch. "I was worried about you, baby."

"I know," Sloan acknowledged. "I'm really sorry."

"Wanna tell me about what happened last night?"

Turning his face into Drew's hand, Sloan nodded. "There was wop at the party and I ended up drinking too much, so Leo and Oliver brought me back to Leo's dorm. I got sick for a while and then Leo's roommate got pizza so there was something in my stomach. I fell asleep on the futon around one thirty," Sloan summarized. "I called you right when I woke up this morning, too. Leo was still asleep when I left."

The look on Drew's face was a mix of disappointment and relief. It reminded him of how his mother had looked when his sister Nancy drove her car into a telephone pole one summer, totaling the car while making it out unscathed. This was a far less dire situation, but Drew looked like that nonetheless.

The hand on Sloan's face slid away, and he remembered Leo placing his palm against his cheek at the party the night before.

"Besides getting sick, did you have a good time?"

"It was okay, but I missed you," Sloan admitted, mirroring the smile that formed on Drew's face. As a reward for this answer, Drew kissed him again, softly.

"I missed you, too, babe. How about we spend tomorrow together, alright? No friends, no homework. Just us. How's that sound?" It honestly sounded fantastic. They had spent little time together since their fight the weekend before.

To show he was content, Sloan smiled. Drew pressed a kiss to his forehead before rising from the bed. "How's your head feeling? Do you need pain meds or anything?"

"It's a little sore, but I already took some," Sloan answered, pulling his knees up and leaning against them. The collar of his shirt pulled tight around his neck, so he reached up to tug it away. Noticing the movement, Drew glanced down at him, brows drawn together. "What?"

"Nothing," Drew insisted. His face said otherwise. "It's just . . . I don't remember that shirt."

Sloan looked down at himself. The night before, when Leo had lent the shirt to him, he hadn't paid it much mind, too focused on being drunk and pizza. It was a dark gray shirt with the faded words *Edgewood High School* on the front in white letters. "Oh."

Drew very well knew Sloan had gone to a high school called *Brookfield,* so he had to know the shirt didn't belong to him. "Ah. Well, I showered after I threw up because I felt gross, so Leo lent me some clothes to wear." He left out the part where Leo supervised his shower to make sure he didn't slip and die. Even though he'd been wearing his boxers, he didn't foresee Drew being happy about that. He would only get the wrong idea.

"Oh," Drew said, his lips not pulling up from his frown. "Well, you're back home now and have all of your clothes here, so why don't you change into something a little more comfortable?"

The shirt from Leo was possibly the most comfortable thing he had ever worn; it was incredibly soft and smelled good. He kept this to himself as well, nodding at the suggestion. Seeing him wearing another guy's shirt was probably upsetting to Drew, even though he refused to let Sloan borrow any of his clothing.

"Sure," Sloan said as he climbed out of bed. He pulled the shirt over his head, folding it carefully and leaving it on the dresser.

As he searched for an acceptable shirt, Drew asked, "Do you want to stay in and watch shows on my laptop until you feel better?" Sloan's fingers stopped on a red T-shirt he knew Drew liked on him.

"I'd like that," he answered, pulling the shirt free from its hanger and swiftly guiding it over his head. The material felt scratchy compared with Leo's shirt. He ignored the unpleasant feeling.

While Drew left to go get his laptop, Sloan returned to bed. He wouldn't mind spending the whole day there with Drew. It wasn't often that they did such things.

As he waited, he checked his phone. There were a handful of messages from his friends.

None from Leo, though.

Sloan read the other texts but, instead of responding to them, he went to his messages between him and Leo.

Sloan: Thanks again for last night

The response was almost immediate.

Leo: It's nothing. How are you feeling?

"Hey, babe, should we watch—" Drew cut off his sentence.

Sloan looked up to see his boyfriend hovering in the doorway, his eyes on Sloan's phone.

Without pause, Sloan clicked off the device. "What do you want to watch?" he asked.

Grinning, Drew joined him on the bed.

Chapter Twenty-Four

Leo

On the Monday after the party, Leo was unusually anxious as he waited for the other students to join him in political science. There was one person in particular he wanted to see, a certain boy with dirty-blond hair who had ruined his shoes last Friday night. After not hearing from Morgan since their two text messages on Saturday, Leo was eager for his arrival. Especially since Colette had said that Morgan hadn't responded to any of her messages, either.

Leo wasn't one to resort to worry, but he kept thinking about what Morgan said regarding his relationship with Drew. It didn't sound like Drew was the kind of person who would hurt him physically, but Leo knew the toll of emotional damage could be just as bad as physical damage.

Sighing, he put his head in his hands. He didn't know what he was supposed to do to help.

Morgan joined him two minutes before class began. "Hey," he greeted, pausing at the end of the table and looking down at Leo with his eyebrows pulled together. "You good?"

"I'm fine," Leo answered, dropping his hands from his face and sitting up straight. The question *Are you alright?* was on the tip of his tongue. He didn't ask it, just eyed Morgan curiously when he took the seat beside him as usual. He looked okay. Actually, he looked better than he had the entire past week. For a while now, whatever was going on with Drew left Morgan openly tired and sad, but right then he seemed well rested and content.

"How was the rest of your weekend?" Morgan asked.

"It was uneventful, I guess. I didn't have any homework to do . . ." Leo trailed off, turning forward so he didn't get caught staring. Still, he glanced at Morgan from the corner of his eye. "What about you?"

Morgan smiled a secret sort of smile that told Leo he didn't want to know what the couple spent their weekend doing. He looked away.

"It was great," Morgan said. "Sorry I didn't respond to your text."

"That's alright," Leo answered. "It's not like you have to respond or anything." It was after he said the words that he realized he was being pathetic and cleared his throat. "So, everything's alright, then?"

"Huh?" Morgan paused in the action of unpacking his backpack. "What do you mean?"

"On Friday you seemed kind of upset with Drew," Leo reminded.

There was a moment of silence, and then Morgan let out a chuckle. It sounded nervous. "Of course everything is alright. Before Drew left that night, we had a minor argument, as couples do, and I was upset. We worked it out, so it's nothing. Just forget what I said."

Leo nodded to acknowledge this, though he felt it was impossible to forget.

Neither of them said anything else for the rest of the class period. It was uncomfortable in a way it hadn't been since they resumed being friends, and Leo didn't know how to fix it.

When class ended and the silence between them became too prominent for Leo to handle, he asked, "How's bio going?" as he swung his backpack over his shoulder.

Morgan seemed relieved that Leo chose to speak. "It's tough, but I can do it," he insisted, moving out of the aisle and starting toward the door. The way he said it gave Leo pause, as if Morgan felt the need to convince him that he was capable.

"I never doubted that you could," Leo said, falling into step beside him.

Wide gray eyes flicked over to look at him. "Oh. Thank you."

I didn't do anything, Leo was going to insist, but he lost track of the conversation at the sight of Colette and Kennedy waiting outside their classroom. Colette raised her hand to wave. "Did you know they'd be here?" Leo asked quietly.

Morgan was checking his phone at the moment and asked, "Who?" His question was answered when Colette reached out and grabbed his arm, stopping him from moving past without noticing them. "Oh." Morgan smiled and tucked his phone into his pocket again. "What are you two doing here?"

"We're going to lunch and wanted to see if you guys were interested in coming," Colette explained.

Leo didn't need to consider other plans possibly conflicting with this. He didn't have any. "I'd like that."

Morgan shook his head. "I have a boyfriend I need to coax out of bed and probably make lunch for. You guys have fun without me." With a wave, he left them standing there.

Leo's eyes met Colette's for a moment. She sighed.

"Well," Kennedy said, smiling at Leo. "Are we gonna go?"

"Yeah," he answered, turning to watch as Morgan rounded the corner at the end of the hallway, disappearing from sight. "Let's go."

After lunch, Leo walked the girls back to their dorm building. Instead of going inside, Colette waved goodbye to Kenni alongside him.

"You're not going to your room?" Leo asked.

She shook her head. "Is it cool if I come to yours? I've got to talk to your roommate."

"Oh?"

Her cheeks flushed. "I'm not going there on a social call. We have a school thing. Sloan didn't mention it to you? He was super flustered when it was assigned."

"Sloan barely talked to me," Leo responded, receiving a heavy sigh from Colette to show her sympathy.

"Our chemistry professor is making us do a lab report with assigned partners, and I got stuck with your roommate," she explained. Despite Leo's newfound suspicions regarding her and Justin, he had to admit she sounded less than pleased with the partnership.

"Fun," Leo offered. Colette scoffed.

She spent the rest of the walk describing their lab, and stressing how important it was for her and Justin to get together to plan beforehand so it wasn't a mess.

Justin must have been able to hear her approaching through the door, because when Leo opened it, his roommate was already turned in his desk chair to frown in their direction. At the sight of Colette, his lips pulled down even farther. "What are you doing here?"

She moved past Leo into the room, her eyes moving over the space to take it in. "Is there some reason I'm not allowed to be here?" she asked. It didn't seem like Leo would have the peace and quiet he preferred to study in any time soon.

He reluctantly closed the door, trapping himself in the uncomfortable atmosphere. Positive he would not get any work done, he went to take a seat on the futon, eyes on the couple.

"I didn't say that," Justin protested, sounding more tired than annoyed. "I was surprised is all." After studying her for one more long moment, Justin turned to his desk again. When Colette ducked under his loft to stand by him, he seemed taken aback. "What are you doing?"

"I'm here to talk to you."

Justin didn't move right away. Slowly then, he leaned back in his chair and crossed his arms. "Why? You made it clear that you wanted nothing to do with me *ever*."

Something was definitely going on. Usually, Leo would mind his own business, but their relationship intrigued him, and the room was far too small for him to ignore them.

"We should plan our lab," Colette explained.

"You actually want to do it together? I thought you'd want to prep separately." Maybe it was Leo's imagination, but Justin sounded hurt.

A pained noise left Colette's throat. "Why wouldn't I want to work with you? You're a good student, even if you're annoying."

"Annoying?" Justin echoed dryly. "I'm pretty sure you're the only person who finds me annoying. People usually love me. *You*, on the other hand, are pretentious."

"I am not," Colette protested, even though she kind of was sometimes.

Neither of them said anything for a couple of seconds, and then Justin grumbled under his breath before sighing heavily. "Alright. Come on. Let's get a study room and work this out quick. If you keep harassing me, we're bound to bother Leo."

"Okay," Colette agreed, moving out from under the loft. "Leo doesn't look all that bothered, though."

"That's just his face," Justin mumbled.

"It's fine if you want to work in here," Leo chimed in. "I have homework to do as well. If you want to be alone, I could go work at the library."

Both of them stared at him blankly for a moment, probably uncomfortable with the word *alone*. Justin closed his eyes. "It's fine. I'd prefer to do it somewhere else, anyway. If she's in here too long, she'll probably find something else she hates about me."

Colette's eyes got large, though she said nothing to refute this.

They left together silently. Leo wondered how uncomfortable their walk was going to be.

He moved to his desk, planning on getting at least an hour of work done.

After only twenty minutes, there was a disruptive knock at the door. For a moment, he considered ignoring it, but he recalled that his only friend—beside Colette now—who knew the location of his room was Morgan.

Leo pulled open the door. He felt a light disappointment to see his assumption had been wrong. "Hey, Leo." Max grinned and stepped into the dorm, eyes looking over Justin's side of the room.

"He's not here," Leo offered. He hesitated with his hand on the door. It didn't seem like Max was planning on leaving, so he swung it closed.

"We were going to get lunch," said Max, poking around at Justin's desk as if searching for clues of his whereabouts. "Where'd he go?"

"Him and Colette had to work on something for a class, so they got a study room together," Leo explained, watching Max drop onto the futon.

Max smiled, the curve of his lips slow and pleased. "Did he tell you what happened?"

"With him and Colette?" Leo asked. Max nodded. "No. Neither of them have, but I know it's something."

"They made out on Friday," Max revealed. Leo recalled Justin's strangeness from that night, putting the two together. "You don't seem as surprised as I thought you would be."

"Well, it makes sense." Leo crossed his arms over his chest. "Were you there when it happened, or did he tell you?"

"I was there. We walked her home, like you asked, and they were arguing the whole time, completely ignoring me, and they got to the door of her building and just started kissing. It was kinda crazy, really. Went on so long that I got sick of standing there, so I left."

It was amusing to Leo that Max's initial thought hadn't been to leave but to stand there and wait.

"So, if they kissed, why are they acting like they don't like each other right now? They *do* like each other, right?" Leo asked.

"Well, I thought so." Max shrugged. "At the party they were being super obvious about it, but Justin said he texted her on Sunday and she had no interest in him and was rude about it. I think he's put out."

Leo didn't respond. He tried to remember if Justin had been acting weird. Nothing came to mind, though he didn't doubt Max's words and wondered whether he could do something to make his roommate feel better. They were kind of in the same boat, both interested in people who weren't interested in them. For the first time since Friday night, Leo thought of Justin's response to his troubles over Morgan. *"I'm not very good at these things, either."*

"Hey," Max said, getting his attention once more. "Do you want to sit, or are you gonna stand there the whole time I'm here?"

"That depends on how long you're staying," Leo replied, throwing a look at his desk. He didn't have another class until two thirty, and nothing was due then. Procrastinating for a bit wouldn't hurt him. When he focused back on Max, the boy was grinning. *Probably.*

"You should come sit down," Max told him, something about his words making Leo nervous. Max wouldn't hurt him, he was sure of it. His dignity and common sense might suffer, though.

He went to sit anyway. "So." Max twisted his body to face him, arm propped up on the back of the futon. "You have fun at the party on Friday?"

"Sure." This answer didn't seem to be enough, because Max continued to look expectant. "It was a party."

"Has anyone ever told you you're very observant?" he teased. As usual, Leo didn't know what to do, so he turned his face away. "Ah, I don't mean it. You know that, right? I know what you're saying."

"You didn't seem like you were having all that much fun," Leo recalled.

"That's because you were giving all of your attention to someone else." Startled, Leo turned back to him. "I only got you for about five minutes." Despite admitting something that had potential to embarrass him, Max looked completely relaxed.

"What are you doing right now?" Leo asked.

Max laughed. "You're super cute, Leo, but you can't take a hint, can you?"

"I can take a hint," he protested. He wasn't stupid. It was obvious Max was flirting with him. He just didn't understand why.

"You can?" Max reached his free hand out to push the hair off Leo's forehead, his body leaning in. "Can you tell what I'm gonna do now?"

Leo could, and he swallowed heavily, eyes shifting to the side where Max's hand came to rest on his cheek. "You're going to kiss me."

"I'd like to," Max admitted. Somehow, he got close enough that Leo could feel his breath against his lips. "Is that okay?"

Was it? Leo dropped his gaze to look at Max's mouth. He wouldn't mind kissing him, he didn't think. There was the soft protest of *Morgan* in the back of his mind, like a whisper, but he recognized he shouldn't think of Morgan in this situation, because Morgan had nothing to do with it. Leo liked Max. He did. He liked how he looked and how he smiled and how he held his gaze consistently through conversation. And Max liked him, too. So, what was so wrong about them kissing?

"Yeah, I guess," Leo answered, his voice coming out dry with nervousness. "I mean—"

It didn't matter what he meant, because Max had officially been given the go, and closed the few inches between them.

The first thing Leo thought when their lips met was, *Wow, it's been so long.* He couldn't even remember his last kiss. It had been with his most recent boyfriend, and nothing between them had been memorable. *This,* on the other hand . . . he'd remember for a while.

Max's lips were warm and soft, kissing him in a gentle way that Leo hadn't expected. It felt good all the way through his body, and he tentatively placed a hand on Max's shoulder, fingers gripping a little tighter when the wet feeling of Max's tongue pressed against his lower lip.

And *oh*. That he felt all the way to his toes.

With a sigh, Leo let his jaw go slack, head tilting to better their angle. He felt Max shift closer, his hand that wasn't against Leo's jaw slipping down to his waist.

Max, Leo learned rather quickly, was very good at this. He knew the right amount of pressure to apply, when to suck, and what places felt good with a light touch of teeth. Leo had never kissed someone with experience, and he found himself embarrassed with what he was giving in return. Thankfully, Max continued to kiss him despite the clumsiness.

It was nice, Leo thought, but even as he was thinking about nothing other than kissing Max, his heart hurt in his chest.

No. Leo's fingers squeezed even tighter on Max's shoulder. *I'm happy right now. Let me be happy.* And he would have been, maybe, if he hadn't already come to accept what it really was that he wanted.

And it wasn't Max.

Unwilling to use him, Leo slid his hand from Max's shoulder to his chest, about to push him away. Before he could, an unfamiliar ring tone interrupted them. Max pulled away first, his head dropping to look at his lap as he freed his phone from his pocket. They were sitting close enough that Leo's face was practically in Max's hair. Breathing heavily, he leaned back.

"Justin," Max grumbled, lifting his head as he answered the phone, eyes on Leo's face. His lips were red, and Leo would bet money his were as well. "Hey, man . . . yeah, I'm here . . . Nothing, don't worry about it . . . sure . . . I'll head over . . . yep, bye."

Max's arm lowered, phone still clutched in his hand. "Justin wants me to meet him at the cafeteria," he explained, sounding completely normal as if a minute ago they hadn't been lip-locked. "Wanna come get something to eat?"

"I already ate," Leo told him. "Thanks, though."

"Alright. Well, text Justin if you change your mind. I'd be more than happy to bring something back for you." He stood and pressed his palms against his shorts. He seemed completely unaffected by what they'd just done.

Am I that bad of a kisser? Leo worried.

"I guess I'll see you later."

"Yeah," Leo agreed, raising his fingers to touch his lips. "Bye."

Max left the room, but Leo could still see his feet through the gap under the door. He wasn't moving, just standing there. *Gathering himself?* Leo wondered. He didn't check, nor did he watch to see when Max left. Instead, he lay on his back and looked at the ceiling.

What the hell just happened?

Chapter Twenty-Five

Sloan

It was nearly eight at night when Drew called him.

It was a Thursday, so Sloan didn't have class. Usually, he'd get together with his friends, but Drew had asked him to clean the apartment, so he'd remained home.

He finished this task a few hours ago and was curled up on the couch writing flash cards for bio with his shark pencil and waiting for his boyfriend to return from golf practice. They had agreed that morning that they would watch the television show they were both invested in while eating dinner, so Sloan anxiously awaited Drew's arrival.

Then the call came. "Hey!" he answered, eyes still on the card he was making. "When are you gonna be home? I made dinner. You might need to heat it up, but it's still good."

"Thank you, babe. Would you put it in the fridge for me? I'm going to the bars with some of the guys, so I won't be home until later."

Drew didn't *ask* him if he could go, he *told* him he was going. Sloan wouldn't have minded, but Drew had been upset at him for doing the same thing in the past. Also, Sloan really wanted to watch their show, and he knew the chances of Drew telling him he could go ahead with the series on his own were slim.

Sloan decided to bring up only the second point, knowing that accusing Drew of being unfair wasn't the way to go. "Didn't you say we could watch the new episode of our show tonight?" Sloan wasn't able to keep the disappointment out of his voice, and he hoped it made Drew feel a little bad. Maybe Drew would actually apologize.

The sigh on the other line told him maybe not. "We can do it another night, Sloan. How about tomorrow?"

"We're going to visit my parents this weekend, remember? You said we could leave tomorrow after you got done with practice," he reminded. "I already told them we were coming."

The noise Drew made then was less than pleased, and Sloan bit his lip, desperately hoping he wouldn't go back on his word. If he did, Sloan wouldn't be able to help getting angry with him, and he had been trying to avoid another fight. "Right. Yes. We are doing that. We'll watch the show later, okay?"

"Okay, okay. I'm sorry," Sloan apologized, thankful Drew hadn't changed his mind about going to see his parents. "It's fine. I need to study for bio, anyway. Have a good time out with your friends." He thought he sounded sincere, but maybe not because Drew didn't hang up right away.

"Are you really that upset?" his boyfriend demanded after a beat of silence, clearly exasperated. "Sloan—"

"I'm not upset!" he was quick to cut in, swallowing all feelings of annoyance for the time being. "Really. Just not excited to do homework. I'm fine, though. Have fun."

When he spoke again, Drew no longer sounded irritable. "Thanks, baby. Don't miss me too much."

Drew ended the call, and Sloan tossed his phone onto the coffee table, then kicked his feet up onto it because he knew his boyfriend hated when he did.

He hadn't been lying when he said he needed to work on bio, but he could no longer focus on it after that conversation. Instead, he reflected on how things had been between him and Drew for the past week.

They were getting along far better than they had the week before, and all tension from their argument over Leo was gone. He was taking Drew's criticism with a more positive attitude than before. When Drew told him something was wrong, he apologized and tried to fix it. When Drew made small comments about things Sloan was unwilling to change, he gave the sincerest *sorry* he could manage and then kept doing them in a less obvious way. Things with Drew were better, yes, but Sloan was already sick of living like this.

Huffing, he pushed his bio stuff off his lap and sat forward to retrieve his phone, the words *Fuck it* on his mind. *He can't expect me to sit here by myself waiting for him the entire night.*

Sloan called Leo, not because he knew it was the person who would bother his boyfriend the most but because it was legitimately who he wanted to see.

The call was answered right away. "Hey, you alright?" Leo asked.

It was nice to hear him. Sloan hadn't heard enough of Leo's voice lately. This was his own fault, he knew. After all, he was the one acting distant.

He wasn't distant because he wanted to be. He just thought it would be easier for him and Drew if he spent less time concerning himself with Leo. That wasn't fair, though. Not to himself, and especially not to Leo.

Sloan was happy he'd called.

"I'm fine. I wanted to see if you were interested in coming over and watching a movie with me. I could use some company." There wasn't a response. Sloan knew that for Leo and Drew, distaste went both ways. "Drew is out with some friends, so I'm here by myself."

The response was immediate. "Yeah, I'll come over. Text me your address, okay? I don't know where you live."

"Great." Sloan smiled. "I'll send you the code to get into the building, too. Don't mention it to Drew, though. He's weird about that."

"I doubt it'll ever come up," Leo said. "I'll be over soon."

"See you then."

Right after he hung up, he sent Leo the necessary information. Then, because it was probably the right thing to do, he texted his boyfriend.

Sloan: Leo is coming over to watch a movie

Drew: Are you asking me if it's okay, or telling me it's happening?

With an eye roll, he typed out another message.

Sloan: Is it alright?

The response took long enough that Sloan was starting to wonder if Leo would arrive before it. He wasn't too concerned. He could see Drew had read the message and knew his boyfriend was trying to make him nervous.

Drew: Yeah, it's fine. Don't let him stay too long. I'd like to fuck when I get home and it'll be easier if you're already prepared

Frustrated, Sloan tossed his phone to the end of the couch before rising from the cushions. He didn't want to have sex. His hips still hurt from the last time.

Because his eyes were dry, and perhaps maybe to discourage his boyfriend, Sloan went to the bathroom to switch his contacts out with his glasses for the rest of the night. Then, he packed the food away in the kitchen like Drew had asked him to.

The distance between his apartment and Leo's dorm wasn't much, so by the time he was putting the food in the fridge there was a gentle knock on the door. Excited, Sloan hurried to let him in.

There was a moment upon opening the door in which they studied each other. Leo cleared his throat. "I like your glasses."

"You've seen me in them before," Sloan reminded.

"Yes," Leo said, his eyes shifting to look into the apartment over Sloan's shoulder. "I still like them."

Feeling flustered from the compliment, Sloan moved out of the doorway and gestured to the inside of the apartment. "You can come in." Nodding, Leo stepped over the threshold and looked around. Allowing him time to take it in, Sloan silently shut the door.

"Well?" he prompted when Leo hadn't spoken for a full minute. "What are your thoughts?"

"On your apartment?" Leo shrugged. "It's nice. Not what I expected from you, though." He was staring hard at the ugly couch as if confused by it.

"You mean I don't seem like the kind of person to have an orange couch?"

Leo's face didn't change, but he did mumble, "*Orange?*" softly, as if the color perplexed him. "That's not what I was talking about. The plants are yours, I'm assuming?"

Sloan confirmed the suspicion.

"I like them," Leo offered, moving toward the small table by the living room window to examine his collection. It was something Drew never took interest in, and Sloan watched his friend out of curiously. Was Leo was actually intrigued, or was he just acting that way because it was something Sloan liked? Did it even matter?

"They're pretty," Leo continued. "I always thought it would be nice to keep succulents. I think I would be so worried about them dying that I'd overwater and kill them." Leo looked around once more. "You have a lot more room than Justin and I do."

"You want a tour?" Sloan offered.

Leo turned toward the closed doors off the living room, eyebrows raising.

Sloan rubbed the back of his neck. "Yeah, I guess that just means, do you want to see the bedroom and bathroom as well?"

"I'm good," Leo assured, which for some reason relieved him. It felt wrong to show Leo his and Drew's bedroom. "You said you wanted to watch a movie, right? Did you have something in mind?"

"Oh." Sloan grinned widely enough that Leo appeared vaguely concerned. "How do you feel about shark movies?"

***

Leo clearly had not been expecting this because he was staring at the television with a shocked look on his face, watching the actress in a bikini swim carelessly in the ocean as the music got more intense. "Ah," he voiced when a shark attacked her, "I get it now."

"You get what?" Sloan asked, looking from Leo to the television. He was watching Leo more than the actual movie. It was hard not to when he was so much more interesting. "The appeal?"

"No, not that. Colette mentioned your thing with sharks to me, and I didn't understand," Leo explained. Sloan wondered if they talked about him often. "Is this movie any good, then? Or is it just a lot of blood and bad acting?"

"Of course it's not good," Sloan answered with a small laugh. "They're awful. Most shark movies are, with a few exceptions. That's why I like them so much. They're funny."

"Right . . ." Leo eyed the television skeptically.

For thirty minutes, they watched in silence, the screams on the television filling the room, as well as soft snickers from Sloan whenever the actors said anything too dramatic. The film seemed to confuse Leo, his eyes squinted as he watched the screen. It was almost as funny as the acting.

"You know," Sloan began after watching the third victim get eaten. After this, the main characters would devise a plan to kill the shark. It would fail the first time and they'd have to come up with something last minute. The plot was all very textbook for these types of films. "I think it would be really fun to make movies."

"Movies like this?" Leo asked, eyebrows arched high.

With a laugh, Sloan shook his head. "No. Not like this. I mean real movies."

"*Real movies*," Leo repeated. "Do you mean *good* movies? Not in the *shark* genre?"

"Yes, that's what I mean," Sloan agreed, amused. "I think it'd be cool. Presenting a story in your own way. Letting people see how you view the world."

"I think you'd be good at that," said Leo. Smiling, Sloan looked back at the television. He'd always thought working in the film industry would be interesting, but it was a dream he'd never been able to share with Drew. He already knew what his boyfriend would say: Making movies wasn't a good enough way to make an impact. Leo, on the other hand, didn't judge him for wanting to do something other than saving lives for a living. It was refreshing.

Another twenty intense minutes passed, and then Leo said, "Hey," softly.

"Yeah?"

Eyes still forward, Leo inquired, "Do you have plans for the weekend?"

Sloan wondered whether his attention remained on the screen because the film engrossed him or he was avoiding eye contact. "Why do you ask?"

He had plans, and the right thing to do would be to say that right away, but he wanted to hear if Leo wanted to spend time with him. More often than not, he was the one to ask Leo to do things, so it would be nice to see Leo express some interest.

"Well, I was talking to Colette earlier today and she mentioned she was going to reach out and see if you wanted to do something. Apparently, you missed Tuesday's movie-watching session."

"Ah, yeah," Sloan confirmed. "They got together today too. I didn't go because I wanted to clean up around here, and on Tuesday I was tired, so I ended up coming back after my labs to sleep."

That was the short version of the story. The long version was that his boyfriend could be rather pushy, and when he wanted to have sex, they'd have sex. It didn't matter how early Sloan had to be up in the morning, so he often sat through early morning lectures and labs completely exhausted from the night before.

"Colette hasn't reached out to me about anything yet. I do have plans this weekend, though. I convinced Drew to come home with me to see my parents."

Leo's eyes finally moved to him. "That'll be nice. Does Drew get along with your parents?"

"For the most part, yeah." Sloan was too embarrassed to admit that Drew complained more than once about their plans for the weekend. It wasn't that he didn't like Sloan's parents; he just preferred they stayed home.

"How have you been doing being away from your parents?" Sloan asked. "I mean, it's not like you can get in a car and drive to see your mom for the weekend." It was a subtle subject change, Sloan believed, and Leo thankfully seemed to not notice.

"It's fine," Leo said with a lack of emotion. This was kind of funny, though not what Sloan wanted, and he made this known with a look of disapproval. Leo sighed. "I barely know my father and his wife, so it's not like I miss them a lot. My dad texts me at least once a week, which is nice. I miss my mom and Lizzy, but I talk to them both over text throughout the day and have calls with them occasionally. It's just weird knowing how far away I am."

"I can't imagine." There was a loud bang on the television that startled them both, and Sloan laughed it off before Leo could be embarrassed. "So, what's going on with Liz? She should be . . . fifteen now, right?"

Not seeming happy about this, Leo grumbled, "Yeah."

"Why do you sound distressed?"

As Sloan watched, Leo leaned to free his phone from the back pocket of his shorts. For about half a minute he searched on it, and then turned the device for Sloan to see.

The picture was not what he had been expecting. The last time he saw Lizzy, she had been ten. A *child*. The girl in the picture did not look like a child. She was tall and tan, with long black hair thrown over her shoulder and a wide smile. It was a Lizzy he was completely unfamiliar with. "She's beautiful."

"Yeah," Leo agreed, turning the phone back toward himself to see the photo. His face changed little while looking at it, but Sloan could tell the expression was fond. It made him think about his own sisters, neither of whom he was close with. Abigail was eight years older, too far away in age for him to relate to, and there was a five-year difference between him and Nancy, who had always treated him like an idiot. His sisters were close to each other, though. Sloan envied both of them, and Leo.

"It's difficult having a pretty younger sister," Leo claimed.

"How so?"

Leo put away his phone. "She's *too* pretty. Where ever we go, people are always looking at her. Most people are respectful, but the idea of her getting unwanted attention bothers me."

Sloan chewed his lip to keep from smiling. It was cute, imagining Leo acting protective. "Do you scare all the boys away?"

Brown eyes rolled. "Oh god, no. Lizzy loves boys. I couldn't keep her away from them if I tried. All I care about is that she's with someone who respects her." Leo cut off then, a smile Sloan was unfamiliar with pulling at his lips. "Her current boyfriend is absolutely terrified of me."

"Really? But you're so . . . *non-threatening*."

As if this was an insult, Leo deadpanned. "I'm starting to worry about how you think of me."

"Why would you want me to find you threatening?" Sloan asked with a laugh. "It's not a bad thing. You should be happy, you know. I thought you said you were a pacifist."

"You clearly think I'm weak," Leo accused. His voice wasn't serious. Content with the light banter, Sloan reached out and placed his hand against Leo's arm.

"No! That's not it!" *You're gentle,* he was going to say, but before the words could leave him, the front door opened.

Both of them turned as Drew entered. At the sight of them sitting together, Drew frowned.

Sloan's hand dropped from Leo's arm. "Oh," he voiced, sounding disappointed before he could catch himself. He checked the time on his phone. "You weren't out for long. It's only been an hour and a half since you called."

"I wasn't having a great time," Drew grumbled, eyes lingering on Leo for a second longer before he swung the door shut and went to the bedroom without another word. When the door closed, Sloan winced at the rudeness. Before he could apologize on his boyfriend's behalf, Leo stood.

"Well, I better head out," he declared. Not wanting him to go, Sloan pouted. Even so, he said nothing. Leo couldn't stay. Not with Drew there, and especially not with Drew's plans for their night.

"Thanks for keeping me company," he offered, rising so he could see Leo off. "I'll see you in class tomorrow."

"Yeah," Leo agreed as Sloan opened the door for him. Before passing through, he looked up to make eye contact. "See you."

When he left, Sloan closed the door behind him.

He knew what was expected of him next. He was supposed to join Drew in their bedroom, but he didn't want to. What he wanted to do was call Leo and ask him to come back, to fall onto the couch beside him and resume their conversation.

He couldn't do that, though. He couldn't even say no, because then Drew would be passive aggressive for days, and Sloan wanted to keep that side of his boyfriend away from his parents.

"You coming?" Drew asked from the doorway of their bedroom. The sound of him opening the door hadn't reached Sloan, so he jerked at Drew's voice.

"Yeah," he answered, forcing a smile. "Let me just turn off the TV."

Drew disappeared into their bedroom, this time leaving the door open behind him as an invitation. Sloan went to the couch, bending over the back of it to pick up the remote.

Pausing, he watched the screen.

It was disappointing that Leo hadn't been able to see the end of the movie.

Chapter Twenty-Six

Sloan

On Monday, when Sloan and Leo left the political science classroom, Colette was waiting in the hallway. "Where are we gonna go?" she asked when they both stopped in front of her.

"The cafeteria?" Sloan suggested. "I figured since we're getting lunch, it would make sense to go to the place that's serving lunch."

"I don't want to eat food from the cafeteria," Colette whined. "It all tastes the same. Right, Leo?"

Leo looked surprised to have been spoken to. Knowing him, he'd probably go along with whatever they decided and would just let them sort it out themselves. "I really don't care."

"You're not very helpful," Colette told him. Leo shrugged, unconcerned.

"All right, then," she continued. "Well, can we pick something up from the convenience store?"

"And eat it where?" Sloan asked. The convenience store had limited seating, and he was positive they'd ruined any chance of getting a table by dillydallying. "One of our rooms? Can't be mine. Drew's probably still asleep."

"Not mine either," Colette added. "Jessica and I are currently in the middle of a passive aggressive roommate war." They fought a lot, so

Sloan wasn't surprised.

There was one option left, and they both turned to Leo. "I guess you can come to my room," he offered.

"Will Justin be there?" Colette asked.

"Probably? He lives there. He won't care if I bring people back. His friends get high in there all the time, so you guys coming to eat lunch is no big deal."

With a sigh, Colette shook her head. "That's not why I'm asking."

There was something weird going on between Colette and Justin, Sloan was pretty sure. She complained about him a lot less lately, and over the past week Sloan noticed her refusal to even look in the other boy's direction. Justin, on the other hand, always seemed to have his eyes on her.

Sloan didn't know how to bring it up, worried that simply asking Colette would be too forward.

"Right," Leo said. "Well, he'll most likely be there. If you don't want to run into him, we probably shouldn't eat there."

"Cafeteria then?" Sloan suggested again.

Colette didn't look happy. "We can eat in Leo's room," she accepted, sounding crestfallen.

The feeling didn't seem to last long. By the time they were walking to Leo's from the convenience store, she was dramatically explaining her roommate troubles to the both of them, clearly not caring that Leo was not listening to her.

She continued until Leo opened the door to his dorm room and her words abruptly stopped.

The first thing Sloan thought was, *God, it smells like weed.* The second was, *What the hell?*

Justin was in the room, and he wasn't alone. Kennedy was with him, sitting on the end of the futon, smoking while Justin lay with his head in her lap, looking completely relaxed. Both of their heads turned toward the door. "Ah, fuck," Justin sighed.

Initially, Sloan was confused by the words. Then Colette turned to push past him, and he saw her face. The expression she wore was a combination of anger and hurt.

"Letti, wait!" Kennedy called. Colette was already hurrying down the hall away from the room. Kennedy scrambled to go after her, nearly knocking Justin off the futon in her haste to rise. Without a word, Leo stepped to the side and grabbed Sloan's arm, pulling him out of the doorway so Kenni could run through. They watched her go.

"Are we supposed to follow them?" Sloan asked Leo.

"Let them figure it out themselves," he answered, moving into the room and gesturing for Sloan to follow.

Taking the bag with their food from Leo on his way to the futon, Sloan said, "I don't get girls." Justin had sat up after being disturbed by Kennedy, so Sloan sat beside him. As he slipped his backpack off his shoulders, he greeted the stoned boy. "Hey, man. How're you?"

"*Fuck*," Justin sighed again. Leo shut the door. "She took it with her, didn't she? If she gets stopped by Campus Safety, she'll get in trouble. Better not say she got it from me." It took Sloan a second to realize he was talking about the joint.

"So, did you sleep with her?" Leo interrogated, stopping in front of the futon with his arms crossed over his chest like a stern parent.

Scoffing, Justin rolled his eyes. "No. Max had a thing with her, so I'm not interested." He sat straighter then, quickly enough to startle Sloan as he unpacked the lunches. "Max has a thing with you too, right?"

Sloan hesitated in his actions and looked up at Leo with interest. Leo seemed embarrassed, because his expression suddenly went deadpan in the way it always did when he wanted to hide his emotions. It seemed like he wasn't going to respond, that Sloan would not find out what Justin was talking about, but then Leo asked, softly, "He told you about that?"

Told him about what? Sloan wanted to demand, feeling incredibly impatient. As he bit his tongue to keep quiet, Leo came to sit beside him, taking one of the containers of sushi they'd bought and opening it carefully. Fresh sushi was the Monday special at the campus store.

"Yeah, man. He told me yesterday," Justin said. "I mean, I'm kinda shocked, but it's not like I *care* necessarily. You didn't break the rule or anything since I wasn't here at the time."

"We didn't have sex," Leo protested.

What did you do? Sloan thought of asking. He wasn't sure he wanted to know.

He learned anyway.

"Well, I don't really want to be there when you're kissing my friends, either," Justin declared. Chest feeling tight for a reason he couldn't quite explain, Sloan turned to see Leo's reaction, hoping it wasn't true. Leo was looking blankly at his wooden chopsticks as he pulled them apart.

The silence stretched on, and Sloan wondered if it was his turn to say something. He hoped not. The only words he could think to say were *Did you really do that?* He felt how Colette had looked as she stormed away and hoped it didn't show on his face.

Unexpectedly, it was Leo who ended up speaking. "Justin, aren't you gonna go after Colette?"

"Why would I do that?"

"Because you have feelings for her," Leo accused, without looking up. Sloan wasn't surprised by this. He suspected as much, given how Justin's eyes followed Colette from the start, but he wasn't expecting to hear it brought up bluntly like that. The atmosphere in the room shifted to something even more uncomfortable.

"Fuck my life," Justin responded dryly. To Sloan's surprise, he actually got up and left.

When the door closed behind him, Sloan squeezed his eyes shut. "What did I just hear?" he asked, mostly to himself. Leo made an amused noise in response. Sloan thought of Max and Leo in the kitchen together on the night of the party, standing incredibly close. *Had it happened then?* he wondered. At the time, he had thought nothing of it, not after Leo seemed so unconcerned with the whole Max and Kennedy thing.

"He's probably going to be annoyed with me later for calling him out like that," Leo said.

"I wasn't talking about Justin," Sloan admitted. "I already suspected he liked Colette. I meant . . ." he trailed off, feeling all too aware of Leo's eyes on his face. *Let it go,* he told himself, but he couldn't. He had to know. "Is it true about you and Max? You have a thing?"

"Oh. No, we don't."

Relief filled Sloan's chest. "So, you didn't kiss then?"

"We did." As if this wasn't a big deal, Leo began to eat. Sloan's own tray of sushi was still in his hand, unopened. He had no interest in it at the moment.

"You're not a thing, but you kissed?"

Leo waited until after he swallowed to respond. "Yeah."

"Do you like him?" Sloan was more afraid of the answer than he should have been.

"I do, just not in the way you're thinking."

"Then why did you kiss him?" He felt ridiculous, but he couldn't drop the subject. He needed to understand. If Leo and Max were potentially going to become something, he had to prepare himself.

Leo corrected him. "He kissed me. He asked first, though."

"Did you say yes?" Sloan was getting impatient. It felt like Leo was vague on purpose.

"Yeah."

"But you don't like him?"

Leo looked at him again, eyes searching his face. "You already asked me that." For a moment, they stared at each other. Sloan forced his gaze away. "Morgan, if you have a question, ask it."

"Sorry," he apologized, raising a hand to rub his forehead. "I guess I'm just trying to understand why you guys kissed when you don't even have feelings for him." When Sloan kissed Leo all those years ago, it had also been done with Leo's permission when Leo didn't have feelings for him. They were only curious children then. This seemed different.

Sloan was worried it was different.

"I don't know," Leo offered unhelpfully. "Kissing is nice."

Kissing is nice. Leo thinks kissing Max is nice. What am I supposed to do if he does it again—

"I didn't like either of my boyfriends all that much in the past, and I kissed both of them while we were dating," Leo added.

"So if he asks you out, you'll date him?"

At that, Leo looked confused. "What? Where'd you get that idea?" Sloan wondered whether he was the only one who realized that wasn't an actual answer. "This isn't important. Why don't we finish the movie we were watching at your place?"

Leo leaned forward to reach his backpack. As he dug through it for his laptop, Sloan considered again what it would be like if Leo and Max started dating.

Could I handle that?

Something else occurred to him. *Why wouldn't I be able to? Why do I feel jealous right now?*

Leo's voice broke through his thoughts. "That's okay, right?"

No. Nothing about this is okay, Sloan thought.

"Is what okay?"

"If we finish the movie," Leo clarified. "The one we started at your apartment."

"Yeah," Sloan answered, smiling at the suggestion, albeit shakily.

It was once they had resumed the film that Sloan really let himself consider why he felt the way he did.

He wondered whether it was because, until then, he only knew for certain that Leo had kissed him. He had, to some extent, still thought of Leo as *his.*

Sloan wanted to change that thinking, though not for the right reasons. He didn't want to just *think* of Leo as his, he actually wanted it to be true, and he wanted to be Leo's as well.

They were bad thoughts. He knew he shouldn't think them, not while he already had a boyfriend. Regardless, when he snuck a peek at Leo and thought of him with someone else, his heart throbbed.

Fuck.

Chapter Twenty-Seven

Sloan

Sloan came to terms with his feelings for Leo but could not come up with a solution to the problem.

Because that's what it was. *A problem.*

He couldn't like Leo, no matter how well Leo treated him. Drew was his boyfriend, and even though things were shaky sometimes, they were still in a relationship. *Besides,* he found himself thinking often, *I don't deserve Leo. I can't even do things right with Drew. How am I supposed to make someone as good as Leo happy?*

"Sloan," Kennedy said, thankfully pulling him from his troubling thoughts. "Are you even listening to me?"

Sloan, Leo, and Colette were at Kenni's for lunch. He and Leo were sitting close together on the futon, even though they had it to themselves, and the brush of Leo's arm against his had him thinking again.

Colette and Kennedy were on the bottom of the bunk beds, sitting side by side with their backs against the wall. They'd apparently made up within the past forty-eight hours. Sloan wondered what happened. He hadn't asked Colette in their classes that morning, worried Justin would overhear.

He thought he'd have the opportunity to ask already, but it would have to wait. At the moment, there were bigger things concerning him.

Kennedy was complaining about how she still hadn't met Drew. Both Colette and Leo seemed to ignore her, but, as Drew was his boyfriend, Sloan could not.

"I'm just saying it's unacceptable that Colette and Leo have met him and Oliver and I have not. I mean, he's your *boyfriend*, Sloan. I see you approximately four times a week. How have I still not met your boyfriend?"

"He's busy a lot," Sloan grumbled. She didn't seem to be satisfied by this answer. "I can talk to him about having lunch with us all. He only has a morning class tomorrow, and Oliver is free on Thursdays, isn't he? Does that work?"

"Yes!" Kennedy exclaimed, while Colette gave a less enthusiastic confirmation.

They all turned to Leo, who seemed surprised by the attention. "Oh. I'm included?"

"Of course you are," Colette insisted. "You are included in the *all*."

"Ah . . ." Leo trailed off. He let out a sigh Sloan was sure he wasn't meant to hear. "Well, I have class from ten to eleven thirty, so if you go after that I'll come along." He didn't sound enthused, though Sloan was still happy he'd be there.

It was selfish of him. He couldn't help it.

Sloan brought up the lunch when he was preparing dinner and Drew was watching television on the couch. "Hey, do you want to eat lunch with my friends tomorrow?"

He knew Drew heard him, because he could see his boyfriend's thumb freeze on his phone screen. Still, he wasn't answering. Sloan left the kitchen and stopped at the end of the couch. "Drew?"

Drew turned his face toward him, distressed. "Why?"

"Because you haven't met all of them and they want to meet you," Sloan answered. Drew's face didn't change. "Come on!" Sloan dropped onto the couch beside him. "They're important to me. Don't you want to see who I'm spending my time with?"

"I don't know . . ." Drew turned back to the television, clearly not interested enough in the conversation to maintain eye contact. "You don't hang out with me and my friends, so it's kind of hard for you to ask me to hang out with yours."

"That's because when you hang out with your friends, you're always going to the bar and I'm only eighteen," he retorted calmly, receiving a groan in response. "*Please*, Drew? It'll be a quick lunch. They want to know you a little better. We can eat and leave. That's all I'm asking of you."

After a pause, Drew grumbled, "Alright."

"Thank you." Smiling, Sloan leaned forward to kiss him. Drew was quick to press two fingers against his lips, halting him.

"You better make sure the potatoes don't boil over on the stove, or there's going to be a mess."

Irritation pricked at him, and Sloan pushed it back. At least Drew agreed to spend time with his friends. Without another word, he returned to the kitchen to check the potatoes.

Their night carried on like usual. They ate together at their small kitchen table, Drew telling him about class and golf and Sloan briefly complaining about bio before getting shut down. When they were done, Drew did about half of the dishes before a show he was interested in came on and he returned to the couch, leaving the rest behind.

Sloan finished them quickly, most likely not up to the high standards of his boyfriend, before slipping into his shoes by the front door. It was a Wednesday, and that meant his and Colette's favorite reality TV show would be airing.

"Alright," Sloan said to Drew, patting his pockets to make sure he had his keys. "I'll be home later."

That got his boyfriend's attention like nothing else had that night. "Where are you going?' he asked before Sloan even had the chance to open the door. With a sigh small enough Drew wouldn't hear, Sloan turned back to the living room.

"Colette's," he answered. "It's Wednesday, and she and I watch a show together on Wednesdays, remember?"

The look on Drew's face told him he did not remember. "Oh . . ." Drew trailed off. Sloan knew that voice. "Well, I kinda wanted to spend the night with you here."

We spend every night together, Sloan thought, his eyes on the television. The show Drew was watching had something to do with a dramatic law firm. It was one of his favorites. Sloan was never able to get into it.

"I'll be back before you go to bed," Sloan told him, shifting nervously on his feet. He really wanted Drew to let him go. It was the season finale of his and Colette's show, and he'd been waiting anxiously to find out how it would end. Despite his eagerness, which he knew was obvious, his boyfriend didn't seem to budge. When Sloan realized he would not win, he toed off his shoes. "I guess I can stay in tonight."

Drew turned back to the television. "I don't want you here unless you want to be," he grumbled, jaw clenched in disappointment. "If you'd rather hang out with your friend, go hang out with your friend."

Honestly, Sloan would rather hang out with Colette, but making Drew angry when he had just gotten him to agree to lunch with his friends the next day wasn't a good idea. It would be best to keep passive aggressive Drew away from Leo and Colette, who were already concerned about their relationship.

If Sloan was being honest, he was worried about their relationship as well. While he had no intent to pursue something with Leo—once again, Leo was *way* too good for him—he wondered what it meant to have gotten feelings for someone else.

Still, Drew stayed with him despite his imperfections. Sloan couldn't just overlook that.

"No," Sloan said, kicking his shoes off the rest of the way. "Of course I'd rather be here with you." Smiling, Drew turned off the television and rose from the couch. When Sloan straightened from putting his shoes on the mat by the door, Drew was there to wrap his arms around his waist, pulling him close.

"I'm glad," his boyfriend said. Sloan closed his eyes, hugging him back. "Why don't we take a shower, hmmm?"

If he made the noise of exasperation he wanted to, Drew surely would have heard. Instead, he pressed his hand to the back of Drew's neck and breathed out a soft, "Sure."

"They're late," Drew complained, crossing his arms over his chest. "You said they wanted to meet me."

"They do," Sloan assured, keeping his eyes on the doors to the cafeteria. They had been waiting only a few minutes and already Drew was getting impatient. "And they're not late. We're a little early."

Drew huffed. "There's not going to be anywhere to sit." Sloan ignored him, raising his hand to tug nervously at his shirt collar. He had done it many times that morning, far too aware of the dark red hickey Drew left on his neck the night before. Before they left the apartment, Sloan attempted to cover it with a sweater. Drew protested.

"*Why don't you want people to know you're mine?*"

Sloan changed into a T-shirt.

"Sloan—"

"What?" he interrupted, the sound harsh. Drew's eyes got wide. "Ah, sorry, sorry. I'm just kind of anxious."

"Why?" Drew asked. "Are you worried they won't like me?"

"That's not it," Sloan mumbled.

Drew reached out to brush hair off Sloan's forehead. "I was going to say that your hair was getting kind of long again. Maybe you should get it cut."

With a frown, Sloan reached up as well, nudging Drew's hand out of the way to feel his hair. He liked it the length it was.

"You know I don't like it too long," Drew reminded.

"Yeah," Sloan acknowledged softly. "Well—"

Before he could give in, Colette and Leo interrupted them. They came together, probably because their dorms were so close. Colette greeted Sloan with a punch to his arm that made him hiss. "I can't believe you didn't show up last night! It was *sooo* good." Her gaze moved down to his neck. "Ah, well, I can see you had some fun of your own."

Sloan didn't even need to look at Drew to know the smug expression on his face, so instead he focused on Leo, who stared back with a neutral expression.

"Is this everyone?" Drew asked, even though Sloan had told him many times who they were meeting.

"There's two more," Sloan reminded.

"You don't sound too excited to be here," Colette said to Drew. "I get it. Eating here is kind of a drag. The food isn't that great."

"Yeah," Drew agreed, as if this was his problem. "We don't come here often. The only time I ate here regularly was freshman year."

Colette smiled, but it didn't reach her eyes. "Well, thank god you made an exception for us." Drew's eyebrows raised in surprise. Before he could respond, Kennedy and Oliver joined them.

As Sloan introduced them to Drew, he thought that maybe, when Drew said he didn't want to come the night before, it would have been best to accept that as an answer.

Sloan spotted Leo sitting alone at one of the eight-person tables toward the back of the cafeteria and went to join him. When Leo noticed him approaching, he smiled at him for the first time that day.

"Hey," Sloan greeted, returning the smile as he took the seat across from him.

"Hi." Leo's gaze lowered to Sloan's plate and his eyebrows pulled together. "Is that the only thing you're eating? It seems like less than usual. Won't you be hungry?"

"I might go back later," Sloan said. Drew had encouraged him to get a salad, so he had, though he was far too hungry for that alone to fill him.

He wanted to start eating but knew his boyfriend would scold him for not waiting for the rest of them. He crossed his arms on the tabletop. "Hey, did you do the reading for political science?"

"Yeah," Leo confirmed. "There wasn't much beyond what we covered in class. Want me to send you a picture of the notes I took?"

"Ah, I would love that," Sloan told him, just as the chair to his left pulled out. Drew sat and, for a horrible second, Sloan feared it was only going to be the three of them, but then Kennedy took the seat beside Leo.

"Love what?" his boyfriend asked. Sloan noted his plate had a burger and fries on it. Desperately, he wanted to reach out and take a French fry. He didn't.

"If Leo shared his political science notes with me," Sloan explained.

The frown on Drew's face told him he didn't approve. "Wouldn't it be easier for you to read the book yourself? Then you'd have a better understanding of the material."

Colette and Oliver finally took their seats, Colette choosing the other open space beside Leo, with Oliver sitting to Sloan's right. "I guess, but I don't really have time to do the reading, and this way I'll at least get the gist of what we're talking about."

"I'll send you the notes," Leo promised. Drew grumbled something that was probably unpleasant under his breath. Sloan couldn't make it out. He wasn't about to ask him to repeat himself.

"So, Drew," Kennedy chimed in, eyes wide from the light tension. "What are you going to school for?"

"Oh." Drew looked pleasantly surprised. He loved talking about school. "I'm in the engineering program. Next year I'm planning to go to grad school for biochemical engineering."

Colette's eyes widened. While she didn't like Drew, it didn't surprise

Sloan that she found his ambition impressive. "Have you applied anywhere yet?" she asked.

Drew nodded. "Yeah. They're all in state. I'd like to end up close. It would be easiest, with Sloan being here." Smiling, Drew raised his hand to Sloan's shoulder. "It's fitting that he's a biology major, isn't it?"

Across the table from him, Leo's composure cracked for half a second, mouth twitching into a scowl. Before anyone other than Sloan noticed, he was deadpan again.

"Oh, for sure," Colette agreed, giving another one of those smiles that didn't reach her eyes. It made him want to wince, and he fought the urge, distracting himself by finally lifting his fork to eat his food.

Oliver cleared his throat. "So, how was your show last night? I know you were really excited for it." He directed the question to Kennedy, though Colette was the one to answer.

"Oh my god!" Colette exclaimed. "It was crazy!" Kennedy nodded in agreement, and Sloan was quick to cover his ears. "He ended up choosing the girl that—"

"Hey! Don't ruin it for me!" he cried.

"You didn't watch it?" Kennedy asked. "You were the most excited."

"Right?" Colette said. "Well, he stood me up."

"Don't be so dramatic. You recorded it, right?" he asked. He hadn't had the chance to and, even if he had, Drew probably wouldn't have wanted to waste a recording on that.

"Who records things anymore?" Colette teased. Sloan nervously glanced at his boyfriend, who did. "We can stream it. You wanna come over and watch tonight?"

Before he could agree eagerly, Drew cut in to say, "You guys can't actually enjoy that stuff." There was an awkward pause in which Colette looked confused and Kennedy angry. Sloan jumped in to do damage control.

"It's kind of like it's so bad that it's good," he defended, breaking the silence.

"I disagree," Colette protested. "It's so *good* that it's good." Kennedy nodded. Colette turned to Leo. "Right, Leo?"

It was immediately clear that Leo wasn't paying attention to the conversation. His eyes were on his phone. At his name, he looked up quickly. "Huh?"

"How do you feel about reality dating shows?" Oliver asked.

For a moment, he actually seemed to think about it. "No opinion, I guess." He glanced back at his phone. "I've never watched one before." Neither had Drew, Sloan knew. Still, he was adamant about disliking them.

"*What?*" Kennedy sounded horrified. Leo seemed alarmed by the outburst. "You've *never* watched one?"

"I don't watch a lot of television," Leo admitted, placing his phone on the table face up. "Just sporadically. I like it, but I don't watch enough to get into anything. I honestly don't know if I've seen a single TV show in its entirety."

While the rest of them, even Drew, looked at Leo like he was strange, Sloan smiled. "I don't know," he teased. "You've seen a lot of that show about how things are made."

"Ah." Leo's lips pressed together to hide his smile. "Those were extenuating circumstances." On the table, Leo's phone buzzed. Even from upside down, Sloan could read the name *Michael* on the screen. Sighing, Leo picked up the phone. "I should take this."

"That's alright," Colette told him. "Go ahead."

"Thanks." When he answered the call, he said something in French. Colette made a surprised face, while Kennedy looked at Leo the same way she had the day she'd opened her door to him. This time, it bothered Sloan. He didn't let it show.

Leo gathered his dishes. Before he left, he excused himself politely.

"It physically pains me that boy is gay," Kennedy groaned, watching Leo walk away. "He is so hot."

"I feel like there's so much we don't know about him," Colette said softly, shifting her gaze to Sloan. "Did you know he can speak French?"

"Yeah," Sloan admitted. "When we met the first time, he was using sidewalk chalk to write in French in front of his dad's house."

"Ah. Well, I'm glad he came to eat with us, even if it was only for a while. He's been acting weird lately," Colette said.

"Justin didn't tell you?" asked Kennedy. At the sound of Justin's name, Colette made a face. "Apparently him and Max made out."

Colette looked horrified. "*Justin?*"

Kennedy's eyes rolled. "*No.* Max and *Leo,*" she clarified. Shocked, Colette's eyes shot back to Sloan. He busied himself with his salad. "They made out on Leo's futon last week."

The annoyance Sloan felt at the words *made out* was great, and he hoped it didn't show. When Justin and Leo talked about it, they only used the word *kiss.* Because of that, Sloan was letting himself assume it had been a quick, closed-mouth thing. He couldn't, nor did he want to, imagine Leo kissing someone with tongue.

"Okay, but it was *Max* who told you that, right? Is it really true?" Oliver asked. They all turned to Sloan then. "Have you heard anything about it?"

He took a drink of water before speaking. "Well, I'm not sure about the *making out* thing, but I know they kissed. Justin brought it up when I was there on Monday."

"No, they made out," Kennedy confirmed. "Max specifically said there was tongue and it went on for a while."

"Does that really matter?" Colette asked. "I want to know if they're a thing or not."

"No," Sloan and Kennedy said at the same time.

"Leo said he wasn't interested in Max like that," Sloan added.

Kennedy gave a mischievous smile. "Also, Max has no qualms about having sex with me, and he doesn't seem like the kind of guy who would cheat."

"Ugh, gross," Oliver accused.

"I don't know, though," Kennedy continued, ignoring her best friend. "I think Leo's at least a little interested. He doesn't seem like the kind of guy to just kiss anyone."

"Maybe he was just curious," Colette suggested.

"Max isn't good enough for Leo," Sloan pointed out. They all looked at him. He could feel Drew's eyes on the side of his face like a burn.

Colette spoke up, her voice soft. "I think Leo deserves to be with the person he wants to be with." To Sloan's surprise, her eyes remained on him, and he looked back in confusion. It felt like she was implying something. He couldn't imagine what.

No, actually, he could, but it was a ridiculous thing to suggest.

"Yeah!" Kennedy agreed. "I mean, if Leo likes Max too, they should totally be together." She continued talking about it, giving a handful of reasons the two boys would make a good couple, despite the fact that it would mean the end of her relationship with Max.

Even though he thought a relationship between Leo and Max may be for the best, Sloan couldn't bring himself to agree.

Drew wasn't in a good mood after lunch, and he made this known with many snide remarks. For the first half of the walk back, Sloan ignored him, lost in his own thoughts. When it became clear that Drew wasn't going to stop, he chimed in.

"Can't you at least try to like them? They're really important to me."

A scoff left Drew. "Why would I like people who take your attention away from me?" he retorted, clearly not seeing anything wrong with the question. Sloan wondered how he could say something like that so openly and not be ashamed of the selfishness. "You're not actually going over to that girl's dorm tonight to watch that shit, are you?"

"I'd like to," Sloan admitted.

Drew scoffed and shook his head. "How can you say you don't have enough time for homework and then go to a friend's room to watch pointless television?"

"I'm going to spend the rest of the afternoon doing bio and stats. I'm allowed to take a break sometimes," Sloan argued with a lack of passion. There was a sharp inhale to his left, but before Drew could say anything, the sound of Sloan's phone ringing interrupted him.

He pulled it from his pocket. His mood lifted at the sight of the word *Mom*, his thumb already moving to press the answer button. "Sloan, really?" Drew snapped. "You know I don't like it when you talk on the phone during our time together."

"It's my *mom*," he defended. This apparently meant nothing, because Drew wrinkled his nose. "Drew, we *live* together. We're together all the time. How am I supposed to talk to my mom if I can't when I'm around you?"

They held eye contact for a long moment. Sloan answered his phone. To show his distaste, Drew quickened his pace, leaving him behind.

That's fine, Sloan thought, watching his boyfriend get farther away as he greeted his mother.

It really wasn't fine. Drew's behavior only conflicted him further.

CHAPTER TWENTY-EIGHT

LEO

On Saturday, Leo got dinner off campus with Colette.

They went to a nice restaurant, and it occurred to him once they had been seated that they probably looked like they were on a date. He wondered what Justin would say if he could see them.

"You're wondering why I brought you somewhere this nice, huh?" Colette asked, gazing at him over the top of her menu. "If it seems like a good first date spot, that's because it is. That's not why I brought you here, though. We're here because I think the best way to counter anxiety is with great food."

Counter anxiety? he thought, confused for only a moment. Of course they were going to talk about Morgan. They hadn't had a chance to discuss him all week.

"You mean because both of us are worried about Sloan?" Leo asked.

She stared at him briefly before looking to examine her menu. "Yes and no." A second later, she snapped the menu shut. "Well, yes, I guess. We should probably talk about that, but that's not the only thing stressing me out."

"Right," Leo acknowledged, annoyed with himself for having only considered what affected him as well. "Justin. What even happened with you two on Monday? He's been in a pretty bad mood since, and I'm too afraid of crossing a line to bring it up."

"Aw." Colette looked touched, and Leo wasn't sure why. "It makes me happy you felt comfortable asking," she said, propping her elbow on the table and resting her chin on her fist. "I'm happy we're friends, Leo. I don't know who else I'd talk to about all this Justin stuff."

"I don't mind you talking to me, but what about Sloan? And aren't you pretty close with Kennedy, too?

"I can't talk to Sloan about it," she denied immediately. "I don't feel like I should talk to him about my relationship issues—that aren't really *relationship* issues—when it's clear he has a lot of things to work out in his own relationship right now."

Lately, whenever Leo thought about Drew, he got angry. He did then as well. "Yeah," he managed. He didn't think he needed to hide his expression from her. Colette already noticed how he felt about Morgan; probably long before even he had.

"And," she continued, "I could talk to Kennedy, but she's so close with Oliver that she tells him everything, and I'd like to keep the number of people who know about my personal life to a minimum. Also, every time I've brought it up to her, she's told me to fuck him, which really isn't all that helpful . . ." This made her smile a little. It quickly faded. "Besides, I don't even know if this whole Justin thing is gonna go anywhere, so I don't want to sound like I'm bragging by talking about it too much and end up looking pathetic."

This made Leo frown. "Why wouldn't it go anywhere? You both like each other, don't you?"

"It's not that simple. He hasn't tried to contact me at all since Monday."

Since Leo was under the impression it was Justin waiting on Colette and not the other way around, this confused him further. "Did he end up finding you that day? He left the dorm to go after you."

She dropped her gaze to the table. "Yeah. He did. He found me and tried to talk to me but he was stoned and I didn't want to have an important conversation with him like that, so I told him if he wanted to talk, he could reach out to me when he wasn't high and we'd have a conversation. I said the same thing to Kennedy when she caught up to me. The difference is that Kennedy came to my room that night to sort things out, and I still haven't heard from Justin." She met his eyes almost hopefully again.

"He really hasn't said anything about it," Leo told her. She sighed. "You want him to reach out to you, right? You want to be together?"

She looked conflicted. The waiter came to take their orders, giving her time to think over his question.

"Well," she voiced once the waiter left to deliver their requests to the kitchen. "I don't know when I started liking him if I'm being honest. I mean, he's always really bothered me because he's so smart and I assumed he didn't try, but once I started paying attention to how hard he works, I couldn't help liking him."

There was a pause. Leo waited. Colette seemed like she had more to say.

"The weed thing . . . I mean, I don't get it, but I'm not going to *not* like him because he gets high sometimes. Kennedy thinks I'm too uptight to be open-minded about those kinds of things."

Leo nodded in understanding. "If you like him, why don't you reach out to him? I don't know this for sure because he hasn't talked to me, but right now he's probably uncertain about your feelings for him, which I'm guessing is why he hasn't called you. People tend to avoid rejection."

"Oh." It was said thoughtfully, as if she hadn't even considered this yet. "You think that'll work?"

"Yeah," Leo said. "I do."

She looked relieved. "Well, what about you then? What are you going to do about your love life? From what I've heard, it's gotten more complicated since we last spoke."

Leo leaned back in his chair. "So, you heard about what happened with Max? I don't know what you've been told, but it wasn't a big deal.

It just kind of happened."

"Were you drunk or high?" she asked. He could tell she thought it was unlikely.

"Completely sober," he admitted. "He asked if he could kiss me, and I went with it."

"That's surprising to me," she said. "I'm not judging. I mean, Max is cute and all … you're just not the person I expected to have a meaningless kiss."

"Well, when it began, I was hoping it would mean something, but the whole time we kissed I felt wrong. Like I was kissing the wrong person."

Colette's expression shifted to sympathy. "He was upset, you know," she said. "That you and Max kissed. It bothered Sloan."

"I noticed," Leo admitted. "I wish I hadn't."

"Why not?"

"Because what does that even mean?" He knew she wouldn't have an answer. If there was a clear-cut answer, he was sure he would have thought of it. Ever since the day Morgan found out about what happened with Max, and Leo noticed his jealousy, he'd been thinking about it. "Does it even mean anything when he's with that—" Anger rose in him again, and he stopped abruptly. "It's emotional abuse, Colette. How he treats him is—"

When she cut in, her voice was low. "I know... I've been thinking of saying something. I just don't know what, and I'm worried he won't listen. What if he pushes me away? Then I won't be there when he needs me."

"Yeah," Leo agreed. "It's so hard to watch. Being with Drew makes him think so little of himself."

"Well, that's how Drew gets him to stay," Colette told him. "He drags him down until Sloan thinks Drew is what he deserves. He's completely unaware that he's settling."

Ah, Leo thought sadly. *So that's what it is.* He knew there had to have been something about Drew to make Morgan stay, but he was hoping it was actually something good. It made him feel worse to think about Morgan going along with Drew because it was all he thought he deserved.

"I don't think I've ever seen you look this angry before," Colette told him.

"I don't know if I've *been* this angry before," he admitted.

Her smile was sad as she reached across the table to pat his hand. "We'll figure something out," she promised him. He wasn't sure he believed her. This entire time he'd been trying to figure things out when it came to Morgan, and nothing had turned out how he expected it to so far.

Leo would not get his hopes up.

When Leo mentioned he was going to get coffee, Justin insisted he wait a few minutes so he could go along. This was fine—Leo didn't mind having company on the walk—but when they got to the coffee shop, Justin surveyed the area and said, "Looks like Max isn't here yet."

"Max?" Leo asked. He had seen Max multiple times since they kissed, and everything thankfully seemed normal between them. It was almost as if it never happened.

"Yeah," Justin confirmed, going to the back of the line to order. "He's meeting us here."

That was how Leo found out they weren't there for a quick coffee run. He could have protested and said he didn't want to stay, though there was no good reason to, so he just sighed and moved to stand behind Justin in line.

They didn't talk, Justin too busy texting Colette—Leo spotted the name on his roommate's phone not long ago—and Leo content enough to stand there silently.

His thoughts, as usual, were occupied with a certain blond-haired boy. He hadn't seen Morgan since class Friday morning, and he spent a great deal of time worrying about him. During class he had seemed fine, but Leo couldn't stop himself from being concerned when he knew Morgan was with Drew.

He was almost to the front of the line when he felt a hand on his shoulder. He turned, expecting to see someone he immediately recognized, and was instead faced with a short girl with wide blue eyes. "Yes?" he asked, wondering if she touched him by mistake.

"Oh god. It is you!" the girl said. In front of him, Justin glanced over his shoulder at them, eyebrows raised. He had to turn forward seconds later to order.

"I think you have the wrong person," Leo told her. She shook her head. "Do I know you?"

"I'm Nicole! Sloan's best friend. I don't think we were ever really introduced that time you came to visit, but Sloan talked about you a lot, so I feel like we were friends! Leo, right?"

"Uh, yeah," he confirmed, squinting a little as he looked down at her. They'd only met once, five years ago, so it was no wonder he didn't recognize her right away. "Nice to see you again."

Justin reached out to touch Leo's elbow, getting his attention. It was his turn to order, so he stepped up to the counter and asked for a latte. After he paid, he moved out of Nicole's way, going to stand beside his roommate as they waited for their drinks.

Apparently, that wasn't the end of the conversation. Nicole joined them once her order was taken. "I didn't know you were going to school here," she said to him, completely ignoring Justin. "Have you run into Sloan at all?"

"I have," Leo confirmed, wondering if it was a bad thing Morgan hadn't mentioned it.

"Oh, that's great! He was practically in love with you when he was a kid, so it's nice you got to reconnect as adults," she continued. Leo didn't know how he was supposed to respond to that, so he just nodded awkwardly. "I'm here visiting for the day. There's actually a group of us meeting Sloan and his boyfriend, but they're running a bit late. You should come say hi. Everyone who came to visit was there the day we met, actually. It's kind of amazing how long we all stayed friends, right?" She pointed to the back of the coffee shop where the couches were, at a group of four people. Leo didn't recognize any of them.

He didn't want to say he would go over there. Nervously, he glanced to Justin for aid, but Justin only met his eyes and snickered, apparently finding the situation amusing.

"Oh!" Nicole exclaimed, seeming to notice Justin for the first time. "Are you Leo's boyfriend?"

This had Leo choking on air. Justin didn't seem at all fazed by the misunderstanding. "I'm his roommate, but sometimes we indulge in certain forms of touching," he answered casually.

Not amused, Leo fixed him with a blank stare.

"So, you guys are here together then?"

"Yeah," Justin confirmed, just as his coffee order was called at the counter.

"Well, can I borrow him for a few minutes?" Nicole requested.

It distressed Leo that she had directed this question at Justin, as if he were a parent or guardian who made Leo's decisions for him.

"For sure," Justin allowed, clapping Leo on the back before going to get his drink. Justin didn't return to them, instead cutting through the line to the seating area. Peeved, Leo looked after him.

So much for thinking he'd be helpful.

"So, you said you've run into Sloan? I wonder why he hasn't mentioned it to me," Nicole mumbled. She sounded a little hurt, as if it bothered her that her friend hadn't shared absolutely everything about his college experience with her. At the counter, Leo's name was called, and he stepped forward to retrieve his latte. Desperately, he wanted to follow Justin. Instead, he returned to Nicole's side awkwardly. She grinned at him, either not noticing his discomfort or not thinking it was valid enough to let him leave. "Do you and Sloan do stuff together?"

Raising his cup to his lips, he said, "Sometimes." The caramel flavor of his drink was sweet on his tongue. "We have class together."

"That's fun." Her name was called, and she stepped forward to accept her drink. "Well, come on then." She reached down and grabbed his wrist, pulling him along.

When he looked back at their destination, he noticed that Morgan and Drew had arrived and were greeting everyone with smiles on their faces. Morgan's high school friends seemed to like Drew, though maybe that was because they didn't really know him.

It took Nicole a moment to notice the addition of her best friend, distracted as she talked nonstop to Leo about something he wasn't listening to. As soon as she looked back toward the couches, she dropped Leo's arm and threw herself at Morgan. Morgan's eyes closed, and he wrapped his arms around her waist to hug her back. Uncomfortable, Leo hovered there, unsure if he should slip away while he had the chance.

Before he could decide, Morgan's eyes cracked open, focusing on Leo over Nicole's shoulder. At first, he seemed surprised, his eyebrows raising. It didn't take long for his lips to pull into a smile. He looked a little different from usual, *older*. It took Leo a minute to notice that Morgan had gotten a haircut.

"And who have you brought back with you, Nicole?" asked one of Morgan's friends, a boy with hair the same color as Leo's.

Leo had been so occupied with Morgan that he hadn't realized everyone else had noticed him as well. The attention embarrassed him and he dropped his gaze.

"It's Leo!" Nicole exclaimed, moving out of Morgan's arms to return to where Leo was standing a few paces behind. She took his wrist again and tugged until he was standing beside Morgan. On the other side of his friend, Drew examined him with a scowl.

"You remember Leo, right?" Morgan asked his friends, his voice coming out a little higher than usual. His cheeks were a shade darker than they had been a moment before, and he cleared his throat. "He, uh, visited the beginning of the summer we were thirteen." As he spoke, Morgan let Drew pull him away from Leo's side to the couch.

"Ohhh, he's the kid you ditched us to hang out with!" one of the boys said. The other three people—two other boys and a girl—wore looks of recognition.

Leo recalled the memory they were referring to. The Sunday after he and Morgan slept in the tree house, they had been on their way to get ice cream when five of Morgan's friends biked up to them and encouraged Morgan to join them. Without pause, he told them no, and when Leo later asked if that had been done for his sake, Morgan smiled and said, "*I did it for myself. I'd much rather hang out with you than them.*"

"See!" Nicole exclaimed, loud enough that Leo winced. "Saying hi was a good idea. I think he was planning on running away from me. Unlike Sloan, I am far more forceful." This made Leo frown. She must have been talking about his abrupt departure that summer.

"If you kissed him, I bet he'd run from you, too," the third boy teased. Nicole looked offended.

"Excuse you, I am a *great* kisser," she shot back, encouraging the banter.

Leo was no longer paying any attention to Morgan's friends. Instead, he was watching the couple, focusing on the mixed expression of confusion and betrayal Drew wore as he stared at his boyfriend. Morgan wasn't looking back at either of them, his eyes squeezed shut as if he wasn't ready to see the damage that simple sentence caused. Clearly, he had yet to mention their kiss to Drew.

Nicole picked up on the tension more quickly than the others and moved to take the seat beside Morgan on the couch. "Aww, don't look so threatened, Drew. He might have been his first kiss, but you were his first everything else."

Drew's dark eyes raised to regard Leo. The look on his face made Leo wonder if he was about to get beat up. Before anyone said anything else, a pair of arms slipped around Leo's waist, pulling him back against a solid chest. He tensed at the touch but relaxed some when he recognized the voice in his ear. "Well, what do we have here?" Max asked, chin dropping onto Leo's shoulder. "None of you are Justin, and I was told I'd be meeting this cutie and Justin."

Cutie? Leo wanted to ask. He saw that Morgan was staring at them, his expression displaying his distaste.

"Ah, Justin must be the roommate you touch!" Nicole accused.

Oh god, Leo thought, squeezing his eyes shut. "He was joking when he said that."

"Thank god," Max said, still pressed against Leo's back. "I was going to be offended that you didn't invite me."

Feeling he had enough of the situation, Leo reached down and pushed Max's arms from around his waist. "Nice to see you all again," he mumbled before leaving to go to the table Justin chose for them, thankfully on the other side of the room.

His roommate was on his phone, but he lifted his head when Leo set his coffee down. "You look awful," Justin said.

Leo took a seat, dropping his forehead onto the table.

"Hey, are you alright? Max, what'd you do to him?"

"I think I embarrassed him," Max claimed. There was the sound of a chair scraping against the floor as it was pulled out. "Leo, you alright?"

He didn't answer. He was embarrassed, but that was only part of the problem. More than anything, he was concerned with the way Drew had looked at Morgan after finding out they'd kissed.

"Leo?"

"No," he managed. "I'm not."

Chapter Twenty-Nine

Sloan

They were supposed to spend the afternoon with his friends, but Drew cut their meeting short. While it upset Sloan, he wasn't about to argue with his already livid boyfriend, so he said goodbye and allowed Drew to pull him back to their apartment by his hand.

Drew's grip was tight, as if he expected Sloan to try to get away, and Sloan stared down at the sight of his hand in Drew's. It looked wrong.

They weren't speaking. Even when they got to their apartment, they silently kicked off their shoes and went to the living room. Sloan sat on the couch, while Drew stood in front of him, on the other side of the coffee table. For a minute, nothing happened. The tension grew more unbearable.

Drew asked, "You're not even going to say anything?"

"I didn't know if you'd want me to," Sloan admitted, staring down blankly.

"Look at me," Drew snapped. Immediately, Sloan raised his head. "Why didn't you tell me you kissed him?"

"I didn't think it was a big deal." Drew scoffed. "It happened when we were kids. I was twelve and he was thirteen. He visited his dad and I kissed him after, like, a week and a half and he was so angry about it he flew home. It means nothing." Even as he said this, Sloan wasn't sure he believed it. Two weeks ago, he surely would have, but he had since discovered his feelings for Leo, and deeming their one kiss as unimportant felt wrong.

"He was your first kiss."

"Yes," Sloan admitted. "But why does that matter?"

"Because you didn't tell me about it!"

Because I knew you'd act like this, Sloan thought. He didn't say it out loud. That wasn't a good enough reason, and he knew it. If he had been thinking about his relationship with Drew, he should have told him about the kiss, no matter how insignificant, and yet he hadn't. Even from the start, he'd been trying to protect his relationship with Leo from his partner.

"Drew . . . it was just a kiss. It lasted a second. I'm dating you now. I live with you, I gave my virginity to you, I *love* you. I'm sorry for not telling you, but it changes nothing." The words weren't coming out right. It felt like he was unraveling.

"It changes *everything*. By not telling me this and spending all that time with him, you were practically cheating on me."

"What?" Sloan asked. "I think that's taking it a bit far now. We're just friends, Drew."

"You hid it from me for a reason!" Drew accused. His voice was so loud that Sloan winced. "This whole time I've noticed something was going on between you two. I've never seen you look at anyone the way you look at him. How long has it been going on, Sloan?"

"I didn't cheat on you," he insisted. "Please believe me, Drew. I wouldn't do that to you—"

Drew cut him off. "I'm not asking that. I'm asking you how long you've wanted him."

Shocked, Sloan stared at the other boy. *How long have I wanted him?* he asked himself. It hadn't been that long since he realized he once again developed feelings for Leo, but when had the feelings started? Had they never gone away from the first time? Had they been dormant all this while? Did he have feelings for Leo again the second he spotted him in political science class?

No. Sloan knew that wasn't true. At the beginning, Leo had just been a friend. He'd felt nothing more for him than that, because there had been no room to feel anything more than that. At the beginning of the semester, Sloan loved Drew and only Drew. So, the real question wasn't *How long have I wanted him* but *When did things go so wrong with Drew?*

"Drew . . ." Sloan trailed off, thinking of what he could even say. "Don't you trust me?"

Oh, he realized as soon as the words left his mouth. *That's it.*

The day of their fight, the morning Sloan returned from staying in Leo's dorm after he had gotten high. It was that day that he realized Drew didn't trust him. That's when they fell apart.

There were good times after that, Sloan thought, though nothing specific came to mind. The closest thing to happiness he'd felt over the past three weeks in his relationship was the weekend he and Drew spent together after Sloan got drunk, and even then, he felt guilty the whole time. There had been the feeling of relief as well, relief that they were no longer fighting. Sloan wondered if the real reason he felt relieved was because they had delayed the ending. *Their* ending.

A relationship without trust wasn't a relationship at all, and by that point, he had been aware Drew didn't trust him. They had resolved nothing, just pushed it off for later.

I wasn't ready for it to end then, Sloan thought. *Am I ready now? Is there even a point in trying to fix this?*

"I don't know anymore," Drew finally said. Sloan realized he didn't really care about the answer. He already knew the truth. Drew didn't trust him, and he hadn't ever since Leo came back into his life.

"I need to think," Sloan told him, standing from the couch.

He started toward the door. Drew beat him there, placing his hand against it to hold it closed. "You can't run away, Sloan."

"You can't keep me here," Sloan protested, pulling at the doorknob even though he knew it would not budge.

"We need to resolve this before you leave."

"Resolve it how?" he asked, his voice pleading. He wanted Drew to fix it. Wanted Drew to give him a way to fix it himself. It would be so much easier if he could go back to being happy with the man who was in front of him, but he didn't see a way for that to happen. "We can't fix trust issues with a single conversation, Drew, especially since you're more interested in hearing what you want to than what I actually have to say. I don't know what you want from me."

"I want you to stop seeing Leo," Drew demanded. Sloan stopped pulling at the door. "Stop being friends with him. If you take that step, then I'll trust you."

He stared at his boyfriend for a moment, not really thinking about anything. Slowly, he blinked, eyes moving back to the door. "Could you move, please?"

"Sloan—"

"Please," he interrupted, voice verging on desperate. Right then, sounding pathetic wasn't a concern of his. He just needed to get out of there. "I need to think about this. *Alone.* Please, let me go."

Walking calmed Sloan down, but he knew his friends were probably still exploring campus, and the idea of running into them right then made him want to cry, so he went straight to Colette's dorm.

She answered the door seconds after he knocked, a smile on her face that faded at the sight of his expression. "What happened?" she asked, reaching out to wrap an arm around him, then guiding him into the room.

Her roommate, Jessica, was in there as well, and she turned to look at him when he entered. "I'll step out for a bit."

"Thanks," Colette said, guiding Sloan toward the futon under her lofted bed. Jessica left silently and Sloan collapsed. Colette sat beside him, her hand resting between his shoulder blades. "Are you alright?"

"I am," Sloan answered. "I'm . . ." He stopped talking. They stayed quiet for a long time as he gathered his thoughts. In the end, the only thing he could think to say was, "Drew found out about Leo being my first kiss."

There was a pause. Colette breathed out a heavy exhale. "He didn't take it well?" she asked. Sloan suspected she already knew the answer.

Shaking his head, he told her, "He wants me to stop being friends with Leo."

"Hell no. Fuck that. He wants you to stop being friends with Leo because you're actually happy around Leo. You're not really considering it, are you?"

"Wanna hear something terrible?" he asked, and her eyes widened. "I thought maybe it would be the easy way out, because then I could keep putting off my relationship problems with Drew."

"Sloan . . ."

"I can't do it, Colette. I can't cut Leo out of my life. Even if it would fix everything with Drew, I couldn't do it. I would rather fight with Drew every day if it meant I could still have Leo."

Colette seemed relieved. "You know those aren't your only options, right?"

Sloan suspected he knew what she really wanted to say. *You know you could remove Drew from the equation.*

"I know," Sloan mumbled. "I think about Leo all the time, Colette, and I'm trying not to because of Drew, but I can't stop." He squeezed his eyes shut. It was his first time admitting it out loud, and while he felt relief from finally being honest about his feelings, he also felt even more terrible about himself as a person. "It's not fair to Drew."

"Oh, *fuck* Drew," she snapped. Surprised, Sloan's eyes flew open. "I'm sorry, Sloan, but your boyfriend is a total prick. You realize your relationship is unhealthy, don't you?"

He dropped his head into his hands. "I've started to realize, yes, but I can't help thinking that it would be better if I tried harder—"

"Sloan." She sounded distressed. "Relationships involve trying, yes, because they're not easy, but it requires it from *both* of you. You shouldn't be putting in effort for someone who isn't willing to put in the effort for you."

"Would Leo be willing?" he asked, mouth working faster than his brain.

Without pause, Colette answered. "Yes."

"God," he groaned, lifting his head. "I'm such a bad boyfriend. I'm still with Drew. I shouldn't be thinking like this."

"Would you think like this if you were happy in your relationship with Drew?"

He sighed. "It's not Drew's fault I'm unhappy."

"Yes, it is," she disagreed. "He constantly criticizes you. It is not your fault you can't be happy in that kind of situation."

Sloan held her gaze for a minute before sighing and leaning against her shoulder. "What do I do? I feel like I can't make the decision myself."

Her hand patted his back. "Well, I'm sorry, but I think you're going to have to. I can't tell you what to do."

While it would have been easier for her to just direct him, he appreciated her saying this. She wasn't pushing him to make the decision she thought was best; she understood that, ultimately, his decision needed to be based on his feelings and his feelings alone.

"That's okay," he said, breathing in the scent of her flowery perfume. It calmed him. "Thank you for being here, Colette."

"Yeah. Of course. Literally any time," she promised. "Wake me up in the middle of the night if you need me, I really don't care." Her hand paused on his back. "And, I know you must already realize this, but I'm not the only one who'll drop everything to help you."

He nodded again. "I know you're not." He felt like he was going to cry, and she must have sensed this, because her voice distracted him.

"Well, would watching a shark movie make you feel better? I'm getting dinner with Justin in a few hours, so we have time to finish at least one and a half," she said. He smiled, lifting his head from her shoulder so she could go get her laptop. Of their friend group, Sloan and Kennedy were the only ones with televisions, so movie nights with Colette involved huddling together so they could see her laptop screen.

"You know just what I need," he said.

"Yeah, weirdo." She freed her laptop from her backpack. "If you're not ready to go home when it's time for me to leave, I can reschedule my plans."

"No," Sloan insisted immediately, not even considering it. "You should go. And when you're ready to talk about whatever it is that's going on with Justin, let me know."

Grinning, she took the seat beside him again, resting her laptop on her knees. "As soon as I know for sure, I'll let you know." There was an unspoken *The same goes for you,* but they were done talking about the boys for the day, ready to focus on less worrisome topics.

He relaxed back against her shoulder, feeling better already. In a few hours, he'd have to return home to Drew, and his boyfriend was surely expecting him to come up with something to say in his time away. Sloan could think about that later.

Chapter Thirty

Sloan

Sloan's school week started poorly.

On Monday, he woke up at 9:10—meaning he slept through chemistry—and only had twenty minutes to get to bio. It wasn't often that his alarm failed to wake him, and it seemed especially strange that morning.

The evening before, after eating dinner by himself in the cafeteria and fully considering what his boyfriend was asking of him, Sloan returned to his and Drew's apartment. They had a brief conversation regarding Drew's proposition, and Sloan informed his partner that he refused to cut Leo out of his life.

"Just the fact that you think that could fix everything shows me how many problems we really have," he said to his unreceptive boyfriend.

Drew had said nothing to him for the rest of the night, and Sloan went to sleep around seven, sick of the tense atmosphere in their apartment.

On top of going to sleep earlier than usual, he slept well, so he hardly believed it when he blinked his eyes open the next morning and read the time.

With only a few minutes to spare before bio began, he fell into his seat beside Colette. "Is everything okay?" she asked. "I was concerned when you didn't show up this morning."

"I slept through my alarm," Sloan told her. "My day fucking sucks. I didn't get to drink coffee, and I realized halfway here that I forgot my backpack. No need to worry, though. My boyfriend hasn't killed or beat me yet." The boy sitting in front of them turned to look at him. Only then did Sloan realize it was Justin. The fact he was sitting there probably meant things had gone well between him and Colette the night before.

Justin's expression was grave. "I'm joking," Sloan assured him.

"Well, it's not funny," Colette grumbled, pulling a pencil from her bag for him to use. She didn't give him any paper, which seemed just as important, but he figured he could ask when he needed it.

"Well, let me know if he hurts you. I'm more than happy to go beat him up," Justin offered.

"Um . . ." Sloan didn't know what to say to this. As far as he knew, Justin and Drew had never met. "I'm not really concerned about him hurting me, but thanks, I guess? Why would you be so willing to do that? You and I barely know each other." Sloan glanced at Colette from the corner of his eye, wondering if maybe Justin was willing to avenge him for her sake.

"Ah." Justin smiled. "I've wanted to punch that fucker ever since he told Leo to stay away from you."

Sloan frowned. "What? When was this?"

"You know about that?" Colette asked Justin.

"Yeah, I know," Justin said. "I was there. I was the one who told that asshole to piss off, since Leo sat there staring at him."

"You know what he's talking about?" Sloan asked Colette.

"Um, yeah. Leo mentioned it to me a while back. It happened before you two were really friends again. It was part of the reason he kept rejecting your offer to hang out."

"Why didn't he say anything to me?" asked Sloan.

"He thought if he did, you'd talk to Drew about it, and that would end up causing you trouble," Colette explained.

Sloan knew Leo had been trying to prevent him from having any conflict, but he assumed that was because Leo thought Drew looked angry when he saw them together, not because Drew went up to him and expressed his distaste.

"Please don't be angry with him over this," Colette begged.

"With Leo?" Sloan looked to the front of the classroom. They should have already begun class, but their professor was still absent. "I'm not upset with Leo at all. It just makes me even more angry at Drew."

Colette shifted nervously in her seat. "If you don't want to talk about it, that's okay, but . . . have you decided what you're gonna do?"

Sloan had no problem talking about it, but Justin was listening as well, and he didn't want to risk anything getting back to Leo. He would only worry.

"Oh," Justin voiced. "If you're worried about me gossiping to my roommate, you shouldn't be. We don't do that. Leo prefers to hear things from the source. Also, I'm pretty sure he only listens to what I'm saying about thirty percent of the time."

With a nod, Sloan explained, "I told Drew I wasn't going to cut off Leo, and he hasn't spoken to me since . . . I don't think I can stay with him anymore. I just don't know how to end things."

"Just tell him that," Colette suggested. Sloan slid his gaze away. It sounded as if she thought it would be easy, though he was positive it wouldn't be. Nothing with Drew was ever easy. They had been together for a year, and Sloan had always been terrible at standing up for himself. Drew would not take it well; he'd fight to keep them together.

"Take your time," Justin advised. "If you need to prepare yourself, take time to prepare. Just keep in mind that everyone is going to be worried about you for however long you're with him, especially if things are as tense as you say they are."

"Thanks," Sloan told him sincerely. "Please don't even mention to Leo that Drew and I aren't in a good place right now. Either of you. God knows that boy has worried enough about me already."

"Okay," Colette said, and Justin nodded in agreement. "But if you think he doesn't watch you close enough to pick up on the fact that something's up, you're wrong."

Professor Larson entered at the front of the classroom. "Sorry, guys," she called out, gathering Sloan's attention. She stopped at the table in front of the whiteboard and set down a stack of papers. "I forgot to print your tests, so I had to do it right before class."

"Test?" Sloan echoed, eyebrows drawing together. "What test?"

Justin turned to look at him again.

"What? She's joking, right?" Sloan asked.

When Justin spoke, he sounded concerned. "Um . . .no."

Horrified, Sloan looked to Colette again. She also seemed worried about him. Taking a bio test without having studied at all couldn't end in anything other than negative results.

"Why didn't you remind me when I went to your room?!" he demanded, his voice at a whisper so he didn't disturb the surrounding students who were frantically paging through their notes. Having forgotten his notebook, that wasn't a luxury he had.

"I thought you knew!" Colette said. "And then with everything else going on, I didn't want to stress you out more. I'm sorry."

"I'm not mad at you," he grumbled, picking up on the panic in her voice. "I'm upset that I'm going to fail this class."

Yeah, Sloan thought miserably. *Today is going to be a shit day.*

The first words he said to Leo that morning were *"I love you,"* which might have been strange, since right before, Leo said, *"You look like you're gonna be sick."*

After finishing—if it could even be called that—his bio test, Sloan went to political science class, where he found Leo waiting for him with a concerned expression and a cup of hot coffee; hence the *"I love you."*

"Ah," Leo managed in response, avoiding his eyes. His ears were pink. Still, he seemed pleased. "Well, Colette texted me and said you looked like you might pass out, so I thought this was the least I could do."

"You're the best," Sloan told him, wrapping both hands around the coffee. "This is the only good thing that has happened to me so far today. Thank you."

Rubbing the back of his neck, Leo assured, "It was nothing. I was going there anyway."

Sloan looked at the table in front of Leo with a smile. "Then how come you don't have a coffee too?"

This made Leo's cheeks flush. "Why hasn't your day been good?" he asked, ignoring the question.

"You know how it goes sometimes. I slept through my alarm and missed chemistry, then I forgot my backpack, and we had a test in bio I completely forgot about, so I didn't study. Not that I had time to study. This weekend was kind of crazy."

"Yes, you got your hair cut," Leo said. "I like it."

"Oh!" Sloan raised a hand to pat his own head. "Thanks. I actually prefer it a little longer, but I guess I don't mind this."

Not meeting his eyes, Leo mumbled, "It always looks nice." He cleared his throat, seeming completely overwhelmed by his own words. "Was it nice to see your friends this weekend? I was surprised to run into them."

Sloan smiled at Leo's cute behavior. "Yeah," he answered. "It was really great seeing them. I'm sorry Nicole abducted you. She gets overly excited sometimes, and she remembers how big of a crush I had on you in eighth grade."

"You had a crush on me?"

"Leo," Sloan began, raising his coffee cup. "I kissed you." As he took a sip of his drink, Leo's shoulders raised in a shrug.

"Well, I figured you liked me a bit, but I didn't know that meant you had a crush on me. Calling it a crush makes it seem like real feelings."

"They were real," Sloan assured. "I liked you the moment we met."

Leo still wasn't looking at him. "I had a crush on you too," he confessed. Class would be starting soon, and Sloan wished for more time. He spent years wondering how Leo had really felt about him that summer.

"Really?" he asked. "But you left."

"Yeah." Leo glanced up to meet his gaze. "Now you know why."

For lunch they went back to Leo's upon Sloan's request. Drew was most likely still in their apartment, and he preferred to avoid his boyfriend for the time being. He'd have to go back eventually to get his backpack before his next class, but he'd wait until Drew was gone.

When they entered Leo's room, Justin looked up from his desk. "Want some chips?" Sloan offered in greeting. He held out the bag he'd bought at the convenience store on the way over.

"Nah," Justin refused, turning back to his books. "I only eat those when I'm stoned."

Leo sat on the side of the futon closest to his bed and pulled a textbook out of his backpack. It made Sloan feel guilty that he was interrupting Leo's study time. Leo didn't seem to mind all that much, and he raised his eyes to look at him. "Come sit down."

Sloan lay out across the remainder of the futon, his head dropping onto Leo's right thigh. Leo studied him for a second with raised eyebrows before bringing his attention back to his textbook. Sighing in content, Sloan placed his bag of chips on his chest.

"How'd you think the test went?" Justin asked him, his back still facing them. Sloan gave a pathetic groan. "That good, huh?"

"I didn't know *anything*," Sloan admitted. "My grade in that class is so low."

"Talk to Professor Larson. I bet she could hook you up with one of those study groups she's always encouraging us to use. You'll be more likely to get a better grade if you show her how hard you're working, so even joining would help."

This was something Sloan had considered many times; there was just a bit of a problem. "Drew thinks only idiots need study groups," he told Justin. Justin and Leo looked at him. "I didn't say I agree with him." They resumed what they had been doing.

They stayed like that for a couple of minutes until Leo reached down to gently tug at a strand of his hair. "Are you gonna eat your chips?"

"Yeah." Sloan reached his hand into the bag and shoved a bunch into his mouth. "You can have some, too." Leo rolled his eyes in a playful sort of way before reaching into the bag to grab a single chip. "You're not going to eat your sandwich?" Sloan asked.

"Not right now, no." Leo looked back at his textbook. "I'm not all that hungry."

Justin's phone rang, and he quickly answered. "No," he said to whoever had called. "Why would you think I was lying to you? Do you want me to bring you lunch or not?"

Ah, Sloan thought, smiling as he watched Justin hang up and gather his things to leave. He waited until the door shut behind him to tell Leo, "I'm pretty sure that was Colette on the phone."

"Oh? Last I heard they hadn't spoken yet. I noticed them texting, though."

"They met last night," Sloan explained. "I don't know what happened, since Colette hasn't told me yet, but Justin sat near us in biology today, so whatever that means."

"Ah." That was all the reaction Leo gave. Sloan recalled Justin saying that Leo didn't like gossip. He wondered whether he should bring up that he now knew about Drew telling Leo to stay away from him, or if Leo wouldn't like it because he hadn't been the one to tell him.

While he considered this, he studied Leo's face for long enough that Leo noticed. "What?"

It was hard to imagine Leo being upset with him, so he went for it.

"How come you never mentioned that Drew talked to you about me?"

Leo's eyes widened. Still looking at Sloan, he shut his textbook and carelessly pushed it off his lap onto the floor. "Did Drew tell you?" he asked. At that, Sloan felt a dark sort of amusement. *Like Drew ever shared anything about himself that made him look bad.*

"No. Justin actually mentioned it in bio. He didn't know I hadn't already heard about it," Sloan explained. "Why didn't you want me to know?"

"I didn't want you to worry. It wasn't a big deal."

"You were going to let that stop you from being my friend," Sloan reminded sadly. To his surprise, Leo's hand came to the top of his head, absently sliding through his hair.

"But I didn't," Leo said. "I know you said it wasn't my problem, but is it so bad that I didn't want to cause you any trouble?"

"No," Sloan answered quietly. They looked at each other for a moment longer. Leo leaned to pick up his book.

As Leo studied, Sloan continued to gaze at him, thinking.

Leo was so good to him, Sloan thought fondly. With confidence, he could say that Leo wanted what was best for him. He wanted him to be happy.

Leo couldn't help Sloan do what he needed to be happy, though. That was something he needed to take care of himself.

Set in his decision to free himself from Drew, Sloan removed his phone from his pocket and began drafting an email to the housing department about moving into a single room as soon as possible.

Chapter Thirty-One

Sloan

The exam scores came back on Friday.

After spending the past three days worrying, Sloan felt ready for the agony of not knowing to be over.

The second he looked at the front page of his exam—more specifically, at the red number written at the top—he wished he could go back. It was kind of nice, not knowing. At least then it was still possible to have hope that things weren't too bad.

He wondered if he'd ever scored in the thirties on an exam before. In high school, he hadn't been the best student, but he'd been alright. This was a whole different level of failure than what he was used to. It didn't even compare with his other poor grades throughout the semester.

Thankfully, Colette and Justin—who had taken the seat in front of him and Colette all week—were discussing their own exams, not paying attention to him at all, so it was easy to slip his test into his backpack, out of sight. It sounded like both Justin and Colette had done well; Justin a little better, judging from Colette's slight pout, though she didn't seem nearly as upset as she would have once upon a time. While Sloan didn't really know what was going on with their relationship, it was clear Colette had warmed significantly to him. He was happy for them.

For their relationship *and* success in biology.

He spent the rest of class thinking about what this meant for his overall grade. It probably wasn't good, and he was thankful he was so bad at math that he couldn't calculate it right then. Ignorance was bliss.

By the time the lecture was drawing to an end, he decided to take Justin's advice and talk to the professor. If he was realistic with his goals, he should stop worrying so much about getting into med school and focus on passing the class. Sloan wasn't even sure anymore if going into the medical field was his dream or the dream Drew made for him.

"Hey," Colette said, bumping his shoulder to get his attention. He realized their professor had stopped speaking and was gathering her things. "I'll walk you to your next class and stop in to see Leo."

"Ah." Sloan avoided her eyes as he tucked his notebook into his backpack. "You go on ahead. I should actually talk to Professor Larson."

"Okay!" She smiled. Nothing in her expression seemed judgmental. "Talk to you later?"

"Yeah, for sure," he answered. He didn't leave his seat until Colette and Justin disappeared through the door together, talking about something that made them both flush.

To his surprise, even though Professor Larson was finished packing up, she was still hovering at the front of the classroom, perhaps assuming he was going to stay after to speak with her. That would embarrass him, so he hoped not. He approached the front of the room with his eyes downcast and his cheeks warm.

After deciding to skip political science, Sloan felt guilty the entire walk to his apartment. *It's fine*, he told himself. *It's not like I'm falling behind in political science, and Leo—*

Leo, he realized, on a completely different train of thought. Just considering him made Sloan pause. He wanted to see him, badly enough that he almost went back. Class had already begun, though, and he couldn't imagine what it'd be like to show up that late. He'd reach out to

Leo later.

As he walked to his apartment, he hoped Drew was still in bed so they didn't have to interact. They'd managed the *no talking* thing until Tuesday, but it wasn't sustainable, so they had begun having short, uncomfortable conversations when they were in the same space.

When he got back to the apartment, he entered silently, toeing his shoes off by the door before peeking into their bedroom. Drew was still asleep, a big lump in the blankets on the bed. It would be easy enough to go lie down beside him. They wouldn't even need to touch each other.

Sloan spread out across the couch instead.

Before falling asleep, he checked his phone. He was only going to look through his email to see if housing had figured out somewhere for him to go yet, but a message from Leo distracted him. It had been sent in the past couple of minutes, after class had started, and Sloan smiled. He'd never seen Leo text during class before.

Leo: You alright?

Sloan: I'm okay. Bad test score in bio. Bummed and tired. I'm gonna take a nap

Knowing Leo, he wouldn't respond again until after class, so Sloan clicked off his phone and placed it on the coffee table. It didn't take him long to fall asleep.

There was nothing going on that night. From what he'd heard of his friends, Colette was hanging out with Justin, Leo was working on a project at the library, Oliver was going home, and Kennedy had plans, so Sloan found himself sitting on the couch beside Drew with nowhere else to go.

For the first time since moving in, he thought their apartment was painfully small. It was only three rooms, which felt huge compared with those tiny dorm rooms without kitchens or bathrooms. Now, with things tense between him and Drew, he realized there was nowhere for him to escape. Until a bit ago, he had been going to sit in the bathroom to get away. It hadn't taken Drew long to get annoyed and begin making a comment about it every time Sloan took a sip of water, so he stopped.

"What are we going to have for dinner?" Drew asked without looking at him.

"I made dinner last night," Sloan reminded. He had the remote and was flipping through channels, but apparently not at a satisfactory rate, because Drew reached over to take it from him.

"Can't you do it tonight as well? I don't feel great."

Crossing his arms over his chest, Sloan grumbled, "I got back a bad test today, so I don't feel that good, either." He felt quite defiant, treating Drew the way he treated his mother when he felt the need to be difficult and knew she would still love him regardless. It was different, though, since he didn't know how much Drew would take before giving up on him. Still, he was only treating Drew the way Drew had treated him for the past year, so if his boyfriend had any self-awareness and guilt, he would suck it up for a little while. At least until Sloan could find another place to live.

"Bio?" Drew asked.

Sloan cringed, knowing where the conversation was about to go. "Yeah."

"You can do it, Sloan. You just need to study harder."

Sick of that type of encouragement, Sloan rolled his eyes. "It's hard to study for something I don't care about."

"You do care," Drew corrected with a confidence that suggested he knew Sloan better than Sloan knew himself. Once upon a time, not even that long ago, Sloan believed he had as well. "You want to be a doctor."

"Do I?"

"Of course you do," Drew said. "Don't be stupid."

"Maybe I am stupid." He said it to piss Drew off, but he felt bad about himself the second the words left his lips. "I got a thirty-eight on my exam."

Drew scoffed. "I don't want to talk to you if you're going to be like this."

That was fine. Preferable, really. Sloan leaned back into the couch, no longer interested in what was happening on the television. He took out his phone to check his email again, hoping to see that housing had reached out to him since he checked last. They hadn't, though there was a small victory in the fact that Drew didn't even bother to snap at him to put away his phone.

They sat there silently for about an hour, the television offering a distraction to the tension that continued to grow when neither of them got up to make dinner. Sloan didn't mind the atmosphere. He'd grown used to it.

To his surprise, it was Drew who found it unbearable first and broke the silence with a reluctant "*Sloan—*"

A knock at the door interrupted him. Neither of them moved. When it became clear neither of them was expecting anyone, Sloan went to see who it was.

Leo was standing on the other side of the door, his eyes wide as if he hadn't expected it to open. There was a pizza box in his hands. "Um . . ." he began. "Hi?"

"What are you doing?" Sloan asked, leaning against the doorframe and smiling at Leo.

"You had a bad day. I thought I might make it better," he answered. It seemed like such an un-Leo thing to do, coming over without asking first, but he was right. It did make Sloan feel better.

"I thought you said you were at the library?"

"I was," Leo said. "I mean, earlier, I was. That was mostly an excuse so it would be more surprising when I showed up. You haven't eaten yet, right?"

Shaking his head, Sloan admitted, "I haven't. Even if I had, though, I'd still eat pizza."

Leo smiled, the expression overcoming the hints of doubt that had been there.

"Why don't you—" Sloan began, but Drew interrupted from the couch.

"Hey, who is it?" he called. The sound made Sloan jump. He had almost forgotten that Drew was there, and he suddenly felt nervous that Leo had come to their apartment. He still hadn't talked to Leo about what was going on with Drew, and he knew it would be obvious that something was up. Still, he wouldn't send Leo away. With a sigh, Sloan waved Leo into the apartment.

"Oh." Drew's eyes shifted to look at the box of pizza. "I don't like pizza."

Sloan expected Leo to ignore this, so it surprised him when he responded with a dry voice. "It's probably a good thing it's not for you, then." The second the words were out of his mouth, his gaze flew over to Sloan as if he expected him to be upset. Sloan just looked back, lower lip pulled between his teeth to keep from laughing.

"How'd you even get in the building?" Drew asked, sounding as if his patience was wearing thin.

The question made Sloan cringe, fearing Drew's wrath when he learned about Sloan sharing the code to the door. Leo seemed to have prepared to be interrogated, because he easily lied, "One of your neighbors was conveniently leaving while I arrived."

One glance at Drew told Sloan it did not fool him, but he didn't give him the opportunity to question it. "Drew, can we use the TV?" he asked, pushing the door to the apartment shut. Drew looked like he was about to disagree, so Sloan added, "If not, that's okay. We can watch something in the bedroom on my laptop."

They held gazes for a long moment. Drew mumbled something including the words *pain in the ass* before getting up and going to the bedroom. The door shut with a click behind him.

Leo's eyes lingered on the closed door. "Are you guys okay?"

Hoping to seem nonchalant, Sloan waved a hand in dismissal.

"We're fine." He took the pizza from Leo and put it on the coffee table. "Take a seat. Do you want anything to drink? The TA who threw that party we went to got me wine coolers."

"Sure." Leo dropped onto the couch, sitting in the spot Drew had vacated. "In case you were wondering, we didn't cover anything important in political science. I made photocopies of the notes for you. I just forgot to bring them."

"Thank you," Sloan said as he reached into the fridge to grab two bottles of brightly colored liquid. "You know you don't have to do that stuff for me."

"It's one less thing for you to worry about, isn't it? Besides, it wasn't like it was hard. I was already going to print something. This isn't like the coffee thing, either. I *actually* needed to print something."

With a laugh, Sloan took the seat beside Leo, handing him one of the chilled bottles while setting his own on the coffee table. "Well, thank you. It'll be nice not to have to worry about copying the notes before next class. I don't have any homework either, so I think I'm gonna spend the weekend wallowing in self-pity."

"You couldn't have done that badly," Leo said, twisting off the top of his drink.

As Leo took his first sip, Sloan leaned over the end of the couch and pulled his test out of his backpack. It was weird that he wanted to hide it from Colette and Justin but didn't mind showing it to Leo. Maybe it was because he knew Leo wouldn't think less of him no matter how poorly he had done.

There was a pause in which Leo shifted his gaze to the test. He sighed and sat forward, pushing open the pizza box and freeing the first slice, which he offered to Sloan in consolation. It was cute, Sloan thought, and he chuckled as he accepted the food. He threw his test down on the coffee table.

"I met with my professor after class and got the number of the TA who sets up the study group."

Leo smiled. "That's great, Morgan."

"Yeah," Sloan said, his cheeks warm. He grabbed the remote as Leo freed a second slice of pizza for himself. "What do you feel like watching?"

"Just put on something with sharks," Leo told him, leaning back into the cushions. He was holding his drink between his legs so it wouldn't spill, both of his hands occupied with his food. "I'm not particular about what I watch."

"Oh, come on," Sloan said, eyes on the screen as he navigated to a streaming app. "Do you really not like television?"

"It's not that I don't like it. I've watched quite a few documentaries that I've enjoyed."

"Leo . . ." Sloan shook his head, lips curling up in amusement. "Sometimes I can't handle you."

"I'm sorry?"

He hit play on a movie he had yet to see. "It's not a bad thing."

The opening scene started. A woman in a one-piece swimsuit was surfing, and Sloan figured he knew what would happen to her, so his undivided attention was not required. "Hey, thanks for coming over. Really, I needed this."

"Yeah," Leo said. "It's no problem. I . . ." He looked at the television. His cheeks were pink. "I wanted to see you after you didn't come to class."

Sloan's heart beat fast at the words. It was the perfect end to a bad school week.

The night wasn't over yet.

They spent their time watching silly movies and talking in low voices, enjoying being together. Drew came out of the bedroom only twice in the hours they sat there, both times to use the bathroom. He said nothing to them, though each time Sloan could feel his eyes on the back of his head.

Eventually, exhaustion—and probably the two wine coolers—got to Leo. He drifted off to sleep, his head lowering closer and closer to Sloan's shoulder with each deep breath. When it finally rested there, his breathing steady, Sloan sat incredibly still. He knew he couldn't stay for long. Drew was bound to come out of the bedroom again at some point, and seeing them like that would most definitely start something.

Sloan only allowed Leo to rest against him for a few minutes before he slipped away. Gently, he lowered Leo's head to a throw pillow and lifted his legs up onto the other side of the couch.

Leo would spend the night there, Sloan decided as he brought the pizza box and empty bottles to the kitchen. Surely Drew wouldn't like Leo staying with them, even for just a night, but Sloan wasn't about to ask for his permission.

After returning from the kitchen, he turned off the television and faced Leo once more. He had shifted some, his knees pulling up and hands curling into fists on the couch beside his face. Sloan carefully covered him with a blanket. A soft humming noise left Leo at the warmth, and Sloan fondly tucked a strand of dark hair behind his ear before leaving him to turn off the lights.

He hoped Drew would be asleep when he opened the door to their bedroom. Instead, his boyfriend was sitting up in bed, his laptop open on his knees. "Homework?" Sloan asked, shutting the door. Drew watched him as he went to the dresser to find a pair of pajama pants for the night.

"Yeah," Drew answered. "Is he gone?"

"No." Sloan moved back toward the door. "He's sleeping on the couch." Drew's mouth opened, but Sloan wasn't finished talking. "I'm going to go change and brush my teeth." Quietly, he slipped from the room to go to the bathroom.

When he returned a few minutes later, Drew had abandoned his laptop. Sloan was expecting him to protest Leo's presence in their apartment, but instead his boyfriend said, "You really shouldn't eat pizza. It's bad for you and it's going to make you gain weight."

Ignoring him, Sloan threw his clothes carelessly in the hamper and turned out the light. Moonlight streamed through the window, and he used it to guide him to the bed.

It was quiet for a couple of seconds after he lay down. He heard Drew shifting on the other side of the mattress.

A hand rested lightly on his hip, and Sloan pushed himself up on his forearms, surprised. Before he could ask what Drew was doing— knowing his boyfriend, he certainly wasn't trying to cuddle—warm lips fastened over his. Incessant fingers pushed at the waist of his pajama pants, and Sloan was quick to grab Drew's wrist.

"Stop," he hissed, his eyes wide as he tried to adjust to the darkness. Drew hadn't wanted sex since they fought last. He seemed to think it was a punishment, like Sloan would suffer from his withholding it.

Easily, Drew shook off his grip, fingers pulling Sloan's pants down his hips. "I want to fuck you," Drew said, leaving his side of the bed to hover over him.

"There's a person sleeping on our couch," Sloan protested, fighting the hands that pulled his legs free of his pants. "*Hey, stop.*"

"We'll be quiet," Drew insisted, hands moving to the backs of Sloan's knees and pulling them apart.

A dry finger threatened to press into him, and Sloan grabbed Drew's wrist tightly. Usually when Drew got like this, he'd roll over and give in. Right then, though, he was angry.

"You only want to do this because he's here," Sloan accused. In the moonlight, he caught of a glimpse of Drew's green eyes. He looked determined. Sloan knew in that moment it was going to happen, whether he wanted it or not. He let out a heavy sigh, his eyes pricking with tears. "Just use lube, please."

There was a huff as Drew climbed off him to get what they needed. Sloan threw his arm up over his face.

This is the last time, he told himself, not nostalgically. Still, it didn't make him feel any better.

CHAPTER THIRTY-TWO

LEO

Leo was a light sleeper. Right about then, it was his least favorite thing about himself.

At first, he wasn't sure what had woken him. He didn't even think about it right away, wondering where exactly he was as he sat up and looked around. Once he wasn't so disoriented, he recalled falling asleep on Morgan's couch.

Also, he was pretty sure it was a sound that woke him. He couldn't hear anything though, so he focused on listening to the silent apartment.

Just when he'd waited long enough that it seemed whatever it was wasn't going to happen again, he picked up on a soft noise. It was a little groan, the sound one would make while massaging a sore muscle or . . .

Leo had never had sex before, had done nothing even close, but he immediately knew that was what he was listening to. Mortified, he lay back down, unsure of what to do. More sounds came from the bedroom, soft creaks of a bed frame and another low groan. It didn't sound like a noise that would come from Morgan, though Leo never saw that side of him, so it was impossible to tell.

He rolled onto his side so one of his ears was pressed into the pillow, his hand bringing the blanket up to his other ear to muffle the sound. It did nothing.

Squeezing his eyes shut, he tried to ignore the tightness in his chest and his pounding heart. He was angry. Angry at Drew for being the one who got to touch Morgan when he didn't deserve it, as well as angry at Morgan for making him endure this.

Leo was about to get up and leave when he heard one last shuddering gasp, followed by silence.

Even though the noises stopped, he wasn't able to sleep.

He didn't know how long he lay there, staring into the dark living room. It was impossible not to think about what just happened, and each second he was there he felt worse. Once again, he considered leaving so he didn't have to face the couple in the morning.

The sound of a door clicking had his body tensing. He forced himself to relax, hoping whoever it was didn't suspect he was awake.

It must have worked because, after a few seconds of pretending, he felt a pair of hands settle on his arm to shake him into consciousness. He rolled onto his back. Morgan was looking down at him.

"Wanna go for a walk?" he whispered. It was easy to pick up his tone in the quiet apartment. Something was wrong.

"Yeah," Leo answered, concerned. Morgan pulled back from his line of sight. Leo sat up to look after him, watching as he crouched by the door to pull on his shoes. "Morgan?"

"Come on."

Silently, Leo got up and went to join him.

Morgan waited for Leo to put his shoes on before pulling open the door. He shut it quietly behind them. Leo could finally see Morgan clearly in the light of the hallway. His eyes were puffy and there was a trail of hickeys on his neck, passing under the collar of his shirt. At some point after Leo had gone to sleep, he'd changed into a pair of plaid pajama pants.

Seeming completely unaware of Leo's gaze on him, Morgan started down the hall. Leo got the feeling that if he didn't follow, he'd simply be left behind, so he trailed Morgan.

They took the elevator to the lobby and left through the front door. Immediately, Morgan sucked in a sharp breath of fresh air, closing his eyes and tipping his head back. If Leo was any good at painting, he would try to capture that image on a canvas. It would be a sad painting, he thought. Beautiful, though not nearly as radiant as one would think art of Morgan Sloan should be.

Morgan cracked open his eyes, staring forward at the parking lot for a long moment before beginning to walk alongside the building. His hands were curled into fists at his sides. Leo was going to reach out and force Morgan's fingers apart, but Morgan shoved his hands into the pockets of his pajama pants.

They just walked around the building, not talking. One lap, two laps, three. They were halfway through their fourth when Morgan slowed to a stop.

Surprised, Leo also paused, looking around in curiosity, wondering *Why here?* They were at the back of the building, in the narrow alley by the dumpster. Leo's mouth opened, the name *Morgan* on his tongue. Only the first syllable was out when Morgan turned to the brick wall and drove his fist into it as hard as he could.

There was no crunch of bones. Even so, Leo was certain the hand was broken. Right after it made contact Morgan cried out, clutched his hand to his chest, and dropped to his knees. He sobbed, the noise utterly heartbreaking. His shoulders shook with it, and Leo, unsure of what else to do, crouched and wrapped his arms around Morgan in an attempt at comfort.

Why? Leo wanted to ask. *Why did you do that to yourself? What did he do to you that made you this upset?*

Leo was pretty sure he already knew what Drew had done. He thought back to what Morgan said the weekend he had been drunk. "*I put out when he wants, even when I don't want to.*" Of course Morgan wouldn't have wanted to have sex when Leo was there, too conscious of the fact he might make Leo uncomfortable. Of course his asshole boyfriend disregarded his feelings and made him do it anyway.

An anger unfamiliar to Leo stirred within him, and he hugged Morgan tighter in response, ignoring the wet tears on his neck and the dampness of Morgan's blood seeping through the front of his shirt. "It's okay," he reassured softly, the sound of Morgan's cries making his own eyes tear up. He felt more useless than he ever had before, clueless as to how to get Morgan to calm down and smile again. Still, Leo was thankful he was there with him. Thankful Morgan wasn't all alone.

Morgan's fingers curled into the back of Leo's shirt, pulling him even closer. Leo hoped he wasn't crushing Morgan's injured hand, but Morgan didn't seem to mind the physical pain. *Shock, probably*, Leo thought.

Leo had no idea how long they were on the ground before Morgan calmed. But right around the time Leo's knees started to ache from kneeling on the pavement, Morgan took a shaky inhale and pushed it out slowly. The grip on the back of Leo's shirt loosened, and Leo pulled away enough to see Morgan's expression.

"Hey," Leo said, taking his friend's face in his hands. Carefully, he tilted Morgan's head until their eyes met.

Embarrassed, Morgan averted his gaze. "I'm sorry," he croaked.

Not looking for an apology, Leo shook his head, thumbs moving across Morgan's cheeks to wipe away stray tears. "What happened?" he asked.

"I can't do this anymore," Morgan claimed. "I don't know if I can wait." There was something Leo was missing, but he didn't ask, not wanting Morgan to cry again.

"Can I see your hand?" he asked. With a shaky breath, Morgan nodded, holding it out. Gently, Leo raised it closer to his face. Morgan was bleeding from a few cuts on his knuckles, though the blood flow had slowed down during the time it took him to cry. While it was a good sign, Leo feared it was the least of his worries. At least two of his knuckles were broken, the swelling already taking over his hand. "We should go to the hospital."

"I'm sorry," Morgan said again.

Leo lifted his hand to Morgan's face again. "I don't need you to be sorry," he told him. "I need you to be okay." He stood, using the wall against his back to steady himself. When he was up, he extended his hand toward Morgan's good one, and Morgan allowed himself to be helped to his feet.

"Do you have your phone?" Leo asked. "Mine was almost dead when I checked last."

Morgan rubbed at his eyes with the heel of his left palm. "Yeah, I grabbed it before we left." He withdrew his phone from his pocket and handed it to Leo.

Immediately, Leo noticed the lock screen. The last time he had seen it, it was set as a picture of Morgan and Drew. Now, a photo of Morgan and Nicole in graduation caps occupied the screen. He said nothing about it, just typed in the passcode when Morgan mumbled it.

As he called the taxi company, Morgan rested his head against Leo's right shoulder, his face turned toward Leo's neck. It was distracting, feeling his breath there, and Leo stumbled over his words during the call. When Morgan chuckled and began to pull away, Leo was quick to wrap his free arm around Morgan's waist. Sighing contently, Morgan relaxed into him as the woman on the phone said someone would be there to get them in about seven minutes.

"Seven minutes," Leo told Morgan once he'd hung up.

"I heard." There was a moment of silence. "My hand really fucking hurts."

"I'd imagine. Besides that, how do you feel?"

Morgan sniffled, and Leo worried he might cry again. "I'm alright. I felt it coming and I couldn't stay there. I—" His voice cracked. "You were awake, weren't you?"

It wasn't hard to figure out what Morgan was referring to. Leo didn't respond. It was answer enough.

"I'm sorry. I told him to stop, but the look on his face . . . I was worried that even if I didn't give in, he'd keep going. I'm sorry."

"It's not your fault," Leo assured. *Fuck.* He was angry. "We should go wait out front for the taxi."

Nodding, Morgan moved away from him. His uninjured hand grabbed Leo's, assuring he didn't go too far. "You don't need to come with me," Morgan said. "The taxi can drop you off at your dorm on the way. I don't want to inconvenience you more—"

"Don't be ridiculous," Leo responded, gripping Morgan's fingers as tightly as Morgan was gripping his. Morgan probably didn't even realize he was doing it, trying to distract himself from his pain. "I'm going with you. How are you going to fill out paperwork with a broken right hand?"

"You sound mad," Morgan grumbled. He must have moved his hand then, because there was a sharp hiss followed by an exhalation of the word "*Shit.*"

They rounded the corner to the front of the building. "I am mad," Leo confirmed. It was still early, though Leo's eyes scanned the parking lot for the taxi with hope anyway. The sooner they could get to the hospital, the sooner Morgan would have pain medication.

"You're mad but you won't let me apologize," Morgan said.

Leo came to a stop. "That's because I'm not mad at you."

Morgan closed the distance between them again, dropping his head onto Leo's shoulder.

"Can I say sorry now?" Leo asked.

"What do you have to be sorry for?"

"For not helping you when I should have known—" Leo cut off, unable to finish.

Morgan raised his head, bringing their faces close together. "It would have been bad for you to interrupt," he said.

"Are you afraid of him?"

A strange look came over Morgan's face. "You know, it's weird to think about," he said. "I mean, it's *Drew.* I've said Drew would never hurt me, but I don't think that's accurate. Drew wouldn't physically hurt me, I don't think. Tonight, for a minute, I was afraid of him. I was afraid that if I said no, he wouldn't stop, so I didn't say no. Drew's manipulative, and he knows me. He knows what he needs to do to get me to give in to him every time, and I'm afraid of that." Slowly, he lowered his head back onto Leo's shoulder. "Don't be sorry. I need to learn to say no to him on my own."

"Okay," Leo agreed, looking up as a yellow car pulled into the parking lot. "Then I'm sorry for not stopping you from breaking your hand."

Morgan offered a weak laugh. "That's not your fault, either."

"I knew you were upset. I should have said something," Leo insisted. The cab pulled to a stop in the middle of the parking lot, and Leo patted Morgan's arm. "Come on. They're here."

He led Morgan over to the car, opening the door and letting him in first. Morgan slid all the way across the back to the other side, making room for Leo to enter after him. "Where to?" the driver asked.

"The nearest hospital," Leo responded. The woman turned to look at them, her eyes moving from Leo, to Morgan, to the way Morgan was holding his hand against his chest.

"Don't get blood in the back of my car," the driver instructed. Leo ignored her, closing his eyes. He wasn't good at staying up late, but he'd stay for however long Morgan wanted him there.

And, judging on the way Morgan was gripping Leo's fingers, Leo was still very much wanted.

Leo filled out all of Morgan's paperwork while the boy rested against his shoulder in the waiting room of the ER. They looked like a mess. Both of them with blood on the front of their shirts. Both of them exhausted. Thankfully, they were the only people there.

"You should call your mom," Leo said as he filled in the last question.

Cause of injury: Punched building.

"Why didn't you say wall?" Morgan asked. "Punched building doesn't sound right."

Leo clipped the pen to the top of the clipboard. "I'm being accurate. If I say *punched wall,* then I'd need to explain interior or exterior. If you punched drywall, that'd do a lot less damage, so they probably wouldn't be as concerned as they should be."

Laughing softly, Morgan straightened to put his weight on the chair instead of Leo, probably expecting him to turn in the form right away. When he didn't, Morgan's tired gray eyes shifted to him.

"Your mother."

"My mother is asleep," Morgan said. "Besides, she'll only worry."

"She could get a call from your insurance company and then she'll be angry at you for not telling her first," Leo pointed out. "I'm going to go turn in the form. I'll be right back."

Morgan watched him go. By the time Leo returned, he was typing something on his phone with his left hand.

"Do you need help?" Leo asked as he reclaimed his seat.

"Nah, it's all typed out already. She's probably going to have a heart attack when she wakes up tomorrow morning and reads that." He returned his phone to the pocket of his pajama pants.

"Morgan Sloan," a nurse called out, his voice ringing through the empty waiting room.

Morgan's left hand clasped onto Leo's forearm. "Come with me?" he pleaded. "I've never been to the emergency room before."

"Sure," Leo agreed, covering Morgan's hand with his own. "I'll stay as long as you want."

An X-ray confirmed three broken knuckles. There wasn't much that could be done with all the swelling, so the nurse said he'd give Morgan a splint to wear for the time being once they cleaned his cuts. This was the unpleasant part.

Leo and Morgan sat side by side on one of the empty beds in the emergency room while the nurse carefully examined each cut, picking out any little fragments he saw with fine-tipped tweezers before washing the wound with alcohol. Morgan hissed but held his right hand steady on the lap table in front of him, expressing his pain by squeezing the hell out of Leo's hand every time it hurt. They'd given him pain killers a bit ago that hadn't seemed to have kicked in yet.

"When will I have to come back to get a cast?" Morgan asked the nurse, clearly fighting the quaver in his voice to come off as unaffected.

"When the swelling goes down," the man answered, smiling at Morgan's bravery. "This might hurt a little. You got something deep in this cut."

"Okay," Morgan grumbled, sounding less than pleased.

"Hey," Leo said, bumping his shoulder lightly against Morgan's to get his attention. "Can I ask when you got your tattoo?" It was an attempt to distract Morgan from what was happening in front of him.

Morgan gave Leo a confused look. "What— *ah, fuck.*" The hand on Leo's clamped down tightly. Even so, Morgan's gaze didn't waver from his face. "My tattoo? How'd you know about it?"

"I saw it."

"When?"

"That night you got drunk," Leo explained, dropping his eyes. It felt strange to admit that he had looked while Morgan had taken his shirt off, even if it was just at his back. "On your shoulder, right? The Cancer constellation."

"Yeah," Morgan confirmed, grimacing at the next splash of alcohol over his knuckles. "I got it last year. Nicole has the Taurus constellation in the same spot. We got them together. We were only seventeen, and Cali doesn't let anyone younger than eighteen get tattoos, so our moms drove us out of state."

"Your mom was alright with it?"

With a small laugh, Morgan admitted, "Oh, Mom was completely against it at first." His eyebrows were still drawn together, but he looked more comfortable than he had minutes before. Leo wondered whether it was the distraction or the narcotic. "She didn't understand why we didn't just wait until we were of legal age. It was our Christmas present to each other and we wanted to do it over winter break."

"Did it hurt?"

"Yes," Morgan admitted with a smile. "I cried. Nicole laughed. I'm never getting another one. I—" The door at the end of the emergency room opened, and Morgan cut off suddenly. Curious, Leo followed his gaze. Drew was being led by a female nurse toward them.

They came to a stop at the end of the bed. "Um, sir?" the nurse began, voice unsure. "This man claims to be your partner." The man who was cleaning Morgan's hand looked up, appearing confused.

Morgan turned away from Drew. "That's right. Thank you."

It was silent for a minute, giving the female nurse enough time to excuse herself and slip away. The man began cleaning Morgan's hand again. "I woke up and you were just *gone*," Drew said, still hovering at the end of the bed, seeming unsure of where to go with Leo occupying the seat at Morgan's side. "I checked your phone's location, and I saw that you were at the hospital. Why didn't you call me? What the hell even happened?"

"It was an accident," Morgan lied. "I fell." The nurse cleaning Morgan's wound knew the real story, and he glanced up at the mistruth. "No need to bother you. Leo's here."

"Yeah, well. Now *I'm* here, so Leo can go," Drew shot back, glaring at Morgan's hand in Leo's.

Leo waited for Morgan's answer, but he said nothing, only gripped his hand tighter. "I think I'll stay," Leo said to Drew. The words made the man look on the verge of throwing a tantrum in the ER.

Morgan's fingers suddenly slipped away. "I'll be okay. We're almost finished here, anyway. You go home and sleep. I'll pay you back for the taxi later."

Leo didn't believe for a second that Morgan actually wanted him to leave, though he could also tell from Morgan's eyes that he desperately wanted Leo to just go with it. "You don't need to pay me back," Leo said, standing from the bed. "We'll talk tomorrow, right?"

"Yeah," Morgan agreed, looking relieved. "Though, I think it's technically today, at this point."

Giving a smile as weak as the attempt at humor, Leo bid one last goodbye and forced himself to leave.

He told himself he wasn't going to turn back but could not resist the urge when he got to the door.

For only a second, he glanced over his shoulder. It was just enough time to notice that even though Drew had taken the seat he'd vacated, Morgan hadn't reached out for his hand. Instead, his fingers were on his own knee, gripping tightly at the pain.

Leo left, despite wanting nothing more than to return to him.

Chapter Thirty-Three

Leo

"Hey, man, why don't you get out of bed? You've been up there all day and it's kind of freaking me out. Wanna go to a party? I'm going with Colette, Ken, and Oliver, and they'd love it if you came," Justin encouraged, standing in front of Leo's loft with his arms crossed like a stern parent.

He was probably right to be concerned. Leo hadn't left his loft all day and didn't feel any motivation to get down. The offer of a party didn't sway him. "I'll stay here," he answered, rolling over in bed to face the wall.

It was nearly nine at night, and he hadn't heard from Morgan all day. It was making him anxious. The events from the night before kept replaying in his mind. Morgan's cries, the way he'd clutched Leo's hand so tightly, the cold way he regarded Drew, his assurance that he'd be in contact. *Did something happen?*

When Justin spoke again, his voice was still close. "Leo. . . are you okay?"

He thought about it. Was he? "Physically, yes."

"Did something happen last night?" Justin continued to pry. It would have been so easy to ignore him, but Leo picked up on the concern in his voice. For him, for Morgan, or both, he didn't know. "You came back really late."

"I'd tell you if I could. I don't think it's my place to talk about it. I think everything's alright. I just haven't heard from Sloan today, and it's making me worried."

"Ah," Justin said. Finally, Leo heard him move away. "I'm sure he's fine. I know his boyfriend's a douche, but he's been handling that for a year now. How was it when you were over there yesterday?"

"They were more tense than usual," Leo explained. "I was expecting Drew to spend the entire time supervising us because he doesn't trust me, but he stayed in their room the whole night. Even when he came out to use the bathroom, Sloan acted like he wasn't there. It was different from what I've seen of them before."

A thoughtful noise left his roommate. "That's why you're worried, then?" It was only part of the reason. Leo didn't really want to specify the rest, so he remained silent. "It'll be okay. Sloan can handle himself."

"Yeah," Leo agreed after a pause. He knew Morgan could manage things on his own, but he couldn't help worrying. The night before, he had seen how Morgan took his frustration out on himself.

"So . . . you still don't want to come to the party?"

"No," Leo said. "I'm really okay here."

Justin sighed, though thankfully didn't say anything else.

It took a couple minutes for Justin to get ready. They only spoke again briefly, right before he left, to exchange goodbyes.

Then Leo was alone.

A part of him—a large one—wanted to stay up until Morgan reached out, even though he might not. Waiting for something that would never happen would just be painful.

Leo wondered what he'd do if he didn't hear from Morgan all weekend, only to go to class on Monday to find him smiling like he had a secret. Would he be able to pretend to be happy for him this time? If Morgan forgave Drew, would he be able to handle it?

Leo squeezed his eyes shut and willed himself to sleep. Overthinking wouldn't change anything. Regardless of his feelings, it was all up to Morgan. Leo only hoped he would make whatever decision was best.

Leo was expecting to get at least four hours of sleep before he was awoken by Justin coming home, so it surprised him when the sound of frantic knocking on his door startled him awake only an hour later. With a groan, he forced himself out of bed, annoyed by the interruption.

It was Justin, he assumed. His roommate had a habit of losing his keys when he was drunk. Leo wondered why he'd be back so soon. Did something go wrong with Colette, or did he leave something behind by accident? Maybe he was just stopping back for more alcohol. Or maybe—

Leo pulled open the door and froze. It wasn't his roommate standing before him. It was the person he wanted to see most. *Am I dreaming?* he wondered, but no, he wouldn't dream of Morgan coming to see him late at night with tear tracks down his face, his hand encased in a splint and the hickeys Drew left the night before still visible on his skin. When he dreamed of Morgan, Morgan was always happy.

"Morgan?" Leo asked. "Are you—" He stopped speaking as Morgan stepped forward and hugged him. Automatically, Leo returned the gesture.

"Housing finally emailed me," Morgan said, his words tickling Leo's neck.

Leo pulled from the hug. He held Morgan at arm's length so he could look him over. He started at Morgan's face and made his way down to his injured hand.

"Housing?" Leo echoed. He didn't understand why Morgan would come all the way there to tell him about housing. "What'd they email you about?" As he asked, Leo got the small ice pack Justin kept in the freezer.

"About where I can live from now on."

Leo paused halfway between the fridge and his dresser. Morgan grinned. Unsure of what to say, Leo just watched as Morgan shut the door. The room was dark. Neither of them made a move toward the light.

"What?" Leo asked, not wanting to get ahead of himself. He stared with wide eyes at the shadow that was Morgan moving closer to him. A hand came to rest on his elbow.

Morgan sounded on the verge of laughter. "I couldn't break up with Drew until I had a new place to live," he explained. Leo still didn't move. His hand was freezing, but he clutched the ice pack even tighter.

"So . . . now that you have a new place to live, you broke up with Drew?" He was trying not to sound too hopeful. The soft smile on Morgan's face made him aware that he had failed. He looked happy, but Leo recalled the tear marks. "Are you okay?"

"I don't know," Morgan admitted. "I don't know. I'm here now and that feels like something."

"Yeah, it does." Leo bit his lip to keep from grinning. "I'm assuming you're not moving tonight, right? You want to sleep here?"

"If I could."

"Of course." Leo looked toward the futon and then up at his loft. "You should take my bed. Let me get something to wrap this in so your hand doesn't get too cold."

As Leo went to his closet to do just that, Morgan clumsily climbed up the end of the loft and collapsed on the mattress. "Ah, fuck. That hurt," he groaned. "Hey, Leo. Why don't you sleep up here as well?"

"There's not much room," Leo pointed out, moving to the head of the bed to offer Morgan the ice pack.

Morgan leaned over the railing to peer down at him. "I don't care," he said, resting the ice pack on his right hand. He didn't lean back, maintaining eye contact as Leo considered this.

There wasn't much room. Leo also didn't mind. Actually, he probably preferred it. "Um . . .do you *want* me to sleep up there?"

"I do," Morgan confirmed without pause. He lay back down then, waiting for Leo to join him.

"What if I roll on your hand?" Leo asked, a valid concern in his opinion. Morgan shook the loft with how loudly he laughed. The sound made Leo smile. "It could happen!" Leo climbed up into the loft and carefully took his place beside Morgan. "If you get uncomfortable at all, wake me and I'll move."

"More comfortable now than I was a minute ago," Morgan claimed, rolling onto his side and draping his left arm across Leo's stomach.

Leo chose not to think about anything as he let the breathing of the boy beside him lull him to sleep.

In the morning, Leo awoke to the sound of talking and cracked his eyes open. He was facing the room and saw Justin first, sitting up in his loft.

"Good morning," his roommate greeted. Something on top of Leo's lower half shifted, and he looked down. Morgan was sitting with his back against the wall, his legs thrown over Leo's.

"Hi," Morgan said. The skin below his eyes was dark. Leo wondered how much sleep he had gotten. He couldn't recall Morgan shifting at all during the night.

With a groan, Leo sat up. "How long have you two been up? You could have woken me."

"It hasn't been that long," Morgan said. "I've been up for five minutes, probably, and Justin just woke up. I didn't want to prevent you from sleeping in if you were tired."

"I'm alright," Leo said. "I slept pretty much all day yesterday. Ask Justin."

"It's true, he did," his roommate testified.

"See?"

Morgan smiled. It didn't reach his tired eyes. "How are you doing?" Leo asked.

Morgan looked away. "I'm okay. I don't know. It's weird. I'm not sad, really. I just feel kind of disappointed."

"Are you talking about Leo's performance in bed?" Justin joked. Morgan let out a weak chuckle, while Leo fixed his roommate with a displeased look. "I'm kidding, alright. I know you two didn't have sex. He has a boyfriend."

Morgan stared at the injured hand in his lap. "Not anymore, actually."

Justin's eyes widened a fraction. "You broke up?"

"Yeah."

Leo shuffled around in bed, trying to free his legs. When he managed, he turned to sit up beside Morgan, their shoulders pressed together.

"Last night," Morgan added.

Leo could feel Justin's gaze on him.

"How did that happen?" Justin asked. "I mean, I know you had been thinking about it, but if I'm being honest, I thought it would take you much longer than this."

Curious, Leo shot Morgan a look. He wondered how Justin knew Morgan was planning on breaking up with Drew when he hadn't.

"I thought so too," Morgan admitted. "But last week I emailed housing about them finding a new place for me to live on campus, and I ended up breaking up with him immediately after I received an email that they have an available room. Friday was a terrible night. Did Leo tell you about it?"

"Nah, of course he didn't," Justin said. "I could see something was bothering him, but he said it wasn't his place to share."

Clearly, Morgan wasn't too worried about Justin knowing what happened, because he explained without pause. "Well, my boyfriend— ha, *ex-boyfriend,* was being a dick and I took my frustration out on the brick wall of my apartment building." To show the damage, Morgan raised his hand from his lap. "We had to go to the hospital."

As if impressed, Justin's eyebrows raised. "Damn, man . . . that's pretty hard-core," he praised. This time, when Morgan laughed, it sounded real.

"Pretty fucking stupid, actually. It hurts like you wouldn't believe . . . unless you've ever broken your knuckles before. Then you'd probably believe it."

Pushing the covers off himself, Leo climbed over Morgan to get to the end of the bed. "I'll go back with you when you get your cast," he offered as he made his way down the loft.

"I think the male nurse was interested in you," Morgan grumbled in response, shifting to watch what he was doing below. When Leo withdrew a bottle of pills from his desk drawer, Morgan said, "You don't have to—" By the time he could finish the sentence, Leo had extended his hand with two pills in his palm. Smiling, Morgan accepted them. "Thank you."

"The nurse wasn't interested in me," Leo disagreed. "You were just high."

"So, how'd the actual breakup part go?" asked Justin. "Did he take it well?" This interested Leo as well. They hadn't talked about it the night before. He'd been too afraid Morgan would cry again.

Reaching his good hand toward Leo when he made it to the top of the bed, Morgan answered, "He did not." Leo took the hand, climbing over Morgan again to return to his seat. Neither of them let go. "There was a lot of yelling, and a lot of crying, and then a fair amount of pleading. He must have called all my high school friends last night, because when I woke up, I had a bunch of messages from all of them asking me what was going on."

"Ah, I'm sorry. It's never easy when the person you've broken up with can't come to terms with it," Justin sympathized.

Morgan shifted his palm against Leo's. "Yeah . . . it's going to make going back there today more difficult."

"You're going back today?" Leo asked.

Morgan turned to him. "I kind of have to."

"Why?" Justin chimed in.

Morgan's cheeks flushed, as if their concern overwhelmed him. "Well, I'm moving into a single room downstairs, and I can't leave all my stuff at Drew's. Some of it I can replace, but I don't have money to buy an entire new wardrobe."

Just as Leo was about to offer to go for him, Justin beat him to it. "Don't worry about that. We'll take care of it."

"Text me which drawers are yours and we'll grab the stuff in them," Leo added. If Morgan was uncomfortable going back to the apartment, Leo would do what he could to help so he didn't have to, even if it meant having to put up with Drew. "You shouldn't go back there if you're worried about it."

"I don't think he's going to like seeing you. Yesterday . . ." Morgan cut off when Leo shrugged.

"I don't care about that. It'll be fine."

Morgan squeezed his eyes shut and nodded. "If you guys don't mind, that would be great. I only need my clothes and my backpack and glasses. Drew owns all the furniture, and everything else I don't care about. While you do that, I can get my key from the resident assistant." With a small, exasperated exhale, Morgan dropped his head onto Leo's shoulder. "I just really wish I didn't have to deal with this shit. I should have listened to my parents and lived in the dorms." He paused. "Ah, fuck. I should contact my parents. Let them know it's done."

"Don't worry about that right now," Leo said. "One thing at a time."

The words seemed to give Morgan some relief, because his body relaxed. "One thing at a time," he echoed. Leo felt very aware of how close they were, and he closed his eyes, trying not to think.

"Well," Justin began, the word loud in the quiet room. "I'm gonna go have breakfast with my girlfriend. Want me to mention to her you two split, or would you like to do it yourself? Also, please don't tell her I referred to her as my girlfriend."

Intrigued, Leo inquired, "Is she *not* your girlfriend?"

"We haven't talked about that," Justin grumbled.

"You can tell her," Morgan cut in. "Could you mention not to text or call me about it right away, though? I already have so many messages I need to sort through. Tell her I'll call her later."

Justin nodded. "That I can do."

It didn't take him long to get ready to go, leaving Leo and Morgan alone for the first time that morning.

They sat in silence, leaning against each other until Morgan sniffled softly. Leo shifted, turning to wrap his arms around him and guiding them to lie down.

They didn't speak, and less than ten minutes later, Morgan was asleep in his arms.

When Drew answered the door to the apartment, he was in the worst state Leo had ever seen him in. His eyes were swollen and he was still wearing a pair of pajamas, despite how late in the day it was. His gaze moved from Justin to Oliver, taking in the empty duffel bags they each had thrown over their shoulders. He looked at Leo then, ignoring the box in his arms to meet his eyes. "Where is he?"

"His new room," Justin answered, pushing past him to get into the apartment. Drew's jaw clenched as he watched Justin walk toward the bedroom without being invited in.

"Ah, pardon me," Oliver mumbled as he entered as well. Leo didn't follow them. Instead, he stepped around Drew and grabbed Morgan's backpack from where it was discarded at the end of the couch before going over to the window. While Morgan hadn't specifically asked for his plants, Leo knew he would want them.

Carefully, one by one, he put them in the small box he'd brought, trying to arrange them in such a way that they wouldn't slide around much. He could feel Drew's eyes on his back the entire time.

"What happened Friday night?" Drew asked after a minute of

silence.

Leo considered ignoring him, but he wanted to hear what Drew had to say for himself. "What?"

"On Friday. What did you say that made him turn against me?"

Disappointed by the accusation, Leo shook his head. "I didn't say anything."

"We were happy until you came along," Drew accused. "This is your fault. You ruined something good for me *and* him, just so you could have him for yourself. I know you all must feel like you're saving him or whatever because we had one disagreement, but we never would have had that disagreement if you hadn't been around in the first place, so this is your fault."

The plants were all packed. Justin and Oliver emerged from the bedroom together, both their duffel bags stuffed full.

"Are you finished?" Leo asked them. They both dropped their heads in nods. "We should get back to Morgan—"

"No one calls him Morgan," Drew cut in, sounding frustrated.

Leo swung Morgan's backpack over his shoulder and picked up the box carefully. He looked at Drew, making direct eye contact before giving Justin and Oliver his full attention. "Let's get out of here."

Chapter Thirty-Four

Leo

Colette: How is he doing?

That was the first message Leo received from her that day, and the second came through almost immediately after.

Colette: I see him in class but he barely talks to me

It had been a week and a half since Morgan and Drew's separation, and Leo received a lot of concerned texts from her. He understood why she was texting him—Morgan wasn't really talking to anyone except for him as he recovered—but even Leo didn't know everything Morgan was thinking. He found it difficult to respond to Colette sometimes. His answers probably weren't enough to reassure her.

For the first few days, Morgan was in a bad mood pretty much all the time. But once the hickeys on his neck—a visible reminder of Drew—had faded, there was a noticeable difference. He'd still be down sometimes, wanting to be left alone in his room as he stressed over his failed relationship and wondered if it was proof that he was as worthless as Drew made him feel, but other times it seemed like Drew was a distant memory, one that couldn't hold him back.

Even on days when Morgan was more closed off, Leo stopped by his room to see him, always bringing food to make sure he was still eating. Some days, Morgan would open the door, take whatever Leo brought with him with a weak *thanks*, and close the door again. Other days—the past three, now—Morgan would open the door wide with a big smile and ask if Leo would like to come in.

Leo always said yes.

This was how he found himself lying across Morgan's bed Wednesday evening, texting Colette with Morgan pressed against his right side.

Leo: It's a good day.

The response wouldn't be enough to satisfy Colette, he knew. She craved details. Even so, he didn't type any more.

"Who was it?" Morgan asked. Leo glanced at him out of the corner of his eye. For the first few days in his new room, Morgan had seemed out of place. Leo was happy to see him looking far more at ease.

It was a small room, like most dorm singles, though Morgan had filled it nicely. His plants were on the windowsill, and there were clothes thrown in places clothes shouldn't be. Only once had he complained to Leo about living there, back when he was still adjusting, and it had been about how he missed having his own kitchen to cook in.

"Colette," Leo answered. "She's still worried about you."

"Everybody's worried about me," Morgan groaned. "You're good at worrying, Leo. I don't want you to worry, of course, because I'm fine, but you don't expect anything from me. You let me do things at my own pace. Colette is a forceful worrier. She wants me to talk everything out and thinks it's best if I do it right away. It just stresses me out because I don't even know how to put some of my thoughts into words right now."

They were quiet for a few minutes. Leo understood that sometimes Morgan just wanted to complain while there was someone there to listen. When he released an exasperated huff a minute later, Leo knew he was over it for the time being.

"Thanks," Morgan mumbled, his eyes slipping closed. Over the last week, Leo heard him say this word a lot. "You're so patient with me, when I know you probably want to shake me with how long it's taking to get over this—"

"I've never once thought about shaking you," Leo assured.

Kissing you, however . . .

"I feel like he fucked something up in me, you know?" For a couple of seconds, Morgan just breathed. "It was always there. Even when we were doing long distance, he still picked at me. The difference is, then he could only do it when we saw each other or when we were on the phone. When I was living with him, it was constant. When you're told you do everything wrong constantly, you start to believe you're useless." Morgan opened his eyes and met Leo's gaze. "Having someone like you willing to stick around makes me feel like I'm not worthless."

Smiling, Leo propped himself up on his elbow. "I'm glad I'm being helpful in some way. I spend a lot of my time thinking about how I could help you more, but I come up empty in this kind of situation."

He'd actually called Ian for advice, since he knew the man had been in a bad relationship before Michael. Sadly, Ian was little help, saying the situations were too different to compare. "*Be patient*" had been his recommendation.

"You've been perfect. I just want to stop feeling like this, you know? I want to go back to normal." Morgan raised his broken hand, now wrapped in a gray cast. "I want *all* of me back to normal."

That weekend they'd returned to the hospital so Morgan could get his cast. Ever since, he had been quite miserable.

"Still itches?"

Morgan groaned. "You have no idea." He glanced at the wrapping with a fury Leo didn't expect from him. "Ugh! I shouldn't have mentioned my hand. Now it's all I can think about." He kicked his legs like a kid and then sat up. "I want to get out. Let's go somewhere."

"Alright," Leo said, sitting up as well. He looked over his shoulder at the bed. "Are you finally going to buy sheets?"

Since dorm sheets weren't something Morgan brought with him to college, he was sleeping with a blanket wrapped around his mattress.

"That's not a bad idea," Morgan answered. "Yeah, let's do that."

As Morgan climbed out of bed to ready himself for their outing, Leo noticed there was the hint of a smile on his face.

After they checked out at the store, Leo used the app Morgan downloaded on his phone—*because who still calls taxi companies, Leo*—to request a car. They waited on a bench outside of the food court, both of them with soft pretzels Morgan had requested they get.

The large bag of bedding was on the ground between them. Morgan had insisted on buying a red set because he thought it went well with Leo's coloring. Leo wasn't sure why this mattered, and he hadn't pointed out that he couldn't even see the color red.

It was warm outside, and Leo thought of what it must be like back home. Lizzy was surely wearing sweaters and scarfs by now. He wondered how his friends were doing on campus and what it would be like when it snowed there. He couldn't imagine going to and from class in that weather.

"What are you thinking about?" Morgan asked. Leo turned to him. Morgan was already watching him. It made Leo wonder how long he'd been looking. "You were just staring at the ground. Your pretzel is gonna get cold."

"Ah," Leo mumbled, finally taking his first bite. It was covered in cinnamon and sugar and was so sweet that his teeth almost ached. "I was thinking about how it must be getting cold back home."

"Will it be snowing when you go back?"

Leo thought of the plane ticket tucked in the top drawer of his desk, the date on it growing nearer at an alarming rate. "Most definitely."

Morgan must have been thinking something similar because he said, "Isn't it weird that there's only six weeks left until the semester ends?"

"Is that all?" Leo asked.

"We're in week nine right now."

That didn't seem right. It felt impossible that they'd been in each other's lives again for that short amount of time. Somehow, it also felt as if he hadn't been in his classes for nearly that long. "That went fast. It's probably a good thing I got my ticket home last week."

A frown pulled Morgan's lips. It was only there for a second before he took another bite of his pretzel. "It'll be weird, knowing how far away you'll be. I don't like it."

"Yeah," Leo agreed. "I'll come back sooner this time. It's not like it's gonna be another five years." The reference to their past made Morgan smile. He was doing that a lot lately.

"Hey, do you ever regret it?" As he spoke, Morgan looked at his almost finished pretzel. It reminded Leo that he also had one to eat, and he took another tentative bite. "Leaving after I kissed you? Do you ever wish you had stayed?"

Not needing to take time to think, Leo answered, "Of course. That summer, I thought about it a lot, actually; in the times I forgot I was trying not to think about it. I kept considering things like, if I stayed, we could have gone to the mall like we were talking about or we could have spent more time in the tree house or maybe we could have even kissed more, but looking back from where I am now, that all seems pointless. Maybe, if I had stayed, all of those things would have happened, and maybe we would have had one of those stupid middle school relationships that just lasted a summer, and then maybe when we had run into each other at the beginning of this semester it would have been too awkward for us to be friends. Maybe I wouldn't have even come back to California."

Morgan shifted closer, patiently waiting for him to continue.

"I think leaving ended up being really important for me in the long run. I mean, I had abandonment issues because of my father, and I think that me leaving you—not because I wanted to, but because I was scared—showed me how people don't always leave because they don't care about you anymore. It's why my father and I have the relationship we do today. Which, admittedly, isn't anything to write home about, but we both try and that's what matters. That summer I also told Michael I had feelings for him and he turned me down because I was thirteen and he was in his twenties, and if that hadn't happened I don't think I would be so close with him and Ian right now. That summer—the time with you and the time spent away from you—all of it was a huge learning experience for me, and I know for sure now that I don't want to run away again."

Morgan was staring at him. Embarrassed, Leo raised his pretzel to his mouth and took another bite, chewing as he waited for a response.

It took a while, but eventually Morgan laughed and said, "I think that was the most I've ever heard you say before."

Leo shrugged.

"I get it, though. Looking back, that summer was a turning point for me, too. You know, I came out to my parents then. They didn't understand why I was so upset about you leaving, and I told them it was because I had a crush on you."

"You're welcome?" Leo said. Morgan chuckled and looked at him with an expression Leo could only describe as fond. Flustered, Leo tried a subtle conversation change. "You know, I never actually came out to my mom."

Morgan finished his pretzel. "No?"

"No. I brought my first boyfriend home one day and introduced him to her. She looked surprised for about three seconds, and then went on like she had known all along."

"You wouldn't have wanted her to make a big deal out of it, right? That's not really you."

"It's not," Leo agreed. There was a minute of silence in which Leo finished his pretzel and Morgan shifted as if there was something he wanted to say and feared he couldn't.

"What is it?" Leo asked when it became clear he wouldn't get there on his own. "You know you can tell me anything."

Morgan chuckled awkwardly. "It's not like I have a secret or anything. I'm curious about your boyfriends, I guess."

"My boyfriends?" Leo repeated, eyebrows drawing together. "Why?"

"Well, you know all about my ex-boyfriend. I want to know about yours."

"My boyfriends weren't important, though. I didn't love them or anything. I dated them because they wanted to date me and I felt uncomfortable saying no," Leo admitted.

The look on Morgan's face was one of skepticism. "They weren't important, but you took one of them to meet your mother?"

"They both met my mother," Leo grumbled.

"*I* haven't even met your mother," Morgan pointed out, sounding genuinely upset.

Leo's eyebrows drew together. "Do you *want* to meet my mother?"

"*Yes*," he said, like it was very important to him. "She raised you. I'd love to meet her."

"Oh. Well, don't judge your importance to me on the basis of whether you've met my mother. She's kind of far away. We can video chat, if you'd like."

"I would," said Morgan, beaming. It was the happiest Leo had seen him look since things between him and Drew started getting shaky. "I'd like that a lot."

Even when their car pulled up, Leo couldn't pull his eyes away from Morgan's smile.

Chapter Thirty-Five

Sloan

Two weeks ago, Sloan finally became free.

That's what he kept telling himself about his breakup with Drew. It wasn't a separation, but an escape. He was free.

Most of the time, he actually felt free. He could watch shark movies in bed and not get yelled at. He could wear his pajamas all day on Thursdays when he didn't have class and no one would tell him off for being lazy. On the days that he had his study group, there was no one to imply he just wasn't trying hard enough.

Best of all, though, was that he could spend all the time he wanted with Leo without feeling guilty. When he was around Leo, he felt like he could smile and laugh more easily. When they were together, Sloan was happy.

His feelings for Leo had grown since he no longer felt the need to hold them in, though he sometimes still had his doubts about Leo's feelings toward him. It was probably ridiculous, thinking that Leo didn't like him. He could see it in the way Leo looked at him. Still, it was impossible not to think sometimes that Leo was just trying to be a good friend and he wasn't pulling away from Sloan's touches because he didn't want to hurt him after everything with Drew. How could someone like Leo realistically have feelings for someone like him? If he really was as worthless as Drew said he was, how could Leo possibly—

Fucking Drew. Sloan was frustrated with himself for letting the man still control the way he thought.

It wasn't something he was able to just turn off, and he found Drew's words coming back to him frequently.

That morning, when he took his seat beside Colette in chemistry, he was thinking about how Drew always told him he looked pale in the light green shirt he was wearing, and how his glasses didn't suit him. It was making self-consciousness rise within him as he worried that maybe Drew had been right.

"Hey," Colette greeted, turning away from Justin to look at him. She was smiling, but it dropped slightly when she saw him.

Oh god, Sloan thought. *I really must look terrible.*

"You alright?" asked Justin.

Sloan thought he was being a little straightforward, asking if he was alright because of how he was dressed. He looked down at his shirt. "Why wouldn't I be?"

"Because you look like you're going to be sick."

"Oh." Sloan relaxed slightly. "I'm fine. Just overthinking like usual. Other than that, do I look okay? Like, my outfit."

Eyebrows raised, Colette looked him up and down, then shrugged. "You look cute. I love when you wear your glasses."

He sighed in relief. "Thanks. Drew would have hated me wearing this, so I feel uncomfortable in it. I was even considering running back to my dorm between classes to change before political science."

"Because of Leo?" asked Colette.

Justin laughed. "I'm pretty sure you could wear anything, and I mean absolutely *anything,* and Leo would still only look at you."

Sloan's face grew hot, though he had to admit the words pleased him.

***

They had a quiz in bio. Even though Colette and Justin completed theirs long before him, Sloan felt incredibly proud when he wasn't the last one to turn in his paper and got to leave ten minutes early. When he arrived at his political science classroom and saw that Leo was already there, he was even more pleased.

Leo was sitting on a bench outside of the room, playing on his phone. It must have been a decent distraction, because he didn't give Sloan his attention until he had sat beside him and reached out to touch his elbow.

Leo appeared startled but relaxed quickly. "Morgan."

"I thought you had class right before this," Sloan said.

"I usually do. It got canceled today. How'd your quiz go?"

Sloan was happy he'd remembered. "It went well, I think. I finished early, so that's something."

"That's good," Leo said, his eyes leaving Sloan's face for just a moment to flick down over his body. The glance made Sloan shift nervously as he thought about Drew's opinions.

"Ah, hey …" He cringed at how obvious his anxiety was. "Can I ask you a question?"

"Alright."

"Just promise me you'll be honest, even if it hurts my feelings."

Leo agreed immediately. When Sloan hesitated, Leo added, "Don't be worried. I won't hurt your feelings."

Sloan shook his head. "No, I need you to tell me the truth."

"I will," Leo promised. "But it's not going to hurt your feelings."

"I haven't even asked the question yet. How do you know your answer won't hurt my feelings?"

Leo smiled. "Because I think nothing negative about you, so no matter what you ask, you're going to get a positive answer." He said this with confidence, and Sloan's heart pounded. He wondered if Drew ever, in their year together, said anything that nice to him.

"So, what's your question?"

"Oh, um." Staring down at the front of his shirt, Sloan asked, "I was wondering if I look bad in this color?" When he didn't receive a response right away, he lifted his head to find Leo squinting him. "What?"

"Uh... light gray?" Leo asked with little confidence.

"What?" Grabbing a fistful of his shirt with his left hand, Sloan pulled the fabric away from his chest. "My shirt," he clarified. "It's green." All expression dropped off Leo's face. "You think this is gray?"

Leo said nothing right away, just stared at the front of his shirt intensely. Then he lifted his gaze to meet Sloan's eyes. "I'm colorblind, so that's not really a fair question, is it?"

This information was new to Sloan, and it took him a little while to process it. By the time he was speaking again, people from the class before theirs were leaving the lecture hall. "I didn't know that about you." They held eye contact for what felt like a long time. Sloan laughed. "You're red-green colorblind."

"Yes," Leo confirmed, smiling. "I can't see the color of your bedding, either." Recalling how he made such a big deal out of the color in the store, Sloan laughed a little harder. Leo's eyes rolled, though his smile stayed in place.

"Oh gosh, I'm so sorry," Sloan offered, raising a hand to cover his mouth.

"It's fine. It's not like it's a sore subject or anything. I'm not offended that you think it's funny."

"I don't think you being colorblind is funny," Sloan said, reaching out to place his palm on Leo's forearm. Brown eyes flickered down to look where their skin touched. He didn't say anything about it, so Sloan didn't pull away. "I'm thinking about your face when I said my shirt was green."

Leo hummed. "Well, I think you look nice today, even if I can't see the color of your shirt. Green is your favorite color, right?"

Sloan wondered how to express himself. Should he be flustered by the compliment or pleased that Leo remembered his favorite color? His face felt hot. "It is." He dropped his hand from Leo's arm, letting it rest on the seat between them. Even though the classroom was empty now, neither of them made a move to enter.

"What's green like?" Leo asked, watching the hand as Sloan absently tapped his fingers.

Frowning, he answered, "It's like grass and leaves—"

"No," Leo interrupted, raising his head. He looked conflicted, and Sloan wondered if it was because of his answer. "Not, what are things that are green. I already know. I mean, what is green *like*? What does it make you think of?"

"Oh." It took some consideration. He'd never thought of it that way before. "Well, I think light green looks like the taste of mint. Like, the mint that makes your mouth feel really cold if you drink water after."

"And dark green?"

"I think of it as like . . . the smell of freshly cut grass or herbs. The taste of basil," Sloan said. "That probably isn't helpful, huh? When you think of those things, you probably already have colors they bring to mind."

Leo didn't deny Sloan's words. All he said was, "It's interesting," with his eyes directed down as if he was trying to imagine it. It was cute, the focused expression on his face, and Sloan watched until he missed the sound of Leo's voice.

"Hey," he started, knocking their shoulders together. "We should stay up and watch shitty movies all night."

"We can try," Leo agreed. The suggestion didn't seem to surprise him, probably because that was how they spent the last weekend as well. It was better than going to a party, in Sloan's—and Leo's, he was pretty sure—opinion. "You know I'm not good at staying up late."

"I do," Sloan agreed. He wondered if it was the right time to tell Leo the reason he loved movie nights so much was because there was almost a guarantee that, by the end, Leo would be using him as a pillow. "That's okay. You can stay over."

Leo didn't meet Sloan's eyes. Sloan figured he was thinking about the intimate way they slept together.

Since Leo still hadn't responded to him, Sloan continued. "How about we order Chinese food?"

Their classmates were arriving steadily then. Leo looked kind of anxious as he watched them, as if he worried someone would break routine and take their seats. "I like that idea," he said. "After class, should we get lunch in the cafeteria?"

Sloan chewed his lip. Ever since the breakup, he had been avoiding going out for lunch, afraid he would bump into Drew. Leo was finally looking at him then, his expression unusually open and hopeful. *It's fine,* Sloan thought. *Drew never eats there. And even if he does today, Leo will be with me.* "Yeah. We can get lunch."

This made Leo smile, and before Sloan could react to the fluttering of his heart, it just beat faster when Leo reached over and took his hand. "Come on," he urged, squeezing Sloan's fingers. "We'll be late."

Maybe, Sloan realized as he rose, Leo hadn't looked nervous about them possibly losing their seats but over taking his hand.

Sloan was expecting it to be just the two of them for lunch, but when they arrived at the cafeteria, Kennedy, Oliver, Justin, and Colette were there. At first, he was nervous, though after about ten minutes of sitting with them, he realized no one had brought up Drew yet because they weren't going to. He relaxed, letting himself laugh and talk like usual among his friends.

"So, you two are officially together, then?" Oliver asked Colette and Justin.

"Yeah," Colette confirmed. She looked happy, as did Justin. Sloan was glad. "We thought it made sense." Her gaze moved to Sloan. She raised her eyebrows in a taunting way, probably thinking about him and Leo. After rolling his eyes at her, he shifted his attention to the boy sitting on his left.

Leo was looking down at his phone beneath the table. Before Sloan could ask, Leo nudged him with his elbow and tilted the screen toward him. Sloan squinted to read what was there.

Mom: How's your day going so far?

Leo: Fine.

Mom: How very descriptive of you. What are you doing right now?

Leo: Getting lunch.

Mom: With your friends?

Leo: Yes.

Mom: Is Morgan there?

Leo: Yes.

Mom: Tell him I said hello!

Smiling, Sloan said, "Say hi for me." The day before, Leo had gone over to Sloan's room and they had video called his mother. It had been enjoyable, though somewhat surprising. Sloan was expecting the woman who raised Leo to be more like him. In reality, she actually reminded him more of Lizzy, comfortable with conversation and unafraid to say what she was thinking, often embarrassing her son.

"Alright," Leo said, typing the message—*Morgan says hello as well*—into his phone. As he did this, a new text came through.

Mom: I'm preparing a care package for you and I'll be shipping it out later today

Before Leo could even send what he'd been typing, a notification for another message dropped at the top of the screen.

Lizzy: Why did I just watch mom put condoms in a box addressed to you?

Beside him, Leo's body tensed. Unable to help himself, Sloan laughed, pressing his forehead against Leo's shoulder as he tried to gather himself.

"What'd we miss?" Justin asked.

Knowing that sharing the contents of the most recent message would only mortify Leo further, Sloan lifted his head and answered, "Nothing." His uninjured hand found Leo's below the table.

No one looked as if they believed him, but that was fine. He didn't care if they knew he was lying or if they thought he should already have fixed what Drew broke in him, or if his shirt made him look pale, because Leo's palm turned against his and their fingers slotted together perfectly. That was all that mattered to him right then.

CHAPTER THIRTY-SIX

LEO

When Leo said he would stay over in Morgan's room Friday night, he meant *only* Friday night. Somehow, he ended up spending the entire weekend there, sharing Morgan's bed Saturday and Sunday night as well. While it was nice sleeping with Morgan pressed against his back, his heartbeat gently pounding against the skin between Leo's shoulder blades, it had been only a few weeks since Morgan got out of his yearlong relationship with Drew. If he ended up regretting anything that happened between them because he wasn't ready, Leo didn't know what he'd do. He liked Morgan far too much to rush things.

On Monday morning, when Leo was awoken by Morgan's 8:15 alarm, he felt Morgan behind him, plastered to his back. It was incredibly comfortable, a little warm and *maybe* too intimate for their relationship. Still, he didn't want Morgan to pull away yet. It would be great if he skipped his first class and held Leo until they both had to get up for their 9:30. This was a thought he only indulged for a minute before shutting off the alarm and reaching back to push at Morgan's shoulder. "Get up," he instructed, only to receive a groan of protest. "Morgan, you're going to be late."

"A few more minutes," Morgan argued into Leo's neck, making his toes curl. The arm around Leo's waist pulled tighter and Leo thought, *Well, I tried.* The mentality was short-lived. In good conscience, he could not let Morgan sleep through his alarm, knowing that he'd be upset with himself for skipping chemistry again.

"You're gonna sleep through chem and Colette's going to kill you." Leo's eyes cracked open as he waited for Morgan's response.

It took a second, but then Morgan sighed and rolled away. Leo's back felt cold. Morgan's right arm was still trapped under his neck and there was no attempt to remove it. "This is torture. Who thought an 8:30 class was a good idea?"

"It's not so horrible," Leo said with a yawn, rolling onto his back and then sitting up. He looked down at Morgan, who still had his eyes closed, hair sticking up cutely all over the place. "You're just not good at waking up."

"You're not allowed to say that, because we both know you're gonna fall back asleep once I leave," Morgan accused, finally blinking his eyes open. Leo climbed out of bed. "What are you doing?"

That weekend, Morgan's parents had visited, bringing along with them a single-cup coffee maker for the dorm room. Leo went over to the machine, taking a minute to put in the correct amount of coffee grounds and water before pressing the brew button and placing a portable mug beneath the spout. He could feel Morgan's eyes on him through the entire process, and sure enough, when he turned to go back to the bed, tired gray eyes were regarding him thoughtfully. "I solved all your problems," Leo said, standing at the bed's edge and holding a hand out for Morgan to take. "Come on, now."

Grinning, Morgan sat up, grabbing Leo's hand with his left and climbing out of bed. "Lie back down," he said, giving Leo a quick hug before moving to his dresser. "I don't care if you stay until you have class."

"Thanks." Leo climbed back into bed. He watched Morgan gather his things from his closet, reaching up to the top shelf to grab his toothbrush from its holder. Beside it, in the same cup, Leo could see his own toothbrush and felt oddly embarrassed. He shut his eyes.

There was the sound of the door opening and closing and coffee being brewed.

He must have drifted back to sleep in the time it took Morgan to change, because he was startled awake what felt like seconds later by the creak of the door opening. "Did you fall back asleep?" Morgan asked. "I didn't mean to wake you."

"It's okay."

Morgan went to the coffee maker on his desk. He grabbed the travel mug and screwed on the top.

"See you in polisci?" Leo mumbled.

Morgan paused with only one foot in a white sneaker. "It got canceled, remember?"

"Why are college classes always canceled?" Leo asked, pressing his face into his pillow. "I actually enjoy going to class."

"It's not college classes that always get canceled, just *your* college classes. Because you're lucky."

"We're both in political science," Leo pointed out. "But yeah, my classes get canceled a lot."

There was a hum, and then, "I'm getting lunch with Colette and Kennedy if you want to come along."

"I'll let you know. I might end up doing homework through lunch. I kind of slacked off this weekend." He also thought it was good for Morgan to get back to doing things with friends other than him, though he didn't say it out loud. "See you after?"

"For sure," Morgan agreed.

Leo rolled onto his back as Morgan pulled his backpack on. "Do you want to do your homework in here over lunch? I'll leave you my key."

As if you ever lock your door, Leo thought, amused.

Morgan continued. "It'll probably be quieter than your dorm, and you'd end up coming over anyway after I get back."

Leo agreed sleepily and Sloan hung the lanyard with his room key over the doorknob. "You're going to be late."

"Yeah, yeah, get some more sleep." Morgan smiled at him one last time before slipping from the room.

It didn't take Leo long to obey, still surrounded by the smell of Morgan's body wash on his sheets. Right before he fell asleep, he had a fleeting thought of how much better it would be if he weren't in bed alone.

When Leo checked his phone after getting out of class at 3:30, he saw he had a text.

Morgan: I forgot to mention that Professor Larson said we had to pick our quizzes up in her office so I'm gonna do that right after class at 4:30. I'll be over after

Leo didn't respond. They both knew he would not protest.

He went back to his dorm to wait, startling the two boys in there when he opened the door. They were under Justin's loft, Justin at his desk and Max sitting on the ground next to him with his back against the drawers. Pinched between his fingers was a joint. "Hello," Max greeted, passing the weed to Justin and climbing to his feet. He went to open the window.

"You still live here?" Justin asked.

Leo ignored him, dropping his backpack by his desk. He unzipped the front pocket to remove his toothbrush, placing it back into the cup on the desktop.

Justin noticed. "Not having a sleepover again tonight?"

"Morgan has lab with you at eight tomorrow," Leo reminded. "It'll be easier for me to sleep here since I don't have to leave until ten. He'll be coming over when he's done with class tonight, so it's not like we won't see each other."

"Morgan?" Max sounded confused. He had taken a seat on the futon beneath the open window.

"That's Sloan's first name, apparently," Justin explained.

Leo sat on the futon beside Max, leaving a few feet of space between them.

"Why is he coming over here?" asked Justin.

Leo was reading a missed text from his sister, so he gave a distracted answer. "Watching movies is more comfortable on the futon." Leo didn't mention that if he spent the evening in Morgan's room, he was almost positive he'd end up falling asleep there again.

"Right," Justin began, sounding amused. "*Watching movies.*" Confused, Leo lifted his gaze from his phone, a frown on his face. Beside him, Max let out a small chuckle. "That means you need us to clear out for a while, right?"

"What?"

Max spoke next, delaying Justin from answering. "We told Jared we would meet him in the library."

"Ah, fuck," Justin groaned, taking another hit. They were ignoring him. Leo found it annoying.

"What do you mean?" he asked again. Both boys turned to him, neither seeming to know what he was referring to. "Why would you need to clear out?"

"The rule, man," Justin answered, as if this explained anything. It did not, and Leo made this known with a blank look directed at his roommate. "Damn. I mean, so we're not in the way when you two are going at it, which I sincerely hope is what you've been doing, because what *else* could you be doing with all the time you spend together?"

Surprised by this accusation, Leo's eyebrows raised. "We hang out. Eat, sleep, watch movies, talk, do homework. I don't know." He shrugged. "Is that what you and Colette do when you spend time together? Have sex?"

Justin didn't answer, only sighed and took another hit as Max laughed. "Justin is getting *no* action. Your friend Colette wants to wait until they know it's serious to do anything."

"Which is fine," Justin grumbled.

There was a pause. "So, are you and Sloan dating then?" Max asked, putting his head back against the futon and closing his eyes.

"We're not."

That got Justin's attention. "You're not even dating?"

"He just got out of a relationship," Leo reminded. Justin scoffed. Max had no reaction to the conversation, despite being the one to start it. "What? He did."

"First off, it's been long enough that it doesn't quite qualify as a *just* anymore. Second, you guys are practically already dating. You spend all your time together, you eat almost all of your meals together, and you sleep in the same bed that is only meant to fit one of you. I know he got out of a shit relationship recently, but the hard part after that is usually emotionally committing and opening up to someone after the last person destroyed you, and he's already done that with you. The only thing left for you guys is to kiss and have sex, and that's the easy part," said Justin.

Unsure of what to say to this, Leo shook his head and looked back down at his phone. All of that made sense and, Leo had to admit, they were acting rather couple-like. Still, that didn't really matter. As Leo saw it, he had no control over his and Morgan's relationship. It was all up to Morgan, and Leo was fine as long as he was happy.

"Hey," Max said on an exhale. "Can I ask you something?"

Leo and Justin exchanged a glance, and then Justin pointed out, "Your eyes are closed, man. We don't know who you're talking to."

"Leo," Max clarified.

"You can ask me something," Leo allowed.

Max didn't open his eyes. His lips parted, then closed after only a sigh left them. He seemed frustrated. "I don't really know how to phrase what I'm trying to ask, so I'll just say it. I've been wondering recently, with everything going on between the two of you, if I ever had a chance?" His eyes cracked open in time to catch Leo's surprised reaction before he tamed it to something indifferent.

Leo didn't even have to think about the answer. Still, he didn't respond right away, searching Max's face. It was something he'd easily be able to lie about, and if he thought that would make Max feel better, he would. He was pretty sure Max already knew the answer, though. If he lied, Max would know, and the knowledge that Leo tried to lie to make him feel better would probably do the opposite.

"Max . . ." Justin began. "I don't—"

"No," Leo interrupted. Max nodded in acceptance. "In any other situation you would have, but the second I saw him again, it was over for anyone else. I was just pretending it wasn't. I'm sorry."

"Ahh, don't do that," Max insisted, dropping his head again. "You can't control your feelings, so don't be sorry for them."

Leo slid his gaze to Justin, who looked back with wide eyes, as if he couldn't believe they were discussing this in front of him. "Hey!" he exclaimed after a moment of silence. "Don't look so bummed, man. You got Kennedy, and she is *way* hotter than Leo."

It hadn't occurred to Leo that Max's reaction was *bummed*. Max chuckled, shaking his head. "Kennedy isn't a romantic interest. She's as big of a mess as I am. We're just friends who fuck."

There was an uncomfortable second as they all thought about this vulgar statement. Justin took the last hit from his joint and put it out on his desk. "Well, at least you're getting laid."

By the time Morgan was knocking on his door, Max and Justin had left for the library. Leo was relieved by this, both because he enjoyed his time alone with Morgan, and because he feared it would be insensitive to flaunt whatever it was they had in front of Max after their conversation.

He pulled open the door, the word *hello* on the tip of his tongue. The only thing he got out was "Hel—" before Morgan thrust a piece of paper at his face. With raised eyebrows, Leo took it from him. It was a biology quiz. Everything was correct.

"Good job," he praised, shutting the door without looking up from the paper, scanning the answers as if he understood any of it. Morgan threw himself onto the futon and pulled his legs up when Leo went to sit, only to stretch them out across his lap. "God, though. Your handwriting with your left is atrocious."

"Right?" Morgan agreed with a laugh. "I wonder if all of them are actually right, or if she just couldn't read my handwriting and assumed."

Leo dropped his hand onto Morgan's leg and lightly squeezed. "Nah, I'm sure they're right. Does it feel as good as you thought it would?"

"Hmmm." Morgan sat up, leaning forward so his chest pressed against Leo's side. He was so close that Leo could feel his breath on the side of his neck. "Even better," Morgan said, a pretty smile on his face. "Did Justin mention how he did?"

"No, but he was stoned," Leo answered, dropping the perfect quiz on the legs in his lap, more interested in the boy beside him.

Morgan chuckled, reaching out with his left hand to pick it up.

"Do you have any homework you need to do?" Leo asked.

"Yes," Morgan admitted. "But nothing is due tomorrow, so I stopped by my room and left my backpack. It can all get done later. Right now, let's watch a stupid movie to celebrate."

Leo agreed, patting Morgan's knee as a gesture for him to move. When he did, Leo rose and went to get his laptop from his backpack.

"Oh, when I was getting my quiz, I talked to my professor for a bit and I think I've decided to drop my major," Morgan said.

Leo glanced over his shoulder at this, his hands pausing on the zipper of his backpack. "Yeah?"

"Yeah," said Morgan, looking back with a grin. Mirroring the expression, Leo pulled out his computer. As he returned to the futon, Morgan continued. "It's just not for me. I'm still gonna work my ass off to get a good grade in the class—or as good as I can get at this point. That way, I know I'm dropping not because I can't do it but because I don't want to."

"I think that's a good plan," Leo said, sitting to Morgan's left and setting his laptop on the ottoman. "So, what are we watching?"

The answer, unsurprisingly, was a somehow overrated shark movie—it only had one star, and Leo was confused which part of the film proved it worthy of even that. Thankfully, the worse the movie, the more Morgan laughed, and Leo welcomed the sound, smiling to himself every time it graced him. It made the film bearable.

About an hour in, the ringing of Morgan's phone interrupted them. Leo actually felt grateful for the opportunity to take a break from the film, but Morgan was quick to apologize, frantically trying to free his cell from his pocket to turn it off.

"It's alright," Leo assured, leaning forward to pause the movie. "Answer it. I don't mind."

There was a moment in which Morgan just looked at him, visibly relaxing as he did. Leo wondered how big of a deal Drew made it when Morgan's phone interrupted them. "Um." Morgan checked his phone. "It's my mom. I'll be quick."

True to his word, it was only about a minute before Morgan said, "Hey, Mom, can I call you later? I'm kind of in the middle of something." She must have agreed, because Morgan smiled and laughed at something she had to say before dropping his phone into his lap.

"How's your mom?" Leo asked. When Morgan's parents came to visit, he sadly hadn't gotten to see them.

"She's alright."

"I haven't seen her in years. Maybe we should visit sometime—"

Morgan interrupted. "Leo, can I just—" He cut off, looking frustrated. Before Leo could ask what was wrong, Morgan leaned forward and closed the distance between them, bringing their lips together for the first time in five years.

Leo froze in shock, his body tensing. He could feel Morgan's lips shifting against his, but he didn't respond right away, too startled and confused. Before he could gather himself, Morgan pulled away, his eyes wide.

"Oh god," he said. "I'm so sorry."

Leo didn't answer, just blinked and watched as Morgan stood and moved toward the door.

"Please forget I did that."

It occurred to Leo that Morgan was going to leave, and he snapped out of his daze. "Wait," he said, rising quickly and throwing himself toward the door as Morgan got his hand on the knob. Less than graceful, he slammed into it. The force made him groan. "Hey, I said wait for a second."

"Are you okay?" Morgan asked, moving his left hand from the knob to touch Leo's shoulder. "You didn't have to—"

"I did," Leo disagreed. "You were going to leave." He took a moment before speaking again, staring at Morgan's chest to avoid any regret or doubt he might see in his eyes. "Why'd you kiss me?"

The hand on his shoulder dropped. "Leo . . ."

"I didn't not kiss you back because I'm not interested," Leo assured. His heart was beating fast. His lips tingled. "I was surprised, is all."

A heavy sigh of relief left Morgan, and he folded forward as if he was suddenly too tired to hold his body up, his head coming to rest on Leo's shoulder and arms making their way around his waist. "You scared me."

"I'm sorry," Leo mumbled, hugging Morgan back. "I didn't mean to."

"I just like you so much," Morgan confessed, raising his head to meet his eyes. "Can I try again?"

Yes, Leo wanted to say immediately. *We can do it as many times as you want.* Despite his desire, he wondered if maybe that wasn't for the best. "Are you sure that's a good idea? You haven't been single for long. I want you to be ready before anything happens between us."

Morgan's eyes remained focused on his, his gaze intense. "Is it okay if I kiss you again?" he repeated.

Leo wondered if he had even been listening to his concerns.

"I don't know if it's still too soon, but I need to know what it's like," Morgan said.

Leo thought about it and realized there was no way he could say no to that. He took a little longer before answering, though, preparing himself for the long-awaited press of lips.

When he finally agreed, dropping his head in a brief nod, he was expecting Morgan to hurry to kiss him again, to rush in his eagerness. Instead, he gave Leo a soft smile and raised his left hand to Leo's face, guiding him closer. *Ah*, Leo thought as their lips finally met. *So this is what it feels like to kiss the person you're in love with.*

His heart hammered so heavily that he felt slightly dizzy. Still, he didn't pull away.

It was so different from the kisses he'd shared with others.

The way Morgan held him was different. Close, as if he was worried Leo would slip away. How his entire body felt hot was different, starting at his lips and spreading all the way to his toes. The way he yearned for more was different.

It was different because he had absolutely no doubts about the boy kissing him.

Morgan's fingers curled in the back of his shirt as his teeth teased Leo's bottom lip, tongue soothing over the skin when he nipped a little too hard.

Morgan pulled back then, breathing heavily as he pressed his forehead against Leo's. "God," he groaned. "I feel selfish because you deserve so much better than me, but I couldn't help myself."

Cracking his eyes open, Leo was unsurprised to find Morgan already staring back. "That's impossible," Leo insisted, his hands coming to rest on either side of Morgan's face. "You're the best I could ever ask for."

Sighing softly, Morgan pressed forward to kiss him again. It was brief, but it left a sweet taste in Leo's month.

"Come on," Morgan encouraged, gripping Leo's hand. His eyes were very bright. "Let's finish the movie."

Chapter Thirty-Seven

Leo

Five years ago

Leo was reading on the porch when Morgan walked over to get him. He hadn't noticed him at first, too busy pretending not to hear his sister as she pleaded to let her join them that afternoon, so he startled when Lizzy called out, "Hi, Morgan!"

Lifting his head, Leo watched Morgan come up the walkway toward them.

"Leo—" Lizzy started to say.

"No," he interrupted.

Huffing, she stomped up the porch steps and went into the house. Morgan's eyebrows raised. "Is she okay?"

"Don't worry about it. Do you have any homework?"

"Not today! I didn't even need to take my backpack out of the car. You've got me all afternoon." That didn't help Leo with his heartbeat, and he found it difficult to fight back the heat that rose to his face.

Overwhelmed, he spat out the first thing that came to mind. "My sister wants to hang out with us."

Morgan frowned. "Oh? Do you want her to?"

"I mean, no, but if you do—"

"Nah," Morgan interrupted before he could get too far. "I'd rather have you to myself. Should we go back to my house?"

Leo nodded and folded his book closed.

As they walked, Morgan talked about his day at school and how excited he was for summer to come. Leo was also eager for this, though he didn't say so. He hummed to make it known he was listening while trying hard not to focus on Morgan's hand brushing against his with each step. Was it purposeful? He couldn't tell. Every time it happened, he glanced at the blond from the corner of his eye for some sign that he even noticed the contact, to no avail. Morgan seemed completely unaffected.

They went inside Morgan's house. Back home, Leo didn't have many friends, none whose houses he had gone to before, so he still felt a little awkward there, unsure of how to act. He settled for silently following behind his friend, bidding Morgan's mother hello when she said it to him first and pausing only to give their old dog a pat on their way out the back.

As soon as the door closed behind them, Morgan reached over to grab Leo's hand and pulled him along. He was talking about summer again, though that wasn't surprising. It came up in most of their conversations, since it was finally close enough to taste. Every day, the list of things they were going to do with their free time got a little longer.

At that very moment, Morgan was suggesting they go to a water park one day. Leo didn't particularly like water parks—that was more up his sister's alley—but he thought it might be okay if Morgan was there with him, leading him around by the hand. Really, anything sounded bearable if Morgan was holding his hand.

"Summer is going to be so fun this year," Morgan continued, dropping Leo's hand to climb the ladder to the tree house. "What do you really want to do? I feel like we only talk about what I wanna do."

"I'm not particular," Leo reminded, waiting until Morgan was almost to the top before following behind him. "Also, I wonder how much of that stuff we're actually going to get done. Most of them are kind of far away and we can't drive."

When he got up to the tree house, Morgan lay down on his back. "My mom doesn't work. She can take us places," he said.

Leo sat beside him.

"Where do you want to go?" Morgan asked again.

"I don't know. Somewhere quiet. Where there's not many people." Morgan turned his head to look at him. "I don't have anywhere in mind, I guess. I just don't like places with a lot of people." He clasped his fingers in his lap and twisted them nervously.

"Okay," Morgan agreed, voice quiet. "I think I'd like that. It'd be nice if we could go by ourselves, wouldn't it? My mom worries too much, though."

Leo imagined it again, Morgan leading him by the hand, only now when he pictured it, it wasn't through a noisy water park but somewhere they could be alone together. "It would be nice."

For a little while, they were silent, just listening to the sound of the leaves rustling in the light breeze. The boards beneath them creaked as Morgan rolled onto his side toward him. "Hey," he began, sounding tentative, as if he wasn't fully committed to the conversation he was starting. "Can I talk to you about something?" He seemed nervous but serious, and it was rare for Morgan to be serious.

"Yeah," Leo answered, lips pulling down. "Are you alright?"

"Yeah," Morgan said, propping his elbow up and resting his head in his hand. "Sorry. It's nothing bad. I just . . . I've been thinking lately, and I think that maybe I'm like you."

Leo didn't say anything right away, trying to decipher what Morgan was telling him. When he came up empty, he asked, "You're like me? Like me how?"

"Uh." Morgan's eyes averted. "I think I might like boys, is what I mean." Shocked, Leo said nothing, watching with wide eyes as Morgan's throat bobbed with a swallow. "Is that okay?"

"Of course it's okay," Leo said. Morgan looked back at him, and Leo wondered if he maybe came off too eager. It was his turn to look away. "I mean, you can like whoever you want."

There was movement to his right, and he turned his head as Morgan sat up. His blond hair was a mess. He kept it long and untamed. It was cute, Leo thought, which was weird, because until this point, the only person he had ever been attracted to was Michael Bradford, who was the exact opposite of *untamed*.

As if Leo wasn't already shaken enough, the next words out of Morgan's mouth shocked him all over again. "Have you had your first kiss yet?"

"What? No," he responded, feeling embarrassed. *Who would want to kiss me?*

"I haven't either," Morgan admitted. The expression he was wearing right then was familiar. It was the one he wore when he was about to do something impulsive, something that his mother would frown upon. He wore it when he convinced Leo to sleep in the tree house, and again when they went to the ice cream shop down the street and he'd ordered an entire pint instead of the scoop he was supposed to. "Can I kiss you?"

There was no way he heard that right. "What?"

"Well, my friend Nicole wanted to have her first kiss, so she asked my friend Keller to kiss her, so I thought maybe it was normal. I won't if you don't want me to. I just thought that it might be easier to do with you because you like boys too," Morgan explained, leaning toward him a little. "Aren't you curious?"

"Um . . ." If he was being honest, he wasn't. Or, he hadn't been until thirty seconds ago when Morgan asked to kiss him. "Well, maybe a little, but don't you think your first kiss should be with someone you like?"

Sounding put out and clearly trying to hide it, Morgan asked, "Are you thinking about that Michael guy?"

"No," Leo said. It was the truth. He didn't think about Michael often when he was with Morgan. "I'm not thinking about him, I'm just—"

"Nervous?" Morgan leaned even closer to him, his eyes dropping to look at his mouth. "Can I try?"

No, Leo thought. *We're friends and both boys and your parents might see us from the kitchen window.* He didn't say no. Instead, he swallowed heavily and nodded. "Sure."

"Really?" Morgan looked delighted. He sat up straighter, leaning so his shoulder pressed into Leo's. Their faces turned toward one another. "Okay. Um, close your eyes." Sighing softly, Leo obeyed.

He had seen enough movies to know what came next, but the gentle press of warmth against his mouth and the effect it had on him still surprised him. It felt like everything had stopped.

All day, Leo had been hot. He had spent his afternoon on the porch in the sunlight, reading as the temperature rose. That didn't even compare to the warmth he felt right then. Kissing Morgan brought on a different heat, like a fire that sparked inside his chest and spread throughout his body. *This is what it feels like to be so close to him.*

Leo was afraid.

Their kiss didn't last long, only a matter of seconds. They stared at each other silently once they pulled away. As always, it was Morgan who smiled first, breaking the tension with a cheerful laugh. "That was kind of nice, wasn't it?" he asked, grinning.

Leo pressed his lips together and cleared his throat. "Yeah."

The rest of the evening was normal, but Leo couldn't stop thinking about it. Every time Morgan laughed, Leo's eyes were drawn to his lips. Every time Morgan smiled, his eyes focused in on his lips. Every time Morgan so much as *breathed,* Leo looked at his lips. It wasn't with a desire to kiss him again, just more of an awareness that it was possible to kiss him because he *had.*

More than anything, Leo wanted to act normally. He wanted to look at Morgan like he always had, but it was impossible. He already knew what it felt like to kiss him and knowing while he was so close was too much to bear.

***

The next morning, Leo watched from the living room window as Morgan climbed into his mother's car to go to school. As soon as the car was down the street, he was out the front door with his suitcase. He had called his mother the night before and, after a fair amount of pleading, she agreed to get him a last-minute ticket to Illinois.

He was going home.

His father drove him to the airport and helped him get checked in, walking him all the way to security where they were forced to part. Very few words had been exchanged, so it surprised Leo when he went to leave and his father reached out to grab his arm. "Dad?"

"I just wanted to say sorry. For whatever I did wrong. I'm sorry for making you want to leave."

There was a pinching feeling in his chest. He swallowed hard. Over the past couple of weeks, Leo had noticed the obvious similarities in personality between him and his father. He now understood that his father, like him, tended to leave things unsaid. His actually addressing the issue made it nearly impossible for Leo to ignore how hurt his dad was by Leo's sudden decision to leave. "I'm not going back because of you, Dad."

"Is it because of Meredith? I thought you got along with her well enough," his father said, eyebrows drawing together in concern.

"It wasn't her, either."

"Did something happen with that friend of yours? The Sloans are good people. If something happened, I'm sure we can work it out with his parents," his father offered, looking hopeful.

Leo averted his eyes and shook his head. "It's something I need to work out on my own, I think. At home."

His father's expression fell in disappointment, but he didn't protest, only nodded and let his arm go. "Alright," was all he said.

As Leo walked to the security line, he considered turning back. His mother would understand. She'd probably actually be happy that he was giving the trip another chance. They could return to his father's house in time for lunch and then, not long after, Morgan would return home . . .

It was the idea of facing Morgan again that pushed him forward.

Right then, he wasn't ready to do anything other than run away.

CHAPTER THIRTY-EIGHT

SLOAN

Sloan got up late on Saturday so, when Leo let himself into his room, he only had on a button-down shirt and a gray pair of boxer briefs. The tan shorts he was planning on wearing were in a crumpled pile at his feet.

Leo paused in the open doorway, looking him up and down before shaking his head and stepping the rest of the way inside. When he turned to shut the door, Sloan noticed that Leo's ears were pink. It made him smile.

Things between them were good lately. They'd kissed five days ago and, since then, they hadn't spoken about it, though it was on his mind often. Leo thought about it as well, he was pretty sure, given the way he would catch Leo looking at him.

It was good. The kiss was good and their behavior toward each other was good and the direction they were going in was good as well. Everything was working out.

"I have them," Leo announced, holding up Colette's familiar set of keys as he moved toward Sloan's bed. Ignoring the pants by his feet for a second longer, Sloan watched Leo drop onto his mattress, grinning to himself as he thought, *God, he looks good in red.*

"I thought we were going to stop by her room on our way out this morning and get them," Sloan said. He realized then that he wasn't sure how late he had stayed in bed. "What time is it?"

"We're still on schedule," Leo assured. His voice seemed strange, and Sloan noticed his flush was spreading to his cheeks. Feeling slightly modest over the reaction—which he assumed was because of his lack of clothing—Sloan stepped into his shorts, pulling them up his legs as fast as he could with his left hand, fumbling a bit with the button. The sound of Leo clearing his throat reached him. "Colette ended up staying over with Justin last night."

As he finally got the button of his shorts, Sloan asked, "So they're at that point, huh?" He took a seat on the edge of his bed, holding out his right arm to fix the sleeve of his shirt. Behind him, he could hear Leo shuffle around and then there was a hand on his forearm, palm warm through the fabric. Curious, Sloan turned his head to look at Leo.

"Did you sleep through your alarm?"

"I did not," Sloan denied, reaching out to squeeze Leo's fingers before continuing to roll his right sleeve. "I woke up with my alarm. I just stayed in bed for a while afterward."

A hum left Leo as if he expected this behavior. Otherwise, it wasn't addressed. "When are you going to be ready to go?" As he spoke, Leo reached out to help him roll up his other sleeve without giving him time to try it himself. With the cast it would have been impossible to do on his own, but Sloan would have put on a show of being pathetic if given the opportunity to.

"I'm ready," he said, eyes on Leo's fingers carefully rolling the fabric on his arm. Maybe it was because he had both hands to complete the task, but he was doing a far better job than Sloan had done on his right arm, the folds perfect and flat. It was going to look uneven. Outstretching his right arm so Leo could see the poor job he'd done, he asked, "Would you—"

"I'll fix it," Leo said, finishing the first sleeve just below his elbow before reaching for his other arm, minding the cast. "How has your hand been feeling lately?"

"It's fine," Sloan grumbled. "Doesn't really hurt all that much anymore. Only when it itches so bad that I hit it on things."

With a chuckle and a shake of his head, Leo said, "You really shouldn't do that." He finished Sloan's sleeve, letting his arm drop into his lap. They looked at each other for a moment. Sloan sighed, relaxing against Leo's shoulder.

"You're okay driving?" he asked.

"As long as you tell me where to go, we should be alright."

It would be so easy to say something then that would make Leo flush, something along the lines of *Since we're together, we'll be alright, regardless.*

For the sake of his dignity, he kept his mouth shut.

They drove for about an hour until they found themselves back in the town where they met.

It was kind of weird, sitting in the passenger seat of a car Leo was driving through his hometown. Once upon a time, he'd pictured something like this, back when he was still a kid and hoped Leo would return for another summer when they were in high school and they could go wherever they wanted, just the two of them. His thoughts hadn't done reality justice. Back then, he'd been unable to imagine an older Leo and completely failed to understand how attractive he would look while driving.

Is that weird? Sloan wondered, watching Leo more often than the scenery outside the car. *Why does he look so good?* Maybe it was his relaxed posture. Or maybe it was the way Leo looked when he was in the sun. It was something Sloan saw often but never for this long, so he'd never been able to appreciate the pretty color of Leo's eyes in the warm light. Or maybe, Sloan considered last, Leo looked good doing everything and this wasn't an exception.

It was around lunchtime when they arrived. They went to the sandwich shop in town, the one they'd walked to as kids to get ice cream on an unbearably hot afternoon. The booth they'd used in the back was already occupied, so they took the one behind it. "This is strange," Leo declared, glancing around.

"Yeah," Sloan agreed, unwrapping his sandwich with his left hand. "Who would have thought that we'd come back here together five years later?"

Making a noise of agreement, Leo also unwrapped his food. "I never really thought I'd come back to California. With my dad flying to Illinois to visit, I never thought I'd need to."

"Are you happy you did?" Sloan asked, keeping his eyes down to better hide his disappointment on the off chance the answer was *no*. "You said you wanted a fresh start, right? Did you succeed?"

Leo didn't respond right away. Sloan appreciated that. He liked how Leo thought before speaking. It showed he was being sincere.

"I am happy that I returned," Leo began. "But it's weird. Can I really call it a fresh start if I just fixed what I broke five years ago? When I said I wanted a fresh start, what I really meant was that something was missing from my life and I wanted to leave everything behind and find it, and I think I did that."

Leo looked out the window. "I'm happy here. It's not that I didn't like it back home, or that I don't miss it. I think I always felt indifferent about everything and I didn't want that anymore."

Sloan picked at the paper cup holding his soda. "So, coming here was a good thing?"

"Yeah," Leo confirmed, smiling. He didn't really smile a lot, but he was doing it more often, especially when it was just the two of them together. Sometimes Sloan felt he lived for those moments. "I'm happy I came back."

Finally picking up his sandwich to eat, Sloan said, "I'm glad."

For a couple of minutes, they ate and spoke about regular college topics like homework and their friends' relationships. It was when Leo had finished explaining how things with Max really weren't all that weird when he suddenly fell silent, a conflicted look coming over his face. "Hey," he said, the change in tone of his voice intriguing Sloan enough that he looked up from his almost-finished meal. "How have you been lately? I've been wondering."

This seemed like a strange question, given that he and Leo were together every day. "Um, good? I don't know. Do I seem like I'm not good?"

"No, that's not what I mean." Leo put his sandwich down on the paper wrapper and wiped his mouth with a napkin. "I know you don't want me to pry and I'm not trying to, but you haven't mentioned how you've been feeling about the breakup and everything lately and I just . . . I wanted to make sure you're alright." It was clear Leo was uncomfortable asking this, probably worried about Sloan's boundaries, but he appreciated the question.

"I'm really okay," he said. "Better than I've been in quite some time. I mean, sometimes I catch myself doing something that Drew hated and panic, and whenever I wear something he didn't like, I feel self-conscious, but it's much better than it was before. It's slowly going away, one thing at a time."

"Good." Leo sounded relieved, and Sloan chewed his bottom lip to keep from grinning, wondering how on earth he ended up with someone so amazing. "The things he made you feel bad about are some of my favorite things about you, so I don't want you to not like them about yourself."

Leo resumed eating as if he hadn't just said something incredibly sweet. With an expression that must have been fond if it reflected any of his feelings, Sloan watched him. The silence between them was comfortable, though charged. It stretched out for a few long moments, long enough for Leo to raise his gaze and look at him again.

"Um," Sloan started, dropping his eyes. He could feel that his cheeks were pink. "Was it awkward having Colette sleep in your room last night?"

Thankfully, Leo took the change in topic in stride. "A little, but it's something I'll probably have to get used to. I'm not worried about them having sex while I'm there or anything. It's just weird to be around couples."

"Yeah," Sloan agreed, thinking about all the times he had been around his sisters and their boyfriends over the years. "Well, you can come to my room if you ever need to. You know that, right?"

Leo took the last bite of his sandwich, so he was unable to respond right away. "I do," he said once he swallowed. "Hey, since we're here, do you want to stop by your parents' house? I know you don't get to see them very often."

This was something Sloan had been considering asking for the past hour, though each time he did, he feared it would be an inconvenience. It was refreshing to be with someone who didn't treat stopping by his house as a chore. While Drew hadn't minded his parents, he never would have offered to stop by just because they were in the area. "Are you sure you don't mind? Today was supposed to be an us day."

"Of course I don't," Leo assured. "I would love to stop at home for an afternoon and surprise my mom and sister, but it's not an option for me like it is for you. Besides, I brought up potentially visiting to say hello last week. Remember?"

Yes. Sloan kissed him right after.

Trying not to get flustered by the memory right then, Sloan quickly moved on. "Would you like to stop at your dad's as well?"

Immediately, Leo's nose crinkled as if he tasted something off. "That's okay. Some other day maybe." His voice sounded strained. Sloan didn't want to pry in case it was a sensitive topic. Thinking back, Leo didn't talk about his father all that often, even though he mentioned they were rebuilding their relationship.

"Alright, sure." Sloan finished his sandwich and crinkled the wrapper. "You ready for ice cream?"

"Yeah," Leo agreed, his voice back to normal. "Definitely."

"Um," Leo began once they were parked on the street outside of Sloan's house. "Are you sure I won't be intruding by going in with you? They must be excited to see you, and I don't want to get in the way."

With a snicker, Sloan pushed open his car door. "Get out of the car," he told Leo, ignoring his misplaced concerns. His parents wouldn't be upset that Leo was joining him; on the contrary, they'd probably be delighted. When they came to visit the weekend before last to bring him the necessities for his new room, Leo had been at the library working on a project. This was distressing to Sloan's mother, who wanted to see him again after how often Sloan spoke of him.

Sighing, Leo unbuckled his seat belt. "Yeah, okay."

They went to the door together, Leo lagging behind a few paces. Desperately, Sloan wanted to grab his hand and pull him forward so they were walking together. He didn't. He wasn't sure how comfortable Leo would be doing that in front of his parents. Instead, he smiled reassuringly at Leo before reaching out to ring the doorbell. "I didn't bring my key," he explained when Leo's eyebrows raised. On the other side of the door, the response to the doorbell came in the form of incessant barking. "Oh. You don't mind dogs, do you?"

Leo's eyes got wide. "Your dog is *still* alive?"

Chuckling, Sloan shook his head. "No. We have two younger dogs now. Molly died right before I turned fourteen." Sloan watched his mother peek out at them through the semicircle window at the top of the door. He waved.

"I don't mind them, really," Leo assured.

The front door opened, and Sloan's mother managed to say, "What are you doing here?" happily, before he stepped inside to hug her. She laughed, squeezing him back. Vaguely, he was aware of the dogs moving past his legs to get outside before the door shut again.

"Just stopping in to visit," he told his mom, stepping back from the hug and turning to look at Leo, who was still standing on the porch. Sloan's mouth was open to continue speaking about their plans for the day but instead, he laughed. Leo was gazing down at the two dogs as they circled him to get his attention. Tentatively, he reached down and made a bewildered face when one of them licked his hand from fingers to palm. "Oh gosh."

Leo raised his head to look at them.

"Come in," Sloan told him.

With one last glance at the dogs, Leo stepped inside. They followed on his heels, excited by the new person.

As his mother pulled Leo into a hug and asked him how he had been, Sloan dropped to his knees to distract the animals. The second he was at eye level with them, they both jumped on him, knocking him onto his back. Laughing, Sloan wrestled them the best he could with one good arm as the two adults conversed.

"Well, thank you for delivering my ridiculous son to me," Sloan could hear his mother saying. Curious, he tilted his head back to look up at them, unsurprised to find them both watching him sprawled out on the floor. His mother kicked his foot. "Get up, you buffoon."

"They missed me," he claimed, pushing the dogs off as he sat up. The smaller of the two, Archie, attempted to lap at his face with a wet tongue, and he ducked out of the way just in time. He reached his left hand up toward Leo to be helped to his feet. Pointing to one dog, Sloan introduced, "That one is Louie. And the darker one is Archie."

At the sound of his name, Archie came and took a seat in front of Leo, looking expectant. "Oh," Leo said softly, reaching out a hand to pet the top of the dog's head.

"He really likes it when you scratch behind his ears," Sloan advised. Leo did just that, gently, as if he was worried about potentially hurting him. Delighted, Archie's tail wagged harder.

"Where's Dad?" Sloan asked his mother.

Her eyes rolled. "The Peters are getting a new roof, so your father went over to watch."

"Ack. That's such a Dad thing to do," Sloan groaned, lowering his gaze to watch Archie lick Leo's fingers while the boy appeared to be mildly disturbed. "You don't have to let him do that. It's not like he'll attack you." Quickly, Leo pulled his hand back and looked at it. To keep from laughing, Sloan chewed his lip.

"Morgan, dear, show him where the bathroom is so he can wash his hands. Do you guys want to have a snack or something while you're here?"

"We actually just ate at Mulligan's," Sloan admitted. "We just wanted to stop when we were in the area."

She frowned, probably upset she wouldn't have the opportunity to show off her cooking. "Well, you'll stay and visit for a little while, won't you?" she asked hopefully. From the corner of his eye, Sloan glanced to get Leo's reaction to this, expecting to maybe catch him looking displeased as Drew would have. Leo didn't seem bothered by the suggestion at all.

"Sure, Mom," Sloan agreed, reaching out to grab Leo's sleeve. "Where's Margo, by the way?"

"Probably napping on your bed. You should stop up and say hello. Come down to the dining room when you're done. I'll make smoothies or something." She went to the kitchen and Sloan used his grip on Leo's sleeve to guide him down the hall.

"Bathroom's this way," he explained. He led him to the half bath and stepped out of the way for Leo to enter.

Going to the sink and immediately washing his hands, Leo mumbled, "Thanks."

Sloan leaned in the doorway, watching him. Leo had nice fingers, longer than his own, though thinner. "You sure you're okay staying a bit?"

Leo dried his hands on the towel by the sink. "Yeah. I figured we would."

"But you were going to sit in the car?"

"I don't want to intrude," he said again, looking toward Sloan once his hands were dry.

"You're not intruding, Leo." It wasn't clear whether Leo believed him, but at least he nodded in acknowledgment.

"Come on," Morgan said. "I'll take you to meet Margo."

"Margo?"

Margo was Sloan's somewhat overweight orange cat with an angry scrunched-up face who loved him almost as much as he loved her. Based on Leo's look of surprise when Sloan turned on the light in his bedroom, that was not what he had been expecting.

As his mother predicted, Margo was napping peacefully on his bed, only to be startled awake by their presence. It took her a moment to fully rouse, and when she lifted her head toward the door, a happy noise left her. She jumped off the bed to come say hello.

"Hi, baby!" Sloan greeted fondly, crouching down to lift the cat awkwardly with his left arm, holding her close to his chest as he turned to Leo. "Margo."

"Margo," Leo echoed, looking back and forth between Sloan and the cat, seeming unsure.

The hesitance made Sloan's lips curled upward. "You can pet her if you'd like."

Seeming determined, Leo reached out a tentative hand and ran it over the cat's fur. In his arms, Margo turned her head curiously to look at him. "Hello," Leo whispered. Right then, Sloan thought that he just might be in love with him.

"You've never had a pet, I take it?"

"I suppose that's obvious," Leo said, pulling his hand back when Margo began to fidget. *It's was about time*, Sloan thought. He returned her to where she had been resting before they interrupted. She never really enjoyed being held, usually tolerating it for only about a minute.

"Maybe a little," Sloan confirmed, taking a seat on the end of his bed and pulling his legs up. He crossed them, since that was the position Margo preferred him in, and sure enough she immediately crawled into his lap. "You seem cautious around animals."

For just a second, he stopped petting Margo to pat the spot on the bed next to him.

As he moved to sit beside him, Leo explained, "My mom was never really interested in having pets." Without hesitating this time, he reached out to pet Margo some more, the look on his face thoughtful. "Lizzy wanted a cat and she fought for one, but to no avail." His fingers moved beneath Margo's chin, scratching gently. Sloan watched as his cat tipped her head back to give the boy better access. Leo wore an expression of pride, as if being accepted by Sloan's animal was a great honor.

"My parents aren't cat people," Sloan admitted, brushing a hand down Margo's back. "Neither is Drew. I was supposed to bring her to school with me, and it was perfect because our apartment allowed one animal, but he said no."

"Are you going to bring her now?" As Leo asked, Margo climbed off Sloan's lap to crawl onto Leo's thighs, throwing herself down onto her back so her belly was open to be rubbed. This made Leo look so incredibly happy that Sloan wondered if it would be okay to kiss him again. He refrained. When he did kiss Leo again, it was going to be after he completely sorted out his emotional damage and was ready for a relationship.

"I don't think so. My mom asked me if I wanted to and I thought about it, but I don't think she would be happy in my tiny dorm room. I'll wait until I get a bigger place."

Nodding, Leo lifted his head to look around, hand still buried in the fur on Margo's stomach. "It's not so bad here. I bet she likes it."

Surprised, Sloan also looked around. His room was what he figured the typical college boy's bedroom looked like. It was probably cleaner than most, since his mother had OCD and obviously came in after he visited last to straighten everything, but it had all the usual things. Queen-sized bed, bookshelf, dresser, and a desk. Various pictures from his middle and high school years were on the back of the door, and on his desk sat a glass shark figurine, right beside a stack of DVDs he recognized as Nicole's.

"Yeah," Sloan agreed. "I suppose it's not awful. She doesn't like the dogs, but I'm pretty sure they're afraid of her, so most of the time they steer clear."

This earned a chuckle from Leo as he gazed down at the cat in his lap with an expression of love, despite having just met her. Sloan felt as if the cuteness physically pained him.

"So, what's our plan for the rest of the day?" Leo asked. "I don't know what's around here."

"Honestly, I haven't thought that far ahead," Sloan admitted, raising his left hand to rub the back of his neck. "I thought it'd be nice to come back to the area together, but there's really not all that much here. We could do something outside. I know we've already driven quite a bit, but we could go to one of the national parks." This idea appeared to intrigue Leo, and Sloan was thankful he'd suggested something suitable.

"I don't mind driving," Leo claimed. "I haven't been to many national parks, so I'd like that."

"We can ask my mom which one she recommends. She's been to more than me." Sloan reached over and scratched Margo's belly, his fingers bumping against Leo's. "We should go down to the kitchen and appease her, don't you think?"

Leo smiled, his eyes still focused on the cat. "Yeah," he agreed. "Let's."

That night, Sloan found himself lying in bed with Leo asleep on his arm. They were in the position Sloan found most comfortable, with Leo curled up on his side facing away from him and Sloan's knees tucked up behind his. As usual, Leo was the first one to fall asleep, but Sloan didn't mind. He was more than happy to trace patterns on the bare skin of Leo's hip where his shirt had ridden up. That was what he was doing when the text from his mother came through.

He ended up reading it twice since the words made him feel so happy.

Mom: I'm happy you two came to visit today. You light up around him like I've never seen before, and the way he looks at you is so sweet. I'm thrilled for you, dear.

Sloan turned off his phone for the night and slipped his arm around Leo's waist. Right before he fell asleep, he wondered if he'd ever felt this way before.

If he had, he was sure it had been five years ago.

CHAPTER THIRTY-NINE

LEO

The first thing Leo did when he was dismissed from class on Thursday was check his phone. There was a message from an hour ago.

Morgan: Lunch this afternoon?

They got lunch together most days, so the suggestion did not surprise him, but it was the first time he'd have to reject the offer. The night before, Leo's father texted that he and his stepmother were going to be in the area and asked him out to lunch. At first, he'd considered saying no, though there was really no reason not to go, and he still felt kind of guilty about not stopping by on Saturday when they were in the area.

They'd be picking him up in half an hour.

It would have been easy enough to text this to Morgan, but Leo liked to hear his voice, so he called instead.

The phone rang for a minute before it was answered. Morgan sounded groggy when he greeted him. "Hey."

"Did I wake you? It's nearly eleven thirty."

"I don't have class today," Morgan answered, sounding slightly off.

"I know," Leo said, trying to think of what was wrong. "Oh. Do you think I'm angry with you for sleeping in? I'm not. I actually feel kind of bad for waking you up. That's why I asked."

"No, no," Morgan said, rustling sheets a background noise to his voice. "I forgot for a second that you don't get mad at me for stuff like that."

This meant it was something Drew would have gotten angry at him for, and Leo felt a brief stab of irritation toward Morgan's ex.

"You shouldn't feel bad about waking me up. Waking up to your voice is all I could ask for . . . actually, it's not. I wish you were here." Morgan had been so honest lately, and every time he was, Leo couldn't help but feel flustered. Luckily, his blush couldn't be seen over the phone. "Are you calling about lunch?"

"Yeah," Leo confirmed, hating how breathless his voice came out. He sounded as overwhelmed as he felt. Before speaking again, he cleared his throat. "I'm actually getting lunch with my father and Meredith, so I can't today. I'll come over beforehand and bring you something from the cafeteria or store."

"Ah. That'll be fun. Don't worry about getting me food. I'll manage on my own," Morgan insisted. "I'm really not hungry. I just wanted to see you. Do you have a little time, or are you leaving right away?"

"They're coming to get me at noon."

He was almost to his dorm building, and he hoped Morgan was about to invite him over so he didn't have to go back to his own room.

There was nothing wrong with his dorm room, it just wasn't the relaxing space it used to be. Since Colette's roommate was so nosy—and incredibly irritating, according to Justin—the couple spent most of their time in the boys' room. It wasn't that big of a deal to Leo, because it gave him an excuse to hang out in Morgan's single the floor below, but it was a little weird when Morgan was sleeping or in class.

"Come over?" he thankfully asked, sounding hopeful, as if there was a chance Leo would say no.

"I'll see you in a minute."

A happy noise left Morgan. "The door is unlocked."

Leo shook his head, amused as well as concerned. "You should really stop doing that. What if someone comes in and steals all your stuff?" As he asked this, he tilted his head to hold his phone with his shoulder, freeing his hands to find his ID so he could unlock the door.

"Do I have anything worth stealing?" asked Morgan with a yawn.

"You," Leo responded, and Morgan snorted out a surprised laugh. "And what about the coffeemaker?"

Not sounding at all worried, Morgan sighed, "Oh no." Leo was in the building now, and he began to make his way up to the second floor. Morgan continued, "Have you ever considered that maybe I'm keeping my door unlocked to encourage you to move in and protect me?"

"Move in?" Leo eyebrows raised. "To your single? I doubt both of our stuff would fit in there. Your closet is pretty full."

"You have, like, six shirts, Leo."

"I don't really get clothes," Leo grumbled in defense, beginning up the second flight of stairs. "I just wear what's comfortable."

When Morgan spoke, there was laughter in his voice. "Well, lucky for you, clothing is strictly optional in this room, so if you're comfortable in nothing, wear that."

Leo knew he was being teased, but he couldn't help letting it get to him, his body feeling uncomfortably hot. As if Morgan was there to watch him react, he chuckled, then suggested, "How about you use your room upstairs as storage, and spend all of your time here?"

"I already spend a lot of time with you," Leo pointed out. He was on the second floor now, making his way down the hall toward Morgan's room.

"So what you're saying is that you don't want to spend any more time with me?"

"No," Leo denied. "That's not what I'm saying at all." Outside of Morgan's door, he came to a stop. "I'm hanging up on you now."

"Wait, why—" Morgan was cut off by him ending the call as he pushed open the door to step into the small room. As expected, Morgan was still in bed.

The lights in the room were off, though it was late enough in the day that the sunlight shining through the window made it easy to see. "That was fast," Morgan said, dropping his phone onto his mattress and pushing himself into a seated position. His hair was all over the place, and he was wearing a tired expression that made Leo want to hug him to see if he would melt into the embrace like he usually did when sleepy.

Forcing his eyes away as he closed the door behind himself, Leo admitted, "I called when I was on my way back."

Morgan scooted back until he rested against his pillows, leaving enough room between him and the side of the bed for Leo to fit. Even though the open space looked inviting, Leo took a seat at the end once he toed off his shoes. Not that he didn't want to sit beside Morgan, but being so close to him right after he woke up and was more prone to cuddling often got him in situations where his heart beat uncomfortably fast.

"So, lunch with your father? How'd that get arranged?"

"He reached out to me yesterday and said he'd be in the area," Leo explained. "I'm a little worried it's going to be awkward, but the week I stayed with them before school began wasn't awful, so maybe not."

"I think you'll be happy you went," Morgan said, blinking his eyes in a way that showed how tired he was.

"What time did you get to sleep last night?" Leo asked.

Morgan's eyes shifted away as he thought. "I'm not exactly sure. I think it was technically this morning when I fell asleep."

"That's why you're so tired?"

Morgan shrugged. "I don't know. Maybe. Or maybe it's because I just woke up and I'm always tired when I wake up. I tried to get up a little earlier, when I sent you the texts, but I fell back asleep."

"Do you want to sleep more?" Leo asked, dropping his hand onto the blanket over Morgan's legs. "I don't mind."

"No. You just got here. Would you come lie by me, though? Your body is always really warm."

With no consideration, Leo agreed. It would be pointless to think about whether it was a good idea. In the end, it didn't really matter, because the result would be the same, regardless.

They ended up facing each other, with Morgan's head tucked beneath his chin. *So soft,* Leo thought, marveling at the way Morgan's body relaxed entirely against him. "Comfy," Morgan praised sleepily. Leo had no doubts that if they stayed like this long enough, Morgan would fall back asleep. "Your heart is beating really fast."

Sighing, Leo pushed his hand through the hair at the back of Morgan's head. "Yeah, I know. I'm sorry."

He made a noise of content, slightly muffled by the fabric of Leo's shirt. "I like it." Pressing even closer, causing his cast to dig into Leo's stomach a bit uncomfortably—though not enough so that he was going to ask for some distance—Morgan claimed, "I like it a lot."

His father and step-mom took him for food about ten minutes off campus at a little place that his stepmother swore was good. Leo wasn't too concerned about the quality of food, more focused on his ability to communicate well after not having seen them for a few months.

He was making a serious effort. The reason they asked him to get lunch was because they wanted to know how college was going. He didn't mind sharing, but he couldn't help feeling uncomfortable doing all the talking.

He was trying to fit in a question of his own after explaining how his classes were, but Meredith once again beat him to it. "And how have you been getting along with your roommate? We didn't get to meet him on move-in day, so I've been wondering."

Leo raised a perfectly crisp French fry to his mouth, thinking about his answer before giving it. "Justin and I get along pretty well. We've both been busy lately though, so we don't spend much time together. He started dating one of my friends, so they're together most of the time."

Across the table from him, a smile Leo didn't quite understand pulled up the corners of his father's lips. "Both of you, you said?"

Leo's eyebrows drew together. "What?"

"You said you've both been busy. He's been busy with his girlfriend, and you've been busy with . . .?" His dad trailed off. It was clear what he was insinuating.

Beside his father, Meredith sucked in a breath and turned to look at Leo with wide eyes. "Are you interested in someone?" She sounded rather excited. Leo averted his gaze.

It wasn't that he didn't want to tell others about what he had with Morgan. He was just unsure of how aware his father was of his interest in men, and he didn't want to shock the man right after he bought him lunch.

Unfortunately, his hesitance came across as suspicious. "Tell us about it!" Meredith encouraged. "No need to be embarrassed. We had our fair share of crushes in college. Right, Peter?"

"Ah, yes," his father confirmed, smiling as if this gave him fond memories. "That's actually where I met your mother, Leo."

This was new information to Leo, and it interested him enough that he lifted his head to look at his father. He couldn't recall them ever discussing his mother before. They were on good terms, Leo knew. More than once back home, he'd seen his father's name appear on his mother's caller ID, but it still felt strange to talk about. He seemed to be the only one who thought so. Even his stepmother appeared at ease with the topic.

"I didn't know that," Leo admitted.

"Yep. She was in one of my classes when I was a sophomore and she was a freshman."

"Oh." Leo didn't know what else to say.

His father met his eyes. "If you don't want to talk to us about your relationship, you don't have to."

Leo fiddled with his straw wrapper. "It's not that I don't want to tell you. You just may not approve." Neither of them said anything, and when he took a nervous glance at them, he noticed them sharing a look. "You remember Morgan Sloan, right?"

"Oh yes," Meredith confirmed. She and his father seemed equally unsurprised. "He's a delightful boy. He's at your school? Are you two dating?"

He didn't respond right away, frowning at his plate as he attempted to grasp the situation. Wasn't it a little strange to be completely unaffected by the prospect of your son liking another boy? Even his mother, who had been incredibly accepting, had initially been shocked when she found out. "Um . . ." Leo spoke slowly. "No. We're not dating, we're just . . . together? Soon to be dating, probably. I don't know. We don't talk about it."

"You're confused," his father observed.

Worried that the man was referring to his sexuality, Leo's heart dropped.

"Are you wondering why we're not more surprised?"

Breathing out a sigh of relief, Leo nodded. "Yeah."

"I didn't know your mother hadn't shared with you that she told me about your sexuality. She probably hoped you could get to a point where you were comfortable enough to tell me yourself," his father explained. "She called me when she first found out, just to have someone to talk to. I don't want you to think she reached out to me because she was disappointed, because she's not. She was worried."

Leo wondered why his mother had gone to his father instead of him to discuss it. "Worried about what?"

"About you, Leo. And rightfully so. As a parent, when something like this comes up, you worry even when you're accepting because you know that not everyone out there is going to think the same way, and the idea of someone you love and want to protect having to deal with those kinds of people is scary," his father explained.

For a minute, Leo didn't know what to say. He thought about how his father had just implied that he loved him, which was something he was pretty sure they never said to each other before.

"I wish I could say that's not a valid concern, but there have been some people who saw me differently after they found out," Leo admitted. "It never really bothered me, though. I guess their closed-mindedness was annoying, but that wasn't my concern. I don't like making people worry, however. Before, if I had known that was a concern you guys had, I probably wouldn't have told my friends or classmates. Now, I feel comfortable telling you not to worry."

He stopped talking to take a sip of his soda, needing a moment to collect his thoughts. "I am currently happy enough that—" He stopped again. It felt like he was saying something too personal. Still, it was true and he didn't want to feel embarrassed about openly expressing his emotions. "I am *really* happy right now, and anything that makes me feel this way can't be shameful."

They both looked at him for a little while with matching expressions of astonishment. His stepmother recovered first, clearing her throat. "And you say that you're not dating this boy, correct?"

"Right," Leo confirmed. "Not dating. We just kind of . . . hang out a lot and eat together, and I stay in his room on the weekends." It occurred to him once the words were out that this was an embarrassing thing to admit.

"That sounds a lot like dating," Meredith pointed out. "Have you not had the conversation yet, or is there a reason you're not together?"

Leo shrugged. "I don't know how to answer that. Both, I guess? We haven't had the conversation and he got out of a bad relationship about a month ago, so he's still recovering from that."

"Give it some time," Meredith encouraged with a smile. "I'm sure it'll work out. It sounds like you guys are well matched."

Smiling down at his food, Leo said, "Yeah. I've been waiting five years already. A little more time doesn't seem like a big deal."

It occurred to him they still didn't know this part of the story when his father echoed, "Five years?" He said it in a way that made it sound like he'd just had a sort of revelation.

Leo remembered they hadn't discussed the true reason he'd fled all those years ago. "Oh," he said. "Yeah. He's why I left that summer. I liked him and I didn't know how to deal with it."

No one spoke right away. His father's expression was hard to read. "I see," he said eventually. "I always thought— "

Leo cut in. "I know." He felt ashamed. "It wasn't because of you. I'm sorry I didn't tell you about it sooner."

His father shook his head and resumed eating his food. "That's alright," he claimed. Leo glanced at Meredith to see her smiling in his father's direction. "It's in the past."

Unsure of how to respond, Leo just nodded in agreement. For a moment, he was worried that no one was going to say anything and the atmosphere would grow awkward, but then his father cleared his throat and asked, "So, speaking of boyfriends, what's up with this Dennis guy your sister is dating?"

Pleased to get away from talking about himself, Leo jumped on the topic of his sister's boyfriend.

He thought that maybe the next time he and Morgan went to visit, they would take the time to stop by his father's house.

After lunch, Leo went to meet Morgan in the library. He found him on the first floor, sitting at a table by the window. Morgan was studying hard, it seemed. Leo almost felt bad for joining him, not wanting to interrupt his concentration. Regardless, he approached, thinking about Morgan's text inviting him.

Morgan didn't notice him until he was standing at the end of the table.

"Oh," he said when he looked up. "You came."

"Yeah." Leo pulled out the chair to Morgan's left and took a seat.

"Of course I did."

Voice quiet to be mindful of the surrounding people, Morgan admitted, "I didn't know if you would." He watched Leo get situated. "I was expecting you to text to see where I was sitting."

"Figured I'd try to find you first," Leo answered, taking out his astronomy textbook. He had an exam coming up that he hadn't prepared for. "I thought it was better to not distract you if you were studying."

"So thoughtful," Morgan said, leaning into his side. He must have showered before leaving the dorm, because his blond hair was still damp. There were a few curls by his temples, and Leo wanted to reach out a finger and trace around the ringlets. He didn't, for the sake of Morgan's concentration, as well as his own.

"How'd lunch go?"

Leo freed his notebook from his backpack. "Great, actually. I'm happy I went."

"I'm glad," Morgan offered. It was the kind of thing people would say to be polite, but with that expression, there was no way Morgan was anything other than sincere.

They spent the next couple of hours studying, their chairs close so their shoulders pressed together. Morgan kept his hand beneath the table on Leo's knee, only lifting it when he needed to turn the page of his textbook, and returning before Leo even had the chance to miss it.

After long enough that Leo's back felt stiff from sitting, Morgan leaned away and then back again, tapping his shoulder against his for attention. Lifting his head, Leo met his gaze. "Are you doing something right now?" Morgan asked.

Leo glanced down at his textbook, then back up again. "Yes?"

"I mean, do you have a few minutes to help me, I should say. If not, it's alright. I can just use my left."

Confused, Leo looked at the blank worksheet Morgan was working on. Often, Leo wrote for Morgan because of his injury. "Oh, I can help you," he said, lifting his pencil. "Just tell me what to put where."

"Well, my name at the top, to begin."

Nodding, Leo wrote *Morgan Sloan* in his best handwriting. As he did, Morgan laid his right arm out across the table, resting his head on his bicep. His left hand remained on Leo's knee. "Read me number one?"

"Oh, your broken hand prevents you from reading as well?" Leo asked, earning in a small laugh from Morgan and a squeeze on his knee. "Alright, alright."

They only got through three questions before Leo spelled something wrong. He was erasing while being teased when Morgan's voice abruptly stopped. Raising his head at the silence, Leo noticed Drew standing at the end of their table.

Drew was staring down at Morgan, his face completely blank. Leo shifted his attention to Morgan as well. He appeared mildly panicked as he gazed up at his ex-boyfriend. It was the first time the two of them had run into each other since the breakup, Leo knew. He found himself happy he was beside Morgan when it happened, able to grip those trembling fingers beneath the table.

"Can I talk to you?" Drew asked, eyes finally dropping. It made him look as if he was regretful. Leo wasn't fooled.

"Um . . ." Morgan began, straightening his back and taking a deep breath. He looked completely composed, though his hold on Leo's hand was tight. "Sure."

Nothing happened. Drew's jaw visibly clenched. "I meant alone," he clarified, sounding impatient.

No, Leo desired to say, not wanting to give him the opportunity to do more damage. He didn't want Morgan to go.

But it wasn't his decision to make, and he could do nothing when Morgan's fingers slipped away from his under the table. "Okay," Morgan agreed, beginning to gather his things. "I'll just . . ." He trailed off as he began packing his backpack with his left hand.

Leo looked at Drew again. The other man stared back. He seemed pleased with Morgan's decision to leave, and Leo refused to give him the satisfaction of appearing uneasy. Instead, he stared back blankly until he felt Morgan's hand fall onto his arm, gathering his attention.

"Thanks, Leo. I'll talk to you later, okay?" He said it like it was a promise. There was an expression on his face that Leo couldn't place. It looked like he was urging him to understand. Leo didn't know what.

"Yeah," Leo agreed. Morgan smiled, fingers squeezing lightly where they still rested on his arm. He stood, pulling away to pick up his backpack. Once again, Leo wanted to protest. He wanted to ask him to stay where he was happy—Leo *knew* he made Morgan happy—but it still wasn't his place to say something like that. This was Morgan's choice to make.

He tried not to, but in the end couldn't stop himself from watching them walk away together.

Leo was lying in bed overthinking when there was a knock on the door.

Justin moved to go answer it, but Leo managed to get down the ladder of his loft before his roommate could cross the room. "Oh," Justin began as Leo grabbed the door handle. As he pulled it open, Justin finished what he was saying. "It's Colette."

The blonde girl was standing there looking at him with raised eyebrows. In her hand was a brown paper bag with a receipt stapled to it. His face must have fallen at the sight of her, because she frowned and said, "Wow. I don't think I've ever seen anyone so upset to see me before. And I brought you *food*."

"I'm not upset to see you," Leo said, stepping away from the door. Instead of crawling back into bed, he went to sit at his desk and put his head in his hands.

He was frustrated with himself for being so rattled. Of course Drew and Morgan were going to run into each other after the breakup, and it made sense that they would want to talk about it, but just knowing they were together bothered him. *Morgan can take care of himself,* Leo thought.

He also thought of Morgan driving his fist into the wall and how he had looked with tears drying on his cheeks. Leo felt as he had after that night, worried Morgan's assumption that Drew would never hurt him was false and afraid Drew would find words that did more damage than actions ever could.

Morgan can take care of himself, but I don't want him to feel alone, either.

Colette placed a takeout container on his desk next to his elbow. A can of soda, a fork, and a fortune cookie followed. He looked up at her. "You brought food for me?"

"Yeah," she confirmed. "I said that when you opened the door, but I don't think you were really listening." She went to sit by Justin on the futon and Leo turned in his chair to look at them. "Justin said you were back to lying in bed freaking out about something and you didn't seem like you were going to talk, so I included you in on our Chinese order. I got you chicken fried rice."

Leo shot Justin a look. His roommate was too busy smiling at his girlfriend to notice.

"Thank you," Leo offered, turning back to examine the food. He hadn't eaten since lunch and was quite hungry. "You didn't have to do this. Text me how much I owe you and I'll send money."

"Nonsense," she said. "It's my treat. I would ask what's bothering you, but I know you won't tell me, so I'm just going to ask you if Sloan's okay."

Of course it was obvious the only thing that would upset Leo like this was Morgan. "I don't know," Leo answered without thinking, not considering how it would sound to Colette until the words were out and she looked at him with wide eyes. "I mean, I'm sure he's alright. It's just don't really know what's going on."

Leo opened his can of soda and took a sip. The carbonation burned his throat.

"Where is he?" Colette asked.

There was no reason not to tell them, so he did. "With Drew." The room was completely silent as he popped the top off of the fried rice.

"With *Drew?*" Justin repeated after the pause stretched on long enough.

Nodding, Leo began to eat. He didn't know what else to tell them.

"Why?" Colette demanded.

Leo swallowed. "Drew wanted to talk."

"That still doesn't explain why Sloan is with him."

"Well, I suppose he wanted to talk to him as well," Leo speculated. "Like I said, it's none of my business."

Colette scoffed. "Oh, like hell it's none of your business. We aren't stupid, you know. You've been in love with him for the past two months," she accused, not in a way that was mean-spirited. It was more like she was urging him to express himself better. When he didn't confirm or deny this, she sighed. "You don't think they're going to get back together, do you?"

Leo paused, the can of soda halfway to his lips. He returned it to the desk before he could take a drink. "No," he admitted, the thought distressing him. "I don't think they're going to get back together."

"Colette," Justin said. "I don't think—"

"I know," she interrupted. "I know. Sorry, Leo. I just . . . you know he doesn't talk to me about these things. You're the only one who really knows what's going on with him. I'll stop asking."

"It's fine," Leo insisted after a tense pause. "I don't mind your questions. It's just, at this point, whatever I say is speculation, and I don't like that." He gathered some rice into his fork absently.

Why hasn't he texted me yet?

Leo thought of his phone still on the bed above him. "It just makes waiting for the truth more difficult."

After finishing his food, Leo forced himself to focus on homework, so he wasn't exactly sure how much time had passed before there was another knock at the door. His body tensed, and he turned to look at Justin and Colette. The couple's attention shifted away from the movie they were watching on Colette's laptop to look back. "Did you invite Max over?" Leo asked.

Justin shook his head, eyes moving to the door. "No."

"Thank god," Leo breathed, rising from his desk to go answer.

To his relief, this time it was Morgan on the other side of the door. He wasn't sure what to expect, though after worrying for so long, it certainly hadn't been Morgan looking so incredibly happy, his lips split into a dazzling grin. For just a second, he considered the possibility that maybe he and Drew actually had gotten back together and thought, *If that's what makes him this happy I should support him,* but then Morgan greeted him with a pleasant sounding, "Hello!" before taking a step forward to close the distance between them and kiss him full on the mouth.

Leo stopped thinking. He kissed him how he'd been thinking about kissing him every day for the past month. Right then, what Morgan and Drew spoke about no longer seemed important. All that mattered was that Morgan was kissing him and he was kissing back.

After what must have been at least a minute, but only felt like a matter of seconds, Morgan pulled back and pressed their foreheads together. Before Leo could become upset about the space between their lips, Morgan asked, using a volume that reached only his ears, "Wanna be my boyfriend?"

Chapter Forty

Leo

His boyfriend? Leo felt his eyes go wide.

Morgan was waiting for an answer. Leo wasn't sure if he had one.

Yes, he wanted to date Morgan. He wanted to date him so badly that he felt a physical ache in his chest when he considered it, but it was still important to him that they waited until Morgan was ready. Before they jumped into something, Leo wanted to make sure this wasn't a hasty decision because of something Drew had said.

"Morgan, I—" he began. That was as far as he got before Colette loudly interrupted.

"What just happened?!" she exclaimed, reminding Leo of her presence. He dropped his arms from Morgan's shoulders to turn toward the couple on the futon, feeling embarrassment burn in his chest. "You two kiss now?"

"Oh, hi, guys," Morgan offered sheepishly. If Leo had to guess, he'd say Morgan hadn't realized they were in the room until Colette spoke up. "Uh—"

Before he could say anything more, Colette cut in. "Don't apologize." Leo seriously doubted that's what Morgan was about to do. "Explain, please. Weren't you with Drew? What happened?"

Also curious, Leo glanced to Morgan. He was already staring back.

Right then, his face was incredibly easy to read. Leo laced their fingers together. "Let's go to your room," he suggested.

It wasn't a surprise when Colette immediately protested. "What? You guys can't leave! Justin, make them stay." In her excitement, Colette sat forward eagerly on the futon so she had to look over her shoulder at her boyfriend.

"What do you expect me to do about it?" asked Justin.

They began to bicker, and Leo grabbed Morgan's arm to pull him from the room while they were distracted. Gently, Leo shut the door behind them. He started leading them toward Morgan's dorm room.

"I didn't know they were there," Morgan was saying, sounding amused. "Did you see Justin's face? I think we really shocked him."

"He'll get over it."

There was a pause. Morgan asked, "Hey, Leo?"

They were going down the stairs now, and Leo continued to move at a pace fast enough that it felt like he was dragging Morgan behind him. "Yeah?"

"Are you alright?" The question caught him off guard. He shot a quick glance over his shoulder. Morgan's eyes were down. "You seem tense right now. I'm sorry for leaving you at the library. I thought—"

"Wait," Leo interrupted, not wanting to have the conversation in the hall. "We're almost to your room."

Clearly, Morgan wasn't getting this, because he continued. "Are you upset because I kissed you in front of Justin and Colette?"

"Morgan, I'm not upset," Leo assured. "I was just worried when I didn't hear from you for so long. I'm okay now that you're here."

They stopped outside of Morgan's room. Leo turned so they were facing each other. "I should have texted you," Morgan mumbled. "I thought about it, I did, but I remembered how angry Drew got when he thought I was paying more attention to my phone than him, and he was already upset. I didn't want to deal with it. I should have done it anyway."

"I wouldn't want you to do that. Never do something that makes you uncomfortable for my sake," Leo told him.

Morgan reached out to grab the doorknob. As usual, the room was unlocked. "Come on," he urged. "Let's talk in here."

Nodding, Leo entered the familiar room. When he heard the door shut, he turned around, mouth open to ask about what happened while they were apart. Before the words could leave him, Morgan kissed him again. "*Ah,* wait, wait." Leo's hands settled onto Morgan's chest, lightly pushing him backward. "I thought we were going to talk?"

"Who says we can't do both?" Morgan questioned with a grin, leaning in to kiss the corner of his mouth. "I want to kiss you right now because I can."

"You couldn't before?" Leo asked, fingers curling in the back of Morgan's shirt when warm lips met his jaw. His inability to say no was probably as unsurprising to Morgan as it was to him.

With a hum that reached a deeper part of his voice than Leo had heard before, Morgan teased, "Are you trying to tell me you wanted to kiss me before?" His mouth was ghosting down his neck now. Leo didn't respond, tilting his head and closing his eyes. It was difficult to focus on anything other than Morgan's warm breath against his skin. "You know, I've wanted to kiss you again every second of every day since we last kissed, but I felt I couldn't until I was ready to begin a relationship. Now—"

"I can't think like this," Leo said.

Morgan pulled back and Leo cracked open his eyes to look at him. "Then don't."

His lips were on his again. Groaning, Leo kissed him back, still holding tightly onto Morgan as they stumbled toward the bed. He was expecting to be gently coaxed onto the mattress, but before that could happen, his foot caught on something and he gracelessly fell backward. "Fuck," he said, raising his hands to cover his face as Morgan laughed.

"Sorry, sorry!" Morgan said, crouching to free Leo's ankle from what he now saw was the strap of Morgan's backpack. "I stopped by when I got back from Drew's and forgot I put that there." Sighing, Leo relaxed against the mattress, squeezing his eyes shut. They flew open again when he felt Morgan climbing on top of him, legs on either side of his hips.

"Wait," Leo demanded, placing a hand on Morgan's chest before he could get close enough to kiss him again. "What happened with Drew?"

Pouting, Morgan rolled off him. "Okay, okay. We talked for a really long time, and it all boiled down to him being upset about our breakup and trying to convince me that I was also upset and just not showing it," Morgan explained. "He said I was pretending to be something that I'm not and that I belong with him." He made a scoffing noise. "More like I belong *to* him."

"Are you okay?" Leo asked.

"Yeah," Morgan said. "I mean, it's complete bullshit. We haven't seen each other since the breakup, so when he says I'm pretending to be something I'm not, he's basing that off of the few hours we spent together today, and what he saw of you and me in the library. I've felt more like myself lately than I have in a year, and I guess him saying that made me realize he never really knew *me*, only the person he pressured me into being."

Suddenly looking fond, Morgan rolled onto his side toward him, dropping his injured hand onto Leo's stomach. "You've never expected me to be anyone other than myself, and you never got angry at me for who I am. I wanted to wait for us to start something when I could completely focus on you and not worry about the past, and I'm ready to do that, so like . . ." His gaze lowered. "Date me?"

Leo smiled, feeling confident this wasn't a sudden decision. "I'd like that."

Morgan hid his grin by tightly pressing his lips together. "Do you think you would like it if we kissed some more?"

"Yeah," Leo agreed, shifting on to his side as well and draping his left arm over Morgan's neck. "I do."

***

Thursday night, Leo slept in Morgan's room, so his Friday morning began with the sound of an alarm that was not Justin's. It seemed to be a good day because, instead of falling back asleep immediately after stopping the noise as he usually would, Morgan pressed a kiss to the side of his neck and crawled out of bed right away.

Leo didn't stir, just let the soft sounds of Morgan getting ready for class lull him back to sleep. He was awakened once more before his alarm when Morgan pressed a warm kiss into the corner of his mouth with a gentle promise of "I'll see you later." Too tired to properly respond, Leo made a noise of agreement.

Later—more specifically, political science class—came faster than Leo was expecting with all of his anticipation. He wanted to see Morgan, his *boyfriend*, from the moment he woke up and, going off the delighted look on Morgan's face when they finally made eye contact, he hadn't been alone in his desire.

"Hey," Morgan greeted as he moved behind Leo's chair to get to his spot. As usual, he had a travel mug of coffee with him, and Leo tried to remember him making it that morning. He came up empty, which wasn't much of a surprise given how tired he had been. They'd stayed up late the night before, after all. "Should we go out on a date tonight?"

Leo smiled, feeling excited for a date for the first time in his life. "Yeah. I'd like that." He paused to consider how fast his heart was beating and let out a chuckle. "I'm nervous."

"Don't be," Morgan said, lifting his backpack onto his lap and unzipping it. "It's just me."

"It's not *just* you, it's *you*," Leo corrected. "I think it's because I've never liked someone this much, so I'm nervous about something potentially changing between us now."

"Yeah," Morgan agreed, shrugging as if this wasn't a big deal. "Things probably will change, but for the better." With a *thwack*, Morgan dropped his notebook on the table. "So we're on for tonight, then?"

Nodding, Leo agreed. "Of course. How are we getting to wherever it is we're going? Oh, and where are we going?"

"I don't know yet. Over lunch, I'll look up places in the area," Morgan said. "And we'll be taking Colette's car. She and Justin kept pestering me in chem about if we were together now, so I made a deal that I'd tell them if Colette let us use her car."

"So they know we're together?" Leo asked, not because he minded but because he wanted to know if he should prepare for Justin to tease him when he went back to the room.

A look of concern passed over Morgan's face. "Ah, yeah. Is that alright?"

"Yeah." He pulled Morgan's open notebook toward himself. Recently, given Morgan's issue with his right hand, Leo had been taking notes in Morgan's notebook and sending himself pictures of the notes at the end of class. "Are you sure we're not inconveniencing them by taking the car?"

Morgan nodded. "Yes. Apparently, they're going to a party tonight, so she said it was fine as long as we find her a better parking spot than the one she already has." This seemed about right, given the current state of campus parking. "Basically, this means a part of our date will be spent driving around looking for a spot."

"That's okay," Leo said. He removed a pen from the front pocket of his backpack. "I should have known they were going to a party. They go to one every weekend now. Is that normal?"

"For some people," Morgan answered. "What, you don't want us to go to parties together all the time?"

He couldn't keep himself from grimacing. "I've been to two, and I feel like that's enough for the rest of my life."

Morgan laughed.

"You threw up on me after the last one, remember?"

"Oh, my god," Morgan groaned. "Why are you even willing to date me after that?"

"It was only on my shoes," Leo dismissed. "Besides, that was just getting even."

The look on Morgan's face was skeptical. "I ruined your shoes. I think I owe you a few more nights of you getting stoned and leaning on my shoulder. It honestly wasn't much of a hardship."

"I don't think I'm going to cash in on those nights. I'm never doing that again," Leo insisted, absently twirling his pen between his thumb and forefinger. "That night was awful. I've never been so afraid that I was going to die before."

"Aw, I kind of feel bad that I got so much enjoyment out of it. I was so happy you chose me to be the one to come watch over you," Morgan admitted with a smile. "Also, you were clinging to me and smelled really fucking good."

Their professor entered at the back of the room, sputtering out apologies for being a few minutes late when, in reality, none of them minded. Leo hadn't even realized.

"I smelled like *weed*."

"Well, yes. Other than that, I mean."

Their professor began to teach, so they fell silent for the time being, though Leo had no doubts that at some point during the lecture, Morgan would get bored enough to engage him in another conversation.

And sure enough, for most of the class Leo found himself too distracted by the boy beside him to pay attention.

After dinner, they went back to Morgan's room to watch a shark movie while sitting in bed.

"Have you seen this one before?" Leo asked. He leaned back against the wall, enjoying the weight of Morgan's head on his shoulder.

"No. It just came out. My mom texted me about it."

Leo's eyebrows raised, his gaze not leaving the screen. They were only about five minutes into the film, and it started with a shark attack, as most of them did. "Your mom knows about this weird obsession of yours?"

"Weird obsession," Morgan grumbled. Without looking at him, Leo knew he was pouting.

"It's interesting," Leo corrected. "You like these awful movies, but you have an interest in making movies that are meaningful. It's an intriguing combination."

There was a pause. Someone on the laptop screamed for help. "Hmm." It was a thoughtful noise. "It may seem like it, but these aren't the only movies I watch. They're not even my favorites. I like them, sure. They're funny and most of them are so similar that you don't really need to pay attention to know what's going on," Morgan said.

"Yeah," Leo agreed. Even at that moment, he was paying more attention to Morgan than to the film, though he was positive that if he began to watch again, he'd know exactly what was happening. "That's true."

Morgan lifted his head. "When you're around me, I find it difficult to pay attention to anything that isn't you for too long. That's why I always choose to watch something like this."

"Oh," Leo breathed, eyes roaming Morgan's face. "I don't—"

"Don't apologize," Morgan demanded, pressing closer to him. "Really. It's unnecessary. I quite like getting distracted by you."

The kiss he gave him then was gentle. Leo didn't let it continue for long. "We're not kissing with a shark movie playing in the background," he protested when Morgan's eyebrows raised in question. He expected Morgan to settle back against his shoulder again. Instead, Morgan laughed as he reached forward to shut the laptop before carelessly sweeping it off the side of the bed. It landed on a blanket with a suspicious-sounding thud. Leo looked after it with wide eyes.

Seeming unconcerned, Morgan climbed onto Leo's lap, arms coming to rest on his shoulders. "Problem solved."

"Aren't you worried you broke that?" Leo asked, finding it difficult to reach the laptop with Morgan pinning him to the bed. Huffing, he straightened, tipping his head back to look at Morgan. "Did you know that blanket was there?"

"It's fine," Morgan said, ignoring his last question. "I've dropped that thing so many times." Before Leo could point out that this didn't make the computer invincible—probably *more* fragile, actually—Morgan leaned toward him again, close enough that the tips of their noses were touching. "Can we kiss now?"

Finding no reason to protest, Leo closed the distance between them with a soft groan.

Kissing Morgan differed from kissing the people he had in the past. He almost found it difficult to control himself, having never experienced closeness with someone he craved this much. Never had he wanted a person as much as he wanted the boy in his lap. It was a strange feeling; undeniable desire. His mind went blank with it when Morgan pressed closer, an unfamiliar warmth filling his chest when he did something right and Morgan hummed softly.

It made him feel good, this noise. An irrational part of himself kept remembering that until a month ago, Morgan and Drew did things like this as well. After a year, Drew had to know all the things that Morgan liked while kissing. Whenever Morgan moaned or gasped, Leo felt incredibly proud of himself. Even without prior knowledge of Morgan's body, he could still make him feel good.

It didn't take long for Leo's entire body to feel hot, fingers curling tightly in the back of Morgan's shirt to prevent them from trembling. Vaguely, he was aware of the state he was in. He kept their lower bodies apart, avoiding the temptation to take things too far. He wondered if this wasn't a concern of Morgan's as well, feeling his kisses grow more and more urgent as they continued.

Leo drowned in it. He let the sensation flood his senses until he had no real thoughts, just moved purely on instinct. It took Morgan moving forward in his lap to snap him out of it, the pressure on his groin startling him enough that he pulled back, gasping for breath.

He hadn't even realized how badly he needed air. It was concerning that he could get so lost in another person. Morgan breathed heavily as well, though he disregarded his own need in favor of bringing his mouth to Leo's neck. Under the assault, Leo went limp, tilting his head back and letting out small sighs when Morgan found the places that were more sensitive than others. They'd spent some time like this the night before as well and Leo praised his memory, gasping out when Morgan showed he recalled the way Leo shook when he gently pulled his skin between his teeth. It felt like he was being taken apart.

He didn't mind until he felt Morgan's hand slip to his waist band. His hand shot down to wrap around Morgan's wrist. On top of him, Morgan stopped, his lips immediately halting. "What are you doing?" Leo asked, cracking his eyes open. Morgan looked at him with confusion. His gaze flickered down between them.

"You're hard."

The stab of shame Leo felt right then made him turn his face away. "Well, yeah," he confirmed, making a flippant gesture between their incredibly close bodies as if to say, *Obviously*. "But I don't expect you to do anything about it."

Now Morgan looked really perplexed, eyebrows drawing together as he sat back on his heels. "But I don't mind," he claimed. "I'm hard too." As if Leo couldn't see this or hadn't felt it against him only a moment before, Morgan sat forward and brought their hips back together. Before Leo could stop him, he rolled against him, eyes focused on his face for his reaction.

"Ugh," he groaned, reaching down to grip Morgan's hips. "Wait." Morgan stopped moving. "Tell me what's happening right now."

Whatever it was, Morgan apparently wasn't comfortable saying it directly to his face because he looked down, hiding his expression. "I just thought that you've been so great and supportive of me for these past four weeks, so I thought I could make it up to you."

Leo filled in the blanks. "By having sex with me." Morgan peeked at him through his lashes. "Okay, well, first off, you don't owe me anything. I wasn't there for you because I thought I'd be getting something in return—"

"I know," Morgan assured, raising his head to fully regard him. "That's not what I meant."

"And second," Leo continued. "I don't think that's a good idea."

There was a second where Morgan gazed at him, eyes wide and glassy. He moved off Leo's lap then, shuffling down the bed to have enough room to lie on his back. Breathing out a sigh, Leo closed his eyes and dropped his head back against the wall. The silence between them felt tense.

"You know I'm not saying no because I don't want to, right?" Leo asked. *Clearly, I want to,* he thought, cracking open his eyes to shoot a resentful glance at the front of his pants.

"You're saying no because you're worried about me, but I'm fine."

"I know you are," Leo acknowledged, dropping his hand to brush through Morgan's hair. "I just want you to actually *want* to have sex with me too. I don't want it to be something we do because you're giving it to me as a *present* or reward."

Eyebrows drawing together again, Morgan rolled onto his stomach, using his elbows to push himself up. "But I'm hard, so it's fine—"

"The more times you use the word *fine,* the better I feel about stopping," Leo interrupted. As if he hadn't even realized he was doing this, Morgan looked at him with surprise before huffing and collapsing onto his chest, face pressed into his pillow. "It shouldn't just be *fine,* Morgan. That's you tolerating it, and you'll never have to do that with me. I don't want to do anything unless you're ready, and right now, you're not ready." While he spoke, Leo shifted to lie on his side beside his boyfriend.

When Morgan finally responded, the pillow muffled his voice. "I'm sorry."

Leo pressed a kiss to the side of Morgan's head. "Nothing to be sorry about."

With a sigh, Morgan turned his head toward him, bringing their faces close together once more. "I guess I don't think of sex that way. When I lost my virginity, it was because Drew pressured me into it, and I wonder if that was traumatic for me, because after that I never really wanted to do it. Even when I got turned on, I didn't want sex. It was never enjoyable for me. I mean, I got off, but it wasn't easy and I would have preferred to masturbate. Drew didn't like me to though, and it wasn't worth listening to him lecture me if I got caught."

"That's okay," Leo assured, averting his gaze. "Take your time. I don't care if you need to do it yourself or anything." The words made his face feel incredibly hot. Morgan let out a soft chuckle before rolling onto his side toward Leo.

"How do you know when you want to have sex?"

"I don't know how to explain it," Leo mumbled. "It's not just *fine*, I guess. If you really want to, it's exciting and something you're looking forward to. Something you've been waiting for."

"Is that how you feel now?"

Leo felt his face heat. "It is."

"And have you ever felt like this before?"

"No." Leo could feel him moving on the pillow beside him, and slipped his eyes closed.

"With your first two boyfriends . . ."

Calmly, Leo admitted, "We didn't have sex. I'm still a virgin." It was quiet for long enough that Leo cracked open his eyes. Morgan was staring at him. "What? Is that no good?" When he received no answer, he rolled to face the other direction.

"Noooo," Morgan protested, following until Leo could feel him pressed against his back, chin on his shoulder so they were ear to ear. "I was surprised! It's not bad."

"Surprised? I thought it would be obvious."

"Well, I suppose it is, but I'd never really thought about it. I never wanted to think of you like that with someone else," Morgan explained. "You know how it works, right?"

Groaning, Leo pressed his face into the pillow, hating how embarrassed he got from a bit of teasing. "Why do you have to ask it like that?"

Laughing, Morgan nuzzled his face into the crook of his neck. "Sorry, sorry. Just wanted to make sure you know what you were doing when you finally fuck me."

There was a misunderstanding. Swallowing heavily, Leo reached back to push at Morgan until he had enough room to roll onto his back again. "Is that how it'll be?" he asked. "I'll be the one who . . ."

Morgan frowned. "Huh?"

Taking a deep breath, Leo forced himself to say it. "You want to be on the bottom?"

"Oh. That's all I've ever done before," Morgan admitted. He sounded unsure.

"Have you ever wanted to do it the other way?"

Morgan rubbed the back of his neck. "Honestly, yeah," he confessed. "Before Drew, I always thought that would be the . . . uh, *role* I filled. Drew never even gave me the opportunity to say what I wanted, though, and when I brought it up later, he refused to even try it that way." Morgan looked lost in thought, and Leo kind of wanted to snap him out of it, feeling slightly bitter that he was thinking about Drew. Instead, he gave Morgan the time he needed to gather himself. "Not that I'm unwilling to bottom, that is."

"No, it's okay," Leo assured. "You don't have to."

"What? No, Leo. If you don't want to, you shouldn't. Then I'd just be doing to you what Drew did to me," Morgan argued, completely neglecting the fact that he would once again end up doing something he didn't want to. Luckily, it was only a matter of miscommunication.

"I want to," Leo explained, and Morgan's eyes snapped to meet his. "What I'm trying to say is that I think I'm—"

Morgan's voice came out loud. "You want to bottom?!"

Leo rolled away again, covering his face with his hands. "Don't say it out loud."

Laughing, Morgan pulled at his wrist. It wasn't enough to get him to budge. "It's not a bad thing!" he insisted. "I mean, I don't want you to think I wouldn't like you if you didn't, because I totally still would, but this is great news for me."

"Please stop talking," Leo begged into his hands. There was more laughter. He felt a kiss pressed into his hair.

"Now I feel bad for assuming you would top just because you're taller and less emotional than me. I gave in to the stereotype. I should be ashamed of myself." Ignoring him, Leo reached down to grab the top of the comforter, pulling it up so it covered his head. "Why are you so embarrassed? You're usually so cool about the things that embarrass you."

"There's only so much I can endure."

The sheets rustled, and the next thing Leo knew, Morgan was beneath them as well. "It's alright," he said, his voice directly by Leo's ear. "Think about it this way. We were going to have this conversation eventually, and now it's out of the way."

Huffing, Leo shifted in Morgan's arms, pressing a little closer. While he was still embarrassed, he was thankful Morgan could maintain a casual attitude.

Neither of them spoke until Leo let out a heavy exhale and finally pushed the covers away from their faces. Morgan blinked at him, waiting for him to speak. "Should we finish our movie?" Leo asked, voice small.

Smiling, Morgan nodded. "Yeah," he agreed. "Let's finish our movie."

Chapter Forty-One

Leo

When Leo returned to Morgan's dorm, he was sitting up in bed, his hair a total mess. "Good morning," Leo greeted. "I went to get us coffee."

"Have I told you that you're amazing recently?" asked Morgan.

Leo flushed. "I got you the raspberry one this time since you kept talking about wanting to try it. Extra whip."

"Those words just turned me on," Morgan joked, holding his hands out toward him. Leo closed the distance to give him the coffee. "Thank you."

Leo set his own drink on Morgan's desk so he could pull off his shorts for the sake of comfort, leaving his phone behind in the pocket. Over the top of his cup, Morgan watched him with half-lidded eyes.

"No, thank you. You paid for dinner last night. I owe you about fifteen more coffees," Leo said.

"No complaints there," Morgan mumbled, scooting over when Leo grabbed his cup and climbed back into bed beside him. With a content hum, Morgan's head lowered onto his shoulder. "So warm."

"Sorry I wasn't here when you woke up."

"It's alright." Morgan raised his head and took a sip of his drink. "It's gotta be alright, because in a few weeks you're going to be in Illinois and I won't be seeing you for a month and a half."

Leo was trying not to think about that too much. When he thought about going home as leaving Morgan, he doubted his decision to fly back, though when he considered seeing his family and friends again, he felt excited. "We'll be okay," he assured.

Morgan made a noise of agreement. "I wasn't worried about that, really." He took a long sip of his drink. "So, what are your plans for today?"

"Well, I have a lot of homework due on Monday, so I'll probably work on that. Maybe I'll call my mom and mention I have a boyfriend. If I wait much longer, she's bound to be angry when I tell her. Beyond that, I don't really know. Why? What are you doing?"

"Colette's going to drive me to the doctor," Morgan answered. Leo's eyebrows raised. "They're gonna do an X-ray and tell me if they can take this stupid thing off." He waved his right hand around, glaring at the cast. It was hard for him to look at, Leo knew. *It's just a reminder of everything that was wrong with my life not long ago,"* Morgan explained once. It would be good for him to be free of it.

Morgan was staring at his hand for a little too long, the look on his face shifting into something that had been far more common in the weeks right after the breakup. Leo wanted to distract him from his thoughts. "You're doing that today?"

Nodding, Morgan dropped his arm. "Yeah. She should be coming to get me in like an hour and a half. Why?"

"I ran into her and Justin while picking up our coffee and she tried to get information out of me about us. I wonder why she asked if she knew she'd be seeing you today." He sipped his drink and hissed when he burned his tongue.

"I don't know," Morgan responded. "Maybe because I haven't been telling her about much lately."

"Are you still not going to?"

"Nah, I'll tell her what she wants to know," Morgan answered. "She deserves that much. All this time, she's been really patient with me. I'll probably talk to her about everything that went on with Drew as well."

Leo raised his eyebrows. "You're okay talking about it?"

"Yeah. I don't even feel anything over it anymore. Not even guilty." Morgan let his head rest on Leo's shoulder once again. "Being with you has made me realize that being myself isn't something I should apologize for," he said. "If being myself led me to have someone as wonderful as you by my side, I think there must be something good about me."

"Not just something," Leo said, turning his face into Morgan's hair. "Everything. You're all good."

"Even with the weird shark movie obsession?"

Smiling, Leo gave an honest answer. "Especially that." The chuckle he got in response delighted him.

As they finished their lattes, they talked in low voices about unimportant things. When their cups were empty, Leo got out of bed to throw them away. Instead of returning to Morgan's side, he stepped back into his shorts.

"What are you doing?" Morgan demanded. "It looks like you're getting ready to leave."

"Yeah, that's right," Leo confirmed. "You should get ready for your appointment, and I was serious when I said I had homework." Morgan groaned a little. Other than that, he didn't protest. "Would you text me about your arm?"

"Yeah. I'll text you when I get back as well. Are you going to spend the night here again?" Morgan asked. Leo paused in putting on his shoes to look at Morgan, finding him with a bright-eyed, hopeful expression.

"I need to sleep in my own bed sometimes," he said. "I already told you I'm not moving in." He finished putting on his shoes and rose, taking a few steps toward the bed, unsure of how they would say goodbye now that they were dating.

As soon as he was close enough, Morgan reached out and grabbed his hand, pulling him closer. "Sleep in your own bed tomorrow night," he told him, head tilted back so their eyes could meet. "Stay here with me tonight."

A large part of Leo felt that if Morgan looked at him like that, he'd do anything he asked him to. "Okay," Leo agreed, ducking to press a kiss to his forehead. "I'll come back tonight."

Morgan pressed his lips to the palm of the hand he was holding, looking quite pleased. "Have a good day."

"You too," Leo said. His palm tingled. He didn't want to leave. In that moment, he would rather fail all his assignments than be parted from Morgan.

His hesitance must have been obvious. "Leo?"

"Oh." He shook his head and slipped his hand free, taking a few steps backward. If he didn't put distance between them, he feared he'd end up spending the whole day there. "I'm going. Just . . . thank you for last night. I had a great time."

"Me too," Morgan agreed, grinning. "Let's do it again." It was hard to tell whether he was talking about the dinner or the kissing afterward. It didn't matter.

Leo wanted to do both again.

Leo tried to do his homework, but his conversation with Morgan from the night before kept pulling his mind away, so he gave up and went to take a shower instead.

He took longer than usual, so when he returned to his dorm, Justin had returned and Max standing in the center of their room with his hands in his pockets.

"I was wondering if you'd be here," Justin said to Leo when he entered. He was standing in front of his open dresser, shirt pulled halfway up his stomach.

"Hey, keep getting ready," Max demanded. Leo shut the door and turned in time to watch Max throw an eraser at his roommate. When it hit the side of his head, Justin made a displeased noise and pulled off his shirt. Leo raised his eyebrows at Max. "He and I were supposed to meet at the library half an hour ago. When I came to get him, he was getting in bed to take a nap."

Leo went to his dresser to throw his clothes and towel in his hamper.

"I was tired," Justin grumbled.

"It's not my fault you hung out with your girlfriend all night," Max said. "Come on, man. I have a lot of work that needs to get done."

"I don't get why you need me to go with you. I don't even have stuff to do."

This seemed to deeply offend Max if his expression was anything to go by. "I don't want to go by myself. It's boring."

"It's the *library*," Justin shot back, voice muffled by the fresh shirt he was putting on. "What do you expect? Excitement?"

Max ignored this. "Are you ready to go now?"

Justin went to the door and stepped into his shoes. "Yeah, just let me run to the bathroom really quick. I'll be right back." Before Max could respond, Justin slipped out the door, pulling it shut behind him.

Oh, Leo thought, staring after him.

He knew he and Max probably should talk, and he was guessing from that sudden departure that Justin had similar thoughts. He probably hadn't even needed to use the bathroom.

Max was the one to actually point this out. "I bet you five dollars he's going to walk into the bathroom, wash his hands for three minutes, and come back."

Leo shut his closet doors. "I'm not in the mood to be losing any bets right now."

Max smiled, but it soon faded. He looked down at his shoes. "So, I haven't seen you a lot lately. How have things been?"

Leo shifted from one foot to the other. "Good. Great, actually." He paused. There was no point in hiding his relationship with Morgan from Max. He'd find out eventually, and then it would be awkward that Leo hid it. "We're together now. I don't know if you heard."

"Ah, yeah." Max cleared his throat and lifted his head. He was smiling, though his gaze was focused elsewhere. "Justin mentioned it to me."

Unsure of what to say, Leo managed a soft, "Oh," before biting into his lower lip. To his surprise, Max chuckled.

"Relax," he told him. "I'm happy for you. If you have any problems or need to talk about anything, I know I'm probably not your first, or even second choice, but I'm here." The look on Max's face was earnest, and Leo smiled. It felt like they were going to be fine, and Leo was incredibly thankful. To him, Max wasn't *just* Justin's friend.

To him, Max was the first boy since Leo was thirteen who actually got to know him and still looked at him like he was worth falling in love with. While that hadn't been enough for them to have a relationship—though, Leo supposed, maybe it would have been if not for the reappearance of the first boy to *ever* look at him that way—Leo was hoping they'd be able to manage a friendship.

"Thanks," he said. "Really."

"Yeah," Max responded pleasantly. The second the word was out of his mouth, the door opened again.

"Ah, I'm ready!" Justin claimed, smiling at them when they both turned.

Max made a scoffing noise. "Were you standing outside the door?"

Blue eyes shifted away suspiciously. "No, of course not." Justin looked back at Leo. "Hey, I'm assuming you probably don't want to because we're super annoying and are going to spend the whole time talking, but you want to come to the library with us?"

Briefly, Leo considered this, but he wanted to call his mother before he got distracted by his homework and forgot. "Um, I actually have a phone call to make," he admitted.

"Ah, well, suit yourself," Justin replied, not seeming at all put out by the rejection.

It didn't take the boys long to leave. Once they were gone, Leo took a seat on the futon and dialed his mother's number.

It rang for a minute, then went to voice mail. He hung up and tried his sister instead. She picked up almost immediately. "Hey," she greeted. "What do you want?"

"Where's Mom?"

"Grocery shopping, I think," answered Lizzy. "Did you only call me to see where Mom was?"

"No. I need to tell you something as well."

There was a pause. When she spoke, she sounded concerned. "What's going on? Do you need to come home?"

"No. It's nothing bad. Um … Morgan and I are dating."

He heard her draw in a sharp breath. "Are you serious? Morgan Sloan?"

Lizzy knew that he and Morgan were friends, but when they'd last talked about him, he'd still been with Drew. He was surprised his mother failed to mention how close they'd become after sending those condoms in the mail, but maybe she'd wanted to leave the news for Leo to share.

"Yes," Leo confirmed. "Morgan Sloan is my boyfriend."

She squealed in his ear, loud enough that he had to jerk his phone away. "Lizzy!" he scolded.

"It's like a movie!" she cried happily. "Who asked out who? How long have you been together? Did he break up with his boyfriend for you? Oh! Does Michael know?"

Leo rolled his eyes. "I'll call him later."

Another noise of delight left her. "Oh, Leo. I am so happy for you. Are you happy? You are, aren't you?"

"Of course I am." He closed his eyes. "He's all I've ever wanted."

The sign she released was wistful. "God. I wish I could go back and tell my eleven-year-old self that Morgan was going to be my brother-in-law."

Leo cringed. "It's a little soon for that."

She wasn't listening. "Hey! Have you two had sex yet? I told you it was gonna happen this year!"

"Elizabeth!"

Chapter Forty-Two

Sloan

For the first Thursday in over a month, Sloan found himself in Kennedy's dorm room with his friends, a movie playing as background noise to their conversation. He was on the futon, wedged comfortably between Colette and Leo, his right hand—now free of the troublesome cast—resting casually on Leo's left leg.

The topic of the group's discussion was the fast-approaching end of the semester and what they all would do after the two weeks were up and they had to return home.

"Oh, that sounds awful," Colette sympathized after listening to Kennedy explain her and Oliver's plan to drive back to Portland together the Saturday after exams finished. "I can't believe you have to drive that far."

Kennedy dismissed this with a simple, "It's fine." She waved her hand. "He's good company and we'll take turns. Part of the reason I went to school here is that it's far enough from home that it's inconvenient. My parents never visit, and when they nag me to come home, I can say I have too much homework and don't have time to make the drive."

"You haven't seen your parents since the semester started?" Sloan asked. "Either of you?"

"No, I have," Oliver admitted. "I went home a couple of weekends back. I actually get along with my parents pretty well."

"Ah, well, going home won't be much of an event for me since I live so close," Colette chimed in. "I'm gonna miss you guys, though. And, like . . . my boyfriend."

With a chuckle, Sloan teased, "Good afterthought." Colette elbowed him playfully. On Sunday, they got lunch after his appointment at the hospital and talked about everything Sloan had been avoiding for the last month. Unsurprisingly, Colette was incredibly supportive, and he thought their relationship was far more comfortable now that there were no sensitive topics between them.

"Oh, Justin's not from around here as well?" Kennedy asked. Her eyes moved to Leo.

He frowned. "What? I don't know where he's from."

Seeming amused, Colette shook her head. "He lives about two hours away from campus. Close enough for weekend trips if neither of us are working, but it'll still feel weird after living with him five minutes away."

Sloan resisted the urge to scoff. He wished Leo would only be two hours away. As if thinking something similar, Leo shifted his leg to press against his.

"And what about you guys?" Kennedy asked.

"I live about an hour south of here," Sloan answered.

"And I'm flying back to Illinois Friday after my finals," Leo added. Frowning, Sloan squeezed Leo's knee more tightly.

Both Kennedy and Oliver looked surprised. "You're from Illinois?" Oliver asked, eyebrows raised high. Nodding, Leo leaned more into Sloan's side. It was something that, before they were officially dating, he would have only done while they were alone. Since revealing their relationship to their friends, Leo seemed more comfortable displaying his affection. "How come we didn't know you were from that far away?"

"Never mentioned it," was Leo's unenthusiastic answer.

Kennedy made an impressed noise. "Damn, though. That's kinda far for a new relationship. Think you two will make it? If not, second semester's going to be totally awkward."

"It's only six weeks," Leo said, sounding completely unconcerned. "The last time I left, I was gone for five years, and things still worked out."

"You better not be gone for another five years," Sloan grumbled. Leo patted the hand on his knee.

They then talked about things Sloan didn't care for much, like the dark marks on Kennedy's neck, so he allowed himself to fully relax against Leo.

Lately, Sloan felt very much like a teenage boy . . . no, that wasn't right. He was a teenage boy, but he suddenly felt like the typical *horny* teenage boy.

It was strange. Last Friday, he had thought of sex as something he could go without and had worried he'd always feel that way, but less than a week later, he could hardly get the desire out of his mind.

He didn't know what to tell his boyfriend. He didn't want Leo to think he was being disingenuous because he'd experienced such a drastic change so quickly.

Would it be alright to say he was okay with it now because he'd thought more and realized sex would be different with Leo because everything was different with Leo, or should he admit he felt far better knowing he wouldn't have to bottom? Or maybe it would be enough to say that lately, when they had been kissing, he understood what Leo said about really wanting it, because he *had*. All of those would be the truth.

Over lunch the day before, Sloan had run this all by Colette. She hadn't given him any useful insight, just reached across the table to pat his hand and say, "You guys are so cute."

At least for the time being, Sloan was going to keep this to himself, to the best of his ability. It was kind of difficult to hide with a boyfriend this hot.

"Morgan," Leo said. Then, when he didn't respond right away, "Did you fall asleep on me?"

Sloan blinked his eyes open, coming to his senses. The others were silent now, and he wondered if one of them had been trying to talk to him while he was zoned out. "Huh?" He lifted his head from where it had fallen on Leo's shoulder. "No. Just relaxing."

"Oh. Sorry. I felt your phone buzz against my thigh," Leo explained.

"Oh." He used his left hand to free it from his pocket so he could keep his right on Leo's leg. Absently, he shifted his wrist to trace the inside of Leo's knee with his pointer finger. He continued this action, forgetting about his phone and the message for a second as he watched Leo's leg tense.

Leaning into his side, Leo questioned, "Who is it?"

"Ah." Sloan dragged his eyes back to his phone screen. "Nicole."

Nicole: What are your plans for today?

Until Monday, Nicole, as well as the rest of his friends from home, hadn't known the details of his breakup with Drew. Or, at least, *his* side of their breakup. All they knew about it was what they learned when Drew called them right after, so on Monday Sloan finally got in contact with his best friend. He'd explained everything, including his new relationship with Leo, and since then she'd begun reaching out daily to see how he was. She felt guilty, Sloan suspected, though she had no reason to. It was his fault that she hadn't known how bad things had gotten with Drew toward the end, not hers.

As he began typing a reply with his left hand, Colette bumped into his shoulder. "What's with this whole *Morgan* thing?" she asked. "Do we all get to call you that now?"

Sloan wasn't surprised other people had noticed. At some point, Leo had abandoned the name Sloan all together and began to refer to him exclusively as Morgan. He didn't mind. Actually, he liked that Leo called him something different than most people.

"No," he said.

"Yeah, why do you go by Sloan anyway?" Kennedy asked. "Morgan is a nice first name."

"I don't mind Morgan," Sloan admitted, finishing his text to Nicole and dropping his phone onto his lap. "That was what I was called for the first fourteen years of my life. When I was a freshman in high school, one of my close friends started dating a girl named Morgan, and they were together for a year and a half, so we all spent a lot of time together and it got confusing. They all started calling me Sloan, and then everyone else at school did, so my teachers started to as well. I just got used to it." He paused. "My parents don't like it."

Colette shrugged. "So go by Morgan again."

"Ah, no," he said without even considering it. "I think I'd be uncomfortable if you all started calling me Morgan all the time."

"So why does Leo get to do it?" Kennedy asked.

From the corner of his eye, Sloan shot a look at his boyfriend, catching his gaze. "Um, well . . ." He glanced away. It would be embarrassing to admit it felt special when Leo called him Morgan. Surely, that would get him teased. "He knew me when I was Morgan," Sloan finally said. He softly added, "And I like the way he says it."

A snicker left Colette, but Leo smiled and put his hand on top of Sloan's, twisting their fingers together.

They left Kennedy's after a couple of hours under the pretense of having homework to do when, in reality, Sloan just wanted to spend the rest of the evening alone with Leo. Leo must have had similar thoughts because the second they entered Sloan's dorm, he spun around to kiss him. Sloan certainly wasn't complaining—if Leo hadn't kissed him, he would have kissed Leo—and he led them in their stumble toward the bed.

Dropping onto his back, Morgan kept his hands on Leo's waist to pull him down on top of him. "Ah!" Leo gasped in surprise, catching himself with his forearms on either side of Sloan's head. "That startled me."

Chuckling, Sloan flexed his fingers on Leo's hips, smiling up at him.

"Kiss me again," he instructed.

A thoughtful look came over Leo's face, his dark eyes focusing on Sloan's mouth. Slowly, he closed half of the distance between them, but before their lips could meet, he froze, eyes snapping back up to his. "Hey, don't you have to watch a documentary for biology by tomorrow?"

Sloan groaned. "Ah, fuck. I forgot about that." He wished Leo hadn't reminded him.

"Oh." Leo rolled off him. "I assumed that was what you were referring to when you told them we had to leave because of homework."

"No. I was just using that as an excuse," Sloan admitted. "I wanted to be alone with you. Does this mean you're going to leave?"

Shaking his head, Leo sat up. "I'll watch it with you. Where's your laptop?" When Sloan didn't respond, still thinking about how he'd much rather be kissing, Leo looked down at him. "Come on." He dropped a hand onto Sloan's thigh.

"Why can't we keep kissing and I stay up until three getting it done?" he suggested. Leo didn't appear to think this was a good idea, features shifting into an *Are you serious* expression for a long moment before he sighed.

"How about . . . every thirty minutes we pause it and make out for five?" Leo countered.

Eyebrows raising, Sloan said, "That's crazy persuasive." He sat up with a groan and leaned over to kiss Leo's temple before climbing out of bed to get his laptop. "You must really like me if you're willing to watch something this unbelievably boring just to hang out."

"That's right," Leo said casually.

Grinning, Sloan freed his laptop from its place hidden under a stack of worksheets on his desk and searched for the blank one he was supposed to fill out. When he found it, he happily returned to his bed and his boyfriend.

"What exactly is this about?"

"Biology," Sloan answered, sitting at the head of his bed with his back pressed against the wall, making sure there wasn't enough room on either side of him for Leo.

"No, I know that. I meant specifically." Leo watched with raised eyebrows as Sloan parted his legs and patted the space between them with his right hand, balancing his laptop on his left. "You're setting yourself up for failure," he accused. Still, he moved to the open gap between Sloan's legs, settling down with his back against Sloan's chest. "Now you're going to be distracted."

Tucking his chin on Leo's shoulder as he settled his laptop in Leo's lap, Sloan assured, "Will not. To be honest, though, I don't know what this is about." With his arms around Leo's waist, he got the video ready. "Thirty minutes?"

"Yeah," Leo agreed, leaning back into him. Sloan rested the worksheet on his own leg where he could still see it.

"You ready?" Leo asked.

"Yeah." It was a total lie, as was his saying he wouldn't be distracted with Leo pressed against him. He couldn't focus on anything beyond that, and by the time Leo was pausing the film, he had allowed his eyes to close and was concentrating on the gentle scent of his boyfriend's laundry detergent. "Have we reached thirty?" he asked absently, turning his face into Leo's neck and letting his lips touch skin.

"What? No. It's been about five," Leo claimed, leaning to the side to get away from the attention. Sloan cracked his eyes open. "I stopped it because we got to the first answer and you didn't write anything down." As he said this, Leo's hand reached out to the touch pad on the laptop, going back about a minute in the documentary. Sloan saw the time. It really had only been five minutes.

"Oh, my god," he groaned. "This is horrible."

Pointer finger hovering over the space bar, Leo disagreed. "It's actually kind of interesting." Then, always the master of persuasion, he added, "You'll be done faster if you pay attention, and then we can make out for as long as you want."

Motivated but not happy, Sloan grumbled, "I thought you said you didn't like bio." As he spoke, his right hand rummaged around in the sheets to locate the pencil he was pretty sure he left there after doing some work that morning.

"I said I wasn't good at it," Leo corrected, reaching his right hand back toward him, a purple mechanical pencil pinched between his thumb and forefinger. "Shall we continue?"

Glumly, Sloan agreed. This time, when Leo pressed play, he did his best to pay attention, catching the answer he missed right away and writing it in the correct spot on the worksheet.

Every once in a while, he would zone out, but Leo, who was paying better attention than he was even though it wasn't his assignment, didn't have to point out any more missed answers. After filling in the first seven blanks, Sloan dropped his pencil. "Hey, what time are we at?"

Leo reached out to check. "Thirty-two minutes," he answered, pausing the video as he spoke. "I'm going to set an alarm on my phone . . ." He trailed off as Sloan's lips attacked the side of his neck, his head tilting to the side. Vaguely, Sloan was aware of Leo's attention on his phone.

He reached his left hand up to press into Leo's cheek, turning his head to the side so he could greet his lips with an open-mouthed kiss. They were getting used to this. At first, Leo seemed a little timid when they kissed, though he was becoming more confident, taking charge sometimes rather than just following his lead.

It drove Sloan insane when he felt Leo grow bold, his tongue pressing deeply into his mouth before retreating so he could catch Sloan's lower lip with his teeth, tugging just enough to make him groan. He did it back, drinking in the sound of Leo's gasp. They could tease each other for hours like this. He *wanted* them to.

It was getting harder and harder to ignore how badly he wanted to touch Leo. His hand moved to the hem of Leo's shirt and slid under to press against the skin of his hip. A soft noise of content left Leo at the touch, shoulders turning so he could better face Sloan and slot their mouths together more perfectly.

His skin is so smooth, Sloan thought, tracing his fingers lightly to Leo's navel, stopping right above the button to his shorts before dragging his fingers upward, over his belly button to his chest. It was obvious that the graze of fingertips was distracting to Leo, the movement of his tongue growing slower, his breath coming out faster. He must have known what was coming, though a surprised cry still left him the second Sloan passed over his nipple.

They both froze at the sound, their mouths still open and pressed together. It felt as if they were both waiting for something, so Sloan repeated the action. Their mouths parted with Leo's gasp.

"*Haaa,*" Sloan breathed, pulling back a bit from their kiss and cracking his eyes open. Leo didn't do the same, his eyelids squeezed tightly shut. A part of Sloan—the only part left of him that wasn't thinking about the movement of his fingers and how fucking hard he was—wondered if Leo did this to avoid looking at him, or if he was lost in the sensation. "You okay?"

Leo ignored him, surging to kiss him once more. Kissing back with half-lidded eyes, Sloan continued his caress, fascinated by Leo's reactions, each one making the situation beneath his zipper even harder to ignore. Feeling experimental, Sloan gave a gentle pinch of his fingers, rolling the skin between his thumb and forefinger. The body against him tensed and pulled away. Sloan's mouth parted, prepared to apologize if he had taken it too far.

Leo didn't give him the chance. He pushed the computer off his lap and turned to straddle him, both arms wrapping around Sloan's head and pulling his mouth back onto his. Leo kissed him so hard his lips tingled. Pleased, Sloan slipped his left arm around Leo's waist while his right hand returned up the front of his shirt.

It was going great, and Sloan was contemplating taking things a step further, when they were interrupted by the sound of Leo's alarm. Leo put some distance between their mouths. For a moment, his face still hovered over Sloan's, his breaths heavy. "*Fuck*," he gasped before climbing off his lap.

"*Noooo*," Sloan protested, hugging Leo around his waist as he settled between his legs once more. "A little longer."

"Thirty minutes," Leo responded, patting his arm with his left hand as he set up the laptop with his right. "You're learning so much . . ." He gestured to the now-wrinkled worksheet sheet on Sloan's leg.

"Ack," Sloan voiced, pressing his face into Leo's neck.

"I won't hit play until you're paying attention and I'm not kissing you until we're at least an hour into this thing," Leo told him.

Groaning, Sloan straightened his back and found his pencil again. "Okay, okay. Hit play," he instructed, rolling his eyes skyward when Leo shifted back against him and pressed heavily on his erection. Neither of them paid it any mind beyond Sloan's sharp hiss.

They got through a few more minutes and one more answer before Sloan's phone buzzed in his pocket. "Ah, sorry."

"It's fine." Leo paused the documentary. "Do you want to check it, or should we keep going?"

Shifting to free his phone from his pocket, Sloan said, "I should check it or I'm going to forget and never respond." This was a problem he often had, and he'd heard enough about it from Colette to be conscious of the habit. "Ah, it's Nicole." Her message was simple, just responding to what he'd texted previously.

"How's she doing?" Leo asked, dropping his head back onto Sloan's shoulder.

"She's good. Happy we're together. I think she said—and I'm trying my best to quote here—*Drew was so hard to antagonize. This is going to be fun*," Sloan recited with a laugh. It was acknowledged with a small noise of distress. "I'll make sure she doesn't tease you too bad."

Leo's shrug could be felt against Sloan's chest. "No, it's okay. She's a lot, but I'll get used to it." As Sloan typed out a response, he continued.

"It's nice that you two talk. I hardly ever talk to my best friend these days."

Sloan tossed his phone to the end of the bed so it didn't have the chance to distract him again, then tangled his hand in Leo's hair, keeping his head tilted back against his shoulder. With his other hand, he played the video. "Well," Sloan said, talking softly. "She's been reaching out recently because I let her know everything that had been going on. She rarely talks to me this much . . . You don't talk to your best friend?"

The head on his shoulder shook. "No. We did the first couple of weeks. I guess we've been busy lately." A hand dropped onto Sloan's knee then. "They went over number nine."

"Oh, sorry. I wasn't paying attention."

This must have been an expected reaction, because Leo lifted his head from Sloan's shoulder and took the pencil from him, writing the answer in himself. When he finished, he handed it back to Sloan.

"I'll pay attention now, I promise. Just . . . can I ask you a quick question?" Sloan asked.

"How quick?"

"I was wondering if you told your best friend about us?"

There was a moment in which the video continued and Leo said nothing, and then his hand shot out to press the laptop's spacebar. "I haven't," he admitted. "He knows who you are as a friend of mine, but he doesn't know we're dating."

This didn't bother Sloan at all, but it made him aware that they'd spoken little about who they shared the news of their relationship with. "Who *have* you told so far?"

Leo turned enough that their eyes could meet. "Michael and Ian, and my family."

"Your dad?"

"I told him I thought we would date at some point but haven't talked to him since besides the usual *how's your day* text. Mom and Lizzy took it well. Lizzy got excited and screamed a lot," Leo explained, and Sloan chuckled. "Is that okay?"

"Is what okay?"

"That I haven't told my friends," Leo elaborated.

Sloan brushed a hand soothingly down Leo's side. "Of course it's okay. Take your time. Tell them when you're ready for them to know."

"It's not that I'm not ready," Leo said. "I'm not worried about them being upset or anything, either. They'll be happy for me, I'm sure. It's just . . . they were there to witness my last two relationships, and I'm worried they're going to assume this is the same when it's not. The idea of them not understanding that I'm serious about you bothers me."

He knew Leo probably wouldn't approve, but Sloan couldn't resist gripping his boyfriend's chin and pulling him into a tender kiss. For the first couple of seconds, Leo kissed him back. He pulled away before it could go too far. "We still have twenty-five minutes before we can kiss again."

Groaning, Sloan tucked his face into Leo's neck. "Alright," he sighed, lifting his head and resting his chin on Leo's shoulder so he could see the screen. "Hit play."

CHAPTER FORTY-THREE

LEO

As usual for a Friday, Leo and Morgan had plans to spend the night together, though, for the first time since they began to date, they would be staying in Leo's room. Justin would be at Colette's for the night, and Morgan suggested a change of scenery.

At the moment, Leo was lying across his mattress as he waited for his boyfriend to join him. They'd arranged to get together earlier, but their plans had changed when a girl from the film department offered to talk to Morgan about the major.

Leo was pleased to see Morgan actively pursuing something he was interested in. Still, it was a little upsetting that they wouldn't have an overlap in courses the next semester. They'd still see each other all the time, Leo didn't doubt, but there was just something fun about sharing a class, even if Morgan did occasionally get distracting during lectures.

The thought made Leo smile. It reminded him of class that afternoon, which had been spent with Morgan's leg pressed snug against his.

The memory of Morgan's skin made him think about what had been on his mind for the past week: *sex*. He felt guilty whenever he longed for it. He had assured Morgan they could wait as long as he needed, but he wanted to try it so badly. For the sake of his boyfriend, he would not bring it up. He would follow Morgan's pace so he didn't make him uncomfortable, even though he was having a hard time stopping himself from taking things too far.

On Tuesday, Leo vented to Colette about his problem while Justin ran to the bathroom, leaving them alone in the room together. She looked both surprised and amused by his confession and suggested that maybe he should mention it to Morgan. Leo was pretty sure Morgan already knew he wanted to have sex with him and he didn't want to unintentionally pressure Morgan to feel ready by bringing it up.

It would feel good, though, Leo thought, squeezing his eyes shut as he thought of Morgan's hand up the front of his shirt the day before. Just that felt better than anything he'd done with his previous boyfriends—which, admittedly, wasn't much. He couldn't even imagine how good it would feel to have Morgan inside of him . . .

Groaning, he rolled onto his stomach, pressing his hips into the mattress. Thinking about it was making him aroused. Briefly, he considered ignoring it but, for the past week, he had been trying something new.

Whenever he had a physical reaction at the idea of having sex, instead of simply waiting for his erection to go away, he helped it along in a way he hoped would prepare him for the day he and Morgan had sex.

It's what he did then as well after going to retrieve his bottle of lube from where it was hidden in his bottom desk drawer. It kept him distracted enough that he didn't notice the message on his phone until a knock on the door interrupted him. Quickly, he removed his fingers from inside himself and checked his phone.

Morgan: Headed over

"Fuck," Leo breathed, glaring at the slight tent in the front of his sweatpants. There was no time to take care of it, so he tucked his erection under his waist band and hoped his boyfriend didn't look at him too closely.

Before he went to open his door, he stopped by his dresser and reached into his bin of dirty clothes to wipe his fingers on a shirt.

When he finally answered the knock, Morgan was standing in the hall with raised eyebrows, hands shoved into the pockets of his shorts. "Hey," he greeted, stepping into the room and leaning forward to press a kiss to Leo's forehead. "Were you asleep?"

"Because I took so long answering the door?" Leo asked, dropping his right hand to grip Morgan's hip while using the left to reach over his shoulder and shut the door.

"Ah, no. I mean, I guess it took you a little longer, but I was asking because you look kind of flushed," Morgan explained, picking at a strand of Leo's hair. "Are you alright?"

"I'm okay," Leo said dismissively, smiling at his boyfriend. "Better now that you're here." They shared a brief kiss. "How'd your meeting go? You're earlier than I expected."

Morgan nodded. "Yeah, we got done faster than I thought we would. Sorry for interrupting your nap." He slipped away from Leo to move deeper into the room. Leo didn't even bother correcting him—a nap was far less embarrassing than being interrupted in the middle of fingering himself. He shook his head to show he didn't mind.

"It went well," Morgan continued. "She was really nice and explained the kinds of things I would study and even showed me the short film she's working on for her senior project."

"Any good?" Leo asked.

"Yeah, it wasn't bad." Morgan slid his backpack off and dropped it beside Leo's desk. "No sharks, but it was very low budget, so that's to be expected, I guess."

Leo chuckled. "Because the movies you made me watch are *high budget*." He received a grin in response. Every time Morgan smiled, he looked exceptionally pretty. It was a welcome sight, though right then, all it did was remind Leo that he was still hard. Flustered, he averted his eyes to the floor as his boyfriend approached him. "That's cool, though.

Do you think you'll like the program?"

"I do," Morgan said. He reached out to grab Leo's hand. "Are you sure you're alright?"

Surprised, Leo lifted his gaze. "Yeah, I'm really okay."

Morgan didn't believe him. He pressed his lips together tightly and narrowed his eyes, still looking at Leo closely. "Hmmm . . . wanna lie in bed and watch something on my phone?"

Nervously, Leo glanced up at his bed, thinking about the bottle of lube hidden somewhere in his sheets. "Why don't we sit on the futon?"

Morgan ignored this suggestion, going over to the end of his loft and beginning his climb up. "While I'd love to relive the time you got stoned, I'm beat from today, so I'll probably fall asleep soon. If I fall asleep on the futon, my back will hurt."

"It's just past six," Leo mumbled, staring blankly at his desk as his boyfriend reached the top of his bed and flopped down, making the loft creak. "You never go to sleep this early." On the bed, Morgan pulled at the sheets. Leo squeezed his eyes shut tight.

"It'll just be a nap. I'm an eighteen-year-old boy, after all. Naps are . . ." Morgan trailed off suddenly and Leo bit his lower lip hard. His heart was beating incredibly fast. For a fleeting second, he wondered if this would be how he died—from shame in front of his own boyfriend. "Hey, Leo?"

"Yeah?"

"You wanna come up here?" Morgan asked. Sighing, Leo nodded, cracking his eyes open. He moved to the end of the bed and climbed. Halfway up, he could fully see Morgan's face, though Morgan wasn't looking back at him, gaze instead on the bottle of lube he was holding as if he's never seen one before. Leo lay down on his side facing him, putting enough distance between them that his back pressed against the cold wall. "So, what were you doing before I got here?"

"I'm sorry."

There was a creak as Morgan also rolled onto his side. "Why are you apologizing?" He sounded truly confused. "You did nothing wrong."

"It's embarrassing," Leo explained, raising a hand to cover his face.

Morgan caught his wrists, preventing him from doing so. "For you, maybe," he said. "I'm honestly trying to think about how you looked when you were doing it." Surprised, Leo's eyes widened a bit. There was no hint of teasing on Morgan's face. Leo swallowed heavily, his throat going dry.

"Did you get to finish?" Morgan asked.

"No," he admitted, uncomfortably aware of the worsening situation in the front of his sweatpants. If Morgan looked down, surely it would be obvious.

For a long, intense moment, they held eye contact. Morgan sucked his lower lip into his mouth to moisten it before asking, "Can I . . ." He didn't finish the sentence, didn't need to before Leo was nodding and thinking, *Yes, god, please.*

Morgan didn't touch him right away. Instead, he took his time lathering his fingers with a fair amount of lube. Nervously, Leo watched and tried to wrap his head around the situation. "Alright," Morgan said once he was finished, tossing the tube somewhere toward the bottom of the bed. "Relax." He shifted closer, wrapping his right arm around Leo's waist.

Leo was expecting him to immediately reach into his pants, but first Morgan leaned forward to kiss him, passing his tongue over Leo's bottom lip until he cracked open his mouth. Humming thoughtfully, Morgan's fingers came to press against the base of his spine. *"Ah."*

"Put your leg over my hip?" Morgan suggested, pressing his forehead against Leo's. He obeyed, lifting his left leg and wrapping it around Morgan's waist. The fingers on his back finally slid down, easily slipping under his clothing.

When the first finger pressed into him, Leo's breath hitched, his hips jumping as he released what felt like a suspicious amount of pre-cum. It felt good having any part of Morgan inside him, and he nearly lost his composure when a second finger quickly joined the first.

"Are you alright?" Morgan asked, voice gentle and breath hot on his face. Leo didn't respond, cracking his eyes open to find Morgan's gaze on him. Even though he was too focused on what was happening to other parts of his body to kiss well, he leaned forward to connect their mouths. The lack of technique didn't seem to bother Morgan much. He kissed him back vigorously regardless, giving more than he was getting in return.

Leo could feel Morgan's hardness pressing against his thigh. Tentatively, he pressed his palm into the front of his boyfriend's shorts. The fingers in him stalled, and their kiss was broken. "You don't have to—"

"Can I if I want to?" Leo whispered, tracing the zipper shyly. The fingers inside of him twitched, meeting his prostate for the first time, and he gasped sharply. Still, Morgan didn't answer. "What's wrong?"

"Nothing's wrong," Morgan said, his fingers carefully pulling out of Leo and instead pressing against his back to push his hips closer. "I'm really trying to control myself here, and I'm worried that if you touch me, I might . . ."

Even more excited now, because maybe, just maybe, Morgan desired him just as badly, Leo forced himself to push back the self-consciousness he felt over what they were doing. "You don't think you could control yourself?"

Gray eyes widened. "What? No. I can control myself. You don't need to worry about something like that with me. It was going to say that I might go a little bit crazy."

"Crazy?" Leo asked, leaning closer so his lips ghosted across Morgan's. "Crazy how? Crazy why?"

When Morgan swallowed, Leo was close enough to hear it. "Crazy from wanting you so badly," he admitted, fingers massaging Leo's tailbone. Moving close enough that their noses were touching, Leo unbuttoned the front of Morgan's shorts, pulling down the zipper next.

He felt bold right then, confident for once. *"Leo."*

"I'm right here," he whispered, eyes staring into Morgan's as he slipped his fingers past his waistband, grabbing his erection. It was an unfamiliar weight in his hand, and he slid his fingers downward carefully and then back up again. They were just light touches, probably not nearly enough, but Morgan still choked. "I'm right here and I want you, too."

"You want me, too," Morgan echoed. It was spoken like a sigh, the words coming out distracted. Leo didn't respond, watching his boyfriend's face as he finally curled his fist around Morgan's hard cock, giving him a couple of firm strokes. "Wait, wait, wait." Leo's hand paused. "You want me, too? Like . . . you want to have sex?"

Pausing, Leo thought of a safe way to communicate his feelings in case he was misunderstanding the situation. "I want you how you want me. When you say that, do you mean you want to have sex with me?"

They were silent for a couple of seconds as Morgan considered this. Suddenly, he laughed. "You just want me to be the one to say it." Reaching down, Morgan grabbed Leo's wrist, pulling his hand free from his pants. At first, Leo thought maybe he had gone too far but, instead of pulling away, Morgan rolled them so Leo was beneath him, thighs parted for him to position himself between. Ducking forward, Morgan kissed him again, sloppily and with too much tongue, before pulling back. "I want to have sex with you. I've wanted to since the day after we first talked about it."

"Me too," Leo admitted, brushing his hands up Morgan's sides, displacing his shirt. "I want to as well, so can we?"

Smiling softly, Morgan pushed himself up and sat back on his heels. "We can," he agreed. "Do you have condoms?"

"Yeah," Leo admitted, propping himself up on his elbows. "They're in the bottom right drawer of my desk. I can—"

"I got it." With a hand on his abdomen, Morgan pressed him back down and made his way down the end of the loft. Leo listened as Morgan rifled through his drawer. The longer he took, the more nervous Leo got.

"Wow, you really put them to the bottom, huh?"

The drawer clicked closed. "Are they the right size?" Leo asked. "I didn't buy them myself, and I guess even if I had, I don't know the size of your . . . well, you know."

"These should work," Morgan answered, sounding amused by Leo's inability to say the word. The bed shook as he climbed up again. "You didn't buy these yourself, you said?"

Leo looked to the end of the bed. "No. They were in the care package from my mom. You saw the message."

Morgan seemed surprised, pausing with one knee on the mattress before continuing the rest of the way. In his right hand, there was a single condom in metallic blue wrapping. "Ah, she really did that?" He laughed and slipped the condom into his pocket. "That's awesome."

Leo made a little groaning noise and allowed his knees to be parted. It felt as if their rhythm had been disrupted, so he was unsure of how to proceed. Morgan didn't seem to share his hesitance. He ducked forward to kiss him again before pushing up the front of Leo's shirt.

"Take this off?" Morgan suggested, thumbing over one of his nipples.

"You first."

He did not need to be told twice. Swiftly, Morgan pulled his shirt over his head and tossed it to the floor.

Leo removed his shirt more slowly, draping it over the railing on the side of the loft. Morgan raised a hand to pat down some of his hair. "Are you okay? If you're uncomfortable, you can call quits at any time and I'll stop."

This was something Leo didn't need to be told. He knew that after what happened with Drew, Morgan was incredibly conscious about not pressuring him.

"I'm not worried about that," Leo assured, eyes drifting down to the bare chest in front of him. Sighing wistfully, he raised both of his hands and settled his palms flat against Morgan's skin. "I'm not even really worried. Nervous would be a better word. As you know, I've never done this before." This was only a part of his concern. Sex was adding a whole new dynamic to their relationship. He didn't know how it would change them.

"It's okay to be nervous," Morgan claimed, leaning forward to press his forehead against Leo's. "As long as you remember that it's us, so everything will be fine."

Ah, Leo thought, feeling warm and reassured. Ducking forward, he gave Morgan a quick closed-mouth kiss. *That's right.* It was always good with Morgan. If things changed, Leo was sure it would be for the better.

Nodding, he lay back again, resting his head on his pillow. "You're right," he agreed, lifting his hips when Morgan's thumbs pushed into his waistband. Morgan paused then, his eyebrows raised. "You can take them off," Leo said.

Morgan did just that, pulling his sweats and boxers down his thighs, eyes following the path of newly exposed skin. Embarrassed, Leo turned his face to the side, curing his fingers in the bedsheets on either side of his hips as Morgan maneuvered both of his legs to one side, making it possible to pull the fabric free. As soon as he was bare, Morgan pushed his knees apart again to kneel between them. "No one's seen you like this before?" he asked. Leo nodded, squeezing his eyes shut at the sound of the lube bottle being popped open again.

A moment later, he felt two fingers, slippery and cold, press into him. He groaned at the sensation, keeping his eyes shut tightly. It wasn't long—probably because of all the prep earlier—before he could easily accept a third finger.

Morgan worked quickly, focusing more on stretching him to take something bigger than exploring his insides. He didn't mind the pace, feeling quite eager himself. Anticipation was driving him mad.

"I'm ready," Leo demanded once accommodating three digits grew comfortable.

"How would you know? You've never done this before," Morgan

teased, but he removed his fingers anyway. For the first time since getting fully undressed, Leo cracked his eyes open to watch the boy between his legs, who was hastily removing the rest of his own clothing. As Morgan fumbled with his discarded shorts, trying to find the condom, Leo let his gaze wander downward to Morgan's erection.

He watched as Morgan finally ripped open the condom wrapper and rolled it on, hissing quietly at the touch.

"Okay?" Morgan asked cautiously after coating himself in lube, his left hand settling on Leo's knee as the right lined his member up to the place he'd soon press into. Huffing at the pressure, Leo dropped his head back against the pillow.

With a heavy swallow, he nodded. "Yeah, I'm okay. You can go ahead—"

Wasting no time, Morgan shifted his hips forward, pushing the first inch into him. Even after being stretched so thoroughly, Leo's breath caught in surprise. It didn't feel unpleasant, and when Morgan paused, lips parting to ask if he was alright, Leo was quick to grab hold of his boyfriend's hip, squeezing tightly. "No, don't stop. Keep going."

Eyebrows furrowing in a way that implied effort, Morgan continued, eyes watching his face for any signs of pain.

There weren't any, Leo was sure. It hurt, of course, but it was an afterthought to the overwhelming feeling of relief that washed over him. They were complete, as close as they could get to each other, connected in a way that Leo had never been connected to anyone before. It was mind-numbingly perfect.

"Wow, wow, wow," Morgan breathed, releasing his hold on Leo's knees to sink down onto his forearms, pressing a kiss to Leo's collarbone.

Unable to speak, Leo hummed, tipping his head back and closing his eyes. Morgan was almost completely in him and one last push brought them flush against each other. The moan that left him was completely involuntary.

His face tucked into Leo's neck, Morgan mumbled in a strained voice, "Are you alright? Is there any discomfort?"

Breathing deeply as he gathered himself, Leo thought about it. The muscles in his back felt tight, and his legs were quivering on either side of Morgan's hips. It was uncomfortable, deep inside of him where Morgan's fingers had been unable to reach, but he was honestly more concerned for the tense boy on top of him. "Are *you* okay?" he managed, practically gasping out the words.

"Feels good," Morgan claimed. "*Too* good. Tell me when it's okay for me to move."

It was more than okay for Morgan to move. Right then, the feeling of him being entirely inside was almost too much to bear. "I'm alright," he assured. "Lightheaded, but in a good way. You should move. Please. I can't stand you not moving. "

Breathing out a heavy breath of what Leo thought might have been relief, Morgan pulled back his hips before pressing in again. Leo's legs came up to wrap tightly around Morgan's waist. "Ah, fuck," Morgan breathed, nuzzling the crook of Leo's neck. "This is crazy. You feel amazing."

It shouldn't have made him feel as good as it did, because it probably would have felt the same inside of anyone, but he couldn't help feeling proud. His thighs gripped Morgan a little tighter as he continued to thrust into him, pace steadily getting faster.

Okay, Leo thought. *I can handle this. I can do this.*

Then, Morgan found his prostate.

"Oh god," he gasped, arms flying to wrap around Morgan's shoulders, holding on as if his life depended on it. *"Morgan."* Making noise felt wrong. It felt somewhat dirty, though at the same time it turned him on even more knowing that Morgan was taking him apart.

"You sound so good," Morgan praised, lifting his head to kiss him. It was hard to focus on, given all the fucking, and the result was sloppy. Leo didn't mind.

Morgan's dick was in him. His tongue was in him. They were so close and it felt so good.

Pulling away from the kiss and throwing his head back, Leo managed a breathless, "Ugh, fuck." A particularly good angle made him arch.

"Leo."

He groaned at the sound of his name, holding on tightly as Morgan sped up a touch more, settling into a rhythm that was on the verge of overwhelming.

"Shit, I'm close," Morgan breathed, reminding Leo of the outcome of this all. That was the goal—to come. It seemed like a weird thing to forget, but at the moment he felt like they could continue forever.

He didn't get to respond. Before he could even consider how close he was to coming, Morgan's hand slid between their bodies to grasp his erection, stroking in time with his thrusts.

It was Morgan who finished first, and just knowing he'd successfully made his partner feel good pushed Leo over the edge as well.

The intensity of his orgasm shocked him, his limbs tightening around Morgan as his vision blurred. *"Ah,"* was all he managed, the sound high-pitched compared with the groan Morgan pressed into his neck.

For a moment, they just held each other and tried to catch their breath. Leo uncrossed his ankles from behind Morgan's back, dropping his legs to free his boyfriend. Pulling out, Morgan rolled off Leo and settled onto his back beside him.

With tired movements, he removed the condom, tying it off and leaving it to rest on his stomach for the time being. "Well," he began, breaking the silence. "We're pretty compatible."

"Guess so," Leo replied, too tired to be self-conscious. He looked down at the mess on his stomach and groaned. "This is gross."

Chuckling, Morgan reached over to take his hand. It was sticky from the dried lube, but Leo didn't care.

Morgan looked satisfied. His eyes were closed as he smiled, hair messy across his forehead. It was getting longer again, the way Leo knew Morgan liked, and he often felt the need to reach out and brush his fingers through it. There was no reason to resist the urge then, so he didn't, letting his fingers settle on soft strands. "You okay?" he asked. Despite the obvious joy in Morgan's expression, Leo wondered if a part of him was upset. It had to be weird having sex with someone new after getting out of a yearlong relationship.

Eyes cracking open, Morgan turned his head into the hand stroking his hair. "That's my line."

"I'm okay," Leo assured. "I feel good."

"Me too." Morgan's eyes slid closed again. "I feel fantastic. All warm and satisfied. You're amazing." His voice trailed off drowsily.

They were going to fall asleep any second, so Leo reached over Morgan to grab the shirt he had draped over the loft's railing, wiping his boyfriend's chest with one side and his own with the other. After wrapping the condom in it with a mumble of, "Remind me to throw that shirt away later," he tossed the fabric over the side of the bed.

Then, because he still wanted to be as close to Morgan as possible, Leo abandoned their regular sleeping position in favor of lying on top of him, his head tucked beneath Morgan's chin. With a sigh of content, Morgan pulled the blankets over them.

That night, Leo fell asleep warm and happy.

Chapter Forty-Four

Leo

When Leo got out of political science on Monday, he said goodbye to his boyfriend and left for the parking lot where Justin was waiting for him. They had run out of the snacks they'd bought at the beginning of the semester, so Justin suggested they go stock up. The lack of food didn't really bother Leo all that much—there was only a week and a half left before he flew home—but Justin thought it'd be nice for them to have stuff there when they got back at the end of January.

They went to the nearest department store. The ride was filled with talk of Justin's weekend and the afternoon he spent with Colette's family. "It's kind of weird," he was saying as he pulled into an open parking space. "I mean, I had a girlfriend for about two years in high school, and I got to meet her parents and stuff, but it feels different now that it's college. My parents met in college, so it feels more serious."

"Mine did as well," Leo said, unbuckling his seat belt. "But they're divorced, so it's probably different for me." Justin looked at him, his expression deadpan. Ignoring this, Leo pushed open the car door and climbed out.

As they cut through the parking lot, Leo asked, "Things are going well with you and Colette, then?"

"Yeah, man, it's great." Justin sounded incredibly happy. "Really great. I like her a lot. I mean . . . the lack of sex takes its toll, but I understand why she doesn't want to do it right away, and I respect her decision." They were almost to the doors then, and Leo shot a nervous look around to see if there was anyone close enough to hear what they were discussing. "What about you and Sloan?"

"What about us?" Leo grumbled. He suspected he knew what Justin was asking and hoped he was wrong.

They moved through the automatic doors. "You guys fuck yet?"

Leo wrinkled his nose at the question.

"I get it, I get it. You don't want to talk about it. I'm asking because I noticed the empty pack of condoms in the recycling bin and wanted to make sure Max isn't bringing people to hook up in there while we were gone."

Leo grabbed a basket by the door, not looking at his roommate as he softly admitted. "He's not."

He couldn't help thinking about that weekend. Justin hadn't ended up coming back to the room until Sunday night, so he and Morgan made the most of the time together, perhaps getting a little carried away. *I need to buy more condoms,* he remembered.

"Ah," Justin said, and when Leo glanced at him, he found a knowing smile on the other boy's face. "I'm glad you two are happy."

"We are," Leo agreed. He raised his head to look around, wondering where exactly he would find condoms, as well as how to separate from Justin so he could go get them. "So—"

"How about I go grab snacks and light bulbs, and you get bottled water and any type of red sports drink?" Justin suggested, taking a second basket for himself.

Leo feared his roommate's faith in him to find red drinks may have been displaced, but he didn't point this out.

He agreed to the suggestion.

"Sweet. Text me if you want anything specific. Otherwise, I'll just grab a bunch of stuff," Justin said.

"Alright." Justin left him, seeming to know where he was going already. Leo stayed rooted to his spot, looking around curiously. He'd never bought condoms before, and after a moment of thought, he started off toward the *Pharmacy* sign.

He wandered until he found the family planning aisle.

There were far more options than he was expecting, and he hesitated, arm stretched out toward a box. Would Morgan consider twenty to be presumptuous? Leo removed a box from the shelf to examine it more closely. *I don't need to tell him how many I bought, and it's not like we have to use them all before break.* He lifted his head again to look back at the shelf. Deciding on the number of condoms to buy was only half of it. There were about ten different options for twenty packs.

Figuring they'd have time to try them all at some point, he tossed the box he was already holding in the basket.

When he turned to wander out of the aisle, he immediately spotted the person standing at the end, staring at him with a clenched jaw.

Shit.

There was a long moment in which he and Drew stared at each other before Drew approached. *How long has he been watching?* Leo wondered, thinking of the box of condoms in his basket. Even if Drew hadn't seen him grab them, it was obvious what he was in that aisle for.

The man stopped a foot in front of him. At first, Leo feared he'd have to be the one to break the silence, but then Drew stated, "This isn't over."

Leo didn't respond right away, taking time to study Morgan's ex. Drew wasn't his usual put-together self. His hair was wild and his stubble unshaved. The last few weeks clearly had not been kind to him. *Good,* Leo thought. *That's what he deserves.*

"What isn't?" he responded, after long enough that Drew looked uneasy. He kept his voice monotone. He didn't want to give the impression he was shaken.

"I've spent the last year shaping him into something better. He was growing as a person with me, and I won't stand by and let you steal him. I know Sloan, better than you ever will, and he's going to come to his senses eventually."

This made Leo angry.

Not because he actually thought Morgan was going to leave him for Drew, but because he'd been hoping that Drew would finally appreciate Morgan for who he was after losing him. That he'd use the experience from their failed relationship to become a better person, so he didn't treat his next partner just as poorly.

Seeming to think the conversation was over, Drew turned his back to him, about to leave. Leo spoke up before he could take a step. "He already has."

Drew turned just enough to look at him. "What?"

"He already came to his senses. That's why he's not with you anymore," Leo said. Drew's eyes widened and he faced him again. He probably expected Leo to be the type of person to stand there and take insults, and most of the time, he was, but he refused to let Drew be comforted by some delusion that Morgan would go back to him. "He's not going to come back to you, and he's not your boyfriend. He's mine."

There was a split second in which Leo registered Drew's surprised look shifting to one of anger, and then another where he noticed Justin approaching them from over Drew's shoulder. Neither of these things seemed important when Drew punched him in the face.

He'd never gotten punched before, and the force of it caught him off guard. He lost his footing, tipping back and sitting down hard. It made the ache in his lower back throb.

There was the metallic taste of blood in his mouth, and he poked around with his tongue until he found where his tooth cut the inside of his cheek. It hurt.

"What the absolute fuck, man?!" Justin exclaimed, putting himself between Leo and Drew and wrestling Drew back a few feet.

A girl wearing the store's navy uniform approached with a roll of paper towels, cautious of the two standing men rigid with tension. She moved around them to get to Leo, crouching beside him. "Are you okay?" she asked. Leo wasn't really listening. He was too busy thinking about how ridiculous he must have looked right then, on the ground with bloody lips and a box of condoms at his hip.

"This is assault!" Justin continued angrily. "I'm gonna call the police."

Drew looked absolutely horrified then—probably because an arrest record wouldn't be a welcome addition to his grad school application—and Leo chimed in with a "No." Both boys looked at him. Despite wanting Drew to face consequences for his actions, he didn't want it to be like this. "No police. As long as you leave Morgan alone, this is settled," Leo said. Drew frowned. "I care enough about him that I would tell him to leave me and encourage him to be with you in a second if I thought that was what was best for him and would make him the happiest, but it's not, and it's never going to be. You had your chance. Now, back off and give up." As he spoke, he was vaguely aware of a drip of blood running from the corner of his mouth. Still, he didn't take the piece of paper towel offered to him by the worker until he finished.

Drew glared but didn't say anything. With a deep breath, he nodded his head twice and backed out of the aisle.

"Shit, man," Justin said, watching him go. When he was out of sight, Justin turned to Leo, holding a hand out to him. "You just needed to buy condoms first."

The girl crouching beside Leo flushed, and he gave Justin a displeased look before accepting the hand offered. "Do you need anything?" the girl asked, rising as well.

"Could I have more paper towels?" He was bleeding far more than he first realized. Nodding, she ripped off a few more pieces and handed them to him. "Thank you."

Awkwardly, she hovered for a moment, so Leo gave her a nod he hoped was reassuring. At the gesture, she hurried off. Leo bent down to pick up the box of condoms. He tossed them into the basket before lifting it.

"Are you okay?" Justin asked. Leo nodded. Despite the pain in his face, he felt pretty good.

"I'm happy it happened. I've wanted to say that for a while." He pressed his tongue against his cheek and groaned. "It hurts, though."

Placing a hand on his back to urge him forward, Justin said, "Come on. Let's grab something frozen for you to put on your face."

Something frozen ended up being a bag of peas, which he wrapped in another paper towel and pressed against his cheek. "Thanks."

"I'm making you pay for those."

"I was thanking you for coming to intervene before he tried to pummel me to death," Leo clarified.

Justin smiled. Despite his concern from a minute ago, he seemed visibly amused. "Yeah, no problem, man. You want to go back right away? I'm cool coming later for this stuff if you want to go lie in bed."

"No, it's okay," Leo assured. "Sorry I didn't grab what you asked me to."

"It's not a big deal. You've already got the most important thing." Justin gestured to the condoms in Leo's basket.

Leo frowned and immediately winced. "Do you think I could get away with not mentioning this to Morgan?"

The answer became obvious the second Justin snorted. "You're probably going to have a big bruise, and even if you didn't, he'd notice when he went to kiss you next." Sighing, Leo grabbed the rest of the paper towel from his basket and spit out all the blood in his mouth. A woman passing by looked horrified by this. "Fuck, man. Are you going to need stitches?"

"No," Leo assured. "The bleeding is slowing down, I think. That had all just been gathering in my cheek and it was getting annoying."

A disturbed noise left Justin. "Fucking gross." Ignoring this, Leo looked ahead. They were approaching the aisle with bottled drinks. "Why wouldn't you want to tell Sloan about this?"

"It's not that I don't want to tell him," Leo said. His face was hurting from the cold vegetables, so he dropped them into the basket with the condoms. "I'm just worried that he's going to think it's his fault because Drew's his ex, and I don't want him to because it's not. He spent a year blaming himself for Drew's behavior, even when he did nothing wrong, and I don't want him to blame himself anymore."

Justin didn't speak right away, busy throwing various sports drinks into Leo's basket. When it was full, he lifted a case of water off the shelf. "Well . . ." he began once they were on their way out of the aisle. "I understand when you put it like that, but I also don't think you should use his past as a reason not to tell him things, because, as you know, it's not really his fault. I think what you should do is tell him why you don't blame him when he expresses guilt until he realizes he shouldn't hold himself accountable for the actions of others."

Leo threw a quick glance at Justin. "That was actually helpful. Thank you."

Justin made a scoffing noise. "*Actually* helpful? Don't sound so surprised."

"Sorry," Leo grumbled, though he wasn't actually and feared that was obvious. Justin's loud laugh made him think it was.

There was just enough time for Leo to lie down on the futon with an actual ice pack before Morgan arrived.

Their door was unlocked, so he entered without knocking. Initially, he didn't notice Leo, too busy removing his shoes as he said something to Justin about having lunch with Colette. It was only once he'd straightened that his eyes found Leo and immediately grew wide. "What happened?!" he exclaimed, crossing the room in long strides.

As Morgan crouched beside him, Leo answered, "I got condoms."

Justin laughed, turning in his desk chair to look at them. "We ran into your ex-boyfriend and he punched Leo in the face," he explained. "And Leo bought twenty condoms."

"Did he really?" Morgan asked. He worried at his lower lip with his teeth.

"I'm dead serious," Justin answered. "Twenty of them. I thought it was a little ambitious, but—" Morgan raised his head to shoot him a dirty look, clearly not in the mood to joke. Justin cut off to laugh, unaffected. "Sorry."

With interest, Leo watched the interaction. It wasn't often that Morgan actually looked annoyed.

By the time Morgan was addressing Leo, his expression had softened considerably. "Leo . . ."

"I'm alright," he promised, smiling reassuringly, wide enough that it could be seen with the ice pack in the way. It hurt to do so, though he thought it was worth it if it put Morgan at ease.

It sadly didn't seem to. "I can't believe he would do something like that. I'm sorry."

"Don't be," Leo insisted, lifting the ice pack off of his cheek. At the sight of the bruise, Morgan's face fell. "You didn't punch me in the face, and as far as I'm aware, you didn't encourage him to punch me in the face, either." Morgan's eyes dropped. "Morgan, I'm really okay."

Morgan nodded, though his expression changed little. "Okay," he agreed. "Tell me what happened?"

"We ran into each other in the contraceptive aisle, and when he referred to you as his boyfriend, I corrected him. He didn't seem to like that very much," Leo explained. As he spoke, Morgan took the ice pack into his own hand and held it against Leo's bruise.

"Did you at least hit him back?"

"No. I don't even really remember getting punched. I just remember being on the floor."

"He didn't even get up right away to fight back," Justin chimed in. "He just sat there."

Morgan's eyebrows raised in question. Leo shrugged. "I'm a pacifist."

Chuckling, Morgan brushed Leo's hair off his forehead with his free hand. "You totally could have kicked his ass," he claimed, which was utter ridiculousness, and Leo displayed this opinion with a snicker.

"Thanks for saying that, but my masculinity isn't fragile, so you don't need to lie to me," he said. It was Morgan's turn to laugh, and he lifted the ice pack from Leo's face to lean forward and press a quick kiss to his lips. "How was lunch with Colette?"

"It was good." Morgan turned his head toward Justin, who had faced his desk once again. "Colette said you can go over there whenever, Justin."

Not looking up from his work, Justin said, "I thought she had to talk to Jessica about some roommate stuff."

"Yeah, well, Jessica bailed, so she's pretty pissed right now. I'd recommend bringing a candy bar or something sweet she likes when you go over to make her feel better."

Even though he'd been told that his girlfriend was upset, a pleased noise left Justin. He pulled open his top desk drawer and removed a chocolate bar he had bought at the store. "I just stocked up."

"You're so smitten it's disgusting," Morgan accused.

"You're one to talk," Justin shot back, rising from his desk and stretching his arms over his head to crack his back. "Alright. I'm going to go then. I'll see you guys later." As he spoke, he went and opened the door, but paused before leaving. Slowly, he turned to look back at them. "Please, if you have sex, don't do it on the futon. I sit there a lot." The door closed. Morgan laughed, clearly less tense than before.

Leo groaned. "Oh god."

"Shall we move to your bed, then?" Morgan asked, voice low. Leo gave him a look. Chuckling some more, Morgan climbed onto the futon, lying down on top of Leo so they were chest to chest. "I know, I know. Your back still hurts. I'm just joking."

The ice pack on Leo's face fell away without Morgan's hand there to hold it. Leo didn't mind. The cold had numbed him, and he was content with their sudden closeness.

"Can we lie here until I have to go to class?" Morgan asked, dropping his head onto Leo's chest.

"Of course."

They were quiet for long enough that Morgan's breathing grew even and Leo assumed he had fallen asleep. This was proven false when the boy spoke once more, softly. "I'm really sorry Drew punched you."

Humming, Leo raised his right hand to push through the hair at the back of Morgan's head, fingers weaving through soft strands. "Really, don't be sorry. It's not your fault, and even if it had been, you're worth it."

A hitch in breath, and then, "How can you think so highly of me?"

"It's not hard."

Fingers curled in the front of his shirt. "Thanks."

There was no need for this, but Leo didn't correct him, just twisted his fingers in Morgan's hair. Another minute passed. Leo continuously prodded the inside of his cheek with his tongue. "I don't think I'm going to go to my last class today," he declared after some contemplation. "Is that bad?"

"Skipping once because you got punched in the face? No. That's not bad." The feeling of a hand cupping his jaw made Leo open his eyes. Morgan had lifted his head to look at him. Tenderly, he ran a thumb over Leo's cheek. "How does it feel?"

"Sore," Leo admitted.

Morgan slid his body up a couple of inches so he could brace his forearms on either side of Leo's head, hovering over his face. "Can I kiss you?"

Leo brought his hands to Morgan's hips. "Why are you asking? If you want to kiss me, you can kiss me."

Looking content, Morgan hooked his thumb on Leo's lower lip.

"Doesn't your mouth hurt?"

"Yeah," Leo agreed. "But it'll be worth it."

Grinning, Morgan dropped his head to kiss him.

Unsurprisingly, Leo found he was right. It was worth it.

EPILOGUE

SLOAN

Sophomore year

"Are you sure this is a good idea, Morgan?" his mother asked, glancing at him through the rearview mirror. He blinked a few times—because *woah, déjà vu*—then smiled and waved a hand dismissively.

School started in a couple of days, and he was about to move into the apartment he'd leased at the end of the previous school year. It was a different building from the one he lived in with Drew, this one a little farther from campus. He wasn't looking forward to having to wake up earlier in order to accommodate the walk, but it was the closest apartment building that allowed a pet besides the one from last year, and he would manage for Margo's sake.

Concerned, he shot a look at the crate his cat was in. While he was extremely excited to be bringing her along with him, he wasn't sure if the feeling was mutual after the hour-long car ride.

"You didn't like living off campus last year," his mom continued. "And you brought more stuff this time. If you decide to move out, where are we going to put everything?"

It was true he was bringing more this time around. He and his new roommate needed to fill the space together, and he might have gone so

415

overboard in his excitement that his parents needed to bring both of their cars to transport it all.

It seemed somewhat pointless to discuss this *what if.* If he changed his mind right then, they'd still need to find something to do with everything he had bought.

He ignored her second statement for this reason. "I didn't like it because I was living with Drew." As he spoke, he stuck his fingers into Margo's carrier to poke at his cat in a way he hoped was comforting. "My roommate this year is much cooler."

"I know," she mumbled. "I can't stop myself from worrying about you." Since he was positive this was all it was—just natural, unavoidable, motherly worry—he didn't bother to reply.

As they drove by campus, he peered out of the window at the familiar buildings.

"Have you heard from Drew at all?" his mom asked.

He actually had. A few months ago, his ex had called to inform Sloan he would be going to grad school out of state, and they no longer needed to worry about running into each other. This wasn't something that happened often the year before, but enough that hearing the news brought him some relief. "Yeah. He reached out to tell me he was moving. No need to stress."

They pulled into the parking lot, and Sloan ducked to speak to his cat. "Are you ready to see our new home, baby?" Margo made an unhappy noise. "I know. I'll get you out of there soon."

"Your father texted and he's a few minutes away," his mother informed, turning off the car. "He had to stop for gas. We should start without him."

They did. Sloan was eager to see his new home, among other things. His mother took a bin, he grabbed Margo, and they went up to the apartment.

Inside, sitting on the couch, was his roommate.

Colette looked surprised when they walked in. She recovered quickly and came to greet them. "You're here!" she exclaimed, throwing her arms around him. "I've been so lonely these last couple of days." She pulled away and went to hug his mother, who set down the bin to accept the gesture.

Colette, as the friend from college who lived closest to him, spent a couple of weekends at his house over the summer. She had gotten to know both his parents well and welcomed his mother with a familiar, "Hi, Eve."

"Hello, dear," his mother responded, smiling as she moved out of the hug. "How have you been?"

"Fantastic. Even better now that I have a roommate and a cat!" As she said this, Colette took the crate from Sloan. Unlike Drew, she was fond of the animal.

"She's not *your* cat," Sloan protested, watching Colette put the carrier on their tiny kitchen table and open it. Gently, she lifted Margo out, hugging her to her chest. "How has living here been? Do you like the building?"

As she carried Margo over to one bedroom, she looked over her shoulder to address him. "Oh, it's great. You wouldn't believe how loud our neighbor is, though. I've only been here for four days and he's driving me *insane*." She crouched to set Margo on her feet, mumbling something about how she needed to explore her new room. It was unclear if she was referring to the room Sloan would stay in or her own bedroom.

When Colette rose, she turned to look at him with a grin.

Warily, Sloan raised his eyebrows at her. "Are you being serious?"

"No." Colette laughed. "Of course not. He's so quiet I've actually gone over there a few times to check and make sure he's still alive. I think he's probably sick of me bothering him."

This sounded more accurate, and Sloan couldn't keep himself from smiling at the idea of the boy next door. "Well, I should go say hello, shouldn't I?"

"I'll join you before I go grab more stuff," his mother said.

Frowning, Sloan turned to her. "Could I actually have, like, five minutes alone with him?"

She appeared put out by this suggestion. Over the past ten months of dating Leo, Sloan's mother grew quite fond of him, impressed with both his manners and the way he treated her son. Sloan knew she was looking forward to seeing him again, though certainly not more than he was.

"Please, Mom? I haven't seen him in a week, and before that it had been two months."

During the summer, Leo spent the first month in California with his father and the last two in Illinois with his mother and sister. He returned to Cali just over a week ago, but he'd only stayed in Sloan's area long enough for them to get lunch before immediately moving into his apartment.

"Five minutes," his mother agreed. "I'll go grab another bin from the car, and when I get back upstairs, I'm coming over to say hello."

"Oh, I'll help you bring stuff in," Colette offered, coming to join them at the door. "Leo said he'd help too, so don't take too long."

As he moved out of the apartment into the hall, Sloan shook his head. "I'm just going to say hello." In response to this, both his mother and Colette wore matching skeptical expressions. "What? I am."

"Five minutes," his mother reminded, reaching out to pat his arm before turning toward the elevator. Colette followed behind her after making an obscene gesture with her hands.

As if you're giving us enough time for that, Sloan thought.

He went to the apartment next door and knocked. His fist remained curled as he waited, fingernails digging into his palm. It felt ridiculous to be so excited, but he could hardly wait to see Leo. Two months of seeing each other only on phone screens made being so close feel like a luxury.

It took a few seconds for Leo to pull open the door. "Ah," he voiced, as if Sloan's arrival was unexpected and they hadn't been texting all morning. "Morgan. I'll come help you move in."

"In a bit," Sloan told him, stepping into the apartment without an invitation to hug him. He'd never tire of the way holding him felt, warm and comforting. "I missed you."

"Yeah," Leo agreed, reaching over his shoulder to shut the door before sliding his arms around his neck. Humming in content, Sloan turned to press Leo up against the closed door.

"Justin's not here yet, right?" he asked, just to be sure.

With hands on the back of Sloan's neck guiding him closer, Leo confirmed, "He'll be here tomorrow. You can kiss me." Before Sloan could even do that, Leo pressed their lips together, the touch both urgent and gentle.

More than content, Sloan let them carry on like that, just slowly kissing since they had no reason to rush. For the next four months, Leo wasn't going anywhere. He'd be right next door.

It took his mother and Colette far less than five minutes to return, a knock on the door interrupting them right as Leo's mouth parted beneath his. Groaning, Sloan pressed his face into Leo's neck. "My mom wanted to come say hello to you . . . I can't believe how fast they were. Not even close to five minutes. So rude."

Leo patted Sloan's back as if he needed comfort and gently nudged him away. "I'd like to see her as well," he said, his hand on Sloan's chest, pushing him back until there was enough room for him to open the door. "We should spend time with your parents while they're here. You know how much they'll miss you." Leo grasped the door handle, but he didn't turn it right away. "We can continue later, right?"

Grinning, Sloan leaned forward to kiss Leo's cheek. "If it's just you tonight, can we have a sleepover?"

"Yeah," Leo agreed without pause. "I was going to ask, but I didn't know if you wanted to spend your first night in your apartment."

Touched by the constant effort to be considerate, he reached out to place a palm against Leo's jaw. "I want to spend my first night back wherever you are."

Brown eyes shifted to regard him directly. "Let's do that then." Feeling warm, Sloan let his fingers slip away.

Leo opened the door. Sloan didn't mind that they hadn't gotten their promised five minutes. It didn't matter. Leo had already agreed to be only his for the entire night.

Sloan's mother only took a half day off work to help him move, so once the cars were unloaded and goodbye hugs were given, his parents started back toward home. The year before when they left, Sloan recalled feeling somewhat sad to watch them go, unsure of when he'd get to see them again with Drew's distaste of visiting his home. It was different this time around.

For lunch, he, Leo, and Colette went to a restaurant near campus that they had frequented the year before. It felt nice to be together, talking casually about their summers while Leo's ankle was hooked around his own beneath the table.

About halfway through their meal, Colette's phone screen lit up with Justin's name, followed by a ring. She excused herself to go answer the call.

Amused, Sloan watched her skip off before bringing his attention to the boy sitting across from him. As usual, Leo had spoken little since they'd sat down, seeming more than content focusing on his food and listening to the extrovert's chatter.

While this was a dynamic Sloan was quite used to, he liked the sound of Leo's voice even more when it wasn't over the phone, and he wanted to hear it. "Have you and Justin been in contact at all this week?"

Leo's shoulders rose and fell. "Not really," he answered, frowning down at his plate. "He texted to ask when I was moving in, and I did the same. That's pretty much it."

Leo and Justin's relationship was interesting to Sloan. They acted as if they weren't close and failed to communicate when it wasn't in person, but then they coexisted so naturally together one would think they were siblings . . . or not. Now that he thought about it, he couldn't think of a pair of siblings who were as unbothered by each other as Leo and Justin were. Their random roommate matching had worked out perfectly for the two of them.

Sloan wondered how his living with Colette would go. She could be rather uptight, and he worried she would be bothered by his distaste for doing the dishes.

It can't be any worse than living with Drew, he thought.

"Hey." The word was spoken softly, and Sloan blinked out of his daze to look at Leo. "You okay? You've been watching me for a while now."

"Yeah," Sloan said, lips pulling up. "Well, it's nice to see your face, so . . ." The concerned look Leo wore shifted. Sloan recognized the expression; it meant he wasn't being convincing. Appreciating that Leo cared enough to not let him blow it off, Sloan reached out to place his hand on top of his boyfriend's. "I'm really okay. I was just wondering how things will go living with Colette, and thought it couldn't be worse than last year."

A huff of air left Leo in agreement. "You two will be fine," he assured. "I'll be right next door if you ever need to get away."

Sloan grinned. "I'm so excited. We're gonna have so much sex."

Leo laughed and shook his head. "You know, I really missed you."

"Yeah," Sloan agreed, amazed sweet words said with such sincerity could still draw the air from his lungs after ten months of dating. Maybe it surprised him because it hadn't been that way with Drew, or maybe it was because Leo said them often enough that he figured he'd be used to it already. "I missed you too. You were gone for a long time. Not five years long, but still."

It was a moment before Leo spoke again. "We have four months to not miss each other now. Summer's just ending."

It was, and there was the typical nostalgia that came with it. With summer drawing to a close came the end of his time spent with his high school friends and parents. He felt sentimental about it all, sure, but he couldn't find any real sadness within himself. How could he? He and Leo had four months to be together as much as they wanted. They could get breakfast together and sleep in the same bed and not have to worry about spotty internet interrupting their conversations.

And while at the end of those four months Leo would travel the 2,000 miles back to Illinois again, Sloan knew he didn't need to worry about him never coming back.

This was just the beginning. They had so much more to do.

"Yeah." Sloan grinned. "It's gonna be awesome."